I0532622

The Mayor's Bride

A Match in Magnolia Falls Romance

By

Tamara LeBlanc

Copyright © 2014 Tamara LeBlanc

All rights reserved.

ISBN-13 (print): 978-0692540442

Publisher's Note: This is a work of fiction. Names, characters, places and incidents are either the product of the author's imagination or are used fictitiously. Any resemblance to actual persons (living or dead), events or locations is entirely coincidental.

Cover design by Tamara LeBlanc

Digital formatting by Lucinda Campbell

Print Formatting: By Your Side Self-Publishing
www.ByYourSideSelfPub.com

No part of this book may be reproduced in any form or by any electronic or mechanical means, including information storage and retrieval systems without permission in writing from the publisher, except by a reviewer, who may quote brief passages in a review.

Thank You

DEDICATION

This novel is dedicated to my husband, Dusty DeStefano, a man with no equal.

I miss you with every breath, every heartbeat. Our time together was painfully short, but memories of your love will fill my heart and soul forever.

Chapter One

Ella Slipper gripped the clubhouse doorknob and groaned when it wouldn't budge. *Why's this locked?* She added a jiggle, a useless twist and then a semi-violent shake. Though she verged on screaming she gave the door a polite triple knock.

Come on… come on… somebody?

A rib squeezing corset, blistering Georgia heat wave, and four hours without a break had sucked her dry. She licked her parched lips, blotted the perspiration off her neck with the back of her lace gloved hand and then hoisted her petticoat. Ready to make the trek back around front and farther away from the kitchen and a gallon jug of sweet tea with her name on it she hesitated when she heard a shout. "Get back here, Thumbsucker!"

Squinting past corkscrew curls and a haze of burning sweat, she glanced over her shoulder, scanning the trees for the source of the nasty voice. A glimpse of blue to her left drew her attention. Three kids pursued a fourth child into the woods.

The largest bully caught up to the little boy in a few steps. "Freak," he barked and shoved him hard onto the ground.

Ella gasped, gathered more of her ridiculous skirt and stormed off the cement porch. Snapping twigs and crushing pinecones under her combat boots, she yelled, "Hey, leave him alone."

Bully Two and Three flashed looks of panic then sprinted out of sight. But the spongy carpet of dead leaves hampered their leader's escape. He tripped into a sprawl with an explosive grunt.

Ella jerked him to his feet. Before she let him run off, she leaned closer. "Pick on someone your own size," she growled.

He nodded like a bobble-head and sped off after his friends.

She smirked and then turned around. The little boy they had been tormenting sat where he'd landed. He didn't move. Nearly huddled in a ball, his little arms wrapped tightly around his shins. His forehead rested against his knees.

He appeared to be the only kid at the Magnolia Falls Civil War festival dressed as Donald Trump. His neatly combed hair, paisley tie and pressed slacks seemed stuffy for a grown man, not to mention a child. And in this heat and humidity he must be sweltering.

"You okay?" She asked and reached for him, setting a lace-gloved hand on his little shoulder.

His forehead swiveled off his knees as he turned to peer up at her. Sad eyes were as green as the clumps of moss hugging the tree bark next to him. Sweat dripped off the tip of her nose, but she gave him a reassuring smile. "Where's your moth—"

"Eric?"

Startled, she jerked in the direction of the masculine shout. Mostly hidden behind a thick web of leaves and overlapping branches, the man called out again. He strode toward a thinner spot in the vegetation. Ella glanced at the boy in time to watch him scramble to his feet and run off.

"Wait. Are you Eric?" Jumping up, a blur of white and a sickening head rush made the ground spin. She flung out her arms to steady herself just as someone gripped her shoulder.

"Whoa there, be careful." The guy from the bushes had obviously found his way through the tangle of vegetation. She wobbled on rubber knees.

"Careful," he warned again. His strong hands supported her shoulders, but she pulled from his grasp.

She barely registered him asking, "Have you seen a little boy back here?" The ten or so Oreos, questionably fresh Twinkie, and can of orange soda she'd inhaled for breakfast came back to haunt her.

I'm gonna puke. I'm gonna puke.

"You okay?"

His deep voice droned like it had been switched on slow speed.

Ella took one step and all went black.

Alexander York caught Scarlett O'Hara mid-fall. Holding her under the arms he lowered her limp body to the ground. He knelt beside her, but scanned the woods.

Where's Eric?

His housekeeper had lost track of his five-year-old son, and while Maggie searched the festival area in front of the clubhouse, Alex had rushed around back to check the woods.

He wanted to resume his search, but couldn't leave Scarlett sprawled unconscious in the dirt.

"Hey," he said, jiggling her skinny shoulder. "You okay?"

Scarlett didn't respond, but a few feet away the club house door opened and a woman dressed in a similar antebellum costume burst out. "Oh my God! Mr. Mayor? What...? What happened?"

"She passed out." Scarlett's bonnet had tipped forward. The lace brim and riot of damp, black curls hid most of her face. He tried to remove the hat, but the ribbon under her chin had been tied in a tight knot.

"Hold on. Let me try." The woman dropped down next to him.

"This heat probably got her." Alex frowned. "It must be one hundred degrees in the shade today?"

"I know. I can't recall a stickier September." The woman struggled with the knot. "She's been in this costume since noon. I should have insisted she take those breaks." She struggled to lift the unconscious woman onto her side. Alex took over and lifted her instead.

"Ella's the best mistress of ceremonies we've ever hired. But she works too hard." The woman untied Scarlett's corset and yanked the laces free. She tugged the rigid fabric out from under her and tossed it aside. Laying her gently on her back again she waved the edge of her own skirt up and down, generating a breeze over the unconscious woman. "We need to cool her down."

Alex patted his suit pockets. "I left my cell in my car down the street. Is there a phone inside? We should call 911."

The woman jumped up and sprinted to the back door. She jerked on the knob, cursed, then shuffled through a ring of keys to unlock it. "I'll call. Be right back." She disappeared inside.

Alex fumbled with the knot under the unconscious woman's chin. It finally came loose and he lifted her bonnet off and tossed it onto the discarded corset. Realizing she wore a wig as well, he eased the hair off her head. Sweat soaked, coal black curls slid from her forehead and cheeks. He grimaced when he finally saw her entire face.

Shit, she looks dead.

He lowered his ear to her pale lips. Felt for breath and watched her chest.

He smiled, relieved that *Ella*, as the woman had called her, seemed to be breathing fine. He pressed two fingers against her thin wrist after pulling her hand from the glove. A satisfying beat vibrated beneath her nearly transparent skin.

"Ambulance is on its way," the woman shouted and hurried back outside with a few more costumed adults on her heels. Concern creased her brow. "How long was she down before I came out here?"

The color seemed to be slowly returning to her skin, but Alex couldn't turn away from the unconscious woman's beautiful face. "Less than a minute," he assured her.

Long strands of hair had escaped the confines of a net cap. He lifted that off as well, hoping to cool her off further. Her hair, thick and nearly white-blonde, pooled around her head like a halo. A fringe of honey colored lashes fanned out above each smooth, porcelain cheek.

She looks like a fairy.

He gently wiped the hair from her face then pried open one of her eyes with his index finger and thumb. Her pupil dilated normally, and one crystal blue iris stared, unseeingly back at him.

"She *does* have beautiful eyes, doesn't she, Mayor York?" The woman asked, startling Alex out of that very thought. He let go of Ella's lids, annoyed.

Shit. The woman's unconscious. Get a damn grip.

And fairies? Had he just been thinking of friggin' fairies?

He shook his head. *Let Scarlett's buddies take over.* He needed to find Eric. He nearly relinquished nursing duties when a rustle of leaves drew his attention to his right. He let out a grateful breath. His son peered at him from behind a nearby tree. "Eric?" *Had he been right there the whole time?*

Big green eyes widened. Though his expression appeared intensely curious the little boy emerged from behind the tree with caution in each step. He stopped before he drew too close. He scanned the small group of adults and then eyed his father warily.

"You okay, Buddy?" Alex asked softly, not wanting to spook his son. He wished he could pull him into his arms and hug away all his fears.

Eric popped his thumb out of his mouth, but didn't answer. His son's silence was nothing new. In fact, Alex expected it.

What surprised him, however, was the way his shy son studied the woman lying on the ground. His head cocked left then right. His eyes narrowed. A few more hesitant steps and he stood less than a foot away, gazing at her. He closed the gap and squatted. Little fingers stroked her forehead, her cheek, and barely grazed her jaw. He reached for her limp hand, taking it into his own.

Alex swallowed in amazement. *Is this really happening?*

Eric cradled Ella's palm against his dimpled face and with a huge smile whispered, "Angel."

Alex fell back completely stunned. Tears stung his eyes and then spilled onto his cheeks, but he didn't give a shit.

Only one thing mattered.

His son had spoken.

Chapter Two

Ella sat at the kitchen table chasing the last bite of her donut with a hearty swig of root beer. Setting down the empty can, she licked chocolate icing from her fingers, one by one.

"What a shock," her mother said as she floated into the kitchen wearing one of the many costumes from their store down stairs. "Another breakfast of champions." She nodded at the can of soda making a set of plastic antennae bounce on the crown of her head.

Ella eyed the black and yellow striped, long sleeve leotard and knee grazing tulle skirt. *Hmm, bumble-bee... must be the organic market's grand opening this morning.*

"Just looking at that mess of calories is clogging *my* arteries," her mother grumbled. "That crap'll kill ya."

"Kill *me*? How 'bout the tobacco tube hanging from your mouth?" Ella countered with a raised eyebrow.

Her mother plucked the half-gone cigarette from her hot pink lips and smashed the smoldering butt into an ashtray. She eyed the empty donut carton on the counter and raised an eyebrow. "There, now do something for me. Eat a *real* breakfast. Maybe some nice *Limone e Basilico uova oltre foccacia* instead?" She chose a frying pan and set it on the stove in obvious anticipation.

"I don't eat things I can't pronounce," Ella muttered, wishing she'd never given her mother that *Recipes of the World* cookbook for her last birthday. "And don't try and change the subject. I thought you quit smoking." She used a napkin to shield her skin as she slid the rhinestone encrusted ashtray to the other side of the table. Standing up she stuffed the napkin in the trash and then glared at her mother.

The woman shrugged, antennae swaying on her head. "I fell off the wagon."

"That would be something... since you never hitched a ride on it to begin with," Ella countered.

Her mother rolled her eyes. "Talk about things you can't pronounce..." She picked up the donut carton and read the ingredients. "All you eat is butylated hydroxyani-whatever and thiamine mononitrate." Her mother frowned. "It's a good thing you exercise." She narrowed her gaze. "How 'bout this... you stop eating your body weight in high fructose corn syrup each year and I'll stop smoking." She thrust out her hand. "Deal?"

Ella refused to budge.

"*Deal?*"

With a sigh, she growled, "Yeah, yeah," and grabbed her mother's palm in defeat. She shook it vigorously and then slumped back into the chair. Resting her elbows on the table she buried her hands in her hair.

"Do you have a new job picked out yet?" Her mother took a bowl of fruit salad from the fridge and joined her at the table.

"Not yet." Ella pulled the want ads off the seat next to her. She reached for the highlighter that had fallen onto the floor and set it next to the paper. She'd circled a few job options earlier, but without a master's degree she could kiss dream job goodbye.

"You should probably nix anything requiring a corset. Looks like employment as a dominatrix is out." Her mother popped a strawberry into her mouth and wiggled her blonde eyebrows.

Ella slapped her thigh, throwing her head back in mock laughter. After a few seconds she eyed her mother and muttered, "You're hilarious."

"Laughter is the best medicine."

Ella scanned the classifieds. "Ha ha, he he, ho ho."

"Okay, I'm sorry. I shouldn't be joking about it. You could have died of heat stroke in that getup."

Chewing on the end of her highlighter, she shrugged. "If you can wear costumes to work in sweltering heat, then I can, too." She peered at her mother and flicked one of the bouncing antennae. "You have the market grand opening today?"

"That's next week. Today I've got the flower shop on Main. They hired me to stand street side, wave at people passing by."

"Too bad it's not tax season. You could be sharing the sidewalk with Mr. Jeffries. Beard and all he makes a lovely Statue of Liberty, don't you think?"

Her mother smiled. "Poor guy. Betty Jeffries sits in that office handling the accounting while her burly husband's outside painted green and dressed in drag."

"And chewing a wad of tobacco the size of my fist." Ella raised an eyebrow.

Her mother chuckled. "Well, I'll try and be a little more ladylike while I'm out there among the people." She poked Ella's shoulder. "But unlike you, I won't be turning down water breaks."

"I didn't realize I needed them." Ella scratched her head. "I was having too much fun with the kids. You should have seen them, Mom. Some of them even dressed in period costume like their parents. They were all so cute."

She had a soft spot for children.

If she ever got married, she wanted three or four.

But she'd probably have to adopt since love and marriage didn't appear to be hovering on her horizon.

A twenty-five year old college student desperate to earn her masters in education had more important things on her mind than romance anyway.

"Well, leave the costume wearing to me from now on, okay?"

"You don't have to twist my arm," Ella said with a smirk.

Her mother grinned. "Good. Now, what's the word? Anything jump out at you?" She pointed at the newspaper.

Ella shrugged, scanning the ads.

"Oh, stop shrugging. You're making my hair droop with all your shrugging lately." Her mother patted the cotton candy fluff of platinum hair grazing her shoulder.

"That's doubtful," Ella muttered. "What's in there? A can and a half of Final Net?"

"Half a can. And you're not funny, Cinderella."

"Don't call me that."

"Then don't knock my hairspray addiction."

"You said you'd never call me that again."

"Your father said he'd never call you that again. I made no such promise." Her mother tweaked her nose with a "honk".

Ella pulled away. "My so-called father could have cared less *what* you called me."

"That's not true." Her mother frowned. "But *I* thought it fit. It's a fairy tale name and it goes perfect with Slipper," she added with a wistful smile. Her expression changed and she popped another strawberry into her mouth. "Just not much of a fairy tale life, huh?"

"I like my life," Ella assured her softly, aggravation dissolved.

"Bet you'd like it even more if we hadn't lost the house." She traced a thin scratch on the Formica, frowned at the cramped kitchen and then glanced back at her daughter. "This is a far cry from a castle."

The distant memory of a two story home with a sunny backyard, an herb garden, her own pretty little bedroom and neighbors on either side with kids her age whizzed through her mind. The house had harbored both good and bad memories, but regardless, she had loved living there as a child. Loved it, that is, until it had been snatched out from under them.

"*We* didn't lose the house. He did." Ella's blood boiled. "He took everything from us. His gambling, his lies, that's all on Clyde Slipper, not you... or me." Ella shook her head and muttered, "Talk about a deadbeat dad."

Her mother set her hand on her clenched fist. She patted it gently until she relaxed. A soft sigh escaped her throat. "I wish things were different."

Ella squeezed her mother's hand. "I don't." Sitting up straighter she added, "I may have a loser for a father, but I won the lottery when it came to mothers."

She brightened. "What did I ever do to deserve such a wonderful daughter?"

"Not a clue." Ella smirked.

Her mother chuckled and finished the last strawberry. She cleared Ella's plate and her own, turning on the faucet. Humming a tune, she wiggled her rear while she washed the dishes. When she finished she turned and asked, "Why don't we go downstairs, and while I open the shop you can decide which elementary school you'll apply to when you graduate? Maybe the one right down the block?"

Ella studied her hopeful expression. Once upon a time her mother had wanted to be a teacher, too, but a worthless man had derailed her goals.

Ella refused to give up on her own dreams. Thanks to Clyde money was tight, but she'd still found jobs that helped finance her education so far. Unfortunately a handful of credits remained on hold. Rent, bills, a few collection agency demands and their little shop downstairs had taken precedence over tuition. She needed more money. She needed a miracle.

"No money. No degree. No career, near or far," Ella mumbled.

"I can dream, can't I?"

Ella flashed a shallow smile. "That's exactly what I'm doing, dreaming."

Her mother tugged the antennae off her head and set them on the counter. She massaged her scalp and then fluffed her blonde bangs. "There's nothing wrong with dreaming. It's giving up on dreaming that's the tragedy."

Ella smiled, nodded and lifted the paper to resume her search. She hesitated when after rifling through the mail her mother muttered, "Hmm."

"What?" Ella asked, setting the newspaper down.

Her mother flicked the corner of a small envelope and then held it out for her to see. "Another one."

"He's persistent, I'll give him that much," Ella said without emotion after reading her father's name on the return address.

"Maybe he's asking for cigarettes again," Trudy said.

"Currency of the realm. What do you think he trades those things for in prison?"

"I have no idea." Her mother tore open the envelope and withdrew a single wrinkled piece of paper. She scanned the letter and frowned. "He's made parole."

"What?"

Her mother opened her mouth to answer, but the ear splitting buzz of their doorbell stole her voice.

"What do you mean he's been paroled?" Ella asked, snatching the letter from her hand.

Her mother snatched it back and stuffed it in its envelope. She set it on the counter. "We'll talk about this after I see who's at the door."

The building they lived in stood on the central square in the busiest section of their quaint town. Their costume/magic shop occupied the rental space downstairs, while the studio apartment they shared made up the entire second floor. No one ever ascended the steps leading to their dwelling, except for Lula's delivery with a family sized mac-n-cheese and a bucket of fried chicken in tow, or stinky Mr. Herbert with the occasional past due notice in his fist.

"Oh God." Ella's heart pounded. "Clyde could be standing on the other side of that door as we speak."

The doorbell screeched again, even longer this time. Her mother waved her hand. "It's not your father. His letter says next week."

She breathed a sigh of relief. Life had been a steaming bowl of crap lately. She didn't need an extra serving of ex-con on her plate as well.

Her mother disappeared behind the huge bookshelf that separated the kitchen from the TV-slash-bedroom-slash-living-room. A few seconds later the metallic swipe of the security chain sliding from its holder preceded the creak of the opening door.

The conversation on the other side of the apartment was unclear, muffled by the rumble of a passing truck on the street below. Ella rose, wanting to read Clyde's most recent letter, but their guest's voice stopped her cold.

"I was given this address. I hope that's okay. I need to speak with Ella..." There was a rustling of papers and then he continued, "Ella Slipper. She lives here, doesn't she?"

She barely registered her mother's reply with the echo of their visitor's deep, sexy voice painting images in her head. *Sprawling plantations, mossy oaks, and sweet iced tea.*

Careful not to scrape the chair against the floor, she left the table. Hidden behind the nine foot high bookshelf room divider she listened to his sexy southern drawl. She would never, ever forget that voice. She knew without a doubt it belonged to the faceless man behind the clubhouse at the Magnolia Falls Civil War Festival.

She slid *The Idiots Guide to Plumbing* off the shelf and peeked through the narrow slot.

Only ten feet away, he stood with his back turned, towering over her mother. *Jeez Louise he's tall.*

He wore a crisp white dress shirt tucked into neatly pressed gray slacks, but the expensive tailoring didn't impress her. His gleaming black hair, broad shoulders, and tight butt, on the other hand, commanded her undivided attention.

Her mother's laughter was like a slap in the face. She jerked out of her trance. The man's hotness factor was irrelevant. The reason for his visit, however... *What the heck is he doing here?* Scratching her forehead, she frowned when little flakes of green fell like moldy snow from her brow and fingertips.

She ground her teeth, squeezing her eyes shut. *Mud Mask!*

Looking down at herself, she bit her tongue to keep from groaning out loud. An oversized T-shirt that advertised, *I do all my own stunts* in big bold print, a chenille *Miss Piggy* bathrobe, and a pair of mismatched knee socks rounded out her morning attire. She looked about as ridiculous as the blonde bumble-bee she lived with.

"I realize it's early, but I really need to talk to her. If that's all right?" He added, drawing Ella's attention.

"Of course." Her mother smiled.

Nooo! Ella glanced left then right. She spotted the dishwasher and wondered if she could stuff herself inside.

"She's in the kitchen."

Mother!

The kitchen had barely enough room for a round table and two chairs. She backed up too quickly, tripping over the braided rug. Grabbing for the table to keep from falling, she missed and tore her mother's silver lamé tablecloth off instead. With a wad of fabric in her grip, she fell on her back, hitting the floor with a bone- rattling thud. The ashtray crashed alongside her.

"Are you okay?" Her mother asked, out of view, a few feet away.

The shiny silver fabric slid off her face and neck. She kept her eyes shut a second longer than necessary, willing the linoleum to swallow her whole.

It didn't.

Damn.

She opened one eye. The other one flew open when she suddenly recognized their guest.

That's Mayor York! He was the one behind the clubhouse? What the heck's the mayor of Magnolia Falls doing in our kitchen?

He knelt beside her, so close she noticed tiny flecks of gold and copper in his sultry green eyes. Widening her focus the luscious bronze of his smoothly shaven skin made her think of sunlight and pure white sand.

Plantations and beaches and sweet tea… Oh my.

Setting the tablecloth aside, his eyes locked with hers. A half smile on his handsome face, Mayor York said, "I need you."

Chapter Three

He took hold of Ella's hand.

Sitting on the kitchen floor, she tried to jerk from the odd electricity zipping from his skin into hers, but he wouldn't let go. His green eyes were unreadable.

With a tug he helped her to her feet, held her hand a few more nerve wracking seconds, and then released his grip suddenly. Rubbing his palm on his slacks like he'd just shaken hands with a leper, he turned away.

So I guess he felt cooties instead of sparks. Nice.

A tad rude, but superbly built, Mayor York snared her attention in their sun-lit kitchen. He bent to retrieve the broken ashtray. His shoulder muscles bulged under crisp white fabric, thighs strained against his slacks. Ella shifted to get a better look at the seat of his pants.

"Go wash up, dear." Her mother's voice slapped her out of a man-candy coma. Coming to her senses, she blushed beneath the mud, muttered a half-assed excuse, and finally ran to the bathroom.

She rubbed the last bits of mud off her skin and splashed her face with cold water. With any luck, the icy liquid would shock her system back into coherence. *Why is our mayor here? Is he trolling for votes? Visiting homes and kissing babies?* She visualized his full lips and wondered if they felt as soft as they looked.

Good grief! Cut it out!

She dried her face and frowned at her bright red cheeks in the medicine cabinet mirror. She'd scrubbed too hard.

Nope, that looks more like sexual heat.

Wincing at her ridiculous thoughts, she yanked the elastic from her lop-sided ponytail, clawed through her long blonde hair and then twisted it into a tight bun. She brushed her teeth and tore off her nightclothes. Standing nearly naked, she realized she'd grabbed nothing to change into. She searched the small bathroom once, twice, three times, coming up empty.

Empty that is, except for one of her mother's costumes slung over the shower curtain rod.

You've got to be kidding me.

She groaned, eyed her goofy pajamas littering the floor and then speared the costume with exasperation. *Decisions, decisions. Either I sit and talk to our illustrious mayor looking like a demented teenager, or Captain Hook.*

"Crap."

She made her choice and hurried out of the bathroom.

"There she is," Her mother said.

Ella lifted her chin and straightened her spine when their guest glanced over his shoulder at her.

Yes she was dressed in a T-shirt, robe and knee socks. And yes she looked silly, but there was no way in hell she would've sprinted past him, rifled through her drawers or their overstuffed closet searching for a change of clothes all while in plain sight of him. So if he had a problem with her attire, too bad. Ignoring the heat flooding her cheeks she strode to the sofa her mother occupied. She plopped into the saggy cushions and quickly covered her bare knees with piggy pink chenille.

"Why's your face so red?" Her mother asked.

Ella glared at her, willing her to drop it.

Thankfully Trudy had been trained in the art of mind reading. Instead of dwelling on her complexion the woman glanced at their guest and smiled. "Well, Mayor York. Why don't you tell Ella why you came?"

The tall man sat on an ancient wicker armchair. His refined attire and movie star face looked so out of place in their apartment Ella almost laughed. He belonged on the cover of *Town and Country*, not in a modest studio loft furnished with garage sale finds and thrift store bargains.

"Well," he said, studying Ella. "I mentioned to your mother a few minutes ago that I'd like to offer you a job."

"A job?" Ella asked, baffled.

"Yes." He rose and the rickety chair creaked its relief. In the middle of the room, he stood a few feet from the neatly made daybed she slept on. If he stepped back, he might stumble onto it. She prayed she'd have the strength to resist flinging herself on top of him if he went down.

What's wrong with you? Stop salivating over the guy. "What kind of a job?"

"I would need you to move into my home. I have a young son in need of a twenty-four-seven babysitter. A nanny."

"You... don't even know me," she said, frowning, "And you want me to take care of your child?"

"I know all I need to know about you, Miss Slipper."

"What's that supposed to mean?" She shifted in her seat, eyeing him cautiously.

"Just that I know you're looking for employment."

She noticed the papers he held in his hand. "What're those?" She pointed at them.

He waved them off. "The festival you were hired for is over. It's a once a year deal. And frankly," his sexy drawl suddenly irritated her, "I was told the pay you earned wouldn't sustain you a few days, much less the year." He raised a raven eyebrow. "You're out of work, correct?"

She squinted at the papers and then glared at him. "What else is written there about me? And where'd you get the info?" Her father was doing time for identity theft. Having this man go behind her back and pry into her life didn't sit well with her.

He folded the papers, slipped them into his breast pocket and frowned. "I spoke with Miss Bartwell... um, the woman who hired you for the festival..."

"I know who Miss Bartwell is," Ella snapped.

"Well she assured me you're between jobs, that you have numerous bills to pay and could use some steady employment. She's actually very concerned for you."

She had really liked the woman, but wished she hadn't answered so many of her endless personal questions. What else had her employer told this guy? Ella sat straighter, raised her chin higher. Their predicament was nobody's business but their own.

"I assure you the pay will be excellent, working for me. But I need an answer right away." He glanced at his watch. "I'm already late to a meeting."

Pessimism strode arm-in-arm with coincidence. Nothing in her entire life had ever come this easy. *Nothing.* In her experience if it sounded too good to be true... it *always* was. She had dear old dad to thank for that bit of wisdom.

She looked Mayor York in the eye and said, "I'm sorry, but I'm not available."

"Ella, that's not true." Her mother stood up and stepped closer to their guest. "She'll take the job."

She ignored her and studied the neatly folded rectangle of papers bowing the fabric of his shirt pocket. *What else is written there?* "I'm unavailable," Ella repeated.

"For how long?" He asked.

"She can start tomorrow," her mother assured him.

Ella threw up her hands. "Will you cut it out, Mom?" Not only was she suspicious of the way he had checked up on her, but minutes earlier she'd been imagining him tumbling into her bed. She'd been drooling over his perfect face, his voice, his butt, for God's sake. Working for him, as a live-in nanny no less, was out of the question.

She opened her mouth to refuse his offer again, but her mother spoke first. "Mayor York, would you mind giving my daughter and me a moment?" She took hold of his forearm and practically dragged him toward the kitchen. He checked his watch and seemed ready to object, but the skinny blonde bumble-bee managed to maneuver him behind the bookshelf partition regardless.

A second later her mother hurried back into the main room. She stopped in front of Ella, that famous, *what the heck's wrong with you,* look on her face. It was no surprise when she whispered, 'What the heck's wrong with you?' through her teeth.

"Mom—"

"Seriously, Ella, what's wrong with you?"

"Um, well, let's see. The mayor of our town, who... might I also add, happens to have a famous senator for a father and one of America's most beloved actresses for a mother is in our house offering me a job while I'm dressed like this." She did a quick Vanna White sweep of her attire.

"So what?

"So what, she says." Ella snorted. "Politician's, an Oscar winning actress? Who needs that drama?"

"You do. His family's loaded. You could use that money."

"I know, but—"

"But nothing. You love kids. He said it pays great. It's perfect. You can put it on your resume and earn money for those last few credits."

"I can't go to school if I'm taking care of his son twenty-four-seven."

"You can take classes on line."

"I can't student teach on line," she shot back.

Her mother opened her mouth and then snapped it shut.

Ella folded her arms across her chest. "Got ya there, Skippy." She stepped closer and lowered her voice further. "And honestly, you don't see anything wrong with him going behind my back, looking into my life, invading my privacy? Our privacy? Remind you of anyone?"

Her mother's brow wrinkled. She looked confused as hell, but then her eyes widened and she shook her head. "Ella, that man isn't your father. He's got a little boy he wants to hire a nanny for. He has every right to do a background check on you. You're being ridiculous. He's not stealing your identity. He's being a good parent."

She didn't have a comeback for that one. Suddenly she *did* feel pretty ridiculous.

"Got ya there, Skippy," her mother mocked with a smirk.

Ella scratched her head. She couldn't imagine *not* investigating an employee that would have complete access to her child. In fact, she'd probably hire a private investigator to do the honors. Especially if she came from a famous family like his. She frowned toward the kitchen. The wall of books blocked her view of their guest. She glanced back at her mother. The woman's hot pink smirk had deepened. *God I hate when she's right. There'll be no living with her.*

"Accept the job, Ella. Work for him as long as it takes to make the balance of your tuition and then put in your notice." She set her hand on her shoulder. Squeezing gently she whispered, "Don't let fear keep you from your goals."

Ella frowned. "Fear? What are you talking about?"

Her mother smiled indulgently. "How 'bout we muddle through that question another day? When there's not a potential employer waiting patiently in the kitchen?"

Before she could argue, her mother turned on her heel and strode into the kitchen.

Ella rubbed the bridge of her nose and took a deep breath before following. In less than twenty steps she rounded the bookshelf.

Mayor York sat at the table, her mother stood at the counter scrutinizing her broken ashtray.

Ella pulled out a chair to sit.

Their guest stood before her butt hit the seat. "I really have to get to the office." He slid a business card from his wallet and handed it to Ella.

"My offer stands. I'm certain you would make a fine caretaker for my son. Do you have a salary in mind?"

Huh? She'd never been given this option before. *Come up with my own salary?* Her mind raced. *Twenty-four-seven, twenty-four-seven... That's a lot of babysitting.* Doing math in her head made her brain hurt. Instead, she blurted a sum, "Fifteen hundred a week, plus room and board." He'd be stupid to agree, but at least negotiations would start high.

"Done."

She nearly fell off her chair.

Something crashed on the floor. Ella eyed her mother as the woman stooped to pick up what was left of the ashtray she'd just dropped. The blonde bumble-bee mouthed the words, *Cha-ching* to her.

Their guest didn't appear to notice and continued talking. "I'm rarely at home so I'll need you to move into my residence full time to take care of Eric. You'll occupy your own suite across the hall from him, plenty of privacy. You won't be expected to clean or prepare meals. Your responsibilities will lie with him alone." He straightened his tie, smoothing it against his impeccable shirt. Pushing in his chair, the corners of his mouth twitched, hinting at a smile. The expression was so quick, Ella wasn't sure she'd actually seen it.

"I expect your acceptance before eight this evening. You can reach me at my office." He pointed at the card she still held in her hand. "Now, if you'll both excuse me"

With those words, he left the kitchen. A few seconds later, the apartment door closed with a soft click.

Ella shook her head. "I expect your acceptance before eight this evening," she mocked, straightening her invisible tie. "Oh, you want fifteen hundo a week? Done. A mere pittance..." She couldn't quite get the accent or the deep timbre of his voice, but she figured she had the snooty attitude down pat. She blew a noisy breath through her lips, ruffling her bangs. "Can you believe that guy? What a conceited ass."

Her mother dumped the pieces of her luckless ashtray into the trash, opened the pantry, took out the cookie jar and set it on the table. She poured them each a cup of coffee and after blowing the steam from her mug, said, "So, when are you moving into the ass's house?"

Ella reached into the container, pulled out a double stuffed Oreo and pried open the halves.

"As soon as I pack," she muttered, and shoved the icing side in her mouth.

Chapter Four

"Here's the rest of it," Wilson Boggs said as he lowered his bulk into a chair.

Alex took the manila folder from his campaign manager. He opened it and withdrew the paperwork, fanning it out in front of him on his desk. "What are all these pictures?"

Boggs shrugged. "You paid that guy a shitload for info this specific. He said he figured you'd want him to go overboard with the telephoto." He raised an eyebrow. "Hey, she's easy on the eyes. I don't blame him for snapping a few, do you?"

Alex frowned at his friend.

Boggs chuckled. "Lighten up, York."

"I'll lighten up when I'm dead," Alex muttered, scanning the images. He could care less about the money. It was the thirty or forty photographs the P.I. he'd hired had taken without his consent that bothered him. He'd be pissed as hell if he found out someone was spying on him. He imagined Ella Slipper might feel the same if she ever got wind of this.

But he had his reasons. For his son's sake he needed to know.

"Like he said when he gave you the preliminaries last week, she's clean," Boggs assured him. "Digging deeper didn't reveal any illegal activity, no drugs, no arrests of any kind, nada. And if she'd stolen a pencil in grade school, his team would've found out about it. Her and her mom are about as law abiding as they come."

Boggs smoothed his comb-over. "Don't be surprised when you see the mom dressed in a bunch of different costumes in those pictures."

"She wore a costume yesterday when I met her. What's up with that?"

"Probably on her way to work. She's got a job at Gwinnett Medical Center's children's ward, dresses up for the kids, tells stories and does little plays for them. Also volunteers at the library for story time in costume. I guess it's a good use of the inventory in their store." Boggs scratched his head, ruffling the thinning copper strands clinging to his scalp. He sat back in his seat. "So mother and daughter are legit, but dear old dad, well..." He chuckled. "Your P.I. wrote that he's far from the worst piece of shit he's ever seen, but said Clyde Slipper's never taken the straight and narrow."

While Boggs spoke, Alex thumbed through the pictures. *Ella sitting in the park with a newspaper in one hand, a highlighter in the other. Ella buying groceries. Ella with her mother dressed as a witch, broom and all, walking into the library. Ella with her mother dressed as a white rabbit, in the hospital parking lot. Ella kicking her car door. Ella sitting in her parked car, forehead pressed against the steering wheel.*

The telephoto lens the investigator had used had captured her expression in the last photo. Her brow was wrinkled, nose red. Tears shined on her cheeks.

Alex frowned and then condensed the glossies into a single pile. He set them on his desk.

"Trudy Bowen, Ella's mom, fell for Slipper when she worked as his magician's assistant."

"He's a magician?"

"Was. Small potatoes. Worked dinner theatre. Used to saw her in half."

"That shop Ella lives above... what's it called?" Alex had trouble recalling the name of the tiny storefront.

Boggs continued. "The Glass Slipper. It's half magic store, half costume rental. Anyway, Clyde started duping Trudy the minute they got married. His magic was going nowhere so he got her to sign half of the shop she'd inherited over to him. It'd been in her family since the sixties. The Glass Slipper was originally called—"

"Bowen's Emporium? In Atlanta, right?" Alex asked, putting the names together. "I remember that place. I bought a costume there for a frat party years ago."

"That's the one... or used to be. It's gone now, mostly. That shop Trudy and Ella live above is all that's left." Boggs noticed a crusty stain on his shirt sleeve and scratched at it with his fingernail while he continued. "They had to downsize when Clyde ran the Emporium into the ground. He'd been skimming profits to pay for horse racing, cards. You name it he bet on it." He inspected his nail. "Their house was next. Clyde had taken out a second mortgage and defaulted. They lost everything because of him."

A knock at his office door drew Alex's attention. "Yes?"

Faust entered. "Your brother just arrived, Sir."

Alex sighed. "Is that camera guy with him?"

"He's alone, Sir."

"Good." Alex massaged the bridge of his nose. Had Conner finally given up on landing his own reality show? "Tell him I'll be out in about five minutes."

"Yes, Sir," his valet said and disappeared into the hall, closing the door behind him.

"No entourage? That's a first." Boggs said, shifting in his seat. "Good thing, too. The last thing your campaign needs is your little brother in a reality show."

"You're preaching to the choir. Conner's all about Conner. You think he cares whether I'm running for governor or not?"

"Just keep praying the networks continue turning him down."

A headache pounded in Alex's skull. His brother's antics needed to stop. "How about we change the subject."

Boggs nodded. "Okay then, getting back to your employee. Soon after they lost the house, Clyde did just shy of a nickel for robbery. When he got out he moved into the studio Trudy and Ella live in now. She was a teenager at the time, Ella that is. You'd think dad would clean up his act, but he applied for credit cards in his daughter's name and started his shenanigans all over again."

"No wonder she can't get a loan."

"Ella Slipper can't get a break much less a loan."

"Where's her father now?"

"Penitentiary, Atlanta. Identity theft. He's up for parole, though. If he's played his cards right he'll be a free man in about a week."

Alex nodded.

Boggs pointed to the files spread across his desk. "It's all there in black and white." He shrugged. "I didn't find a single reason why she shouldn't watch Eric."

"Good."

"I have a few errands to take care of before we go over your schedule for the week. I'll be back later this evening." He strode to the door, opened it, but turned back before leaving the room. "Oh and word to the wise…"

Alex glanced at him. "Yeah?"

"Keep your eye on the ball, not on her."

"Who, the nanny?"

"Yeah, the nanny. You're a good looking guy. She's a good looking girl. And that blonde, blue-eyed slice of cheesecake is gonna be living under your roof. All I'm saying is don't take a bite. Push that plate aside and concentrate on winning the governor's seat."

Alex shook his head. "I never eat desert."

"Never say never."

"She's here for one reason… Eric. Good looking or not, she's my employee. My only interest in her is how well she'll take care of my son."

His friend nodded. "Glad to hear it." He turned and strode into the hall and called out, "This is your moment, York. I can feel it," as he disappeared out of sight.

Alex gathered the P.I.'s report and straightened the pile.

One of the pages was skewed so he withdrew it. The image printed on its surface snared his attention. A black and white copy of Ella's driver's license smiled back at him, long hair draped over her shoulder, lips full and inviting. He didn't need color to instantly recall the incredible blue of her eyes.

A sudden craving for cheesecake assaulted him.

Shit.

He condensed the pages and shoved them all in their folder. As he stowed them in a bottom drawer he heard a racket in the hall.

Alex sat back in his chair and rubbed the pain pulsing in his right temple.

"Lex, I think Faust might have added a second stick to the original he had shoved up his—?"

Alex cut him off. "Don't say it."

His younger brother grinned. "Did you and your valet get a two for one deal on stick implantation?"

Alex continued rubbing his temple. "Why are you here?"

Conner sat in the chair across from Alex. "Now is that any way to greet your favorite brother?"

"You're my only brother."

Conner grinned. "Got that right, and good thing, too. Who else but me would put up with you?" His smile turned to a frown when he realized Alex wasn't in the mood. "What?"

"No camera crew today? Is it possible you've finally given up on the show?"

Conner frowned. "Hell no."

Alex sighed. "Then where's your shadow? Not that I miss him."

"Oh, he's sleeping off a gallon of gin. Later he'll help me edit some of the footage we shot. The networks are gonna realize soon enough I've got a great concept. Plus, mom's got connections."

"So riding her wake for the rest of your life is okay with you?" Alex asked as he stood at the lunch cart Maggie had brought in earlier. He eyed the coffee pot. "Why don't you do something productive with your life and money instead?"

Conner's response consisted of another shallow shrug.

He lost interest in the coffee and took a step closer to his brother. "You're nearly twenty-eight years old. Don't you think it's time you got a job? A real job?"

"The show will be my job."

"Yeah, keep telling yourself that." Alex shook his head. "Even if you're lucky enough to get it, don't forget that it can be snatched right out from under you when you least expect it."

"If I'd have wanted a lecture I would've visited mom and dad."

"You don't listen to them either."

Conner ruffled his jet black hair. He scrubbed the back of his neck and then dropped his hand. "Don't you wanna know why I came here to begin with?"

"You mean it wasn't to piss me off and interrupt my day?"

He rolled his eyes. "Just listen. I think I found a nanny for Eric."

Alex sat back in his seat assessing his brother. *This should be interesting.*

"You're looking for another one, right?"

"I found one already." Alex strode to the window. Watching the wind ruffle the leaves he added, "And she's not some pole dancer you met at shoe show."

"I didn't meet this chick at a strip club."

"At a bar then."

"It was a pub if you want to get technical," he muttered.

"Well that makes all the difference. Sorry I doubted you."

"This her?"

Alex turned from the window. His brother held one of the photos from the pile he'd left on his desk. "Put it down."

Conner whistled and an eyebrow rose on his forehead. "No wonder you picked her." He nearly salivated over Ella's picture. "Thinking you'll get a little somethin' somethin' on the side, maybe?"

Alex took the picture from him and set it back on the others, face down.

"That's right, bro. Hide it for later. Just make sure you lock the door so Maggie doesn't walk in on you while you got your junk in your hand."

"Don't you have to leave now?"

"Yeah, yeah," Conner said, standing. "Just stopped by to offer my nanny finding services." He dug in his pocket to retrieve his phone. After a quick check of its screen he smiled at his brother. "Your loss. Lolita loves kids."

"Lolita?"

"Yeah, the nanny I was talking about. She's from Madrid." He stepped closer and whispered as if the office were filled with nuns. "That woman can do this thing with her mouth that...." He shivered. "Let's just say you won't walk right for a week after she's through with you."

"Thanks for the tip."

"So it's a yes?"

"Um... no."

"Hey, I tried." He strode toward the door and opened it. "Where's the little guy anyway?"

"Taking a nap."

"I would've liked to see him."

Alex smiled for the first time since his brother arrived. "You know he's always liked you." The list of Conner's faults was a mile long, but hating kids had never been on it. He'd always gotten along with Eric. Back when his son still spoke Conner used to take him fishing or to the movies. He'd make a decent father one day if he'd stop partying and learn some responsibility.

"I like him, too. Nothin' wrong with the strong silent type."

Alex nodded, grateful for his brother's words. "I've always appreciated the time you've spent trying to get through to him." He envisioned his parents. How they seemed uninterested in Eric. They never visited him or even asked about him. "It makes me mad that mom and dad are nowhere as diligent."

"Give Hades and Medusa a break. You know those two. They're uncomfortable with anything they can't control."

"So you're sticking up for them now."

He chuckled. "Hell no, but mom said she'd get me an audition for Bruckheimer's next flick, so I'm playing the dutiful son until then." He moved into the hall and took a few steps before hesitating. He pointed at Alex. "Hey, make me proud."

"Of what?"

"What's that saying? Dip your pen in the company ink?"

"It's *don't* dip your pen in the company ink."

"Whatever, Bro. Just promise you'll live a little while the hottie's on your payroll."

"That's not why I hired her."

"Yeah, we'll see."

"Goodbye, Conner," Alex said, giving his brother a shove toward the stairs.

"Okay. Smell ya later douche bag."

Alex returned to his office with a smirk on his face. He could never stay mad at his brother. No one could. He supposed that's why he got away with so much.

He took a seat at his desk.

Eric's photo caught his eye. His son smiled back at him. But the expression on his little face was nothing more than a moment caught in time. Time he suddenly realized he'd never get back.

His humor was immediately extinguished.

He loved his son more than anyone on Earth, and he wanted to tell him so. He wanted to play catch with him, go to the park with him, read him stories at night and tuck him in. He wanted to talk... to him...

He swallowed hard. His mouth went dry again.

He had accused his parents of being absent from his son's life, but he was more at fault of emotionally neglecting his child than they could ever be.

Guilt tore a hole in his chest.

He had failed his own flesh and blood.

He needed to make things right, but had no idea where to start.

Taking hold of the small framed photo of Eric, he drew in a deep breath and then let it out slowly. After a moment he set it back on his desk and accidentally hit the pile of pictures the P.I. had taken. One of the rectangles slid off the top and onto the blotter.

He turned it over.

Ella, crying in her car.

He ran his index finger across her image.

He smiled grimly.

Maybe Ella Sipper would be that start he was searching for.

Chapter Five

Ella took a left onto Verdant Court. Rain pelted the windshield, distorting everything beyond the furiously swishing wipers. She squinted through the windows, gaping at the homes she passed. Her 1980 Volkswagen Beetle, lovingly named "Pepto" thanks to its a-*Bismol* Pink paint job, skimmed the curb and she jerked the exhaust-belcher back into its lane. She shook her head, annoyed, and glued her eyes to the wet pavement.

Jeez, they're just fancy houses. Get a grip.

She had spent the previous day knowing she had no choice but to accept the job Mayor York had offered. *Sure*, the man was arrogant and rude, but fifteen hundred bucks a week for a few months would cover her last semester and a whole lot more.

"Call the man, Ella," her mother had finally said, handing her back the thick embossed business card.

Ella had growled her displeasure and though the guy rubbed her the wrong way, she had called.

But instead of the mayor an abrupt female secretary answered. The woman had given Ella directions to the house and the time she was expected to arrive. "Don't be late," the secretary concluded. "Mayor York cannot abide a tardy employee."

Ella glanced at her watch after she slowed in front of the right house number. *Perfect timing. Eight fifty on the nose. Ten minutes to spare. Boo yaa!*

She turned into the driveway and stopped in front of an impressive iron gate. The ornate perimeter fence seemed about six feet tall, and each delicately wrought but rigid black picket ended in an arrow shaped spike. Elegant shrubs and a forest of mature hardwoods rose out of the landscape just beyond its intimidating boundary.

She cranked down her window, leaning away from the rain to speak into the intercom. Before she could say a word a small black camera perched on the intercom pillar focused in on her.

Cheese.

Her hesitant smile wavered. An electronic buzz heralded the opening of the gate.

Vibrating violently under the continuous downpour, red and gold leaves formed a fiery canopy that blocked out the slate sky as Pepto lurched ahead. She drove past stately Oaks and ancient Dogwoods until a break in the trees revealed her destination.

Pulling into the circular driveway she braked in front of an enormous brick home and cut the engine. While it continued to sputter and cough like a cranky old woman she ducked her head and craned her neck, straining to see all three stories rising above the windshield.

Crap. That's not a house. It's freakin' Tara.

Once Pepto wheezed its last, Ella grabbed the overstuffed duffel that held clothing, toiletry items, and a framed photo of her mother wearing a Sombrero. The heavy bag wedged against the steering wheel as she scooted off the seat and by the time she jerked it free, hoisted it into her arms, and sprinted up the front steps, she'd been soaked.

Dropping her bag on the porch, which sheltered the front and wrapped around the sides of... *Scarlett O'Hara's mansion*, Ella wiped the rain from her face. She squeezed a gallon of water from her ponytail. Frowning at the bag, she muttered, "Where's a butler when you need one?"

The words were barely out of her mouth, when the front door swung open. And there stood... *Lurch.*

The tall elderly man's expression looked as dry as her mother's recent attempt at Meatloaf.

"Miss Slipper, I presume?"

"Yes," she replied, trying not to seem amused by the way his beaked nose bobbed as he enunciated each word in a cultured British accent.

"May I take your belongings?"

"It's just the one, but it's pretty heav...y..."

Before she could reach for it, he grabbed the frayed strap and lifted the bag like it was filled with bubbles. "This way," he commanded and turned into the house.

Ella had expected grandeur, but not like this.

Her apartment would fit inside the enormous foyer with room to spare. Ornate moldings lined the walls, and a large round table took center stage.

Crystals dangled like suspended raindrops from the arms of a chandelier hanging high above. The fixture cast a soft glow throughout the foyer. As they ascended an impressive double staircase, what Ella thought to be stone turned out to be trompe l'oeil. She stopped to gape at the illusion.

"Jeez Louise, that's gorgeous." She ran her fingers over the wall.

"Young lady, please do try and keep up."

She tore herself from the wall and hurried to catch up with Lurch.

"Where's my bag?" She asked at the top of the stairs, when she noticed he no longer held it.

"It has been taken to your room by a member of the staff."

"Missed that." Ella shrugged.

"When one stands about with one's mouth hanging open while ogling a man's possessions, one tends to miss things, yes."

She chewed her lip. *I've made a friend.*

Lurch proceeded down the hall. Ella followed, wondering what she'd gotten herself into.

Alex stood at the bank of windows in the rear of his office, watching the rain.

He hated rain.

It brought gray skies and gloom, and sometimes even death.

Today, however, the rain brought a bit of hope. *A brand new start.*

Ella would walk through his office doors any second. He'd been informed of her arrival.

Hiring her elated and disturbed him at the same time.

His son had spoken.

Angel.

One word had shifted his world in a whole new direction.

Eric had seen doctors all over the country after the accident. Not for cuts, concussions or internal bleeding, but for a broken heart.

Psychiatrists had offered treatment for his emotionally scarred son, but none were able to break his silence or heal his wounded soul after his mother's death.

Until Ella Slipper came along.

She'd somehow succeeded where everyone else had failed, including him.

He'd move heaven and Earth to hire her.

And he'd nearly screwed that all to hell.

He'd been a jerk at her apartment. He couldn't help it though. Part of his rudeness developed out of urgency. The sooner she moved in, the sooner she might get Eric to smile again. And if she could make him smile, maybe she could also encourage him to say something more.

Unfortunately, another part of his shitty behavior stemmed from an urge of a different kind.

When he saw her lying on her kitchen floor it had taken enormous restraint to keep from lifting her into his arms and pressing her warm, rose scented body against his chest.

She'd been covered in green mud, but he still recognized desire smoldering in her unusual eyes. A shock wave had rocketed through his veins. Touching her hand had only tripled the electricity. He'd forced the sexual reaction from his mind, but his effort didn't last. Later, she'd walked across the room, sunlight streaming through her apartment windows, highlighting long toned legs beneath the short bathrobe she wore. He couldn't take his eyes off her smooth, pale flesh. He'd wondered if her skin was a soft as it looked. And then he'd wondered how it would feel to bury himself deep inside her.

Lusting after an employee was a huge mistake. An unethical mistake. Plus, the opportunity to be hurt by a woman again wasn't high on his list.

He'd been there, done that, got the fucking T-shirt. And he'd be damned if he'd go through that pain again.

So he'd smothered his craving and feigned indifference.

A knock at the door ended frustrating thoughts.

Faust walked in at his bidding, his crooked nose a little higher in the air than usual. "Miss Slipper," the valet stated blandly.

Faust stepped aside and Ella entered the room.

Alex drew in a breath. *Maybe she'll bring Eric back to me.*

Her hair was soaked. Her skin glistened with rainwater. Her t-shirt and cargo-pants clung to every curve, though there weren't many. Small, firm breasts and hard nipples were perfectly outlined beneath the soggy fabric.

Or... maybe she'll just give me a chronic case of blue balls.

It was a struggle to shift focus from her body, but once he met her gaze, the fight ended.

She blinked. Though her hair and skin were pale white, nearly colorless, her eyes were a completely different story. The color of Tahitian water, deep oceanic blue, nearly turquoise, they sparkled with life and warmth.

Christ. Those eyes are gonna kill me.

Alex had never felt such a powerful attraction toward a woman. Not ever. Not even for his wife.

Ella Slipper had consumed his every thought since he'd met her.

That knowledge terrified him. He clenched his fists. Bringing her into his home could turn out to be the best—or possibly the worst—thing that could ever happen to him.

Chapter Six

The door clicked behind her. Checking over her shoulder, Ella realized the butler had left. She glanced back at her host. They were alone. She shivered, but doubted the goose bumps had anything to do with the thermostat.

To fill the awkward silence, she smiled and said, 'What's with the undertaker?' jerking a thumb at the door.

Mayor York narrowed his eyes.

She chewed her lip, but jumped when something poked her shoulder. She spun around. Lurch stood behind her holding out a thick white towel. "Jeez, you scared the crap out of me."

His crooked nose twitched. He handed her the towel then spun on his heel like a soldier. In a few steps, the undertaker left the room as soundlessly as he'd re-entered.

Ella glanced at her employer. *Good job, Miss Blurt Without Thinking. Nice way to start your first day.* "I'm sorry. I shouldn't have shouted at him. Your butler's—"

"Faust isn't a butler. He's a valet. He's been with my family since I was a kid." His words were monotone, without the melodic tenor she'd salivated over in her apartment. He seemed annoyed with her, put out. Her discomfort shot to the ceiling.

He strode to his desk. Without looking at her, he said, "The towel was offered for a reason." He glanced up as he took a seat. "You're dripping all over the carpet."

She squeezed her hair in the plush fabric, but the terry loops caught one of the sapphire stud earrings her mother had given her for high school graduation. She tried to tug the fabric away and winced. She realized he watched her.

"Is there a problem, Miss Slipper?"

Annoyed by his tone, she ignored him and kept tugging. Unfortunately the towel didn't seem to want to leave her ear.

He stood, rounded the desk and closed the distance between them. She turned from him and tugged some more.

"Don't pull so hard, you're going to rip—"

"Your fancy towel?" She interrupted with a sarcastic snort.

He stepped in front of her, blocking the light from a nearby lamp with his towering frame. Pinned by his shadow, she stopped tugging. Standing eye level with his chest, she slowly peered up.

She was growing accustomed to the unreadable slash of his full lips, but his eyes narrowed in a surprising smile of their own. "Your *ear*," he replied softly. "You'll rip your earring out of your *ear*." He reached for her. Though his melodic tenor had returned, she flinched, taking a step back. His voice, his body, that clean soap scent drifting off his skin wove disturbing thoughts through her mind.

Bodies.

Their bodies.

Entwined together.

Sting's lyrics, "Don't stand so close to me," popped into her head. An embarrassing flush scalded her cheeks and she wanted to bolt, but two words chained her in place.

"May I?" He moved even closer, raising his hand.

She couldn't speak. Couldn't breathe. She just stood there like a water-logged deer in headlights.

His gaze touched her eyes, her cheeks, her lips. It roamed her face, then focused on her jaw and ear. She couldn't help feeling like she'd just been visually caressed.

He brushed aside the soggy ponytail that lay against her neck and gently loosened her grip on the towel. Heat scorched her skin in the wake of his fingertips, and his touch ignited sensitive nerves and unfamiliar desires. She nearly dropped her head to the side to give him better access but harbored just enough willpower to keep still.

He grasped the towel in one hand and her earring in the other. His eyes, the deep green of summer leaves, focused in on the task. His warm breath kissed her cheek and throat, sending goose bumps on a mad scurry up her arms. A little closer and she could bury her face against his chest and inhale his simple but mesmerizing scent.

Thankfully, before she had the chance, the spell was broken. She was free.

His eyes flicked back to hers. He inhaled sharply, then leaned away with a grimace.

She frowned, resisting the urge to sniff her armpit. *Did I forget deodorant this morning?*

He pulled the cloth from her neck, then strode toward his desk. Dumping the towel in a wad on the polished wood, he sat down. "Faust will show you to your room. Change and report back here in ten minutes." He said all of this while focusing on some papers.

What the heck's wrong with you? She wanted to yell, but bit her tongue. First day of work and all. But she couldn't help wondering how she could want to jump his bones one second and kick his balls through his throat the next.

And therein lay her quandary.

She needed this job, but the man obviously couldn't stand her. Her attraction to him, though irrational and skin deep, was also an issue. She couldn't work for a guy she found so incredibly sexy. *It's not professional. It's not fair to his son. It's moronic... and he's rude.*

She made up her mind.

"I'm sorry, Mayor York. I can't work for you." She spun around, flung open the door and ran down the stairs.

She hurried through the foyer and noticed Lurch, Faust, whatever the heck his name was, standing at the open front door. He held her bag extended from his body like it contained biohazard waste. Ella sneered at him. "Eavesdropper," she accused, grabbed her bag, and ran out into the pouring rain.

Water pelted her as she grabbed Pepto's handle. The door sometimes stuck at unfortunate moments, usually when she rushed home to pee after a long day at school or work. Another unfortunate moment kept her yanking at the door as she and her two-hundred pound bag got re-soaked.

"Damn." Alex flew after Ella. He'd never made a habit of begging for anything. Never had to. But right now, if it came down to it, he'd drop down on his knees to bring her back into his house.

What's the matter with you? Get over the fact that this woman disturbs you on every level and just focus on Eric's needs.

He rushed down the stairs and past Faust, who stood at the open door with a raised eyebrow.

He ran into the downpour and caught up with her. "Come back."

Rain fell steadily on their heads. It soaked their clothes and hair.

Ella glared at him as she yanked on the door of her ugly pink car. Her lagoon eyes had darkened to the hue of a stormy windswept sea. "This isn't a good fit," she shouted, trying to be heard above the din as she hoisted her bag around onto her back. She grunted, playing tug-o-war with the car handle.

"I'm not a nanny. I'm not... I'm not good with children." The way she choked on her words made her declaration sound like a lie. "Your son is better off without me." The bag swung forward and hit the car with a thud. With a disgusted curse, she dropped it on the ground.

The rain suddenly slowed, making it easier to see and hear. He set his hand on her icy fingers. She stopped tugging and stiffened.

"I need you." He ran a hand over his face and through his wet hair. "My son needs you," he clarified. "Come back inside." Defiance flared in her eyes and he hastily added, "Please, Miss Slipper. Please, just come back inside."

Jerking her hand from beneath his, she frowned at him. "I told you. I'm not right for this job."

"You're exactly the person for it."

"Why would you say that? You might have checked up on me, but you don't know me, not really. Not as a person."

"I didn't just check up on you. I needed to be sure so I went deeper. " He regretted his words the minute they came out. Her eyes widened and her jaw dropped. She looked like her head might explode.

"You what? How did you... what do you mean, deeper?" She blurted the questions, then resumed tugging on the handle. The door sprang open, throwing her off balance. He reached for her, but she slapped his hand away and grabbed for her bag. He snatched it up first.

"Gimme that!" She barked.

Alex jerked it from reach.

"Are you ten years old? Give me my bag!"

"Come on. I needed to know everything about you. You'd be taking care of the most important person on Earth to me." He held the bag behind his back like a bully on a playground. Playing keep away with a grown woman wasn't his idea of chivalry. The words Jack-Ass and Dick-Head came to mind, but none of that mattered. If taking her bag hostage gave him enough time to convince her to stay, it was worth it.

She stood still. The rain slowed to a heavy drizzle and rivers of water traced their way down her face and neck. Her snug black t-shirt adhered to her body like a second skin. Her nipples pebbled beneath the fabric, and he prayed the rain would never stop. He needed the frigid shower to douse the fire smoldering under his skin.

"I'm sorry I invaded your privacy... but I did it because I love my son."

She wiped water from her face and looked away, seeming to contemplate his words. When she finally focused on him again she said, "It pissed me off at first. Hearing you talk at my apartment like you knew everything about me. I got over that, though. But now you tell me you dug even deeper? You could have requested a resume. We could have sat down and had a proper interview. You could have asked permission to pry into my private life."

"That would have wasted time."

"Wasted time?" Confusion clouded her stormy eyes. "What's the rush?"

He drew in a deep breath and rubbed his forehead, wishing he had a jacket to cover her shivering body. "Can we discuss this inside? Out of the rain?"

She folded her arms across her chest. "No. I'm not afraid of a little rain." She scanned his wet clothes. Her scrutiny ended at his feet. She glanced back up at him. "You afraid your snappy shoes might drown?"

He noticed his handmade Italian loafers were more than wet. The custom shoes were now a pair of custom crap.

"I don't care about my shoes, Miss Slipper," he challenged.

"Because you can buy another fifty pairs?"

"The only thing I care about is Eric. Nothing else... nothing."

He scanned the house toward the east wing. Last night while Eric slept, he had visited him. Nighttime was the only time he could really spend near his son. The little boy wanted nothing to do with him when he was awake.

He'd pulled the covers higher on his small body and kissed his forehead, trying his best not to disturb him. Sitting in the rocking chair next to his bed for nearly an hour, he'd watched him sleep.

He initially thought Eric's sudden communication occurred after seeing a costumed character. But as far as he knew, his son hadn't uttered a word to *Scarlett O'Hara*, or whoever she'd been dressed as. For whatever reason he was only motivated to speak when she'd been stripped of her bonnet and wig.

Alex glanced at her. He jammed his hands into his pockets to keep from pulling her into his arms. His happiness and hope for his son's recovery was so strong he wanted to crush her into his embrace. But hugging her, even in appreciation, would be a mistake. He doubted he'd want to let go.

"Eric saw you at the festival behind the clubhouse. In the woods."

Recognition flared in her eyes. "He's Donald Trump's Mini-me."

Alex smiled grimly. "He saw you when you were unconscious."

She bit her lip. "That must have scared him." Her expression shifted from defensive to concerned in the blink of an eye.

He shook his head. "No. Actually, it helped. He hasn't spoken in a little over two years."

"What do you mean?"

"His mother was killed in a car accident. She was hit by a drunk driver."

"Was he with her?" She whispered through her fingers.

Alex swallowed the painful lump that formed in his throat. "He was at home with me. She was alone." He shrugged, trying to make her understand. "He hasn't spoken a single word since that night. He never smiles or laughs. Until he saw you, that is."

A scarlet leaf fell from the tree above and landed in her hair. He shoved his hands deep in his pockets to keep from removing it, from touching her.

"I'm sorry for the way I've acted. You don't deserve it. I hope you can accept my apology." He took a step closer. "You being here..." he drew in a deep breath, "You being here might bring him back to me. And that's all I want. It's all I've ever wanted. Don't hold my behavior against Eric. He needs you more than you know."

She didn't say a word, didn't move. The storm in her eyes had abated, but he braced for another surge.

She reached for the strap draped over his shoulder. He drew back slightly and challenge flared in her blue gaze. *Don't be a jerk, York.* He grudgingly handed the duffle over. She hoisted the bulk under her arm and took hold of the car door.

Alex figured he should start by prostrating himself. If he had to kiss her combat-booted feet, he would.

Before he could flatten himself on the wet ground though, she smiled. The change in her eyes stole his breath.

"Well... let's get inside then. No reason to stand out here in the rain like a couple of ninnies." She slammed the car door shut, shifted the duffle under her other arm and walked toward the steps.

She hesitated on the front porch for a second, glanced over her shoulder at him, nodded and then disappeared inside.

He couldn't help thinking the fresh start he'd been hoping for had already begun.

Chapter Seven

Faust held out a clean dry towel as Ella stepped back into the entry hall.

This guy's good. Nosy, judgmental, stiff, but good.

She took it and dried herself, careful to avoid her earrings. Mayor York strode past, accepting his own towel.

"Can you please take Miss Slipper's bag to her room?" He asked while he dragged the cloth across his neck and back.

"Of course, Sir." The lanky man obeyed and ascended the stairs.

Ella watched him for a second then turned to her employer. He stood with his back to her, wiping water from his hair and face. He kicked off his ruined loafers, leaving them in a puddle on the polished stone floor.

The mayor's snowy dress shirt clung to his skin in all the right places. He wore a white under-shirt as well, but the wet, transparent fabric couldn't hide a set of broadly developed shoulders and the defined V of his back. The sculpted muscles, beautifully proportioned and lean, were like an Olympic swimmer's at the height of his sport. Ella wondered how it would feel to touch those gorgeous ridges. Run her hands across his bare skin. Taste the moisture on his chiseled belly and...

"Miss Slipper?"

She re-focused. Mayor York's shirt re-appeared and her quickie fantasy shot from her thoughts with the sting of a slap. *What are you doing? Jeez, you're like one of those sweaty construction workers that whistle and hoot at anything with two legs and a heartbeat. Stop it. What's gotten into you?*

"Everything okay?"

"Yep," she said, nodding. "Yep. I'm good." *Just imagining the mayor of Magnolia Falls shirtless is all.*

"I'll introduce you to Eric now."

She followed her boss, glad he couldn't see the blush that crept into her cheeks.

This is gonna be tough.

Mayor York pushed through a swinging door, entering the kitchen. The huge room gleamed with stainless steel appliances, granite counters, and polished cabinets. Ella couldn't help smiling from ear to ear when the room's decadent aromas filled her nostrils.

Bacon, her second favorite breakfast food after fried dough, popped and sizzled next to fluffy, honey colored pancakes on an island in the middle of the room.

Standing at the flat griddle and singing off key stood a rosy cheeked, red-haired woman. The plump lady turned each piece of bacon with tongs while The Dixie Chicks sang, "Cowboy Take Me Away," from a small CD player on the counter.

"Miss Butterfield..." The older woman jumped at Mayor York's loud address.

"Son-of-a-biscuit!" She stooped to retrieve the bacon slice she'd dropped on the floor. "What's wrong with you, boy?" She asked with a deep southern twang. She tossed the greasy mess into the sink. "Are you trying to scare me to death sneaking up on me like that?" Her chubby hand patted an even chubbier bosom.

Mayor York strode to the stove, eyeing the bacon as if it were Anthrax. "This isn't for Eric, is it?" He asked.

"How long have I been working for you?" She snorted, giving each strip a shake before setting it on paper towels. "I'm well apprised of the rules around here. No junk food for him." She flipped a pancake. "The little Master's oatmeal is over there bubbling on the burner alongside my cheese grits." She tucked a stray wisp of gray streaked red hair behind her ear and smiled sweetly at her employer. Ella had never met the woman, but she had the distinct impression Miss Butterfield had fibbed.

"So this is all for you?" He asked, crossing his arms over his chest with a raised eyebrow.

Miss Butterfield mimicked his pose. "Yeah it's for me. How else do you think I got all these sexy curves?" She grinned, patting her plump middle. "You got a problem with that?" She waddled around the island and pointed the tongs in his face. "And there's no good reason for you to be dripping all over my newly polished floor asking silly questions either." She looked him over. "With a brain like the one you got, I'd think you'd have enough sense to get yourself out of the rain."

Ella smiled, liking the woman immensely. Miss Butterfield seemed to have no fear of her boss.

"And you, young lady?" Ella straightened when the woman finally addressed her. "Are you Master Eric's new nanny?"

"I am."

The woman shook her head. "He has no manners, our employer." She ended her sentence by stabbing the mayor with a steely gray gaze. "What are you thinking, coming in here blustering about bacon instead of doing your duty and introducing our guest?"

He glanced at Ella and then at Miss Butterfield. "I just—"

"Hush now." Waving a chubby hand in dismissal, she returned to her post behind the island. "I don't wanna hear your excuses. Don't you have work to attend to?" She lifted more bacon from the griddle, dropping it alongside the others on their bed of towels. "You haven't been home for a stretch this long in years. I'm beginning to think you might actually like it around here."

Mayor York ignored Miss Butterfield's comment. "I planned to introduce Miss Slipper to Eric after she changed. She needs to be acquainted with his routine and the rules, but if you have it covered, I'll allow you the honor."

"Sure, I've got it covered. Now git, you green eyed giraffe."

Mayor York appeared unaffected by the woman's bullying. He simply turned from her, nodded impersonally at Ella then left the room without another word.

"Come now," Miss Butterfield said to her. "Take a seat and eat something. You're skinnier than a book of matches."

Ella noticed the upholstered seats. "I'm still wet."

"A little water never hurt anything."

"But what about your polished floors?"

Miss Butterfield smiled. "You just let *me* worry about the furnishings." She stooped to lift the edge of the floor length fringed tablecloth and peered into the darkness beneath the fabric. "We've got a guest here, Tadpole. If you come out, maybe she'll share some breakfast with you."

Ella watched the blackness under the table with bated breath. After a second or so, a child appeared in the opening.

She recognized him immediately. The sad little boy from the festival hesitated under the table. Without moving he glanced at Miss Butterfield and then finally at Ella. Large green eyes set in a cherubic face studied her intently. She wondered if he might retreat back into his hiding place, but after a moment he seemed to make up his mind, slowly taking Miss Butterfield's hand. With her help, Eric scooted out of his sanctuary holding her pudgy fingers. The thumb of his other hand hid in his mouth.

They had both lost a parent. They shared a common bond. The difference, however, was that Clyde Slipper *chose* to leave. Eric's mother hadn't had that luxury.

How does a child his age cope with tragedy like that? The thought twisted her heart.

Eric stood straight and glanced at Miss Butterfield who smiled kindly down at him. He turned toward Ella and his serious expression changed. A small smile broke the suction on his thumb, but his finger stayed between his teeth. He giggled and his grin grew huge.

His sweet laughter was infectious.

Ella knelt, opening her arms.

His thumb left his mouth and he ran across the floor to fly into her embrace. The impact nearly knocked her off her feet.

God, I love this.

Pulling back, she grinned. He was beautiful beyond reason. A perfect little nose, huge dimples, and bright green eyes smiled back at her. Father and son were nearly identical. Like raven haired clones. Although she had no idea if the elder York had such appealing dents in his cheeks. The man had yet to smile.

"Hello, Eric," she finally said.

The little boy continued to grin, wrapping his fingers over her shoulders.

"Do you know who I am?"

"You're the *Angel*," he whispered.

Chapter Eight

A gasp caught Ella's attention.

Miss Butterfield stood near the table clutching her chest. "Mr. York said the boy spoke after seeing you, but I had my doubts." She plopped in a chair, dabbing tears with the skirt of her apron. "How foolish I was."

Ella decided to give her a moment and focused on the little boy. "Will you eat breakfast with me?"

Eric nodded. She took his hand and led him to the table. With a small boost she helped him into a chair. To Miss Butterfield she asked, "Can I help you serve?"

"No, no. Let me." The woman swiped the tears on her cheeks. Waddling to the island, she grinned from ear to ear. "If I could give you a million dollars, for inspiring the little tadpole to speak, I would. Seeing as though I have yet to win the lottery, or that dang Publisher's Clearing House, I'd like to give you the next best thing. A meal prepared with my own two hands." Hesitating in piling a plate high, she cocked her head. "You *do* eat, don't you?"

"Ravenously."

"And you're not in to that health food, no carb, fat free hooey, Mr. York's so fond of?"

"What's food without fat or carbs?"

The woman exhaled. "Cardboard." After she'd filled the plates and set them on the kitchen table she added, "It's always nice to be in the company of a fellow food lover."

Eric eyed his meal with relish, swinging his little legs beneath the chair.

"What did Mayor York mean by rules?" Ella turned her attention on Miss Butterfield. She'd joined them at the table with her own full plate.

"Eat, eat." The woman nodded while forking a hearty slice of pancake into her mouth. "I don't live by formality. There's nothing wrong with talking with your mouth full as long as nothing flies out of it while you do so," she

35

mumbled as she chewed.

Ella bit into a piece of thick cut bacon. *Mmm.* She smiled with her mouth full and asked, "The rules concern Eric?"

"Well, first of all, you can call the man Mr. York instead of Mayor York. He might seem all high and mighty on the outside, but deep down he's just a country boy at heart." She swallowed another bite and then said, "Okay, now let's go over the rules." Miss Butterfield patted Eric's head and grinned, but as she named them one by one her smile faded to a frown.

"Eric isn't allowed junk food of any kind. You may not be into health food, but our employer is. He runs and exercises and eats... well, he eats cardboard all day long." She grimaced and shoveled another bite of pancake into her mouth. "I normally abide by this rule. I'm not one to rock the boat, but on occasions such as this, when a special guest is to be arriving... I make exceptions." She winked at Eric. The little boy grinned back at her. His round cheeks so full of food he looked like a squirrel.

"Number two. No skipping his lessons."

"Lessons?"

"Eric already knows how to write. He's quite adept at arithmetic, can print all fifty states and their capitals, and can look up most words in the dictionary faster than some adults I know."

"That's amazing." Ella glanced at Eric, who scooped a mound of grits into his mouth. He seemed completely oblivious to their conversation, chewing with relish.

"Is he in pre-K?" Ella asked, impressed with the little boy's apparent intelligence.

"Not yet. Some of the doctors thought it would be too much stress. Faust tutors him." Maggie grimaced. "He also insists on dressing the boy."

Eric grinned at Ella, still chewing. She focused on his clothing—a starched white oxford, blue tie cinched at his neck, a pair of pressed dress khakis and a brown leather belt. Just like at the festival. *Where does he even get ties that small?*

Maggie leaned closer, hand at her mouth and in a conspiring whisper continued, "I think Faust was born with a telephone pole up his petute, if you want my opinion. It works out though. The tadpole's father, well, he's much too busy with business and such to contribute in that area."

"Really?"

"Let's just say, the man is barely ever home."

"He works that much? What about Eric?" Ella mouthed the latter question, not wanting him to hear, though the boy seemed interested only in his breakfast.

Miss Butterfield glanced at Eric. Her eyes grew soft. "It's not my place to say." She rose from her seat and poured two glasses of milk. The third glass she filled with carrot juice and set it in front of Eric. She squeezed back into her chair.

"Anything else?" Ella inquired with a frown.

"No pets."

"Okay."

"Mr. York hasn't the patience or time to deal with an animal. Never owned one."

She'd never owned a pet either, though she'd always wanted one.

"Oh, and there's a locked bedroom upstairs. The room's off limits."

"Hmm. Okay."

Miss Butterfield pursed her lips and then ate the last bite of her breakfast.

"What's in the room?" Ella couldn't stifle her curiosity.

Maggie glanced at Eric who shoveled pancake into his mouth then wiped his lips with the back of his dimpled hand. Maggie eyed Ella. "It's not my place to say. Don't like rocking the boat, you understand."

Ella cocked her head.

Miss Butterfield met her curious gaze. "Can I be frank with you?"

"Sure."

"There've been nannies before you. They come in and out of here with no success at all in breaking his silence. What's worse, not one of them had any personality to speak of. Oh, sure they had impeccable qualifications... spotless credentials, but... I think one needs a bit more than a crisp diploma to steal the heart of a child." Her gaze shifted out the bay window. The rain had ended, leaving a sunny day in its wake. A male cardinal landed on a nearby feeder. It pecked at the seeds and then flew off.

Miss Butterfield focused on Ella with bright determination. "Mr. York gave up praying his son would come out of his terrible depression... until you came along."

She took Ella's hand, squeezing gently. "When I heard him talk and what I see in his demeanor now? Well, that's a miracle *you* performed. Whether you're a believer in the Lord or not, I assure you He had a hand in bringing you here to us." Maggie nodded. "You're here to heal hearts, Ella Slipper."

She blinked, trying to digest her words.

Hearts? Plural? If Maggie referred to their employer she had been misinformed. Men didn't have hearts.

Even if Mr. York *did* possess a ticker, Ella wasn't Mother Theresa. She couldn't perform miracles. A perpetually absent father who thought work was more important than his child was beyond help.

"I'm a bit of a psychic, you see. Have been all my life. I've got a gift for seeing things others miss and I can see determination in you. I can see it in those lovely blue eyes of yours. Use that spirit, that personality. Use it and heal this family." The woman let go of her hand. She took their empty dishes, got up from the table and stacked them in the sink.

"I'm not a therapist, Miss Butterfield—"

"There'll be none of that formality around me. You'll call me Maggie from now on."

"Okay... Maggie, but that doesn't change the fact that I'm not qualified to heal anyone." Ella glanced at Eric. He'd finished eating and was sniffing his carrot juice like it was bug spray.

"And this is only temporary. I'm studying to be a teacher," she clarified softly, beginning to feel overwhelmed. Too much responsibility was being heaped on her shoulders. *I'm just in this for the money. Don't these people understand I'm not staying long enough to heal broken hearts or mend souls?*

"That may be so, but while you're here I'm sure you'll do plenty of good. Why, in less than five minutes you've made this one smile from ear to ear." Maggie nodded toward Eric. "That's no easy task. I assure you."

A brilliant grin swept over Eric's angelic face. His eyes twinkled. Ella couldn't help smiling back at him.

"It's good to see him so happy. It's been much too long." Maggie winked at the little boy. She focused on Ella with conviction in her gaze. "Listen to me. Just be yourself and everything will work out fine."

Ella chewed her lip. She noticed Eric's near empty plate. Something occurred to her. She'd give him one hundred percent of her care, but there was nothing wrong with a little fun, too. Taking his fork, she trailed it through his gooey leftovers. "Tell me Eric, do you like wearing these clothes?"

He set down his juice, pursing his lips. Hooking a finger inside his collar, he tugged at the snug fabric with a grimace. He shook his head back and forth.

"Uncomfortable, huh," Ella prodded Eric.

"Faust might as well dress the boy in a straight jacket," Maggie mumbled at the sink.

He pulled on his tie and stuck out his tongue comically.

Ella laughed. "Your shirt's too clean. Too starched and grumpy," she said, mimicking Faust's cultured accent. "Right?"

Eric covered his mouth with his hand, an endearing giggle escaping his throat. He nodded.

Ella grinned, scooped a bite of pancake with the fork. She swung it from the plate and slapped it against Eric's pristine white shirt.

Surprise couldn't describe the look on the little boy's face. Both arms extended, eyes and mouth as round as saucers, he watched the sticky mess slide down his shirt and tie. It ended up plopping onto his khakis.

For a split second, Ella regretted her juvenile attempt at fun. But in the next moment she had her reward. Eric laughed. Not just a giggle, but true split your sides hilarity that was so infectious, Maggie bent over, cackling with glee as well.

After the woman caught her breath she set a hand on Ella's shoulder. Between giggles, she managed to get out, "It's like I told you, be yourself and everything will work out just fine."

Chapter Nine

After stripping Eric of his stained tie and dress shirt, Ella left Maggie to her duties in the kitchen and followed the little boy to his room.

He held her hand as they strolled through the house, past a library, numerous impeccably decorated sitting rooms, and one vacant bedroom after another.

Why do people need such excess?

To her, money had and always would be a necessary evil. It paid for food and rent and even school, but... it was also a powerful corruptor. The lure of wealth had been her father's downfall. She felt sure it always would be.

Her thoughts skid to a halt when they came to the only room hidden behind a closed door. Was this the mysterious *locked room?*

Before they passed it, Eric, thumb securely hidden in his mouth, let go of her hand. He stopped in front of the door, laid his cheek and free palm against the white paneled wood and closed his eyes. He remained that way for only a heartbeat and then, trailing his little fingers along its surface, walked away.

He reached for Ella's hand. Taking it, she hesitated, wondering about the room behind the door. Before she could satisfy her curiosity, he tugged softly, leading her away.

Eric led her into the very next room. She drew in an awed breath. The blue painted walls were overlaid with wispy white clouds and airplanes of every era racing among them.

More astonishing than the incredible artwork was Eric's bed. Standing nearly floor to ceiling, his bed had been modeled after a helicopter. A quilt-covered mattress lay within the cockpit, complete with controls and a windshield at the pillowed end. Propellers up top and a set of runners bellow completed the authentic look.

Ella gaped in wonder. She'd never seen anything quite so remarkable in her life.

"Your pardon, please."

Her mouth snapped shut and she spun around. Faust stood in the doorway, his lips pinched like he'd just sucked a lemon.

"Yes," she managed.

"A fresh set of clothing." A starched blue dress shirt, green tie, and pressed khakis dangled on a child's hanger gripped in his extended hand.

The President should hire this guy to keep tabs on Al Qaeda.

"He's fine, thanks."

"A gentleman is much more productive when dressed appropriately."

"Hold up a sec." She raised her index finger and glanced at Eric. The little boy had climbed into his helicopter, thumb in mouth, watching Faust with a wary eye. "Eric, do you like wearing those clothes?" She asked him.

He vigorously shook his head no.

Ella shrugged at Faust. "He's the boss."

The man eyed her with disdain, sniffed imperiously and turned on his heel out the door.

Ella spun around, catching Eric's smile. "You are too cute for words."

Dampness and chill prickled her skin beneath her long sleeve-T, but the cool air felt good against Ella's face as she jogged under a canopy of leaves. Glowing lamps lit the winding path on her way to the wrought iron fence. When she reached the gate it opened like magic, closing behind her as smooth as silk.

Nearly through with her first week as the York nanny, Ella had risen at six a.m. to go for a run. Her employer allowed one of her favorite morning regimens as long as Maggie consented to picking up the slack if Eric woke before she returned.

With her charge in good hands, Ella turned left instead of right, wanting to explore the other side of the neighborhood Mayor York lived in.

She normally ran in less urban areas and though city streets offered plenty of views, she realized she also enjoyed the scenery this neighborhood offered.

Until he came along.

He startled her at first, coming up from behind her in the dark and then jogging at her side. She hadn't even heard his footfalls. "What are you doing?" She asked the mayor while she continued jogging.

He stared straight ahead as he matched her step for step. "What does it look like I'm doing?"

"It looks like you're horning in on my *me* time. That's what it looks like."

He continued his pace, focused on the road. "You don't have any *me* time. You're on the clock right now. You're actually running on *my* time, if you want to get technical."

She rolled her eyes and increased her speed, pulling a few inches in front of him. "You okayed it. You're the one who gave me this *me* time... if you want to get technical," she said over her shoulder.

Suddenly he was next to her again, keeping pace.

"What are you doing?" She asked, exasperated.

"I thought we cleared this up already."

"If you want to get *technical*, you never answered that question the first time I asked it."

He ignored her sarcasm. "I'm running."

"That's obvious, Einstein. I meant, why are you running *with* me?" She sped up, pulling forward once more.

"I'm not running with you." He closed the short distance between them.

"Could have fooled me. What do you call this, then?" She glimpsed him out of the corner of her eye.

"I call it going on a run in *my* neighborhood, on *my* street, and happening to pass you by." He pulled about ten feet ahead.

The last thing she wanted was to exercise with her employer. Especially this employer. The nerve of him ruining the only time she had to herself all day. She'd always looked forward to her solitary runs. The hour or so spent pounding the pavement gave her time to daydream about the life she wanted for herself and her mother. Her runs renewed her desire to succeed.

Now all it was doing was renewing her desire for her boss.

He jogged in front of her, illuminated by street lights, muscular shoulders and arms clad in snug athletic wear, feet gliding over the asphalt like they were winged.

He looked like a Gatorade ad.

Or... like a God...

She nearly let him pull farther ahead, if only to watch his perfect body move with strength and grace down the street.

But his words echoed in her head, *and happening to pass you by*.

She might normally daydream on her runs, but she was no slacker. She consistently ran between six and seven minute miles. And though her fastest time of five minutes and thirty-eight seconds was nowhere near Olympic caliber, it was better than most people could do.

She wasn't about to let him *pass her by*. This might be *his* neighborhood and *his* street, but as far as she knew he hadn't been crowned Verdant Oaks resident Speedy Gonzalez.

She blew past him like he stood still.

The brisk air whipped her bangs off her forehead and though her lungs burned slightly she grinned from ear to ear with the knowledge that she'd left him in her dust.

"Is that the best you can do?"

Her jaw dropped as he pulled up next to her. She gritted her teeth and stared straight ahead.

If there'd ever been a day to break her mile record, today was it.

I'll show you what I can do you big, overgrown moose.

Her sprint impressed even her as she left him behind. Elbows bent, fists relaxed, her arms alternated back and forth next to her body, driving her forward. She lengthened her strides, heel-toe, heel-toe, eating up the pavement like the Roadrunner.

The end of the block was in her sights. But suddenly, so was he, right next to her, again.

She'd been proud that the frequency of her breathing hadn't increased much until she realized he wasn't huffing or puffing at all.

"Will you stop following me?" She growled up at him.

"I go this way all the time," he growled back. "I'm not following you."

"Yes you are," she shouted. The burn in her lungs increased. Her legs were on fire, but she continued her sprint alongside him. She glared at him and nearly opened her mouth to call him a show off when he shouted, "Watch out!"

He grabbed for her arm, but she eluded his grip the same instant something knocked her feet out from under her. She tripped and fell forward at full speed.

"Ooomph!" She hit the asphalt like an avalanche, skidding across its rough, black surface.

It all happened in an instant. The fall and then the pain, like knives cutting her hands, her knees, her chin.

"Jesus, Ella." He suddenly squatted next to her. "Are you okay?"

He helped her to a seated position. She bent her legs to examine her wounds, wincing. Her palms were scraped raw. Her sweatpants were torn. Her knees bleeding. She gingerly touched her chin. Blood stained her fingers.

"Owwwaaah," she breathed.

"You're all cut up." He took hold of her left leg and scrutinized the vertical red scrapes.

"What'd I trip over?" She peered over her shoulder.

"A branch." He jutted his chin indicating the nearest house. "Must've fallen from that oak."

The leafy length of wood sat inconspicuously in the street. The street lights were too far apart to fully illuminate its mottled bark. She'd been running so fast and had been so focused on beating *him* that she'd never noticed the obstacle.

She tried to get up. He set his hand on her shoulder. "Wait a second. Let me run to the house and get the car. I'll drive you back."

She finally met his gaze. His brow wrinkled. His green eyes probed hers. The concern drawing his lips into a frown seemed genuine.

She shook her head, "I'm fine," and winced as she rose from the pavement. She stood up, a little hunched over. Straightening her legs hurt. She touched her chin again. The blood had coagulated but the cut stung.

"Sit down. Wait here and I'll run back and get the car," he repeated. The heat of his hand on her shoulder made her shiver.

She stood straighter. "It's just a few scratches for goodness sake."

"More than a few. Jesus, didn't you see that thing lying there?" He scratched his head, eyeing the branch.

She scowled at him. "Sure, I saw it, but I thought skidding across the road would be oodles of fun."

He smirked. They walked a few yards and he shook his head. "I bet you flew ten feet. I can't believe you didn't rip your whole face off."

Embarrassment heated her cheeks imagining what she'd looked like tripping at full speed. "Yeah, laugh it up, Fuzz Ball," she muttered, limping away from him in the direction of his house. "I bet it was hilarious."

He caught up and walked slowly beside her. "It wasn't funny. I'm sorry I didn't grab you in time."

She shrugged.

They walked a few more feet and he asked, "Fuzz Ball?"

She shrugged again. "Star Wars reference... I tend to quote the movies. Hopefully you won't mind if Eric starts echoing my Darth Vader impressions."

"Eric can echo Princess Leia for all I care. As long as he's speaking."

She glanced at him. He wasn't smiling. Wasn't poking fun. His hand sought her back. His fingers splayed over her shoulder-blade. His thumb gently pressed against her upper arm. His warmth radiated over her flesh, seeping under the fabric of her T-shirt. She wanted to pull away. She didn't like the sensation his touch aroused.

Or... to be honest... she liked it too much.

She limped slowly up the street, wishing she'd turned right instead of left.

"Do you have a phone with you?" Alex asked.

"No," she answered. "You?"

"I'd be too tempted to do business if I took it with me. It's at home. And we've got more than half a block to go. Why don't you let me carry you the rest of the way?" He offered.

Blue fire shot from her eyes. Her expression said, *Carry me? Are you high?*

He held up his hands. "Whoa. Got it. No carrying."

Besides the rustle of leaves in the chilled breeze, a dog barking in the distance was the only other sound as they continued further down the street.

He wanted to break the awkward silence, say something. But what? He'd already apologized. Asked if she was okay. If he could carry her. What else could he say?

Can I bury my face in your hair? Run my fingers through it? See if it's as silky as it looks.

Yeah, say that to her, York. See if she doesn't bitch slap you for your trouble.

"Do you run every morning?" She asked, tugging him from his thoughts.

"Uh, yeah. I do... when I'm not too busy at work."

She said nothing more as they passed a few more houses. Small talk. She'd probably wanted to break the uncomfortable silence as much as he did.

"Maggie said you're barely ever home."

He glanced at her. Her focus was riveted on the street. Her lips were tight, pained. He fought the desire to scoop her into his arms. "You two were talking about me?" The idea sent a damn thrill through his veins.

"No." She dragged out the ō. Studying the road again she added, "She told me your rules for Eric's care... the first day I got here. And then your absence came up in conversation. She said you're away more than home."

"I've had to step back from law, but my firm keeps growing. Overseeing its progress keeps me pretty damn busy. And even without that, my mayoral duties are monumental. I'm running for governor in about eleven months. I have a million responsibilities. It's hard to find time to—"

"Spend with your son," she finished for him. She didn't frown at him when she spoke, didn't wag a finger in reprimand or slap him on the wrist. She didn't have to. The four words had been enough to make him feel like a jerk all on their own.

He opened his mouth to defend himself, but couldn't think of a single thing to say that wouldn't bury him further.

She stopped limping, propped her foot on the curb and then bent to examine her left knee.

Maybe the conversation had ended.

No such luck.

"A career is incredibly important. Believe me, I get it," she said, spreading the torn fabric of her sweat pants to probe her wound with her index finger. Wincing she added, "Anyone who says otherwise is a fool." She checked the other knee with a little less interest and then straightened. She scanned the houses and then the tree tops. After a long stretch of silence she glanced his way. "I've taken a bunch of psych courses. Most of them aren't even necessary for my major, but I've always felt that knowing why a person, or a child, acts the way they do would help me be a better teacher. Anyway, one of my developmental psych professors, a cliché with way too many tweed vests in his wardrobe, began every class with a quote. One of them really stuck with me." She narrowed her eyes. "Want to hear it?"

He shrugged. "Sure."

"To be in your child's memories tomorrow, you have to be in his life today."

He drew in a slow, deep breath and then let it out silently. He had nothing to say to that.

She turned and limped away. He didn't follow her. Shame shifted into annoyance. "I do the best I can," he called after her.

She stopped and turned to assess him with stony eyes. A slow, bitter smile finally crested her lips. "Whatever helps you sleep at night," she said and resumed limping away from him.

He clenched his jaw. He'd said those exact words to his father a few days earlier after he'd invited the man over to visit Eric and he'd given some flimsy excuse why he couldn't stop by. He figured he'd probably even given the senator the same derisive look Ella had just shot his way.

He shook his head. "Shit," he muttered. *See what you get for stalking her, dumbass? What happened to the promise you made yourself? No interaction with the nanny. None.*

Before this morning he'd done a pretty damn good job of keeping that vow.

He ran nearly every day, whether he was home or out of town. Exercise helped clear his head, and a good sweat eased tension. He knew the nanny ran too, but he'd made an effort to avoid her, altering his regular time and route to keep from bumping into her.

But this morning he happened to leave at the same time she had. He couldn't be sure if that had been a conscious or unconscious decision. To be honest, he didn't feel up to dissecting the impulse in his mind. Either way, he'd ended up following her right through the front gate of his property. He could have turned right then. He should have turned right, but something unseen and emotionally foreign urged him to go left... and trail about twenty feet behind her. He'd admired the smooth stride that carried her forward, her proud posture, her blonde ponytail swishing side to side like bound silken thread.

He'd watched her run for a couple hundred feet until he realized what he was doing was creepy. That's when he'd sped up, deciding to pass her, but...

He couldn't help himself.

He had slowed next to her and, true to form, screwed everything to hell.

Now, up ahead, Ella continued to hobble along toward his house. Her limp seemed to be worsening.

Fuck it.

He strode up to her and scooped her into his arms. She squeaked in shock and then growled, "Put me down."

"Shut up," he said, holding her close against his chest, one arm supporting her shoulders and upper back, the other snaking beneath her knees. She was tall and fit, but surprisingly light.

She squirmed against him. "Mr. York, put me down, now!"

"Jesus, you're stubborn." He squeezed a little tighter to keep her from jumping out of his arms. "You're walking too slow. Eric's going to be up any minute and I want you home in time to greet him. I'm not doing this for you, I'm doing it for him."

She glanced at her watch and then at him. "It's barely six thirty. He hasn't woken before eight since I've been here." She pushed against him, grunting when he tightened his grip. "You're the stubborn one. Let me down or I'm gonna—"

"What? You're gonna what?" He asked, striding down the street, challenging her heated gaze. Her eyes flashed blue fire in the hazy light of early dawn. But her anger didn't repel him.

It did the opposite.

"I'll scream," she hissed.

"So scream." He smirked.

"I'll wake up your neighbors. I've got a set of pipes that'll shatter glass."

"Give it your best shot."

"They'll call the police on you."

"For what?"

"For holding a woman against her will."

"I'm the mayor. I'm doing my civic duty and carrying a wounded woman to safety... my neighbors won't call the police. They'll give me a medal, throw a parade in honor of their illustrious leader's gallantry."

"Illustrious? Gallant? Full of yourself much?"

He walked a few more yards, nearing the gate surrounding his property. "I'm still waiting for that glass shattering scream, Miss Slipper."

She glared at him. She'd draped one arm around his neck. The other had reached across his chest. Her hands met at his shoulder, fingers clasped. He figured she was just holding on because her rigid body language indicated she had no clue her embrace made his blood race faster than any sprint.

He continued to stare straight ahead, hoping she wouldn't wise up.

"You're infuriating," she said and looked away.

"Thank you."

"That wasn't a compliment."

He shrugged, smiling. He enjoyed bantering back and forth with her.

The gate swung open. Its facial recognition software had been money well spent. He stepped onto the cobbled driveway and strode toward the house.

"You can put me down now," she growled.

"We're almost there. Maggie'll clean you up when we get inside."

She pulled her arms in and crossed them defiantly over her chest. Her scowling face was in profile.

She smelled like flowers.

He swallowed hard and breathed through his mouth.

After a good minute of silence she said, "He needs you, you know." She didn't look at him when she spoke, though the hard line of her lips had softened.

He swallowed again, but this time with guilt. He walked another ten yards, reaching the circular driveway, unsure what to say. He knew his son needed him. He needed Eric, too. But he had no idea how to bridge the gap that had steadily grown between them.

Her head turned. Her blue eyes searched his. She raised a pale eyebrow, obviously expecting a reply.

"I know he needs me," he said, feeling two inches tall.

"Then why did you hire me?"

"He needs a nan—"

"No... listen to me," she interrupted, shifting in his arms to look him in the eye. "It's obvious you love him. The way your face lights up when you talk about him, the way your eyes shine. You adore that little boy. I know that. But hiring me isn't going to show him how you feel. I'm a buffer, a wall between the two of you. Don't you see that?"

He shook his head. "You don't understand."

"So make me understand."

"He's afraid of me."

She frowned in confusion.

"Ever since the accident."

Her frown deepened.

"He blames me for what happened."

"He's five years old. I seriously doubt he blames you for anything."

"Like I said, you don't understand. There are circumstances..."

The front door opened, drawing their attention. Maggie hurried off the front porch, wiping her hands on her apron. "Faust saw you from the window. He said you must be hurt. What happened?"

Ella planted her hands on his chest and pushed away. Grudgingly he lowered his arms to release her. She slid from his grip, feet barely grazing the cobbles. The warmth of her body blazed a trail of fire down his torso. His blood raced faster.

Let go of her.

Why weren't his hands obeying?

"Mr. York..." Ella said softly, looking up at him.

Let go of her you idiot.

"Mr. York, I'm on the ground." Her hands had remained on his chest, fingers splayed. She pushed again, but not very hard. He noticed something before he finally let her escape his embrace... she had liked being there. Her smoldering blue eyes and blushing cheeks told him so.

She wants you.

The next instant her smolder fizzled. She stepped back three or four feet, assessing him warily as Maggie waddled up to her.

"I told you I'm fine," Ella said to him, raising her chin and straightening her spine. She appeared suddenly unaffected by what had just happened between them until she started brushing at her shirt as if his contact contaminated her clothes.

She's repulsed by you.

That's probably more like it.

"What on Earth happened?" Maggie asked Ella and then glared up at him.

"What're you looking at me for?" Alex shrugged in exasperation.

"Well, she's cut to ribbons." Maggie took hold of Ella and tugged her closer.

Ella spoke up before he could defend himself. "Maggie, I'm okay. I was running and there was a branch in the road. I tripped and fell."

Maggie shot him a heated glare.

He sputtered a laugh. "You think I put it there?"

"Of course not, you pig-headed hayseed." Maggie maneuvered Ella toward the house. "But how many times have I told you to bring your phone with you for emergencies?"

He opened his mouth to respond, but his housekeeper beat him to it. "You're a stubborn mule, Alexander York," she accused, shaking a finger at him.

He sighed and then called out, "I thought I'm a pig-headed hayseed... whatever the hell that is."

The pair had reached the front steps. Maggie helped Ella up the stairs. The older woman frowned his way while her charge limped into the house. "It's a fool and you're both," she shot back and then closed the door behind her.

Chapter Ten

"Here, sit down," Maggie said, directing Ella to a high kitchen stool. "I have an old family liniment I keep on hand. It'll heal those cuts quicker than you can say Neosporin."

Maggie disappeared inside the cavernous pantry. The shuffling of boxes and cans accompanied her incoherent mumbling. A few seconds later she emerged triumphant. "Hah!" She brandished a mason jar filled with greenish-black tar and a bottle labeled Witch-hazel. Waddling close, she scrutinized Ella's chin. Drawing her brows together she shook her head. "This might sting, but I need to cleanse the cuts before I apply Granny Tallulah's remedy. Okay?"

Ella smiled and nodded yes though her scrapes were on the periphery of her mind.

His strong embrace.

His clean, cotton scent.

His warm breath.

All she could think about was her boss.

Why did he have to pick her up and carry her?

And more disturbing, why had she let him? Why had she let herself like it?

Maggie's eyes narrowed in concentration as she gently wiped the cut on Ella's chin with a cloth dipped in Witch-hazel. "It's not deep," she said. "Shouldn't scar that pretty face of yours at all."

Biting her lip, Ella focused on the older woman's freckles. Counting the cinnamon specks helped distract her from Mr. York... at least for the few minutes before he stepped into the kitchen.

Still dressed in his running clothes he clutched something in his hand. He buried whatever it was into his pocket when Maggie turned to see who had invaded her domain.

His housekeeper frowned at him.

"Come on, Maggie," he said. "I promise I'll take the phone with me from now on."

"Too little too late," she muttered and then resumed cleaning Ella's chin.

Before anyone could say more, Faust pushed in through the swinging door. Mouth pinched, spine like a plank, Mayor York's valet looked straight at Ella and announced, "The young master is awake."

Ella hopped off the stool, but Maggie set a hand on her shoulder. "Oh, no you don't," she said, directing her back into her seat. "You're in no shape to handle a little one at the moment. Sit right there and don't worry about Eric. I'll take care of him." She pointed at Mr. York and ordered, "You help her cleanse those wounds and slather them with the ointment." Maggie moved closer to him and stabbed her plump finger against his chest. "And none of that hokum. Granny's recipe is all she needs, you hear me?"

Her boss saluted with a playful grin. "Yes, Sir."

Maggie scowled, poked his chest once more and then spun on Faust. "And you and that stick up your petute can get out of my kitchen."

One of the valet's gray eyebrows twitched, he shot Ella a final imperious glare and then exited the room.

Maggie slapped the jar into Mr. York's hand, wagged her finger at him and then left as well.

Her boss set the tar on the counter and then stepped closer to Ella.

He knelt in front of her.

Her heart thumped wildly. *Too close, much too close.* She shifted on her seat. She scanned the floor, the ceiling, the counter, anything to avoid eye contact. Her gaze zeroed in on the jar and she grabbed it. "Maggie wants me to use this." She spun the lid off. "And I can do it myself," she added, but wrinkled her nose when an awful stink wafted from the container.

"Yeah," Mr. York said, eyeing Maggie's family recipe. "Smells like crap, doesn't it?" He smirked.

Ella curled her lip at the concoction. It smelled exactly like crap... with a hint of two day old corpse mixed in. Another whiff assaulted her nose and she slammed the lid on tight. "Holy cow," she blurted. "That's horrible." She shoved the jar at him.

He held up a hand. "I'm not touching that." With a chuckle he added, "Put it on the counter."

Ella set it on the granite and pushed it as far away as she could. "What is that stuff?" She stifled a gag, amazed at the stink's pungency.

He smiled as he reached for the plastic bottle. He sloshed Witch-hazel onto the cloth Maggie had used earlier. "It's an old southern secret," he mocked playfully, imitating his housekeeper's falsetto twang. Returning to his deep southern drawl he added, "She's been pushing that goo on us since we were kids."

"We?"

He sloshed a bit more fluid onto the cloth. "I have a younger brother, Conner."

She would have asked about his sibling, but lost her voice when without asking permission her boss peeled aside the torn gap at the knee of her sweatpants. He gently cupped her calf with one hand and dabbed the Witch-hazel onto her cut with the other.

She should have rejected his help.

She should have informed him she could clean her own wounds.

But she didn't.

She couldn't.

Say something, dummy.

He knelt in front of her, scrutinizing her knee as he swabbed the vertical cuts with the damp cloth.

Goose bumps rose in the wake of his touch.

Too close.

She couldn't speak if she tried. Her leg twitched from his grip.

Concern knitted his brow. "It stings?"

"Yes," she lied, trying to cover her reaction to his nearness.

Feather-light he blew on the wound. His breath fanned her skin. A second wave of goose bumps rose in its cooling wake.

He met her gaze. "Better?"

She gave him a shallow nod as he set the cloth aside. He reached into his pants pocket and withdrew a small yellow and white tube. The one he'd hidden from his housekeeper earlier. She recognized it immediately, Neosporin. He set the cap on the floor and then squeezed a small greasy blob onto his finger.

"Maggie hates this stuff," he said.

"How come?"

He dabbed the medicine on her skin. With a delicate touch he smeared the ointment onto each scrape. "Because her Granny Tallulah didn't invent the recipe."

Ella smiled.

He studied her other knee, but the scrapes were superficial. Straightening he stood up.

She rose along with him and turned, wanting to check on Eric, but Mr. York stopped her.

"Hold on. Let me get your chin," he said.

"It's fine. I'll do it later."

"I'd put this stuff on now if I were you." He smirked, holding up the Neosporin. "Take it from someone who knows. If that redhead finds out you didn't cover every cut with at least some kind of goo, she'll force that old southern stink on you."

Ella frowned.

"And that stink doesn't wash off easy. It lingers for days, weeks even."

She raised an eyebrow. "You're making that up."

"When he was ten, Conner cut a slash right here," he pointed to his forehead, "when he fell out of a tree. Maggie smeared that stuff on the cut. Not only did he smell like a truck stop toilet for a week, but he had to go to school with a big black X on his face."

"An X?"

"Yeah. It stains your skin and she thinks if you draw an X with the medicine it'll work better, like it's X-ing out the germs." He shook his head. "I don't know, some kind of hillbilly superstition." He raised an eyebrow. "I'm saving you from a similar fate."

Ella smiled again. "She won't be upset that I used... hokum, instead?"

"Sure she'll be upset." He smiled as he dabbed another blob of ointment on his index finger. "But you can blame it on me."

Ella rewarded him with a small smile. For some reason he'd been craving the expression. Ever since she'd smiled at him the day she'd first arrived, in the rain, right after he'd stolen her bag, he'd been recalling the gentle curve of her full, pink lips.

All right, York, dial it down.

"Hold still," he said.

Her humor faded. She swallowed visibly, her posture rigid, but she lifted her chin obediently.

He figured she didn't realize she still smiled at him... in a way. Her mouth naturally curved upward at the corners. A perpetual grin of sorts.

Shit, York.

He nearly told her to do it herself. She was a big girl. There was no reason at all he needed to be tending her wounds.

She raised an eyebrow, probably wondering why he stood there so long without moving.

Fuck it.

He stepped closer. "Lean your head back a little more."

She lifted her chin a hair, her lips a straight line, the corners of her mouth betraying her apparent indifference.

In contrast to her porcelain skin, the cut glowed angry red. With his index finger he gently smeared the ointment onto the raw scrape.

She winced.

"Sorry," he said, lowering his hand.

"It's okay." She waved it off.

He noticed something. "Your palms." He reached for both of her wrists and turned her hands over.

"It's nothing."

"They're as bad as your knee." He lifted her right hand and reached for the cloth soaked in antiseptic.

She tugged her wrist from his grasp.

"Ella." He frowned. "There's gravel embedded in your skin."

She stepped back but the island stopped her from retreating further. "I can take care of it myself."

He took a step closer though he knew it wasn't a good idea. "I know you can." He shrugged lightly. "But I feel responsible."

"You didn't trip me," she whispered.

"I know, but I saw it lying in the road. I should have pulled you out of the way sooner." His heart beat a mile a minute. Why was he moving closer? Why couldn't he stop himself? Why was he ignoring every instinct screaming in his head? Why was he so incredibly drawn to this woman?

She set her palm against his chest.

He shouldn't have, but he covered her hand with his.

For a moment they both stood there, unmoving, their eyes locked in an embrace that needed to be broken.

"Daddy."

His gaze jerked to the left.

It hadn't been a figment of his imagination. His tiny son stood in the doorway. Maggie stood right behind him, hand to her mouth, gazing at the boy with a mix of amazement and joy.

"Eric?" Alex said, barely finding his voice.

His son backed into Maggie's skirt. His thumb returned to his mouth. He clutched his favorite model airplane by the wing with his other hand. His rumpled footy pajamas and messy hair melted Alex's heart. *He spoke to me.*

Alex wanted to run and scoop him into his arms, but stifled the urge. He lowered to one knee. "Did you have a good night's sleep, Buddy?"

Eric's green eyes darted toward Ella.

Alex couldn't see the nanny from his vantage point, but after a moment his son looked at him. The little boy nodded and then shied into Maggie's skirt.

Alex's heart swelled. He never thought he'd get his son back. He'd been sure he'd lost him forever… until now.

Now there was hope. So much hope.

"Eric? Why don't you let your daddy take you up stairs to get dressed?" Ella's voice came from behind him. At that moment Alex wanted to kiss her.

But Eric shook his head no. Not a violent shake, just a soft refusal. He turned his face away from Maggie's skirt long enough to point to his nanny. "I want, Ella," he said very softly, hesitantly.

Elation buried disappointment. His son had progressed more in one week than he had in two years. He was talking. Saying full sentences. He called him daddy. It had been an eternity since he'd called him that. Awe couldn't begin to describe his feelings.

Alex glanced over his shoulder at the woman who had made all of this possible. "You heard the little man." He smiled at her.

Concern drew her pale brows together. "Are you sure?"

"Completely," he said as she came up next to him.

The smile he couldn't get enough of brightened her face. She set her hand on his shoulder and squeezed gently before leaving his side. She neared Eric. His finger popped out of his mouth and both arms extended up to her. Lifting him into her embrace she hugged him close and left the kitchen.

Maggie, tears in her eyes and a hand lingering at her mouth, gazed at Alex. "Did you hear him?" She whispered through her fingers. "Did you hear the little tadpole?"

Alex stood up. "I heard him, Mags," he assured her, holding back his own tears of joy.

She dabbed her cheeks with the skirt of her apron as she made her way to the island. Her gaze then fixed on the jar of stink sitting on the countertop.

Alex figured she'd give him an earful for disregarding her orders, but instead she turned and asked him, "Why are you home?" Her teary blue-gray eyes narrowed.

"Huh?" He frowned. "I live here."

After another quick swipe at her cheeks and a loud sniff she folded her arms across her chest and raised an orange eyebrow. "I know you live here you big hayseed."

"So that's it? No more Alex? Hayseed's my new name? What does it mean again?"

She shook a finger at him. "Look it up on your fancy phone... the one you never have on hand for emergencies." She stepped closer. "And do it on your own time. Right now I'm expecting an answer to my question."

"What'd you ask again?" He grinned.

"You know you're not too old to get your hind quarters tanned. I bet there're some nice sturdy switches to be had right there in your backyard. So unless you want to go pick one out, stop fooling around and answer me."

He shrugged. "I don't know what else you want me to say. I already gave you an answer. I'm home because I live here."

"You've always seemed to prefer a hotel room to this place."

"Not always," he said, turning serious.

She sighed. Taking a few steps forward she held out her hand.

He set his palm against the roughened warmth of her own. She squeezed tight. "I know it's been hard. The Lord knows I've seen you struggle. Staying away has been your... coping mechanism."

"You've been watching Dr. Phil again."

She smacked his knuckles with her free palm. "He's a brilliant bald Texan. Now hush and listen to me." Her crow's feet lengthened. Her forehead wrinkled. For a second he thought she might cry again. His grin faded.

"Something's happening between the two of you," she said softly.

"Me and Eric."

"Course, you and your son, but that's not who I'm talking about."

He tugged his hand from her grip. "Stop Maggie."

She frowned. "Don't you see it?"

Of course I do. It's scaring the shit out of me.

"She's my employee," he assured her... and himself.

"She's your savior."

"Savior? Come on, Maggie, you romanticize everything." He started to pull away, but she stopped him.

"Hasn't it occurred to you why your son is so drawn to *your employee?*"

Because she's beautiful and smells like flowers...

"When your wife still lived she used to tell the child that an angel watched over him," Maggie continued. "The statue in the room next to his, the room you had locked up after his mother passed? Recall the one I'm talking about?"

An image of the foot tall statue popped into his head. Pale skin, blue eyes, long platinum hair... and wings. "I remember."

"Remind you of anyone?" Maggie cocked her head.

Ella. The statue of the angel Deidre had brought back from Switzerland and then set on a shelf in Eric's playroom looked remarkably like Ella.

"Make sense now?" Maggie raised an orange eyebrow.

Alex said nothing. He'd wondered why his son had responded so quickly to the nanny, but he'd been so thrilled that Eric had spoken that he really never questioned the cause further. *Angel... he'd called her Angel.*

"Your son is drawn to her for his own reasons. What are yours?"

"I don't want to talk about this, Maggie." A knot tightened his gut.

"Your son is on the mend... why don't you accept some healing, too."

"She works for me," he repeated, wishing she'd drop it.

Maggie waved away his statement. "Pah. She's a woman." She stabbed his chest with her index finger. "Angel or not, she's living under your roof. And you might think I'm a meddling old lady, but since she's arrived, you've been under that roof, too."

"I'm here for Eric."

She waved a hand. "Whatever helps you sleep at night."

"Why does everyone keep saying that?"

"Saying what?"

"Never mind."

"You may be here for Eric, and it's been wonderful having you—except when you traipse across my polished floors with dirt on your shoes—but there's another reason you've been hanging around day in and day out, and it's not because that old, bald coot irons your boxer shorts."

Ella.

He adored his son and wanted to witness his recovery, but... he also wanted to be near Ella.

Maggie was right about Eric. The angel in his playroom had to be the reason his son was so drawn to his nanny.

But what about him?

Her resemblance to a hand painted statue that once collected dust on the shelf of a European church gift shop hadn't even occurred to him until now. And though his parents attended regularly he barely ever went to mass anymore.

Religion had nothing to do with his attraction to Ella.

And though his body ached for her and he imagined burying himself inside her, his desire for her... felt so much deeper.

He realized Maggie was still talking to him. "...trying too hard," she said. He lost the rest of her sentence when those three words triggered a thought.

Maybe that's it. Maybe I'm trying too hard to see something that's never been there in the first place.

Lust.

That explained everything. He'd been walking around with a hard-on for a week now. He hadn't been with a woman in a while and he was just horny.

He needed to blow his load on someone other than his employee. Then he'd get sex off his mind and realize there was nothing at all between them.

That's it.

"Maggie," he blurted, grabbing her shoulders. "Thank you!" He gave her a big kiss on the cheek. "You're amazing."

She glared at him. "Have you lost your mind? I was in the middle of a breakthrough."

"So am I," he said over his shoulder and pushing through the door made a vow to steer clear of the nanny.

Chapter Eleven

Two full weeks had passed since her accident and Ella's cuts were all but gone. She continued her jogs every morning and though she'd been keeping an eye peeled for stray dead fall she hadn't seen her employer on the road in all that time. She told herself it was best they kept their distance, but she'd found herself hoping he'd emerge from the shadows and sweep her off her feet again.

Not only was her morning routine the same, but each day her job had been repetitious, though totally endearing. She was offered whatever she wanted at mealtime, but opted to share Eric's Organic health food so he wouldn't feel bad. She'd eaten egg whites, turkey bacon and sprouted grain toast the last seven breakfasts in a row, but to her surprise, the stuff actually tasted pretty good. She and Eric read books together, played computer games and he'd take a nap. They ran in the backyard, swung on his swings or played hide and seek. Tofu burgers for lunch, more reading then dinner, a bath, bed and the next day they started all over again.

And in fourteen full days she hadn't seen hide nor glossy black hair of Eric's father.

The man set her on edge, made her blood race through her veins and her heart slam against her ribs with just a simple green eyed gaze in her direction, but the longer he remained absent, the deeper she buried her feelings of longing. Anger overshadowed desire.

He should be home for Eric. He should be here to see his progress. He should be sharing dinner with him, ruffling his hair and then tucking him in at night. He should be telling him he loves him.

Ella went so far as to confide in her new friend, "Where is he? Why doesn't he visit Eric, Maggie?"

The woman said little, just, "He's a busy man," and then she'd change the subject.

Ella worried that his ambition came at the expense of his son's well-being.

Eric seemed happy, but she refrained from asking the little boy how he felt about his father's absence. What if he turned the tables and asked his own questions? She didn't understand Mr. York's neglect herself, so how could she explain it to a five year old? And was it even her responsibility?

She just hoped at least her own presence was still making a difference in the child's life.

"So what's the verdict, Ella? Do you prefer employment as Scarlett O'Hara or Mary Poppins?"

Ella smiled, holding the receiver against her ear. She sat in her gorgeous bedroom across the hall from Eric's. Decorated Country French with soft, butter colored walls, delicate furniture, and Wedgwood Blue accents, her two-room suite belonged in Windsor Castle.

A few hours and adorable yawns earlier Eric had fallen asleep on his window seat after watching three Cardinals squabble over the contents of a nearby feeder.

Ella had gazed at his beautiful face for a moment, amazed at how fond she'd grown of him in a few short weeks. Lifting him carefully, she'd placed him in bed.

Sitting in a rocker, craning her neck so she could see him through the doorway, she laughed at her mother's question on the phone. "Call me Miss Poppins. Practically perfect in every way."

"So I'm right about you, huh?"

"Right about what?" She asked, settling more comfortably into the chair.

"Don't play dumb. Face it. It was good that you took this job. You need to be near children. Mother knows best."

"Uh huh."

"And how's the mayor?"

Ella grimaced. "I like to refer to him as the invisible Mr. Hyde."

"Hyde?"

"You know, Jekyll, Hyde? My boss is the grumpy one."

"He that bad?"

"You met the demanding, egotistical giant? Not my cup of tea."

"That leads me to my next question, Darling. Who exactly *is* your cup of tea?"

Ella glanced at her watch. One thirty. Shouldn't the woman be organizing the shop's inventory instead of giving her the third degree? "You know my type. It mirrors yours. A loving, attentive fairy tale prince who only exists on the pages of a book."

"The real ones aren't all bad, you know."

Ella frowned. "Who are you, and what have you done with my mother?"

Her mother ignored her. "Don't you dream of getting married one day and having children of your own?"

"Of course, but I don't need to be married to some guy to have kids. I desire a family, not wedding bells."

"Why not?"

"Because I happen to know what it's like. I'm practically married to *you*. Every morning we eat breakfast, read the paper, go to work, come home, chat about our day, eat dinner, and then sit on the couch and watch reruns while shoveling popcorn down our throats. We sleep in the same room, share a bathroom, kiss goodnight. Jeez Mom, you *are* my husband."

"Why do *I* have to be the husband?"

"I give up," Ella groaned.

"You know, loving someone isn't all that bad."

"I love you, Mom."

"Come on, you know what I mean. Loving a *man* isn't so bad. There're plenty of good guys out there. You just have to weed through the bad to find the good."

"Like you did?" Ella squeezed her eyes shut, wishing she hadn't said that. It wasn't fair.

Her mother continued, unruffled. "I didn't make the best choice, but that doesn't mean *you* won't someday."

"Like I said, who *are* you? You never worried about this before," Ella added, shaking her head.

"I'm your mother, and I've *always* worried about your happiness."

"I mean your sudden urge to push me into a relationship."

"I know what you meant," her mother countered. "I'm not pushing. I'm just getting older. I guess time is melting the layers of ice."

"That's a pretty quick thaw."

"Plus," she added with a snort, "You're my daughter. And I..." she hesitated. Bitter emotion crept into her voice. "And I've been teaching you nothing but mistrust since you were a teenager. It's not right. Look what it's done to you. You don't give love a chance. I'm afraid you never will."

Ella sighed. "Why go through that pain? Looking for Mr. Right is a waste of time. I'm perfectly content being married to you."

"And what if I'm hit by a truck tomorrow? Would knowing and loving me have been just a waste of time, too?"

Ella said nothing.

"Of course it wouldn't. We would've shared memorable times holding hands and feeding each other popcorn in our sexless, mother-daughter marriage."

"Um, when *you* say it, it sounds really gross."

"You brought it up."

"I wish I didn't."

"Okay. I get the hint, but think about it. If all men are dogs then why are there so many content women in the world?"

"Prozac?"

Her mother blew out an exasperated breath.

Ella traced the carved arm of the rocking chair. Leaning back, she glanced across the hall into Eric's bedroom again. His dark head snuggled against his pillow, and his little butt jutted in the air in a vertical fetal position.

"Ella?"

"Uh huh?"

"Can you just do me one favor?"

She shifted in her seat.

"Can you just try to give people a chance? Men… a chance?"

"Why?"

"Because I want you to be happy."

"I am." The two words stuck in her throat.

"Tell the truth." Her mother was a master bullshit detective.

"That is the truth," she lied.

"Yeah, right." Bullshit radar on high alert.

A pause in the conversation gave Ella the chance to change the subject. "What's the word on Clyde? He's not really being paroled. He's full of it, right? He's not getting out so soon?"

"You'd rather go down that road?"

"If it takes the heat off of me, then yeah."

Her mother sighed. "He was telling the truth. It took a little longer than he said it would and over the last few weeks I thought he'd been blowing steam up our skirts, too, but he was finally released two days ago."

Ella shoved her fingers into her bangs and rested her elbows on her knees. "You're kidding."

"I don't kid about Clyde."

"So he's out?" Ella asked, incredulous. "He's free?"

"As a bird."

Ella shot out of her chair. Her fingers remained buried in her hair, the heel of her hand pressed against her temple. A sudden headache thudded in her skull. "Has he contacted you? I mean other than a letter?" She dropped her hand. "Has he called you?" Her gut twisted. "Has he shown up at the apartment?"

"He called."

"Son-of-a… what did he say?"

Another sigh. "He asked if he could see me."

"I can't believe this!" Ella slapped a hand over her mouth. She stepped into the hall to check on Eric. Her outburst hadn't woken him. She back pedaled into her room and closed the door with a soft click. Lowering her voice she said, "You can't let him—"

"I won't."

"I need to come home. I can't stay here."

"What are you talking about?"

"I can't leave you there alone."

"Ella, stop it. I'm a big girl. I appreciate your concern, but I can handle Clyde. He's not picking up where he left off. I made that clear."

Ella shook her head. "I don't know…"

"It may have taken me years to grow a spine, but I've got one now, and it's damn sturdy. I can handle your father, Ella. Don't worry."

"You'll let me know if he shows up? If he bothers you?"

"You'll be the first I call."

Ella stopped pacing. She drew in a deep breath. "Good."

"So don't leave your job."

Ella nodded. "I won't. I wouldn't."

"See, you like it there."

Her shoulders drooped. "Not this again."

"Awe, come on. A conversation that includes you and your handsome boss is very appealing."

"Handsome bosses can also be dead-beat dads," Ella muttered.

"What?"

"Nothing. Can we just drop it?" She opened her bedroom door again to look in on Eric.

"Okay. I suppose I've done enough mothering for one afternoon."

"That'll be the day."

"Ha ha."

"It's time I get back to work anyway."

"Hey, speaking of work, when are you gonna bring the little guy to see me? I don't think I'll ever get grandchildren of my own, so I might as well borrow one."

"Such a comedian." Ella glanced at Eric as he shifted in bed. "Soon. Maybe later today."

"I've got homemade pecan brittle."

"He has to eat healthy food. It's a rule. We follow rules around here."

"Rules are meant to be broken."

"It's a wonder I turned out so well with such a principled role model."

"You'd be lost without me."

"Mom, I gotta go; he's waking up. I'll call you later. Love ya, bye." Ella hung up as Eric sat up in bed. He rubbed his eyes with dimpled fists. She reached his doorway.

He smiled at her. His thick black hair stuck out like a porcupine's quills.

Thumb in mouth, he stepped out of the bed. His rumpled T-shirt and wrinkled cargo pants made her smile. Because of that, she ruffled his spiky hair, knelt at eye level to him and said, "How 'bout we take a ride?"

Chapter Twelve

"Oh Lord, it's a good thing Mr. York isn't home to see this. He'd probably have himself a coronary," Maggie giggled.

Ella smiled as they both watched Eric trot around the kitchen. Actually, a huge, fluffy Golden Retriever trotted; Eric just straddled its back for the ride.

After her mother's phone call, she'd had every intention of bringing Eric over for a visit. But on second thought, she had decided against it. Her mother's sudden surprising outlook on the merits of men would be much harder to deal with face to face.

Yet another worry, her father. What if she ran into the man slinking around the apartment? She had offered to help her mother keep Clyde at bay, but the last thing she wanted was a reunion. She hadn't seen him in four years and wouldn't mind if that trend extended another forty.

So instead of a visit to the costume queen, Ella had opted for a day outdoors. She'd loaded Eric, booster seat and all, into her car and off they went to the park.

They ate the vegi-wraps Maggie had packed, flew a kite, fed the ducks, climbed monkey bars, swung on the swings and then played tag.

Finally home now Maggie asked, "So what's her name?" She scratched the gentle dog's wooly ear.

"Well, actually, *she* is a *he,* and Eric named him."

"Did he now? And what's *his* name?" Maggie asked, turning her attention on the child.

"Eric?" Ella smiled, encouraging him to answer for himself.

Sprawled across the dog's back, the little boy grinned at Maggie. "Chewbacca," he cried with glee.

Maggie held her chest and stared at the boy like he'd walked on water. "Good Lord." She gazed at Ella, gathered her into her chubby arms, smothered her in a soft embrace, and kissed her on the cheek. Pulling back she smiled. "I'll never ever get tired of hearing that adorable voice of his."

Ella didn't know what to say. She hadn't really done anything except take the woman's initial advice and be herself. She glanced at Eric, feeling embarrassed and unworthy of her praise. "It's one word, Maggie." She whispered the rest. "He's only said a few words all day. I'm not a magician. I haven't done anything special."

Maggie knelt, patting Chewbacca. She smiled into Eric's happy face. "He's speaking. He's smiling." She glanced at Ella with tears in her soft gray eyes. "To me, you're an angel. Everything you do is special."

After some thought, the woman rose, scratched her head and cleared her throat. "There's a bit of a problem though. You remember the rules?"

"No pets. I know." Ella nodded in agreement. "Chewbacca's not staying." She knelt and let the animal lick her face. "He wouldn't leave us alone at the park. He followed us everywhere, wagging that furry tail of his. We asked everyone if they lost a dog, no one claimed him. When we got into my car, he kept climbing in, too. I figured we'd take him home, put up some flyers and find his owner." She ruffled his fur and the dog's heavy tail swished back and forth like a windshield wiper on high speed.

"I already told Eric Chewbacca can't stay. He understands. He just didn't want to leave him at the park all alone." Ella glanced at the little boy. He smiled up at her as she fondled the macaroni necklace he'd given her that morning. They'd made the craft a day earlier and Eric had proudly offered her the gift. The smooth elbow pasta and red yarn had become her favorite piece of jewelry. She knew she wasn't supposed to bring the dog in the house, but after receiving such a wonderful present she couldn't refuse him.

A blast of sneezes from beyond the kitchen halted her thoughts.

"Son-of-a-biscuit-eating-monk," Maggie yelped, grabbing Ella's wrist and yanking her to her feet.

The door swung open and Mr. York strode in holding a handkerchief to his nose.

The island helped hide the yellow animal, but Maggie shifted her bulk in an effort Ella assumed meant to further camouflage the dog.

"Mr. York I wasn't expecting you for dinner." Maggie jerked Ella closer. "It's not even dark yet."

Pinching his nose in the folded cloth he glanced at them. His eyes were bloodshot and puffy. He looked awful.

"Maggie—" Covering his nose and mouth with the cloth and turning away he sneezed three times in a row. With a noisy blast, he blew his nose and faced them again.

"Yes," she asked nervously and grabbed Ella's hand.

"Is there—" another sneeze, "A dog—" and another, "in this house?"

"Of course not." Maggie chuckled a little too loudly. "I know the rules round here. I'm not one to be rocking boats. No boat rocking. Not me. No siree!"

The woman lied with as much grace as a drunken ballerina. She stuttered, looked everywhere but at her employer and squeezed Ella's hand so tight her bones ground together.

He focused on Ella after blowing his nose again. "Miss. Slipper." Two sneezes. "Has a dog been in this house?"

Ella cringed. Normally she would have straightened her spine and challenged the guy. He denied his son junk food and pets, and was continually absent.

But uncharacteristic sympathy snuck into her heart. Either Mr. York had a severe head cold or he was very allergic to dogs.

Ella patted Maggie's hand, the one crushing her own. She smiled at the older woman, "Let me show him," she whispered. Maggie frowned and then grudgingly released her grip. Ella stepped aside.

She couldn't read Mr. York's puffy poker face.

She glanced down at the dog hidden behind the island. Chewbacca lay on the floor, sprawled on his back, tongue lolling out of his mouth like a pink slide. Eric stood beside the furry animal. His thumb had returned to his mouth. He watched his father. His wary expression spoke volumes.

"Miss Butterfield, get rid of the dog." To Ella, Mr. York continued, "Miss Slipper, Eric probably needs dinner, a bath, and then bed. After he's taken care of, report to my study." He glanced at Chewbacca, then at Ella and left the kitchen.

She let out a breath and glanced at her red-haired accomplice. "Maggie?"

"Yeah, darlin'?"

"What happened to all the other nannies you told me about?"

The woman eyed the still swinging kitchen door and replied, "They were canned."

Chapter Thirteen

Raising his blanket to his chin, Eric snuggled into his bed. His expression worried Ella. On the verge of tears, the little boy struggled to keep them at bay.

"Eric, what's wrong?" She gently smoothed his freshly washed hair.

His head moved back and forth against the pillow. He wouldn't speak.

"Are you sad about Chewbacca?"

His watery green eyes pierced hers. His bottom lip quivered.

She smiled gently. "You know... it's okay to cry if you're sad. Sometimes it helps you feel better." Maybe it was just Eric's nature to be stoic, but Ella had a feeling the trait had been learned from his father. The man seemed very adept at indifference.

A single tear slid down his cheek despite his effort. He brushed it away as if it burned.

"Tell me what's wrong."

He stayed silent.

"Come on," she prodded.

He frowned, and she almost gave up... until he opened his mouth. "I don't want you to go away," he said, and a few more tears escaped.

Ella kept her expression neutral. She didn't want to spook him into silence with the happiness brimming in her heart. Another full sentence. She was so proud of him. "What makes you think I'd leave?"

"Daddy." He sniffled and rubbed his nose. "People leave."

"Who?"

His little brows knitted together. "People I love."

A stinging lump formed in her throat. She wished he wasn't going through such an ordeal so young. A dead mother, an absent father, poor little boy. She'd fallen head over heels for little Eric York and wanted only the best for him. "I don't plan on going anywhere."

He brightened and whispered, "You'll stay with me?"

"I will," she assured him. In fact, she planned on fighting for her job. Regardless of the way she felt for the boy, she didn't want to give up on the money. She'd only received three paychecks so far.

His smile broadened.

She tweaked his nose and said, "honk".

He giggled. "Why do you do that all the time?"

"Do what?"

"Honk my nose," he said, wriggling it.

"Because you make me smile. It's my way of telling you I think you're wonderful." She honked his little nose again and was rewarded with another giggle.

"You okay now?"

Eric nodded.

"I promise I won't leave you." She hoped she'd be able to keep her word.

Twin dimples emerged on his cheeks.

Ella kissed his forehead, said goodnight, tucked him in, and left the room.

Yep. She'd broken the rules. But rules were meant to be broken. Just ask Trudy Slipper. Anyway, children needed flexibility within boundaries—strict rules sometimes caused rebellion.

Heck, look at Anakin Skywalker. He wasn't allowed to get it on with Padmé so he fell to the Dark Side and became Vader. I could be wrong but I don't think Mr. York wants a five-year-old evil Jedi Lord on his hands.

Ella smirked at the useless *Star Wars* trivia always floating in her head, but then frowned. She'd had no intention of keeping the dog. She only took the thing home temporarily. Plus, the animal had made Eric so happy. And she'd had no idea Mr. York's reasons for keeping a pet free home were because he had allergies. She wouldn't have brought the dog home if she'd known that. If he would have outlined the list of rules himself.

With that in mind she knocked on his closed study door, hoping her boss would see her reasoning.

Alex sat at his desk, eyes on the door. He heard the soft rap but decided to make her wait.

He'd managed to get home early again today, but instead of catching a glimpse of Eric he'd been busy decontaminating himself in the shower. Talking his surly valet into vacuuming every stray dog hair from his house took up another twenty minutes.

He checked his watch. He'd still had time to look in on Eric, but hell if he'd leave his office until he got his allergic reaction completely under control.

He might run into *her.*

It was bad enough Ella brought a dog inside. Even worse, she'd witnessed his snot symphony.

His whole life he prided himself on staying in control in any situation. He could debate politics or argue a case without breaking a sweat, but introduce a little dander and yellow fur and he turned into Puffy the Eighth Dwarf.

After his wife's death he'd never worried about his appearance to women. He had no interest in finding someone new. He had enough career stress to deal with without introducing relationship drama into the mix. But as Ella knocked again, this time with insistent force, he wondered how he looked as he sat at his desk.

The allergy meds and scrubbing had helped his symptoms. His eyes remained bloodshot and the scratchiness in his throat persisted, but other than that he looked fine.

Didn't he?

Women found him attractive. He wasn't blind or deaf. He could see their looks, hear their sexual remarks, but did *she* find him attractive? Did Ella Slipper want *him* the way he still wanted *her*?

And he still wanted her, even after assuring himself his attraction to her was nothing more than a need to get his rocks off.

Shit.

He rubbed the bridge of his nose, annoyed with his thoughts. He didn't care what the nanny thought of him. *She's a goddamned employee, that's it.*

"Hellooo." She knocked again, her voice strong and clear through the door. "You asked to see me." After a moment, "Are you in there, Mr. Mayor?" She stressed *May* and then *Yor* accentuating each syllable with sarcasm.

He hated when she called him that. Sure he'd earned the title, but he'd much rather hear her purr his first name against his ear or whisper it against his lips.

But thinking of Ella doing anything to his ears or lips, much less purr against them, pissed him off. *Why can't I just get her out of my mind?*

He closed his eyes in frustration, realizing why—because since the moment he'd met her she had monopolized every thought in his head. And on the rare occasion he forced her image from his brain, the goddamned smell of roses in the air forced it right back. He'd inhale that scent, *her scent,* and lose his fucking mind. Late last night when he had gotten home from work he wanted to tear through the halls, break down her door, join her in bed and not only inhale her close up but kiss, lick and taste every inch of that beautiful fragrant body. Instead, he'd locked himself in his room and had doused himself in an ice cold shower. He'd never taken so many cold showers in his life.

He didn't want her in his head and he certainly didn't want her in his office. He put his head in his hands, squeezing his temples. He slammed his fist on the desk. "Go away!"

Shifting uncomfortably in his seat to adjust the painful erection straining against his pants, he was surprised when she shouted, "Why?" through the door.

He couldn't remember what he'd said to her. "Why what?"

"Why should I go away?"

"Because I want you to leave," he shot back, recalling his demand, hating how he always felt like a horny teenager in her presence. He lost control whenever she was involved. He couldn't stand it. He grabbed a pencil and tapped it against the leather blotter like a drum. *Get it together York.*

The hall beyond his office remained quiet for a minute or two. *Good. Don't come back.*

The doorknob jiggled.

The pencil snapped in his fingers. *Did I lock it?*

Another jiggle and the door swung open, hitting the bookshelf behind it.

There she stood, dressed in one of her ridiculous outfits—camouflage cargo pants, a Boba Fett T-shirt and a pair of faded converse high tops. A thick leather cuff encircled her thin wrist. Her hair, gathered in a loose ponytail, draped over her left shoulder and brushed the underside of her breast. Thick satiny bangs and wisps of white-blonde hair framed her face.

She was a beautiful, irresistible mess, and Alex gritted his teeth, knowing Ella Slipper would be his undoing.

He sat behind his desk glaring at her. Ella jammed her hands on her hips and tapped her toe against the hard wood floor.

"I told you to leave," he ground out.

Her toe stopped tapping. *God he looks pissed.*

Pushing her apprehension aside for Eric's sake, Ella stiffened her spine. Before he fired her, she'd let him know what she thought of his parenting skills. "How dare you."

"How dare I what?"

"Why don't you pay attention to your son?"

"That's none of your business."

"I'm his nanny!"

"A glorified babysitter who can be replaced."

Fury boiled her blood. "Am I fired?"

"I never said that."

"Maggie said—"

"I'm your boss. I say who stays or goes." He'd stabbed a finger against the desk top and then got up and strode within feet of where she stood. "And don't think for a minute I haven't thought about it."

"So then why are you keeping me around?"

"For Eric. He's the only reason you're still here. He needs you."

"That's right," she said, glaring at him. "That's what you said when I first came here. And you know what? It's true. He needs someone other than an absent father. And on the rare occasion you show up you don't seek him out. You didn't even acknowledge him in the kitchen earlier. You neglect him. That's child abuse."

The dark look in his eyes turned into a pained stare. "I would never hurt my son," he whispered hoarsely.

"There are more ways to hurt someone than with your fists. He's just a little boy. He needs you."

"I'm here for him."

"No. I mean by his side. In this house," she explained. "I've been here three weeks, and you haven't visited him once in the last two."

His Adam's apple bobbed as if he wanted to say something. She hesitated but continued when the moment passed. "You're not here when he wakes up and you're not here when he goes to bed. And tonight you had a chance to tuck him in, and instead you close yourself up in here, hiding. What are you afraid of? He's your son, not a land mine."

"I wasn't hiding." He ran a hand through his short black hair. "I don't like... I don't want people to see me like..."

"What?" She demanded.

His green eyes burned a hole in her. "I don't like losing control."

A humorless laugh escaped her throat.

"What's so funny?"

"You are." She shook her head. "A couple of sneezes aren't a sign of weakness."

"I'm not weak."

"That's your problem."

"What is?"

"I never called you weak, but that's the conclusion you just came to. Is that why you're campaigning twenty-four-seven? Because you don't want to appear inadequate?" Agitated, she turned from his piercing gaze and strode toward a wall full of diplomas to keep from screaming at him. She skimmed the calligraphy and Latin print without really seeing it. And then she noticed a framed picture on a bookshelf. She took hold of it to get a better look. Her boss stood on the steps of an immense courthouse. She recognized the unsmiling man posing with him from newspaper articles and TV. Senator York, his father, appeared forbidding and cold standing next to his son. Her boss seemed just as aloof at his side.

Do they even like each other?

A thought tickled her brain and she faced him. She held out the picture. "Or maybe it's just him you're trying to impress."

"That's none of your business." He snatched the frame from her and slapped it on his desk face down.

"He's a powerful man. Probably plenty intimidating. Lots of people spend their lives trying to get lesser known parents to notice their accomplishments. I can't imagine your pressure."

"You're crossing the line."

She knew she was, but for some reason she couldn't shut up. "There're plenty of fathers out there who should never be allowed to raise children. Some of them push too hard, but the worst are the ones that are neglectful and indifferent." She narrowed her gaze. "Which one is your father? Or more importantly, which one are you?"

"You think you're an expert after taking a few psych courses?"

He closed in on her, but she wouldn't end her observation. She couldn't. She'd been merely fishing, but his angry outburst assured her she was on to something. "You said it yourself, you don't like losing control. Maybe your son's illness makes you feel inadequate, too."

"You don't know what you're talking about. You have no clue what's going on here."

She backed into a shelf unit, palming the books. "Maybe you're looking for a way out."

"You're out of your mind."

"For the longest time he didn't speak to you," she persisted.

"Stop it," he growled.

"Or smile at you."

"Stop!" He slammed his hand against the shelf beside her head. A book toppled off its perch and thumped against the floor next to her shoe.

She flinched but kept on. "And you think you're weak because you have no real control over his depression. You can't fix him, so you figure it's easier to just stay away."

He stood too close, his face inches from hers. His breathing, erratic and angry, scorched her skin while a blend of fury and something else she couldn't comprehend flooded his gaze. Her knees turned to jelly. Her head spun. She closed her eyes unsure of his intentions but couldn't erase the thrill of standing in the shadow of his towering frame.

An electric charge skittered over her cheek. Her eyes flew open. "What are you doing?"

His mouth hovered near her lips, barely a breath away and though he didn't touch her, she felt the impending kiss all over her body. Her stomach, her nipples, between her legs. The sensitive skin there jumped in erotic anticipation.

He drew back barely an inch. With the lightest touch he cradled the loosened base of her ponytail and slowly let the strands slip between his fingers. His gaze followed the path of cascading hair. He drew in a breath and focused on her face. His eyes held hers captive. Gently, he swept her bangs aside and then his finger tips caressed her cheek. He hesitated there unmoving.

Time stood still. Her heart continued to slam against her ribs. Her blood continued to speed through her veins. She touched his shirt, just barely, and he flinched. The warmth of his fingers faded from her cheek as he pulled back.

The anger had disappeared, but the other emotion she hadn't been able to decipher still lingered. She had no prior experience with men, and even less desire to give in to their cravings, but instinct was a powerful thing. The intuition passed down from ages of womankind helped her finally recognize the look of longing and hunger in his eyes.

He dropped his hand from the bookshelf and took a step back. His fist bunched at his side. The muscles in his jaw clenched. "Go to your room before I do something we'll both regret."

The threat in his voice vibrated straight down to her toes, but her feet wouldn't budge. Her brain wouldn't work. She should have been terrified. She should have run, but desire paralyzed her.

"Go," he barked.

She flinched, regained her senses, and ran out the door, nearly barreling into Maggie.

"Sorry," she said, helping the woman steady the loaded tray she held and then hurrying off toward her room, eager to lock the door behind her.

Alex glared at Maggie as she entered his office with what smelled like his dinner. "Eavesdropping?" He grumbled.

The red-haired woman set the tray on his desk before turning to gaze at him. "I don't make a habit of listening in on people's conversations."

He snorted. "Since when?"

She folded her plump hands in front of her. "If the people in question happen to be yelling at each other in a room with the door wide open, a room that I happen to be outside of because I'm a conscientious employee and I'd never be late bringing up a tray of food for my employer, then, yes, I suppose you might accuse me of eavesdropping."

Alex dropped into his seat behind his desk. He lifted the lid on the main dish, thankful for the distraction. What the hell had come over him? What had he nearly done?

Maggie shifted in his periphery.

"You plan on watching me eat?" He muttered.

"Yep."

Alex picked up his fork and scowled at her. "Why?"

"Wouldn't want you to choke."

"Choke?"

"Yeah, you know, on a big, steaming, mouthful of lies."

He set the fork down. "What are you talking about?"

"Are you aware of how idiotic you've been acting lately?"

"Maggie, calm down. Close the door."

She jammed her hands on her hips.

He rose and shut the door himself. In a few strides he stood in front of her. "What lies?"

"Why would you allow her to think you're neglecting your son?"

"Maggie—"

"No. I'd like an answer. You want to act like a child? I'll treat you like one. You're not leaving this room or eating in peace until you've given me a reason."

"Jesus Chri—"

She smacked his face, hard. "That's for blasphemy. I might have raised you, but I don't recall teaching you to take the Lord's name in vain."

He said nothing.

"Now, talk," she said, holding out a hand to indicate he sit in the closest of the two chairs positioned in front of his desk. She took a seat in one and then nodded at the other.

He drew in a deep breath and sighed. After rubbing the back of his neck he took a seat.

"Look at me," she asked him.

His elbows rested on his knees, his hands hung out in front of him, fingers lightly clasped. He didn't want to look at her, didn't want to explain his actions to her. She *had* basically raised him and he'd never liked disappointing her.

"Alex…"

He lifted his head. "Yeah?"

"Why are you letting Ella think you're a bad father when the truth is just the opposite?"

Sitting up he rubbed the knot in his neck and then scratched the back of his head.

She waited patiently.

He dropped his hand. "It's best for both of us."

"Both of whom?"

"Ella, me, it's best for both of us."

"And why would letting that sweet girl think you're a horse's ass be best for the both of you?"

Just drop it, Maggie.

"Why feed her such rubbish?"

"I explained already."

"No you didn't. All you said was that under no circumstances was I to let her know that you've been home most days all along. So I've been acting as though you're out of town even though you've been visiting Eric every morning while he sleeps and Ella's out running. I haven't told her that you watch your son from an attic window on the days you can get away from the office while they're out back playing together. Or that you sit, soundless, in that rocker next to his bed for hours every evening after midnight before you finally retire." She shrugged. "It's a good thing this house is as big as three or four put together." Her gray-blue eyes narrowed as she leaned forward. "What good are these secrets doing anyone?"

"It's complicated."

"Okay… umm, this is what we're going to do now. I'll ask you a direct question and you'll respond with an answer that doesn't dodge the gall-darned truth. Sound good? So I can soak my feet and then get to bed some time before sunrise?"

He studied the floor, though all he saw was blonde hair and blue eyes. "I can't get her out of my head."

Maggie remained silent for so long that he glanced at her. The accusation hardening her expression had softened with sympathy. "Your feelings for her have grown."

"I never said I have feelings for her."

She cocked her head. "It's as obvious as the nose on your face."

He exhaled a derisive laugh. "Well then there it is. If it's obvious to you it's probably obvious to her. I don't need her thinking I've got a thing for her. "

"Why not?"

"She works for me."

"It's a lawsuit you're avoiding, then?"

"It's not that."

Maggie contemplated his words. Sitting back in her chair she scratched her head. Her freckled brow wrinkled. "I think my brain's working a little slow this evening. I don't get it."

Neither do I.

"So... then... you want her to think you're a horse's ass?"

He shrugged. "Yeah, I guess that's exactly what I want."

Her brow rose. She set her hands in her lap and smiled, though it was clear she wasn't happy. "Well at least you're consistent."

"What's that supposed to mean?"

She waved him off.

"Maggie. What do you mean consistent?"

She stood up, refusing to acknowledge his question. When she reached the door she set her hand on the knob, but stood still. After a long stretch of silence she finally made eye contact with him. "When you were born I was beside myself. You had a smile that lit up the room, even as a baby." Her expression softened.

Alex stood.

Tears gathered in her eyes. She held out a hand to stop him from moving closer. Lowering it she continued, "I never had little ones of my own, so working for your father and mother was a dream." She lifted her chin. "I had such high hopes for you both, you and Conner, and prayed for the strength to help raise two respectable, reliable, polite young men."

A knot formed in Alex's throat when her proud shoulders sagged and despair dimmed the sparkle in her eyes.

"Conner has his faults, but he's a good boy at heart. You on the other hand exceeded all my expectations... except, it seems, for the most important one of all." She took a step forward and set her warm calloused hand against his cheek. "You reject love."

"Maggie..." He wanted to embrace her, let her know he adored her, but the words stuck in his throat.

She lowered her hand. "You push people away. You always have... and I'm not sure where I failed you in that regard. You keep everyone at arm's length and I fear your son has suffered the worst for it."

Guilt tore his heart to shreds.

"I know what you're afraid of," she whispered. "I can't imagine the pain you felt when your wife and son stopped believing you hung the moon and the stars."

He turned his head, ashamed.

"Look at me."

He met her gaze.

"Rejection is a frightening thing, especially when it comes from someone you love."

"Maggie... I don't want to talk about this."

"I know you don't." She nodded and walked to the door. Opening it she turned to smile softly at him. "To heal, though, to move on and begin a life with your son, filled with happiness instead of regret and pain, well... you're going to have to confront those demons at some point." With another nod she stepped over the threshold and left the room.

She waddled down the long, dark hall and then disappeared down the stairs. She never once looked back at him.

Turning, he strode into the center of the office. His dinner plate, sitting on his desk untouched, continued to throw off wisps of steam. It wafted into the air and should have made the room smell like rosemary baked chicken and brown rice.

But another scent, delicate and floral, filled his senses instead. He had breathed her in. Touched her. He'd been intoxicated by her hair, her skin, her eyes. In those fleeting moments, while she'd trembled just inches from him, he'd imagined telling her how he felt.

But he'd sent her away.

He'd never considered himself a coward. In fact, he'd always prided himself on his strength, his fortitude, in business and in politics.

But Maggie hadn't accused him of shying away from court or blowing a speech. No, that kind of criticism he could take.

Her blame cut much, much deeper.

He'd never considered himself a coward… that is… until now.

A few feet away something caught his eye. He picked the book up and slid it back into its spot on the shelf. He vaguely recalled hearing it thump against the floor when he'd cornered Ella against the wall unit.

He shook his head.

She didn't deserve to work in this environment. She didn't deserve to be carried or cornered or caressed.

She deserved his respect.

She deserved his composure.

She deserved an apology.

He left his office determined to give her all three.

Ascending the stairs and then traveling to the left wing of the house, he finally reached her hallway. Determination spurred him on. An apology for his behavior would be a start. Though it pained him to do so for Eric's sake, he also made up his mind to allow her the opportunity to leave his employment. No doubt he'd made her job stressful, what with worrying her boss might try and take advantage of her on a regular basis. He wouldn't blame her if she sued.

Her door was closed when he reached her room. Eric's was nearly straight across the hall from hers. His door was cracked and he went to check in on him first. After smoothing the soft, close cropped strands at the nape of his neck and chancing the softest kiss on his sleeping son's forehead, he stepped out of his room and moved toward Ella's.

Lifting his hand, he hesitated before knocking. Her voice, somewhat muffled, but still discernible caught his attention.

"I know, Mom, I know. And I understand that, but I love his little boy."

Alex lowered his hand.

"But Mr. York…" Ella's voice trailed off.

He knew he should leave, turn around and walk away, but he couldn't. *She loves my little boy?*

"I... I hate being near him. I hate it."

Her words cut like a knife.

"But I can't leave Eric right now. I don't want to leave him. He's progressing so much."

Alex closed his eyes. *Walk away York.*

"And I'm not a quitter," Ella said, continuing the one sided conversation. "I won't do it. I've never quit anything in my life, never given up. I'm not gonna start now."

Walk away.

There was a long pause and then, "No.... I don't want an apology. In fact, if he'd leave me alone all together, it'd be heaven here with Maggie and Eric."

Alex drew in a deep breath. He stepped back. *Leave her alone.*

He walked away, resolved to do exactly that.

Chapter Fourteen

A day after the argument between her and her employer, Ella relaxed stressed muscles in a tub of hot, bubbly bathwater. Twelve or so lit candles, puddling in various states of melt, cast a warm glow against the bathroom walls.

Though it would seem she had all the ingredients for a peaceful evening, she felt far from soothed. Waking an hour earlier from an odd dream she couldn't quite recall she'd checked the clock and sighed when she realized the time—eleven p.m.

She'd peeked in on Eric, who slept soundly, thumb in mouth, rump in the air, then tip-toed through the dark house to the kitchen. She was glad she didn't run into Alex, but was surprised to find Maggie up. The woman sat drinking a cup of cocoa, reading a romance novel at the counter.

"Is the story any good?" Ella raised an eyebrow at the scantily clad heroine draped seductively in her hero's embrace on the cover of the book.

"Uh huh." Maggie grinned. "The hero's the perfect man—tall, dark, handsome, completely attentive and a devil in the sack as well."

"Too good to be true, wouldn't you say?"

Maggie smirked. "You're too young to be so cynical."

"Not cynical, just realistic. No man is perfect."

"I don't know many perfect women, either." She smiled, but her expression turned skeptical before she said, "You've never gotten your bloomers in a twist over *any* man?"

"Not a one." Then, hoping to change the subject, she reached for the last slice of pecan pie sitting in a tin on the counter.

"Oh, that's for..." Maggie hesitated then waved a chubby hand in the air. "Never mind. You go right ahead."

"You sure?" She hesitated taking the last piece.

"If there's anything I'm sure of, it's food. Take it with my blessing."

Ella grabbed a fork and ate right out of the tin.

They sat together, discussing Maggie's favorite books until Ella yawned.

"Time to go back upstairs."

Maggie promised to bring the novel up to her as soon as she finished. She assured her the hero would change Ella's views on men.

"I've got less than a chapter left before the happy ending." Maggie had winked and licked her finger to turn the page. "Reading this might make you *want* to fall in love. Or if nothing else find a sturdy buck to have a steamy tumble with. A girl your age, with your figure and pretty face, should be beating suitors off with a stick."

"When I need a stick, Maggie, I'll let you know." Ella had kissed the woman on the cheek, said good night and left the kitchen.

In the bath now, she recalled their discussion and smiled. Finding a sturdy buck to have a steamy tumble with sounded ludicrous.

She scooped a handful of the few remaining bubbles and blew them to the other side of the tub.

That is, until I met Alex.

Her stomach knotted.

After she left Alex's office last night, she had run straight to her room and closed and locked the door.

What happened between them had been shocking *and* sexually thrilling at the same time. She couldn't suppress the crazy urge to run back to him and learn exactly what it was he'd promised she'd regret. Dragging the dresser in front of her bedroom door had come to mind. Problem was, she didn't know if she'd be barricading the room to keep him out or her in.

And her subsequent conversation with her mother hadn't helped either.

So many emotions warred in her brain. She'd been thrilled by his touch, his nearness, his warm breath caressing her face. She'd gripped the bookshelf just to keep from threading her arms around his neck. But the minute he'd kicked her out of his office, and the heat of his body left her skin, and the tingling in her toes had diminished she had come to her senses and realized she'd been lucky. She'd been balancing on a precipice and had nearly fallen in.

To make matters worse, she had no doubt their argument had been useless. For a whole day, there had been no sign of him. Obviously Mr. York cared more for his career than he did his son.

And poor Chewbacca. Faust had informed her that he'd taken the sweet dog to the pound this morning. The pound of all places! The whole thing stunk. It made hardening her heart against her employer that much easier.

She shifted uncomfortably, sloshing water over the edge of the tub. The soothing heat had fled, leaving a tepid bath in its wake. She stood, grabbing a towel as she stepped out of the diminishing suds.

With a bottle of lotion in hand, she strolled into the bedroom and sat on the bench in front of her bed. She dotted the rose scented crème onto her shoulders and arms. Her favorite flowers were yellow roses. But since pricey bouquets weren't in the budget and the apartment didn't have property for a garden, she made do with smelling like them. The drug store lotion might be inexpensive, but the scent was lovely and very comforting.

She stood and lifted her foot onto the bench to reach her knees and heels.

She rubbed lotion into her skin reveling in its silky feel and didn't hesitate when a brisk knock rattled the door. *Boy, Maggie, you're a fast reader.*

Ella smiled. The fragrance relaxed her senses and the turmoil in her head. Curling up with a good book would round out the evening. Thoughts of Mr. York floated from her mind like the bubbles gurgling down the drain. Maybe she'd get a good night sleep after all.

She called over her shoulder, "Come in," then focused on her calves and thighs.

Her quick response to his knock pissed him off. At a little after midnight he expected his son's nanny to be snoring away, dreaming up new ways to disrupt his life. He wanted to jar her from a sound sleep. Disorient her. Force her to feel as unbalanced as he did in her presence. Instead, she'd just called out to him like she didn't have a care in the world. To make matters worse, he'd promised himself he'd steer clear of her after nearly jumping her bones in his office, but damn it, here he stood.

Bursting into the room, he yelled, "Who the hell do you think you are?" He shut the door behind him so he wouldn't wake his son.

Ella spun toward him, wide eyed.

"I just got home. I'm tired and hungry and pissed with all the damn delays at the airport. Since I landed I've thought of only three things—a slice of Maggie's pecan pie, the comfort of my own house, and the sight of my son."

Before she could speak, he strode into her room—*his* room to be exact. Yes, this woman lived in it, but it was still *his*. The whole house was *his* along with everything in it, including his son, right down to the last hair on his little head. Ella Slipper needed to be reminded of that fact.

"There's an empty pie tin in the kitchen, the constant smell of that stuff," he pointed to her bottle of lotion, "in the house is getting on my nerves and the sight of my son..." He shoved a hand through his hair. "The sight of my son..." He couldn't seem to get the words out.

"What? What's wrong with Eric? I just checked on him a little while ago." She hurried forward, worry wrinkling her brow.

He held up his hand. "He's fine, Miss Slipper. He looks like a science experiment gone to hell, but, other than that, he's just fine."

Her brow quirked at an odd angle as if she hadn't a clue what he was so furious about.

"Green. My five year old has green hair. What the hell's wrong with you?"

"Oh," she laughed. "We went with my mom to the children's hospital today. She works there, so we decided to dress up, too. He wanted to be The Incredible Hulk. Did you know his favorite color is green?"

"That's it? That's your answer?" He glared at her, annoyed with her fidgeting. She'd been fidgeting ever since he burst into her room, grabbing at her... grabbing her... He stopped short. She was grabbing at a towel. A bath towel wrapped around her body. Her blonde hair was piled on her head, the tendrils around her face and neck damp against her soft creamy skin.

Holy shit.

"Why aren't you dressed?" He barked.

"I just got out of the tub," she fired back.

"Why'd you let me in?" *How the hell did I miss the towel?* Anger must have blinded him. Yet another instance this woman caused him to lose control. He'd promised himself he'd leave her be. He vowed he wouldn't come within ten feet of her ever again, and here he was... an arm's length away and in her friggin' bedroom.

She shifted the towel, hiking the thick white fabric higher under her arms. Her thin fingers gathered the cloth tighter around her thighs, but not before a slice of ivory skin peeked out, seducing him, rendering him temporarily speechless.

"I guess our argument last night had no impact on you at all," Ella said.

Noticing a robe slung over the back of a chair, he'd been about to command her to put it on, that is, until she'd blasted him with the accusation. And she was dead wrong. Her visit *had* impacted him more than she could possibly imagine.

He'd woken early that morning with a tented sheet and the lingering image of an erotic dream starring a pole dancing Miss Slipper. Today on his day trip to Texas he could think of nothing but Ella. Learning about the media group in Austin interested in backing his campaign, he thought of nothing but Ella. At lunch with the widowed owner, a spectacular brunette with a rack that spilled over her D-cups and a hand that fondled his crotch beneath the restaurant linen, he could still think of nothing but Ella Slipper.

"Your son misses you. He needs you, and after all I said you still stayed away." The color in her cheeks rose, and he realized she hadn't been talking about the sexually charged moment they'd shared in his office. She'd been referring to his son. He shoved a hand through his hair. Shame tightened his heart.

Sure he had important business today. Meeting with the brunette was necessary. Securing her financial backing and the support of the media empire she now controlled was vital. But could he have rescheduled so he might spend some much needed time with his son... quality time, time that didn't include watching him through windows like a gargoyle or whispering words in his ear while he slept? Definitely. He was a grown man. He could do whatever the fuck he wanted, but did he? No, and probably because Ella and Maggie were right. He was a coward. Terrified if he pushed too hard Eric would revert back into silence, or worse, his own son would reject him as completely as he had two years earlier.

The consequences that possibility revealed, denial, aversion, rejection had already scarred his heart beyond repair. He couldn't go through that again.

So to deal with his fear, he simply stayed away. How Ella had come to that conclusion, he had no clue, but her grasp of his failings had been nearly dead on.

Fear perpetuated the mistakes he'd been making all of his life. He wanted to grow, to break the cycle, but felt powerless to do so.

"I was in Austin on campaign business." Though true, his excuse sounded lame even to him.

"I see. So he needs to make an appointment." She strode to the desk, holding the towel tightly in place with one hand and grabbing a pen with the other.

"Exactly how long will he need to wait? A month, two months? Should he expect the glory of your presence at all this year? You know, since you're so booked up."

"Ella," he said softly, moving closer to her.

"No really, I'll write it on the calendar so we won't forget. Do you have a morning or afternoon preference?"

"Ella, please. You have to believe me. I love Eric. I love him more than anything. He's a part of me. The best part..."

She said nothing, though her glare lost some of its heat.

"He retreated from me two years ago. Wouldn't come near me. Wouldn't talk to me. But I think the worst part was the way he'd look at me. His heart was broken, Ella... losing his mother was... Jesus, I can't imagine the pain he's suffered."

"You lost her, too."

"He's just a little boy. He adored her. The strength of his loss, his sadness, can't be compared to mine."

Sympathy tugged at the perpetual smile that graced her lips.

"I know it's wrong. In my heart I know that keeping my distance from him might form a permanent wedge between us, but I do it to spare him more pain." He swallowed hard. "I've already caused him too much."

"Alex..." she whispered, seeming to want to say more.

He gently removed the pen from her hand and set it down. Her eyes, furious seconds earlier, seemed unreadable now, but the color—their vibrant blue—mesmerized him as they always did.

"I would die for him, Ella... I'd do anything for him."

"Then show him. Show him you love him." She took his hand and squeezed gently. "Don't you think he feels for you what he did for his mother? You're his father. Like you said, you're a part of him. Trust in the love I know he has for you."

Easier said than done.

Her grip loosened, but he wouldn't let her hand fall from his. She gazed at their clasped fingers and then at him. Crystal eyes searched his.

He had complained about her perfume, but the truth was he couldn't get enough of it. She smelled like summer in his mother's garden. And this close, her fragrance seemed to embrace him. At that moment, with the soft lamp light, the scent of flowers in the air, and the crackling electric charge that coursed from his hand into hers and back again, something broke down. He couldn't resist. He had to taste her.

He captured her lips with his own. The motion so quick and undeniably necessary her teeth nicked his skin.

He plunged his hands into her hair, loosening the knot that secured the mass on top of her head. Opening his mouth against hers, he ran his tongue across her lips then deeper, tasting her warmth, honey sweet.

She laced her hands through his hair, and a thrill shot through him as she kissed him with equal passion. He lifted her into his arms, carrying her to her bed.

Gently, he set her on the mattress. Her lips were parted, still pink from his kiss. Her ivory skin appeared softer than the fine sheets she lay on. He wanted her more than he'd ever wanted anything in his life.

Descending on her, he pressed his lips against hers, kissing her deeply. She moaned softly in the back of her throat. He shifted on top of her, covering her smaller body with his larger one, supporting his weight with his arms.

He kissed the corner of her lips, brushing his mouth against the perpetual smile he adored.

"It's wash out," she said softly, when he'd shifted focus, kissing her jawline.

He drew back, frowning. "Huh?"

She smiled sheepishly. "Eric's hair. It's wash out color, the green." She lay beneath him, biting her lip. "I just wanted to clear that up."

"That's good to know," he said, smiling. Something in her eyes stopped him from picking up where he'd left off. "You okay?"

The worried expression vanished like it had never been there. She pulled his face close and kissed him so deeply his erection swelled to granite.

All thoughts of green hair disappeared from his mind.

Chapter Fifteen

Ella's skin caught fire wherever his fingers touched—her neck, her face, her arms. Goosebumps rose in the wake of his lips as he kissed the column of her throat and lingered at the hollow above her collarbone. Her nipples tightened, chafing the soft terry cloth, which had managed to stay in place, *somehow*.

Nerves had nearly derailed the passion that sped through her veins. She was practically naked, kissing a man in her bed. This was a first, terrifying and thrilling at once.

She chased her fear realizing that she wanted to experience what came next.

She arched against his body, molding her belly against the center of his hips. *Rock hard.* She'd never felt anything like it, but knew the firm ridge scorching her skin was evidence of his arousal. A painful stab of desire pulsed between her legs.

He groaned against her lips while his fingers found their way to the edge of her towel. With a gentle tug he peeled the terry cloth back.

Cool air bathed her breasts. Moist heat replaced the chill when his skilled tongue licked a fiery path over her skin. He kissed and nipped and then drew her nipple into his mouth, suckling the hardened flesh. She bit her lip, pressing her head deep into her pillow. The electric sensation in her breasts matched the foreign pulse between her thighs, liquefying into white-hot arousal.

A gentle knock at the door nearly stopped her heart. She stifled the moan building in her throat and shot a glance toward the sound. Alex slid the towel lower, licking the sensitive skin against her ribs. She closed her eyes and reveled in the feeling.

Another gentle rap tore her from her ecstasy.

"Alex," she whispered.

He peered up at her. The want she saw reflected in his eyes turned her brain to mush.

He kissed her deeply, caressing her mouth with his tongue.

Another knock re-solidified her gray matter and she pulled away. "Alex," she whispered again.

He kissed her breast. "Say my name again, just like that."

"No. Alex..." she whispered fiercely and pushed at his shoulders. "Someone's at the door."

"Ella, I brought the book for you. May I come in?" The muffled voice came from the hallway.

Alex finally realized someone *was* there. His expression would have been comical had Ella not been freaking out.

"Hold on, Maggie." She jerked upward and shoved Alex hard. He fell off the bed onto the wood floor with a loud thump as she hopped to her feet. His hands flew between his legs and his face screwed up in pain.

"Sorry," she whispered, realizing her knee had connected with his crotch.

"Ella, are you okay?" Maggie called out.

"I'm fine... just... fell off the bed," she yelled back and grimaced. She sounded like a moron.

"I'm so sorry," she mouthed, righting her towel and kneeling next to him.

"It's okay," he whispered in an amusing falsetto.

She smiled and helped him to his feet. Not moving fast enough and still holding his offended organ, Ella yanked him toward the double doors leading out onto her balcony. She threw them open and shoved him through. He opened his mouth to say something but she shut the doors and turned the lock. She flung the heavy drapes closed, dropped the towel and grabbed her robe. Shrugging into it, she ran across the room as she tied the belt and reaching the door, took a deep cleansing breath. She turned the knob.

Maggie stood leaning against the jamb smirking. Her cinnamon eyebrow cocked high on her forehead. Holding the book out she said, "Fell off the bed... did you now?" Her eyes twinkled.

Ella raised her own eyebrow. "I was sleeping. You startled me. I fell." *Jeeze Louise. You're as bad a liar as she is.*

"More like a... *tumble*... wouldn't you say?"

She bit her lip and accepted the book.

"Enjoy the novel, and good night to you." Maggie turned to leave and then hesitated, frowning. "Too bad the hero is only a figment of the author's imagination." She smirked. "Cause the real thing is so much better. Wouldn't you agree?"

She tucked the book under her arm. "Guess I'll have to just read and find out," she answered with a shrug.

"Do that with my blessing. Sleep tight."

"Good night, Maggie," Ella said softly and closed the door. She glanced at the balcony doors and set the book on her desk. Not a sound came from beyond the glass panes.

Her body still tingled where he'd touched her. Kissed her. Licked her. She wanted to run to the doors, fling them open, and continue where they'd left off. Instead, she strode to the bathroom, bolted the door, turned on the shower and tugged off the robe. She stepped under the spray. The cold water doused the fire. She proceeded to scrub her body with a surgeon's proficiency hoping

Alex would use his seclusion outside to cool off as well.

The last few minutes with him had been so exhilarating, so erotic… and completely uncharacteristic of her. She'd never felt such overpowering want. The few dates she'd gone on had left her wondering… *Are all guys so self-centered? What about my feelings? My desires?*

Remaining a virgin for twenty-five years hadn't been hard at all. Not with those experiences.

So the way she responded to Alex physically and mentally surprised her.

She scrubbed away the evidence of his kisses and shut off the water. Her head, however, continued to flood with thoughts.

She'd been so sure of his neglect. Completely positive he was an uncaring, uninterested father. But his heartfelt admission, that he loves Eric, would do anything for him, had made an impact on her. He'd been telling the truth. She'd gotten very good at spotting lies over the years. The look of anguish in his eyes and on his face had been real. But he was also holding back. There was more to the story of his wife's death. She wished she knew what it was.

Could she ask him? Push harder to learn the truth? Maybe then she could help reunite father and son.

She frowned. Alex had been right. All the classes she'd taken didn't make her an expert. She wasn't a psychiatrist.

But she was Eric's nanny and as she'd told Alex before, her involvement in their lives was, in effect, like a boundary separating father from son. She took care of the little boy. She interacted with him daily, played with him, ate with him, bathed him and put him to sleep at night.

Alex needed to be doing those things. He needed to face whatever it was that kept him from connecting with his son.

She noticed her reflection in the bathroom mirror. If I quit my job, would Alex step up, face his fears and be a father to his little boy?

She contemplated the thought, though the possibility of losing so much money made her stomach knot up.

That and the fact that she'd fallen for Eric… and possibly even his father, made the prospect of leaving even less appealing.

She turned off the light and left the bathroom.

Striding into the room, toweling dry on her way, she pulled open a drawer. She yanked out sweat pants and a sweatshirt. Wiggling into granny underwear, a shapeless sports bra, and the baggy sweats, she headed for the balcony doors.

She couldn't leave Alex out there all night, but neither did she want to pick up where they'd left off. She had a decision to make. Rolling around on her bed with her boss wasn't going to make her choice any easier. She'd let him in and point directly toward her bedroom door. No wham, no bam, and definitely no thank you, Ma'am. But if somehow he got a hold of her and started the undressing and the licking and, oh God… the kissing part was really, really good…

She stopped and smacked herself in the face. *Get it together woman!*

She cleared her mind knowing she mustn't let the obvious attraction she felt for him, or that he felt for her, go any farther.

Flinging open the curtains she then yanked open the doors ready to fend off his advances and stifle her own desire.

The balcony was empty.

A chilled breeze floated in fragrant with pine and Earth. It ruffled her damp hair as she stood alone craning her neck over the railing to search the moonlit yard.

Not a whisper of sound or flutter of movement caught her attention.

Alex had disappeared.

She wondered if the best decision she could make concerning her own future would be to disappear, too.

Chapter Sixteen

"Would you prefer the blue tie or the red this morning, Sir?"

Alex ignored Faust's question and continued wiping Neosporin onto his face.

His valet, ever-dutiful, had set out his briefcase and a suit for today's business. Alex watched him in the reflection of the bathroom mirror. The stone faced man set a pair of trousers pressed to a knife's edge into the bag, followed by perfectly creased and folded underwear.

Why the hell does he insist on ironing my boxers?

He shook his head. A compulsive old man was lowest on his list of worries.

Ella, on-the-other-hand, had earned the number one ranking.

Second, he wondered if the cuts on his face were slathered in enough ointment.

Responsible for the turmoil in his heart and the perpetual erection he found himself the uncomfortable owner of, Ella was also responsible for the numerous pride-killing scratches he'd sustained last night after being shoved and then left on her balcony.

Actually, to say his son's nanny was solely responsible might be an exaggeration. He supposed her involvement could be deemed indirect. She didn't force him to climb over the balcony railing after he tried her locked doorknob. She didn't make his foot break through the lattice on the flimsy trellis. *Why the hell do movies always show grown men climbing down that particular escape route?* She couldn't be blamed for planting, watering and growing the roses beneath the balcony leading into the room *he'd* chosen as her suite. And she certainly didn't make him fall right on top of them. Face down.

He counted the scratches, five large and a bunch of small ones. It was a toss-up as to whether the deepest needed professional medical attention. And those were the ones just on his face and arms. He had no idea how many lacerations he'd sustained on his body. Not to mention the ragged tears in his dress shirt. Faust had frowned at the garment before tossing it back into the trash where Alex had originally shoved it.

To tell the truth, however, he didn't give a rat's ass about the shirt, and the scratches—though plentiful and surprisingly painful—would heal.

He just didn't know if his heart would fare so well. The thought of Ella caused his chest to swell, filled with such passion he thought it would explode.

Jesus. What's happening to me? When did he start dissecting his feelings? Why was he even thinking about *swelling passion* for shit's sake?

If an excess of emotion wasn't bad enough, he had the rigid state of his dick to consider. The underused organ between his legs was at constant attention now that Ella had moved in. Underused that is, for the last two years since his wife's death. Of course, that didn't include their abstinence before the accident. Altogether, he could honestly say he hadn't had sex in nearly three years.

It hadn't really been a sacrifice. He just hadn't been interested. Granted, he'd had plenty of opportunities. There were a handful of divorcees in his own neighborhood that had propositioned him over the last few years. And yesterday the busty media mogul had come right out and asked him to bang her in her limousine. He could have. He should have. But the only thing swelling the organ in his chest and the insistent one between his legs was Ella Slipper. Both body parts might be out of practice, but they sure as hell knew what they wanted.

Alex looked at the mirror without really seeing his reflection. Instead, he imagined Ella stretched beneath him. His name on her lips. Her skin silky smooth and as pale as ivory against his fingers. Her gorgeous legs parted in invitation, wrapping around his waist, urging him closer.

God, he'd never wanted a woman so badly.

To add to his misery he'd finally accepted that it wasn't just a physical desire he felt for her, but a mental desire as well. Most women in his social circle drank tea with their pinkies raised—not to mention their noses. They wore Chanel like a uniform and wouldn't be caught dead in camo or screen T's. They said things like, "How do you do," and "So pleasant to make your acquaintance," when in reality they plotted to stab the recipient of their gentility in the back. They spoke their minds only if it benefited them personally.

The women he had come in contact with all his life had no character, a skewed sense of morality and an absence of endearing eccentricities. They were bland and predictable.

Not Ella.

She had no fear. Not in her choice of clothing, not in the way she spoke, and definitely not in her actions. Dyeing his son's hair green was bold. The way she'd melted against him last night had been downright mind-blowing.

He wanted Ella, body and most certainly soul. And he knew now he'd do anything to have her.

After bathing Eric and returning his hair to the shade God originally intended, Ella led him toward the kitchen for breakfast. She prayed Alex had already left for another business trip, or meeting, or whatever it was he did every day to avoid his son. Running in to him this morning after their fling last night would be crazy awkward. With that in mind she had intended to give her notice, but after some playful tub time, a bit of infectious giggles and a few more hesitant words with sweet little Eric this morning, a motherly instinct dampened her will. How could she leave this child she'd fallen in love with? And more importantly, would her abandonment affect the progress he'd made?

She debated also whether she could leave the man she had... fallen for. Oddly, it hadn't taken long to come to that conclusion... that she'd *fallen for* Alex. Though she had tried to discount her feelings, her heart wouldn't hear of it. Falling asleep in the same bed he'd kissed and touched and lain next to her in didn't help. But her emotions for him were a betrayal against everything she'd believed all her life.

She pushed through the kitchen door with that thought in mind.

"Good morning." Maggie said, smiling at her. "Any more... tumbling last night, or did you finally settle to sleep?" The woman stood at the stove stirring a blissful smelling concoction in an iron skillet.

Ella shot a warning look at the red-head who chuckled pleasantly and started dishing out the meal.

"Here you go," she said, scooping out one steaming spoonful after another, "Mag's skillet sensation—hash brown potatoes, scrambled eggs, three cheeses, and homemade sausage all fried, baked and then melted into a the most mouth watering concoction ever created. Got some homemade buttermilk biscuits there on the table, too. I woke up this morning craving calories, so I decided to share this masterpiece instead of subjecting everyone to yet another pot of boiled oats." Maggie set a heaping plate in front of Eric, whose tongue wagged like a gluttonous puppy. She placed another in front of Ella. Joining them, she sat at the table with her own plateful.

"Good morning," a masculine voice broke in.

Plantations and beaches and sweet tea, oh my.

Alex pushed through the swinging door.

Maggie shot out of her chair, grabbing Eric's plate and the forkful of sausage he nearly had in his mouth. "Land sakes what's gotten into me? I've given you the wrong plate of food." She clanked his dish down next to hers and hurried to the pantry. Flinging the door open she grabbed a canister. "How 'bout some nice organic Muesli?"

"Maggie, sit down, eat your breakfast. Let Eric eat what you made him." Alex gently slid the egg casserole back in front of his son.

The little boy hesitated. He swung an unsure glance Ella's way.

"Go ahead," she said, handing him another fork.

The skepticism in Eric's green eyes lingered on his father for a second and then dissolved. A small smile hooked the corner of his mouth. He nodded at his plate then scooped up a bite. Ella patted him on the head and then glanced at Maggie.

The woman stared at Alex with her mouth hanging open. "What the heck happened to your face?"

Ella sucked in a breath after studying him more closely.

"Cut myself shaving," he stated blandly as he poured himself a huge mug of coffee.

"So you're using a rabid cat these days instead of the Gillette to trim your whiskers?" Maggie blustered.

Ella bit her lip to keep from smiling at Maggie's comment. It *did* look like he'd been wrestling a crazed feline. But the urge to laugh faded to shock when Maggie raised a cinnamon eyebrow her way. The woman grinned and winked. Ella's jaw dropped and she kicked Maggie under the table. The state of her employer's face was a complete mystery to her.

It obviously happened after he left my room. He must have climbed down the balcony... or... fell... off. She cringed. *Jeez Louise. He must have fallen into the rose bed.*

Alex stood oblivious to her dismay, blowing on his steaming coffee and then taking a sip. She wanted to apologize for leaving him outside, but she'd be revealing their ill-fated liaison in front of Maggie and Eric.

"And speaking of ill-tempered beasts," Maggie said, rubbing her shin and halting the turmoil in Ella's head. "What are you doing here, might I ask? Didn't you and Mr. Boggs have a meeting to head off to this morning?"

"I'm taking the day off."

"A day off?" Maggie stood. "Come here." She waved him over. He didn't obey so she waddled closer. "That rabid cat's given you a fever. Bend down and let me feel your head."

Alex ducked her hand, nearly spilling his coffee.

He moved a safe distance from her and set his coffee on the granite. Leaning against the counter he studied his son and then said, "I'd like to spend the day with Eric."

Eric ceased chewing, chipmunk cheeks full. His brow knitted together, green eyes narrowing. He seemed to be contemplating his father's plan.

"That is, if you'd like to spend some time with *me*," Alex added, his lips turning up in a half smile.

Eric glanced at Ella, big green eyes searching for approval. She kept her face neutral. She wanted the child go willingly to his father without encouragement. Eric needed to feel comfortable with Alex, and Alex needed to feel comfortable with Eric. This was exactly what she'd been hoping for.

Eric blinked, appearing to mull the situation over. He chewed once, twice, barely deflating his rounded cheeks. After a moment he managed a smile on his compressed lips and with a shy nod accepted the invitation.

It was a start.

Maybe the start of something big between father and son. Ella could only hope.

She glanced at Alex. He locked eyes with hers. A shiver skittered up her spine. The involuntary electrical surge awakened the most private parts of her body. Realizing she was in danger of throwing herself into his arms, she shot from her seat. "Well, look at the time. The day's a wastin', and I need to get over to the admissions office. See about my final semester."

"But it's Saturday. Is the building open today?" Maggie asked.

It didn't matter if it was closed. She'd go for a walk, go to the library, visit her mom, play Twister with Faust. Anything to give father and son some alone time together.

Ignoring Maggie, she glanced at Alex, but pinned her attention to his chest. Making eye contact with him again might jump-start another sexual surge. And this time she couldn't guarantee she'd be able to keep her hands off him. "Since you're taking Eric today, could I have the day off, please?"

He stood rigid. She focused on the polo pony embroidered on his shirt. *Don't look up. Don't look up.*

"May I have the day off, please?" She repeated when he still didn't answer. "Sure. That's fine..."

His strange tone dampened her resolve. She lifted her chin. His green eyes held... what? *Disappointment?*

She turned to break the pull of his gaze and kissed Eric on the cheek. "I'll see you later, Little Man." She ruffled his dark hair and then honked his nose. She smiled and waved bye to Maggie as she nearly ran out of the room.

I need my mom.

Trudy hadn't merely earned the title Bullshit Detective, she'd also been awarded Mother of the Year on more than one occasion. The woman had been guiding her through rough times all her life—in regards to Clyde, money, or a lack of it, school, their dwindling family business, or even on the rare occasion a loser happened to break through her defenses long enough to take her out.

Only, Alex York wasn't a criminal, a bill collector, an admissions officer or a loser. He hadn't stolen money from her, insulted her intelligence, stalled her dreams, or abandoned her. He simply happened to be her boss. And though he hadn't proven himself fully to her, she'd still warmed up to him pretty darn quick.

But dissecting the issue further reminded her that both his mother and father were in the public eye.

How would it look if Senator Robert York found out about his son's little late night employer/employee liaison? Or if Alex's campaign team found out? Or the media? Or some seedy tabloid? Screwing around with the help might not be Earth shattering news, but it might make a political hopeful look like a fool to voters and campaign contributors. And she'd be considered a gold-digger. Or worse, a slutty gold-digger.

Giving up her job might not be the best option, yet, but it had become increasingly obvious there were just too many downsides to keeping it.

She hurried upstairs to grab her purse and then tug on her high tops. She sat on the edge of the bed, the mattress shuddering beneath her. The innocent bounce conjured the previous evening. Her finger slipped from the heel of her shoe as a warm shiver ignited a frenzy of sparks in her belly. She closed her eyes, replaying what she let Alex do to her, right in that very spot. The magic of his fingers, his lips, the firm, heavy weight of his body against hers... Her lids flew open. She stood up and turned around. Her vision blurred on the mattress. A devastating realization doused the fire in her veins.

What if he's just a horn-dog?

What if he's the type that just wants to get into your pants?

And... you almost let him.

"Ella."

She accidentally knocked her macaroni necklace and keys off the nightstand. As she stooped to pick them up Alex stood in her periphery. When she finally rose she looked right at him.

God he's gorgeous.

She bit her tongue trying to skew her traitorous thoughts while she draped the necklace over her head, carefully smoothing the pasta beads.

Shoving the keys into her purse, she slung it over her shoulder and stiffened her spine. "You gave me the day off." The words came out harsher then she meant.

"I know." He took a few steps closer.

She took a few steps back.

"I wanted—"

She held up a hand. "Don't say anything. What happened last night was a mistake. A huge mistake. One I'll never make again."

His hands slipped into his pants pockets. His expression was unreadable. "If that's how you feel."

"That's how I feel," she responded quickly and moved toward the door. He stood in the way. She stared at his chest, refusing to look at him. *Just let me leave.*

He didn't.

The heat of his body radiated around her, pulling her toward him like a magnet. She stiffened, fighting the attraction but feeling his eyes on her. *Don't look up. Don't look up.*

"Have a pleasant day," he said, without the cheerfulness the statement should have implied. He stepped aside into the hall.

Ella hesitated for only a heartbeat then strode out of the room and down the hall.

She couldn't feel his eyes on her anymore.

Chapter Seventeen

Cinderella's fairy godmother had been unable to solve her problems with a wave of her wand... or in this case, a wooden spoon sticky with red velvet cake batter.

"If you're that uncomfortable at his house, you need to quit," her mother had reasoned. She had frowned and then set the spoon down. "This cake won't be ready for a while, but I have some nice leftover fried chicken in the fridge. You want some? It'll make you feel better."

"How about a nice Ring Ding?" Ella had mumbled.

Her mother had hugged her and smiled. "I've got those, too."

Ella mulled over their visit as she drove back to Alex's house. She hadn't given Trudy all the details. She'd left out the steamy looks, the attraction, the kisses. And she hadn't had the courage to mention that she cared for Alex. She had trouble accepting the emotions herself. Instead, she had simply told her mother she was unhappy.

She should have confided everything to her, like she always did. But she didn't think she could handle the *There're plenty of good guys out there, Ella. You just have to weed through the bad to find the good,* speech again.

Instead she'd eaten the last of the Ring Dings and polished off a container of mint chocolate chip ice cream.

Her stomach churned now.

She didn't know if the discomfort originated from the gobs of thiamine mononitrate and trans fat she digested, or the difficult decision she had made.

Quitting a job that not only made her money, but had earned her the friendship and love of a little boy and a cheerful housekeeper upset her deeply. What upset her more, however, was the fact that her decision had been dictated by a skillfully seductive man. She'd never made an advance toward her boss. He'd been the instigator from the start. He was the reason for her dismay, and she blamed him for taking advantage of her.

She blamed him, even as her body and soul cried out to be near him.

Pulling into Alex's driveway, she shut off the engine. Pepto continued sputtering and hacking, voicing her own derogatory opinion of the matter. Gripping the fur wrapped steering wheel she set her forehead against her knuckles. *Why can't this be easy? Why can't I just not care?*

Finally climbing out, she slammed the tricky door, stiffened her spine and walked toward the front porch.

Her mission lay before her.

She'd find another job.

She'd finish school with honors, graduate and do what she loved, teach.

A bright future on her own terms.

Exactly what she always envisioned for herself.

What she didn't envision was a life someone else determined. If she stayed and gave in to the seduction in Alex's eyes, the pleasure of his touch, she'd be selling herself short. Her goals and dreams would be extinguished as she hoped for something between them that would never happen.

She wouldn't do that to herself. She deserved so much more.

Pressing the doorbell, she raised her chin.

"I need to talk to Mr. York, Maggie. Where is he?" Ella found the housekeeper on her hands and knees dusting the baseboards. She rose with Ella's help and stretched her back.

"This old body isn't what it used to be."

"Why won't you let me help you? You shouldn't be on all fours like that."

"I told you already. I'm delighted by your constant offers, but I pride myself on this work. I've been doing it since I was your age. I come from a proud family of housekeepers." She waved her pudgy hand. "Besides, I'd go crazy if I were to sit idle. I'm fine, just a little stiff is all." She waddled to an elegant sofa and plopped down, taking a deep breath. She gazed at Ella, who took a seat next to her.

"You've caused quite a change in this house. You know that?"

She stiffened worrying the woman might bring up her suspicions about the previous night's *tumble.*

"Now, now, don't get your bloomers in a twist. I'm referring to the change in father and son," she said, reading Ella's mind.

"Oh."

"Mr. York took the little tadpole this morning and hasn't left his side since. In between dusting and sweeping I've done my share of eavesdropping. At first Eric stayed real quiet. But by and by he warmed up to his daddy and well... they've been getting along finer than frog hairs split four ways."

Ella smiled at her colorful way of putting things. "That's wonderful to hear, Maggie, but what does it have to do with me?"

The woman's eyes widened. "Since you took the job the boy is talking. He's sleeping through the night. He's eating like a horse. He even stopped sucking his thumb." She grinned. "That progress is due to you and you alone."

Ella shook her head, but Maggie held up a hand and continued. "It was the death of his mama," she said, and quickly crossed herself. "God rest the woman's adulterous soul." She frowned at the polished floor. "That tragedy caused his depression, and Mr. York hasn't known what to do about it. I believe his way of dealing with the heartbreak of watching his only child withdraw was to stay away. Drown himself in work." She leaned in close to Ella. "The Lord in all His infinite wisdom failed to make the human male very emotionally intelligent. When it comes to love they're dumber than a sack of soap."

She smiled, but cocked her head, deciding to question something the woman had said. "What did you mean just now, *adulterous soul?* About Mr. York's wife?"

"I didn't say that."

"Yes you did."

"Ah well, sometimes my lips flap before I have a chance to zip them up." She rocked to the edge of the sofa and stood. "Best be getting back to my chores. You said you wanted to talk to Mister York? He's in the backyard, with Eric and... an attractive blonde."

Blonde? Ella frowned. Why had Maggie lowered her voice like that? Like she referred to someone scandalous.

An old girlfriend? A new girlfriend?

The *getting into her pants* scenario suddenly gained momentum.

Maggie dusted a console table, humming a tune. Ella nearly questioned the woman further, but thought better of it. What did she care if her boss's wife had been cheating on him? And if he'd invited some chick over? She was just an employee who was about to quit. It was none of her business.

Over the last week Eric's infectious giggles had become a regular occurrence. As Ella maneuvered the wide path between the stone pool deck on her left and the sprawling, dormant flower garden on her right she recognized his laughter immediately. The winterized pool and its surrounding deck sat between the back of the house and a gorgeous stretch of sky high evergreen shrubs that hid a wide swath of manicured lawn at the rear of the expansive property. The elegant layout and mature vegetation made pinpointing father and son's exact location difficult.

As she moved closer to an opening cut into the leafy wall, a hearty chuckle caught her attention. Though she'd never heard his laughter before, and still couldn't see him, she knew instinctively the humor belonged to Alex.

The trellised branches within the opening formed a high arch that served as a doorway to the rear of the property. She stepped through and finally caught a glimpse of father, son... and blonde.

Wide eyed, Ella cupped her mouth in disbelief.

Alex sat in the grass, back facing her, about twenty-five feet away. His long legs were bent, arms draped casually across his knees. A little red wagon had been overturned nearby along with a couple of baseball gloves and a plastic bat. She couldn't see his face, but knew he watched his son running back and forth in front of him by the way his head moved side to side.

Eric ran laughing, smiling, black hair glinting in the afternoon sun, while being chased by not a woman, but a large wooly yellow dog.

The scene tugged at her heart. She couldn't help it. Tears sprung up in her eyes.

Eric stopped short, turned and Chewbacca barreled into him. Boy and dog fell into the grass. The Retriever righted himself and with a huge pink tongue licked his playmate's face. Eric broke into a fit of giggles as the dog bathed his cheeks and ears and neck.

Alex's laughter came out warm and hearty. He leaned forward and surprised her by rubbing Chewbacca's floppy ear.

Eric got up and wrapped his arms around the dog's neck. With his eyes squeezed shut he smiled from ear to ear hugging the animal. When he opened his eyes they widened. He noticed her standing there.

He let go of the dog and tore off running toward her. Ella squatted low to welcome him. Chewbacca followed, wagging his furry windshield wiper tail. He brushed against them and licked her cheek, nearly knocking her down. Eric hugged her tight and then pulled back to smile at her. "Daddy got Chewbacca back," he whispered.

"I see that," she said, so happy for him she could burst. Standing up she took Eric's hand. She gave Chewbacca a quick scratch and then shifted focus to Alex.

He'd risen as well and stood in the sun, gazing at her.

She couldn't help feeling drawn to him. Her heart slammed against her ribs. Her stomach fluttered with the beat of a thousand butterfly wings. What had she come to discuss with him? She couldn't remember.

Eric reached for her hand again, breaking into her thoughts. He tugged her fingers, encouraging her to follow. She tore her gaze from his father for just a moment as they navigated the tangle of roots underfoot and left the shade of a towering Magnolia. A breeze lifted the hair off her neck. The day had been chilly, but she didn't notice the cold now as she locked eyes with his father again.

Alex smiled at her. "You're back."

Eric led her closer to him. A few feet away she stopped. "I'm back," she said, needlessly.

The little boy scampered off to chase his playmate. The dog's friendly 'woof, woof' accompanied his bright laughter.

Close up she realized Alex's eyes were bloodshot. His nostrils were rimmed in pink, too. She frowned. "I thought you didn't like dogs."

"I never said that. I've always wanted a pet, but being able to breathe is kind of important to me." He shrugged. "Scarfing allergy meds won't be so bad. I'm on some pretty hefty doses right now."

She caught a glimpse of Eric zigging and zagging nearby as he tried to outrun the animal. Looking back at Alex, she asked, "What changed your mind?"

"Eric did." He gazed at his son and chuckled when the little boy sprung out from behind a tree to surprise his playmate. He glanced back at Ella with a smile lingering on his lips. "I asked him earlier if he had liked having a dog. And you know what he said to me?"

She shook her head.

"He said, *yes, Daddy, I liked it a lot.*" Alex's smile reflected in his green eyes. "He called me Daddy again, Ella. That's all I needed to hear. If the pound had already given Chewbacca away I would have gotten on my knees and begged his new owner to give him up. I would have done anything to get that dog back... just to hear that little boy call me Daddy again."

A lump formed in her throat.

He stepped closer. His gaze caressed her face. "What you said to me last night. Wanting me to show Eric I love him... and trust that he loves me... it made a difference, Ella." He took another step closer, narrowing the gap between them.

His nearness sent her pulse on a mad dash through her veins.

With a gentle touch he brushed a wisp of hair from her cheek. His fingers lingered there. "It gave me the courage to do the right thing." He lowered his hand. "You make me want to do the right thing."

No one had ever said anything so sweet to her.

"I've missed out on so much with him." He glanced at his son. Eric extended his arms wide like the wings of a plane as he weaved in and out of trees. "Vroom, vroom, vroom," he cried while his dog chased him. Alex smiled softly and shook his head. "Never again."

A day without her interference and Alex had already taken a step in the right direction. Some time alone with Eric had been all he'd needed. That and a little prodding on her part.

Now that things appeared to be on the mend between father and son, something occurred to her. She'd been intent on quitting. And the reason for her earlier dismay was very quickly fading from mind. But she realized that sticking around might not be in the best interest of their little family.

As Eric's nanny she'd be doing the things—helping him dress, sharing meals with him, bathing him, playing with and reading to him—that would better be left to his father. Those activities would help cement the bond growing between them.

And the way Alex gazed at her now, with an intensity in his expression that her good sense resisted latching onto, she knew her continued employment might take some of his focus off his son.

She didn't want that to happen. Not now, after they'd come so far.

But another part of her, her heart—the resister of logic and reason—wanted to grab hold and hang on tight. Her heart urged her to stay, forget college. Witness Eric's complete recovery and spend countless stolen moments kissing his attentive father instead.

To hell with her mantra, *Men aren't worth it.*

As far as her defiant heart was concerned, this one was.

Alex couldn't take his eyes off her. He'd been fighting his feelings for Ella since the moment he met her and the emotional war waging in his head was ripping a chasm in his heart. He didn't want to avoid her anymore. He didn't want to hide his emotions for her.

He wanted to pull her close, kiss her deeply and breathe in her scent for the rest of his life.

"Ella, I want you to know—"

The big dog barreled into her. A mass of fur shoved her forward into Alex's arms. He kept her from falling at first, but tripped on something when he stepped back. A flash of metallic red at his feet. *The wagon.* He fell into the grass, dragging her along.

They burst into laughter as the dog made his apologies with a slobbery tongue.

Alex caught a glimpse of Eric out of the corner of his eye. His son giggled behind tiny fingers, sharing their humor. Chewbacca barked, licked Ella once more and then joined the little boy.

"He's got the cutest laugh," she said. "I love hearing it."

Wisps of the long hair that framed her face tickled his neck. The ends of her thick blonde ponytail draped over his shoulder and chest.

His chuckles faded.

So did hers.

Her rapid heartbeat thumped against his ribs. Sky-blue eyes seduced him. Lips parted, her breath fanned his cheek with warm huffs. He buried his fingers into the pale silk of her hair, gently rasping his thumb against the hollow behind her ear.

"Alex." She blushed. "We should…" she rolled off of him while she spoke, but he shifted his weight to carefully lie on top of her.

She smirked. "I was going to say we should get up, not trade places." She craned her neck, awkwardly scanning the lawn behind her. "Where's Eric?"

"He's over there, playing tag with Chewbacca again." He nodded in their direction. "I can see him." He smiled when she gazed back at him. Brushing her bangs from her brow with his fingertips he added, "I don't think either of them is interested in us right now anyway."

Worry faded.

She plucked a blade of grass from his hair and let it fall to the ground. Her smile grew. "I'm so happy for you both."

"I have you to thank for this." He craved the taste of her lips and nearly dipped his head to kiss her, but Chewbacca ran up and kissed her instead.

The dog was relentless, licking them both, one and then the other. They finally rolled out of reach and stood up.

"Ella, push me." Eric stood by the swing. Chewbacca pivoted left and right beside her, yipping like an excited puppy. She ran over and helped him onto the seat. She pushed him slowly at first and then harder to help him gain height.

Alex couldn't help smiling. He never thought this would be possible. He never imagined Eric's life would change so drastically.

He watched Ella.

Dressed in a Star Wars t-shirt, snug gray hoodie, ripped jeans, and heavy black combat boots she was about as unconventional looking a nanny as they came. But he didn't care about her clothes. He cared about the woman wearing them.

She'd changed his life. Changed his son's life. Neither of them would ever be the same again.

Eric dragged the toes of his shoes across the grass. His swing came to an abrupt stop. He hopped off and ran up to him. A smile lit his face. Twin dimples dented his cheeks and his green eyes sparkled. "Did you see me?" He pointed at the swing set. "I went high."

Alex squatted. "I saw you. I think your toes might have touched the clouds. Like a plane."

Eric nodded, grinning.

Ella joined them. The smile he craved drew her lips into a gentle curve. She ruffled Eric's hair.

Chewbacca ran up and resumed licking Eric's face. The little boy fell into the grass, giggling.

Alex stood. "What?" He asked, realizing Ella was smiling softly at him.

"This," she said. "You and your son... together. You're making memories."

To be in your child's memories tomorrow you must be in his life today. He recalled her quote and agreed with its importance.

He took her hand, wanting to pull her closer, but hesitated when he noticed Eric frowning at something behind them.

Alex glanced over his shoulder.

Boggs strode toward them, stone faced.

"Daddy, who's that man?"

Alex focused on his son. "Don't you remember Uncle Wilson? You've seen him before."

Eric's green eyes narrowed. He shifted past Chewbacca's wagging tail to get another look at the visitor. His bottom lip stuck out. Alex couldn't tell if he was disgusted or confused.

Before he could decipher his son's expression the little boy sprinted to a nearby tree at the rear of the lawn. His loyal friend followed. Eric hid behind the wide trunk and peeked around the bark on one side. Chewbacca's wagging tail and rump stuck out on the other. They'd become a boy-dog hybrid.

Alex would have chuckled at the illusion, but his happy mood had been doused. He drew in a deep breath, stood and turned to face his friend. "Wilson."

"Hello," Boggs said. He'd been eyeing Alex, but after a quick perusal he shifted focus to Ella. Alex stepped in front of her, shielding her from the man's unsmiling scrutiny.

"I'm gonna go check on Eric," she said, behind him. The crunch of dormant grass let him know she'd left.

He strode toward Boggs. "I told you I took the day off. The *whole* day."

The man didn't respond. He gazed past him in the direction of Ella and Eric. His expression had soured. He watched the pair silently for a good thirty seconds. "Looks like you've developed a craving for cheesecake after all." He shifted back to Alex. "You know... even though you never eat desert."

"What's your problem?"

"With desert? Nothing. I'm a champion cake eater." He nodded toward Ella. "With her, where do I start?"

"She's none of your concern."

Boggs scratched his head. "Am I missing something here? Did you can me and forget to send me the memo?" He stepped closer. "I thought you hired me to help you become governor."

"I'm not so sure that's what I want anymore."

"What?"

"Lower your voice."

"The hell I will. Where's this coming from? Her?" Boggs pointed at Ella.

Alex took him by the shoulder and steered him toward the archway.

"I'm not done talking to you, York."

Maneuvering him beneath the latticed branches onto the other side of his property, Alex said, "I don't want your yelling to upset my son. We'll talk here," he added, directing him onto the pool deck.

"You sure it's just your son you're trying to protect and not the blonde?"

"Where's it written that I can't be with a woman? I'm mayor, not pope."

"Exactly. You're mayor. The goal here is to make you governor. When the hell did you stop wanting that?"

"I've done a lot of good in Magnolia Falls and I want to keep doing good. This is a thriving community and I'd like to think a lot of its progress is due to me."

"You're right. This is a beautiful little town, Alex, and you've put it on the map, but it's nothing more than a blip on the political radar. Winning governor'll set you up to take your father's seat. And, shit, after that you can take the damn presidency one day. You want to give that up?"

"Eric's started talking. He's laughing and eating and calling me daddy again. He's happy."

"I'm glad to hear that, but your son has nothing to do with your career."

"The hell he doesn't. He has everything to do with it. I've finally gotten him back. Finally reconnected with him. That's all I ever wanted and now that he's better you think I'm going to jeopardize his health by working twenty-four-seven in a higher office?" He stepped closer, anger flooding his veins. "Governor suited me before, when I thought I'd lost him. Now, all I want is to raise my son, keep him safe and be a part of his life. I can do that right here, in this town. Find someone else to run." He flung up his hand. "Hell, Conner likes the limelight."

"Are you out of your mind?" Boggs's face reddened. "Your brother's a dumbass!"

"His IQ is one-forty-four. He's a pain-in-the-ass, not a dumbass."

"Jesus Christ. A week ago you were gung-ho." He ran a hand over his balding head and then let his palm slide down his face. His focus shifted suddenly toward the play area beyond the arch and then zeroed in on Alex. "This is because of *her*, the blonde, isn't it?"

"She means as much to me as my son does."

"She's got you brainwashed." He paced. "Your fucking opponent probably sent her to derail your campaign."

"You know how stupid that sounds?"

"She's a piece of ass, swaying in your face."

"Watch yourself."

"You're the one who needs watching. You're father won the majority by landslides both times he ran. And you know what? You're more popular than he ever was. You've got the world in your hands right now and if you play your cards right, you can set up shop in the White House one day. But one seemingly meaningless infraction, something that to you might seem petty and insignificant right now, can and will bring it all down. I've been around long enough to see it happen to lesser men than you."

Alex chuckled. "And you think she's the wrecking ball?" He shook his head. "Come on."

"It's not what I think, it's what I know. She has no pedigree. No money. No career. Her father's been in and out of jail since she was a kid. He's a criminal, a loser. The girl's a detriment. She's nothing more than poor white tra—"

Alex poked a finger into the man's chest. "You're crossing the line old man."

Boggs narrowed his gaze. "Christ, are you seriously defending her?"

"Call her that again and you'll know just how serious I am."

Chest rising and falling, nostrils flared, Boggs stepped away. He ran a hand through his hair and then returned to his spot on the deck. "Why her?"

"Because she's the most amazing woman I've ever met."

"Maybe so, but she's not the *right* woman. Hell, your neighborhood alone is full of the *right* women. And I've seen the *right* women flirt with you, bat their eyes at you, slip you their numbers. Jesus, Alex, they drool at your feet. And every last one of them have money and family and influence and connections that will further your career instead of ruining it. Why not fall for one of them instead?"

"I told you. I'm happy right where I am. My career doesn't need furthering right now."

"Have you banged her yet?"

If Boggs wasn't fifty-seven years old and a triple chili cheeseburger away from cardiac arrest, Alex would have grabbed him by the shirt and tossed him across the deck. The white trash comment alone would have gotten a younger, healthier man the ass kicking of his life.

"I can see it in your eyes, York. You wanna punch my lights out, don't you?"

"The thought crossed my mind."

"Of course it did. I know you, son. I know your temper. I said that to piss you off."

"You figured you haven't pissed me off enough already?"

"My point here is that if I got to you... *me,* someone you know and like," he shrugged, "Most of the time at least... then what if some dirt bag reporter does the same thing?"

Alex shook his head.

"You're a volatile guy, passionate. You're protective of the people you care about." Boggs slapped a bug on his neck and then flicked its corpse into a nearby planter. "And that's a good thing. But if you end up defending her, like you just did to me, but with some dickhead shoving a mike in your face instead, and you fly off the handle on camera, what do you think that's gonna do for your career... even as mayor?"

"You're acting like I'm some lunatic that needs anger management courses."

"If you were, you wouldn't be in contention for governor. I'm not saying that at all. But think about your reaction when the press gets wind of this relationship. You think voters are gonna give a shit that she's a nice girl? No. They'll see some floozy who conned her way into your home posing as a nanny. And you know where they'll get a lie like that? From your damn opponent. You're squeaky clean, Alex. He's had nothing to discredit you so far, but once he finds out about her he will. Her name will be leaked. Her backstory will become public knowledge. Her father's crimes will become fodder for speculation on your platform and values. People love celebrity dirt. It's a friggin' American pastime. Your family's famous, Alex. It's that reason alone the public will give a shit."

"You're blowing this out of proportion."

"The hell I am. I'm telling you right now, that blonde has and will screw up everything!"

"Daddy, look at this."

His son's voice came from behind him. Alex turned and immediately noticed two things. Eric stood less than ten feet away, smiling and holding a stem full of red berries in his outstretched hand. And Ella, holding his other little hand, stood rigid beside him. Her worried frown made it clear she'd heard Boggs's outburst.

"I'm sorry," she said, sweeping Eric into her arms and holding him close. "He ran over here to show you the berries he picked for me." She started walking toward the house. "We didn't mean to interrupt."

She nearly passed him, but Alex took her hand. She stopped walking, but didn't look at him.

"Ella?"

She turned his way. Her smile seemed genuine, but her brilliant eyes had dimmed. Why couldn't Boggs keep his big mouth shut?

He tore his attention from her when Eric held the berries under his nose. "See what I picked for Ella?" The little boy asked him.

"I do. They're very pretty."

Eric handed him the stem. "Smell it."

Alex obeyed. "Mmm." He reached out and gently tucked the small cluster into Ella's hair. "How about we put it right here?"

His son smiled. "Do you like it, Ella?"

She nuzzled his nose. "I love it. Thank you for picking it for me."

Her sweetness toward his son warmed his heart. Everything about her felt right. There wasn't a single doubt in his mind. Giving up governor for her... for his son, was a sacrifice he'd gladly make.

"I'll take him inside for a bath now," Ella said. She smiled softly at Alex, nodded respectfully at Boggs, waved Chewbacca over and then all three left the deck.

Boggs watched her until she disappeared into the house. Then he shoved his hands in his pants pockets and studied the planter.

"Look," Alex said, rubbing the back of his neck. "It's getting late. If that's all, I'd like to get back to Eric now."

Boggs sighed. "So that's it?"

"What else do you want me to say?"

"That you're gonna forget about her and focus on the election."

"That's not happening."

"She's that important to you?"

"Yes."

Boggs tilted his head back, eyeing the sky. He exhaled a noisy breath and lowered his chin. "I've always thought of you as a son. I'd be lucky as hell to have raised a man like you. And I honestly believe you deserve to be happy." He shook his head. "If you were just some Joe Shmo I'd be first in line to congratulate you on finding the girl of your dreams. But you're not, Alex. You're a born leader, destined for greatness. Destined for bigger than mayor of a small southern town." He focused on the planter again. "I can't watch you sabotage your future."

"So you're putting in your notice?"

He snorted. "Hell no. I'm not that smart."

"Well that's good to hear. Because even though you piss me the hell off I still like having you around."

Boggs smiled grimly. "Yeah, yeah." He hoisted his waistband up over his protruding belly. With a chuckle he said, "My pants might be a forty-three, but my vision's twenty-twenty. I'm cursed with seeing every aspect of things." He scratched his head. "Maybe I can wear blinders when it comes to her." With a shrug he added, "Or burn my eyes out with red hot pokers..." He backed away and then turned to leave. He hesitated after five or six steps. "Hey, Alex?"

"Yeah?"

"I hope she's worth it."

"I know she is," he said, and meant every word.

Chapter Eighteen

When Alex said he'd feed Eric and then read him a story after she'd given him a bath, Ella had gladly relinquished the tasks. She wanted to give them more one-on-one time, but she also needed some privacy to think.

After he'd returned from the yard without the man he'd been speaking to, she did her best to avoid his gaze. He seemed like he wanted to talk to her, maybe discuss what she'd overheard, but she wasn't ready for that. She didn't know how to process it. She'd excused herself and retreated to her room, hoping a hot shower might soothe the tension she felt.

Drying off she stepped onto the bath mat. She brushed her hair and then separated it into sections. With a practiced hand she braided a length. Her vision blurred as she recalled images of father and son together. She felt fortunate to have witnessed the strengthening of their bond. Eric had opened up to his father, laughed and talked with him, as if he'd been doing so all along. The joy on Alex's face with each word, each dimpled smile, each and every hug had been nothing short of magical.

Just as amazing were the changes in Alex. His scowl had vanished. His stony demeanor had softened. She finally knew what his smile looked like. Dimples and all, it might be his best feature.

Her happiness for father and son, however, had been tarnished by a stranger's outburst—*her father's crimes will become fodder for speculation on your platform and values. People love celebrity dirt. Your family's famous. The public will give a shit.*

And worse—*I'm telling you right now, that blonde has and will screw up everything!*

He'd obviously been referring to Alex's political career and made it clear he thought she would ruin it. Or… that her father would ruin it. *What if he's right?*

Winding an elastic around the ends of her hair she quickly braided the other side. When she finished she focused on her reflection.

Alex had appeared angered by the man's statement. He obviously didn't agree with him. At least that's how it looked to her.

She wished she hadn't overheard. She wished the memory would stop looping in her mind.

She left the bathroom with a frown, but blushed the instant she set eyes on the bed. Now every time she looked at the queen-sized mattress she couldn't help the ripple of passion that zipped over her flesh.

The memory of the man's threat washed away, leaving only Alex in its wake. She imagined him standing behind her, whispering in her ear, running his warm fingers across her neck and shoulders. Turning her into his embrace and kissing her lips. And then lifting her into his arms and taking her to bed.

Another thrill shot through her body.

Last night this fantasy had been a reality. She had welcomed his touch and melted with each kiss. She had been his in every sense of the word. If they hadn't been interrupted would she have let him go further?

Yes.

There was no doubt in her mind. *Oh yes, yes, yes!*

She'd been building a wall for twenty-five years, but over the last twenty-four hours the barrier she'd laid brick by brick had been ravaged by desire and quickly crumbled to dust. She felt no regret for its destruction, only certainty and happiness.

She wanted her first time to be with Alex.

She dressed quickly, worried her decision might invite impulse. As much as she wanted him, begging him to join her in her bed right now wouldn't fly. Instead, fully clothed, she'd go downstairs and fill her need with some of Maggie's fresh baked bread and honey butter.

In the hall she decided to peek in on Eric first.

Hidden behind the jamb she tried to remain inconspicuous. Alex had mentioned trying to put him down for a late nap. She'd expected to see the little boy nestled in bed, rump jutting in the air. Instead she'd intruded on something even sweeter.

The curtains had been drawn across the wide bank of windows, but filtered late afternoon sunshine managed to keep the darkest shadows at bay. Alex sat in a rocking chair, head resting back, eyes closed, rocking slowly. On his lap Eric slept curled in a ball, his little head snuggled against his father's chest. He looked so peaceful, thumb nowhere near his mouth. She barely remembered the shy, silent little boy he'd once been. His progress amazed her.

Happiness warmed her heart.

Alex shifted his long legs then settled again. His eyes remained shut. He seemed to hug his son tighter within his embrace.

She glanced toward her room. She should call Trudy, let her mother know she'd been on to something after all when she'd told her, *There're plenty of good guys out there, Ella. You just have to weed through the bad to find the good.*

After all this time could she finally give up weeding?

Peering back into Eric's room her heart skipped a beat. Alex's eyes were open. He winked at her and then stood up, careful not to wake his little bundle. He set his son on his bed, tucked the covers around him, smoothed his erratic hair and then kissed him on the forehead. Appearing satisfied he slept soundly he exited the room and shut the door behind him with a soft click.

"I knew he'd need a nap. He kept saying he wasn't tired, but he fell asleep at the table," he said. "Maggie couldn't even rouse him with a cookie."

She smirked. "A cookie?"

"Oatmeal... I might go a little overboard, but I'm not a complete monster." He grinned.

"I bet he's exhausted."

"He'll probably be down for a while." Sexy green eyes twinkled.

"Where's Chewbacca?" A nervous shiver skittered up her spine. She'd been bold with her thoughts earlier. But now that they were alone, and only steps from her bedroom and her illicit bed, and their only responsibility might be asleep for a good long while, her nerve started to crack.

"I ordered a dog house for him." He stepped away from Eric's door.

Ella retreated into the center of the hallway.

"He'll have to live out back." He shrugged, moving closer. "A shower and a bottle or two of Benadryl does wonders, but I'm not ready to share my recliner with him yet."

His eyes were still a little bloodshot, but not as bad as earlier. And though he'd sneezed off and on while they were with the dog, the redness on his nostrils had practically disappeared.

In fact, he looked too handsome for her own good.

She backed up another step and bumped into the door jamb to her bedroom. He moved closer until he stood in front of her.

His eyes lingered on her face and then lowered. He lifted her left braid and twisted the end gently between his fingers. He stroked the strands beneath the elastic band with his thumb and then gazed at her. "You're beautiful," he said, softly.

Sultry green eyes hypnotized her into silence.

His fingertip glided across her jaw. "I've tried to do the right thing and keep my distance from you. I've tried to look the other way and ignore my feelings... but I can't." His lips brushed her forehead, feather-light.

She closed her eyes. A thrill of passion weakened her knees.

He lifted her chin with a gentle nudge. Her lids fluttered open.

"I know it's not right. You work for me... this isn't what you signed up for. And it's not what I planned either." He drew back. His gaze searched hers. "Say the word, Ella, and I'll leave you alone."

Her heart beat like a drum, filling the silence in the hall.

A hint of a smile tugged the corner of his mouth. "It won't be easy." The smile faded. "But if you want me to back off, I promise... I will."

His sultry southern drawl woke the butterflies in her stomach.

"I want you to be happy," he said softly.

She'd been terrified of the range of feelings she'd had for him since the day they met. Criticism, disapproval, animosity... understanding, craving, desire... she'd had no idea how to process such a disparity. The mixed emotions had been tugging her in opposite directions for a month.

Now… she finally felt peace.

She *was* happy. And though she never thought she'd say it, her happiness was due to a man. It had everything to do with Alex.

She slid her hands around his waist and gazed up at him. "I am."

Pinning her gently against the wall he cupped her face in both hands. "Ella." The way he said her name, hardly more than a whisper, made it seem like the air itself held its breath in anticipation. Raw emotion darkened his green eyes. He leaned in and pressed his lips against hers.

Their first kiss had been rough and hungry. They'd fallen into bed in a frenzy and he'd wasted no time separating her from her towel.

This was different.

He took his time, like he wanted to savor every second. The softness of his lips, the gentle pressure against her mouth, the warmth of his fingers sliding into her hair, spun the butterflies into a vortex of frantic fluttering in her core.

This kiss was different, but just as thrilling and sexually intoxicating as it had been last night.

Her lips parted beneath his, inviting his tongue to caress the recess of her mouth. Her brain and knees were made of bubbles. She held on tight so she wouldn't float away.

"You're pardon, Sir." The stern voice barely registered in the euphoria that clouded her senses.

"Jesus," Alex growled.

Jesus? Her puckered lips unpuckered. Her lids took an extra second to flutter open. Her nipples were tight and the blood continued to race through her veins. She blinked, having trouble coming down from heaven. She blinked again, regaining her senses. Alex hadn't stepped away, but she realized he glared at something to their left.

She turned, jumped and blurted, "Yee-ikes!"

Faust stood less than two steps away, scowling, looking slightly more constipated than usual. He peered down his crooked nose at her with a bushy gray eyebrow raised high on his forehead.

A short, humored exhalation of breath escaped Alex's throat after he'd shot her a smile and then glared at Faust. "What're you doing sneaking around up here?"

"I assure you, I have never sneaked anywhere in my life, Sir," the valet sniffed.

Embarrassed, Ella ducked out of Alex's arms. He caught her hand before she could slink into her room.

"Don't go," he said softly.

She stayed put, not really wanting their tryst to end either, but she let his big body shield her from the old man's accusatory expression.

"Eyes on me," Alex said to the valet.

Faust's gaze shifted immediately. "You're pardon, Sir."

"Did you need something?"

Faust cleared his throat and stood taller. "Yes, Sir. Mr. Boggs visited earlier."

"I know. I saw him." Alex waved the information off.

"He said he had forgotten to remind that you are expected at the charity ball this evening, Sir. I assured him you will be there."

"Charity ball?

"Yes, Sir. Your mother's organization is sponsoring the event. It is this evening. I reminded you last week."

Alex sighed. He rubbed the back of his neck. "Damn it," he muttered. He shifted, glancing at Ella.

"Sir, you must not be late. Miss Lhuillier, your date, is expecting you promptly at eight. I have your tuxedo set out."

His attention had been riveted on her during his valet's briefing. At the mention of *your date*, Alex had closed his eyes for a breath longer than a blink. His mouth thinned into a grim line. "Thank you, Faust."

"But, Sir..."

"That's all."

The man clicked his heels, nodded, and stalked off.

Ella's focus fell to the floor.

A date?

Is that what that guy had been referring to outside? That she was going to screw up Alex's date?

Did her boss just ask this Miss Lula-whatever out? No, Faust said he'd reminded him last week. He'd known about the rendezvous while he licked her breasts last night. And kissed her senseless just now. Her heart dropped and shattered into a million pieces. *So stupid, Ella.*

Her attraction for him evaporated into thin air.

"Ella, it's not what you think."

"I have no idea what you're talking about," she said, forcing a smile.

"I forgot all about tonight. This charity thing is a big deal for my mother's—"

"Our relationship is purely business, Mr. York." She made sure to keep her voice low, not wanting to wake Eric.

"Will you stop calling me Mr. York?" He asked, annoyed. "And as of a few minutes ago it was a lot more than business."

"That's your name."

"What?"

"You told me to stop calling you Mr. York. It's your name. What else am I supposed to call you?" *Liar, Jerk, Mr. Try-To-Get-In-The-Nanny's-Pants-With-Some-Pretty-Words-And-Kisses?!* She forced her knees to keep from buckling and turned to escape into her room. He grabbed her wrist. She tried to pull free and glared at him. "Let go." Her skin tingled within his grasp. She tugged harder annoyed by the way her body betrayed her mind.

"Ella, I'd cancel, but... last minute like this? It's a black tie event. This woman means nothing to me, believe me, but I have an obligation to her. What kind of man would I be if I broke it?"

"Please refer to me as Miss Slipper from now on. And I haven't said a thing about breaking your obligation. Go with her. Have a blast. It's no big deal to me. Now let go." She tried to pry his fingers from her wrist.

"Ella, come on."

"Miss Slipper," she corrected. "Get that through your thick skull. I work for you. I'm your employee. What you do in your spare time is your business."

With a final jerk, she freed her wrist. She turned and strode into her bedroom, shutting the door behind her.

Only then did she allow herself to cry.

Chapter Nineteen

She flung herself on her bed and wept quietly into the pillow, not wanting Alex or his nosy valet to overhear. The feathers took the brunt of her despair. After a while she flipped onto her back and let the warm drops stream down her temples, wetting the fabric further.

Blinking wet lashes, she scrubbed away the moisture with her fists.

Stop it. Get a grip.

She sat up in bed, swinging her legs off the mattress. A breath in and then out shuddered in her chest. She grabbed a tissue and blew her nose. *Enough with the waterworks. This shouldn't surprise you.*

"Miss Lhuillier, your date. I reminded you last week."

She drew in another breath, but this time in anger.

Faust had reminded him of his date, as recently as last week.

Since then he'd kissed her, more than once. He'd caressed her, said passionate things to her. He'd made her fall in…

She squeezed her eyes shut.

No. Never.

A lifetime of bias had been undermined. Passion had erased her mantra.

And look what it got her—the incorrect belief that a man could exceed expectation and rise above the faults of his gender.

She stood up, strode to the bathroom and splashed cold water on her face. She noticed her braids in the mirror, recalled the way he'd gently stroked the ends of her hair and told her she was beautiful. She scowled at her reflection and quickly pulled the elastics off. Raking through the strands with her fingers she then swept the mass into a high, lopsided bun.

"Beautiful… yeah, right. And what do you call Miss Lu-la-whatever, Alex?"

She tossed the hand towel at the mirror and then left the bathroom.

"This is good," she said, tugging on a wool sock. "Eric is much better, now. He'll be fine without me. And his dad can have his damned career. I'm not going to be here long enough to screw anything up." The other sock was inside out. She yanked it on regardless and then strode to the bedroom door.

She hesitated at the knob. Was he still in the hall? Had he gone back in with Eric? She didn't want to run into him. For a split second she wondered if she should hide out in her room.

"No."

She hadn't done anything wrong. He was the one who should be hiding...

"In shame."

Besides, she had a sudden craving for Double Stuff Oreos, and the only way to get them was to venture into the kitchen.

She nodded in determination and opened the door.

No bastard boss. No sour servant. The hall was empty.

She came to Eric's door. It was closed. She didn't want to open it and find *him* sitting in the rocking chair. But she felt duty bound to check on the little boy. She carefully opened his door.

No bastard boss there either.

Just an adorable sleeping angel.

Anyway, Mr. York was probably getting ready for his date.

She growled as she descended the stairs. Nothing the man did should concern her anymore. *Stop thinking about him.*

She recalled her desire for milk and cookies and easily pushed him from her mind.

Another floor and a bunch of steps later she found Maggie in the kitchen spraying whipped cream into a malt glass. The whoosh of air as the sweet, white fluff expelled from the canister made Ella's stomach rumble. Oreos had been on the menu, but this would certainly do.

"Milkshake?" The woman grinned at her.

Ella hadn't even had lunch yet and the Ring Dings and ice cream she'd stress eaten at her mother's earlier were long digested by now. She wondered if Alex would eat on his date with, Miss... what the heck was her name? Lula-frigger, Lula-ma-jigger, Lula-man-snatcher.

There you go again. Stop thinking about him.

"I'd love a milkshake, Maggie. Make it a double."

Two minutes later Ella sat at the counter in ecstasy, sipping thick chocolaty goodness through a straw. Her extreme pleasure ebbed only when a brain freeze split her skull in half. She welcomed the pain. It numbed her mind.

"Here you go. Use a spoon. It's too thick," Maggie said.

"Thank you."

Alex entered the kitchen as a spoonful of milkshake nearly reached her mouth.

He wore a pristine tuxedo obviously custom fit to his height and broad shouldered build. The rich black fabric matched the color of his neatly combed hair. The memory of its silken texture against her naked skin ignited those pesky nerve endings. She shivered.

Her crotch felt wet.

Squirming, she glanced down.

Ice cream had ended up on her sweat pants instead of her tongue.

That's what you get for staring.

She scraped the soupy mess off with the spoon, thankful Alex checked his watch and hadn't noticed her idiocy.

But Maggie had.

The woman grinned like a redheaded Cheshire cat. Ella rolled her eyes.

Alex opened the fridge, peered inside, then closed the door. He gazed out the window, shoved a hand through his hair and then glanced at her. She avoided eye contact, grabbing a napkin to continue blotting her pants.

"So why are you still here?" Maggie inquired, fishing a cherry from the jar and popping it into her mouth. "I thought you were going out with that high falootin' snob... I mean... that nice young heiress."

"I was," he answered.

"Was?" Maggie asked, chewing a handful of cherries.

"I just got off the phone with her. She twisted her ankle this morning playing tennis. She cancelled."

Ella shifted in her chair, uncomfortable with his penetrating gaze.

"Serves you right."

Alex shoved a hand through his hair. "Maggie, I had no choice and you know that."

"It's none of my business. I'm not saying another word. Don't like rocking the boat, as you well know."

"Sure. You'd rather turn the damn thing over," Alex countered. He drew in a deep breath and sighed. Stepping closer he glanced at Ella. "This date with Chloe was arranged something like three months ago."

"Chloe. How regal." Ella scooped another bite into her mouth, wincing at the brain freeze, though she bore the pain better than the casual use of his date's name.

"Miss Lhuillier," he clarified. "She's my mother's friend's daughter. The two of them set everything up. I didn't have anything to do with any of it, but I promised I'd go."

"Mr. York." Ella set her glass on the counter. "I already told you, your personal life is none of my business."

"Will you stop being so stubborn and just listen? I forgot all about the ball until Faust brought it up earlier."

"He said he reminded you last week." She bit her tongue. *Don't say another thing to him.*

"You've heard the guy talk. He drones on and on and on. I barely listen to anything he says. It must have gone in one ear and out the other."

"That's a good one."

He shoved a hand through his hair and scrubbed his palm across his neck. "None of that matters now anyway."

She tucked a few stray wisps of hair behind her ear then leaned back in her chair and continued devouring her shake.

Alex stood motionless. Though she concentrated on the dwindling ice cream, she still felt the heat of his gaze burning into her.

"Because I'm looking for another date."

She nearly fell off her chair.

Maggie spoke up. "It's a tempting offer, but I've given up seeing younger men. They can't seem to handle my girlish charms." Maggie winked at Alex and sipped her milkshake. He winked back.

Ella pretended to study the chocolate stains on her clothes.

Faust stepped into the kitchen at that moment.

"Your pardon, Sir."

"What now?" Alex growled.

"Mrs. Diane York on the phone, Sir." He handed a receiver to his employer.

"Hello." Alex turned from Ella's view.

She noticed Faust eyeing her with derision. She smiled sweetly, then crossed her eyes and stuck out her tongue. He wrinkled his nose and turned away.

"I said I would... No... No... You'll see when I get there... Yes... Okay... Goodbye." After the one-sided conversation, Alex handed the phone to the valet, who shot one more look Ella's way and left.

"How's Mrs. Diane?" Maggie asked him, popping another cherry in her mouth.

"Demanding as ever."

Ella sprayed more whip cream into her shake. The smile on her face as she swirled it into a mountainous spiral and then took a spoonful could be mistaken for gluttonous ecstasy. In fact, she grinned in triumph. *Ha! You deserve to be pestered by your mother.*

"Well then... I've got an idea. Since I'm just too much woman for any one man, why don't you take Ella?" Maggie suggested.

Ella spit whip cream across the counter.

"That's what I had in mind, but I doubt she's willing."

"Of course she's willing," Maggie countered.

Ella mopped the counter with a napkin and demanded, "How 'bout you guys stop talking about me like I'm not here."

Ignoring her, Maggie wondered, "Does she have an evening gown?" She shook her head and answered her own question. "Of course she doesn't. Not here at least."

"And that's a good thing cause I'm not going," Ella argued.

"What would she wear?" Maggie scratched her head.

"You'll figure something out," Alex offered.

"Am I invisible?" Ella waved her hand. "There's no way in hell I'm going."

"Of course you are. Now hurry and come with me." Maggie held out a hand.

"Nope," she said, grabbing her glass. "I'm already on a nice date with this milkshake. We're about to round second base."

Maggie thought for a second and then waddled toward Alex.

Ella could almost see a light bulb glow above her red head.

Maggie whispered in his ear. He shrugged and handed her his wallet. She unfolded it and peered inside.

"You mentioned yesterday morning you needed to replace some doohickey on your car, but hated to use your savings," She said, cinnamon eyebrow raised.

"Yes," Ella confirmed, drawing out the s.

"Well then, will you change your mind and go out with him for three hundred dollars and..." Maggie snapped her fingers, nodding at his pants pocket. He dug into the tux. There was a jingle of change. He held the coins in his palm for Maggie's scrutiny.

The woman looked up and the Cheshire grin returned. "And forty-six cents?"

Chapter Twenty

At first, three hundred dollars and forty-six cents sounded like a pretty good deal. Get dressed up, go to a fabulous party, eat loads of food, and pay for the maintenance on her car, all while ignoring her date. *Easy peasy lemon squeezy.*

A win-win situation.

As she gazed at herself in the full length mirror, however, the win-win situation looked destined to fail.

Twenty minutes earlier, Maggie had pointed her to her room and told her to fix her hair while she went to the basement to find something "snazzy" for her to wear.

"Here we go," she'd said, unzipping a garment bag.

Black and intricately beaded, the halter neck, form-fitting dress turned out to be the most beautiful piece of clothing she'd ever laid eyes on. It fit nearly perfectly. With heels it skimmed the floor a hair too much, and the bodice could use some padding, but it fit everywhere else.

"Where'd you get this?" Ella asked, lifting its gossamer train in awe. She noticed a price tag attached under her left armpit.

"Well, that's the thing," Maggie mumbled nervously.

"What's the thing?"

"It belonged to someone."

"It still has the tags on it." She squinted at the price. "Three thousand dollars? Three... *thousand*... dollars?" She jerked toward Maggie, eyes wide, jaw hanging open.

"Yeah. She never wore it. Bought it and hung it in the closet to collect dust. She often did that. Spent money like it grew on trees."

She turned from the mirror and frowned at Maggie. The woman avoided eye contact, grabbed scissors and quickly clipped off the tags. She crumpled them up and stuffed the evidence in her apron pocket.

"Who's... *she*, Maggie?"

"Well it belonged to the laaaann Mrrmm Yooorrrm," she mumbled, turning away.

"You're gonna need to repeat that," Ella said, narrowing her eyes.

Maggie sighed. "The late Mrs. York."

Ella spun to see her reflection as a flash of lightening lit the darkened sky and a clap of thunder shook the bedroom walls.

For a split second, she could have sworn she heard the macabre melody of organ music.

"Nope. I'm not going." Dancing in a circle she tried to unzip the zipper under her arm.

"Of course you are. Don't be a horse's petute." Maggie tried to grab her shoulder.

Ella ducked her grip. "I'm *not* wearing Alex's dead wife's dress on a date with him!"

"Now who said it's a date? 'It's just a business arrangement, that's all. Remember? Besides, she never wore the gown. Never even tried the thing on. It's like I just picked it up for you at the store. Alex doesn't even know I held onto it. I told him I got rid of all her things. But this..." She held Ella by the shoulders to position her in front of the mirror. "This is art. I couldn't give this away. There're others down there wrapped in plastic that were never worn either. We'll just keep that to ourselves though, won't we? Don't need to be rocking boats. Anyway, remember your car and the three hundred dollars he's paying you?"

"It's not worth it."

"It is and you know it."

"This is creepy and he's a... jerk."

"It's not creepy. And if you want my opinion, I think it's admirable he meant to follow through with his obligation to that woman. He's never liked her. And sure she's as big a snob as they come, but my guess is that even a she-devil has feelings to hurt. He did the honorable thing. Now stand still so I can clasp this."

Ella turned and gripped Maggie's hand. She swallowed hard. "I still can't go... not with him."

Maggie reached up, touched Ella's cheek and then tucked a stray wisp of hair behind her ear. "Why not?"

Another flash of lightning illuminated the darkening sky. A rumble of thunder, less intense followed. Ella shifted focus from the window to her friend.

"I know, sweet-heart... I know," the woman said softly, as if understanding the look of anguish in her eyes. "The human heart is an odd thing. It makes us feel one way, when our head is telling us to feel another." She beckoned Ella lower and then kissed her on the forehead and patted her hand. "You'll be fine. I promise you that."

Ella nodded with a half smile. She doubted her troubles could be solved so easily, but accepted the woman's vote of confidence, none-the-less.

"Now, how do those spiked heels fit?"

Ella grimaced. "Like sardine cans."

"That's no good."

"You're telling me."

"So what will you wear instead then?" Maggie asked, scratching her head and scanning the room.

"Those." Ella pointed in front of her bed where a pair of shoes sat.

"Lord help us." Maggie crossed herself. "Just promise me when you sit down try not to expose your feet. I don't think upper crust society can take such a shock."

Ella smiled, "I promise."

"That's good. Now let me fix your hair, before you go to him."

"What's wrong with my hair?" She patted the bun she'd bunched on top of her head.

"Nothing at all. That is if you want to look as if you styled it with a pine cone."

Ella grinned and let Maggie do her magic.

Alex paced the foot of the stairs.

What the hell am I doing?

Ella didn't want to go with him. Her feelings were obvious. She'd accepted, but reluctantly, and only because she wanted to get her car fixed.

If he'd had a grand in his wallet he would have given it to her. Hell, he'd buy her a new car if that's what she needed, but that wasn't the point.

What he cared about was she didn't want to go out with him in the first place.

Can you blame her?

Christ, last night he'd undressed her, would have made love to her if given the chance. And the next thing she knows, he's got a date with another woman?

He'd never forget her face. She'd lifted her chin as if Faust's news had no effect, but she couldn't hide the hurt. Those expressive eyes. They broadcast her feelings in HD.

He shoved his hand through his hair. *Damn it. This whole situation sucks.*

If his mother had mentioned the event recently it must have gone right over his head. And learning that Faust had reminded him only affirmed his current theory. If it didn't have to do with Ella or his son, it didn't matter.

Just like Chloe didn't matter. The self-centered woman bored the hell out of him. But he'd consented to the arrangement in an effort to curtail his mother's constant nagging.

Why couldn't the woman be as diligent about more important things... like his son?

He stopped pacing and pictured Eric. His smiles, his hugs... his voice. His son had amazed him today. Very little in his life lately had achieved such rank. His heart felt so full he thought it would burst with love for the little boy.

He hadn't thought he was still capable of that emotion. But it seemed to be making itself known more and more each day.

For so long he'd felt dead inside, a lifeless shell going through the motions. But no more.

He'd wasted too many years, missed too much of his son's life trying to avoid causing him pain. He'd not only squandered precious time with his son, but he'd wasted his own existence as well.

He could thank one person for such a momentous revelation.

An electric charge in the air drew his eyes toward the second floor landing. There, at the top of the stairs, she stood.

He knew at that moment he loved Ella Slipper with the remainder of his heart... the part his son hadn't already stolen.

Alex maneuvered his Mercedes into the valet parking line at the Botanical Gardens main building. Even forty-five minutes late, the back-up of cars jammed the curb. Out of the corner of his eye Ella sat next to him, rigid, hands clasped knuckle white in her lap. Her body language spoke volumes even though she hadn't said a word the whole way there.

I'm sorry, he wanted to say, but stayed quiet. He sucked at apologies.

They pulled under the overhang and out of the rain. A uniformed valet accepted his keys. Another helped Ella from the car. Taking her hand, the kid guided her onto the sidewalk. His eyes lingered on her lithe body until he noticed Alex's glare and quickly looked away.

Alex touched her wrist as they walked into the Grand Lobby. She pulled away, clasping her fingers in front of her. With a scowl, she turned to him. "This is a business arrangement, Mayor York. I'm here as your employee. Got it? I really have nothing else to say to you this evening so the sooner we get this over with, the better." Her intriguing blue eyes flashed resentment.

Alex nearly smiled. The sparks in her voice only fueled the fire in his heart.

He'd wanted to tell her how beautiful she looked. Her thick hair had been arranged in a loose side bun. Tendrils of golden silk floated in the breeze, caressing her cheek and the bare curve of her shoulder. Against the ebony of her gown, her skin shone like fine porcelain. Her perfume, the warm rose scent that always clung to her, drove him crazy.

He'd wanted to tell her how beautiful she was as she had descended the stairs earlier.

But he hadn't.

Voicing emotions as well as apologies had never come easy. Loving words always stuck in his throat. His wife had complained of that fault more times than he could count.

Standing in front of Ella, however, her radiance barely dimmed by her anger, he couldn't help but break convention. The impulse was too strong.

He leaned close, nearly a breath away. Their eyes met. "You're beautiful," he whispered.

"Drop dead," she replied calmly and left his side.

He smiled. At least he'd gotten her to talk to him.

Chapter Twenty-One

"So what's it like living with the dime?"

Alex sipped his single malt and then glanced at his brother. "Dime?"

Conner rolled his eyes. "Your grasp of slang sucks ass. *Dime*, you never heard that one before?"

"Can't say I have," he muttered, impatient.

"Ten... it means ten, old man. Like, that chick's a ten? She's the whole package. Get it?" Conner shrugged. "Dime sounds better, though."

"Whatever you say." He took a deeper swig of Scotch. The smoky burn pooled in the pit of his stomach.

Conner raised an eyebrow. "So?"

Alex sighed. "So, what?"

"What's it like? You know," he raised a dark eyebrow, "Living with *her?*"

Tilting the glass back, he downed the rest of his drink in one gulp and then followed Conner's gaze. Ella stood across the ballroom next to five other women.

As if on cue, the group laughed at something one of her companions said. All, that is, except Ella. She smiled politely, chin held high, but didn't join in. Alex raised an eyebrow. Genteel wit could bite like a rabid Pit Bull. He wondered what the woman had said that had Ella looking less than amused.

He drew in a deep breath and let it out slowly. The evening wasn't going as he'd planned.

He'd been duty bound to make the rounds. For the last hour he'd been busy glad handing government officials, movie and television stars, pro athletes and other less notable supporters. He had always enjoyed speaking with people, no matter who they were. Getting their views on hot button issues and listening to their concerns gave him the incentive and drive to be a better politician.

But tonight he'd been distracted. He'd wanted Ella at his side and she'd been doing her best to avoid him.

He shook his head, pissed. He'd finally gotten a little time alone and had been about to try and reason with her, but his younger brother had cornered him. And it didn't look like his harassment would end anytime soon.

"I'm talking to you," Conner persisted, poking his chest with a stiff index finger.

Alex eyed the younger man. Conner resembled a less serious version of himself. They matched each other physically—black hair, green eyes, six feet and change. Yorks from head to toe. But disposition wise they were in different galaxies. His brother's immaturity level stretched as wide as the cocky grin frozen on his face. The expression mirrored his personality perfectly.

"She's even better looking than that picture you had of her in your office," Conner marveled, admiring Ella.

Little brother also chased anything in a skirt and embraced promiscuity as his religion.

"She's not your type," Alex muttered and accepted a glass of champagne from a passing waiter. He deposited his empty tumbler in its place on the tray as he noticed their mother join Ella's group.

"I didn't ask if she's my type. Hell, I've banged chicks that swore they weren't my type. And later they *swore* I was the best thing they ever had." Conner grinned.

Alex rolled his eyes and downed the champagne in one gulp.

"So are you two serious?"

He didn't answer. Ella held his full attention.

"Doesn't matter. This'll come in handy regardless." Conner grabbed his hand and slapped something in his palm. "Knowing you, you're not carrying."

Alex sighed and opened his fingers. When he realized what he held he hid it in his fist. "Jesus, Conner." He tried to hand the square back, but the younger man backed up a step, waving his hands.

"Take it," Alex ground out.

"Hell no. You look all stiff and mad all the time. It's because you don't get enough pussy."

Nearby a woman gasped, pressing a hand against her chest. She speared them both with a scathing glance.

"My apologies. He's drunk," Alex said to her. He glared at Conner. "Will you shut up? We're in public," he whispered.

Conner ignored him and called after the woman, "Don't knock it until you try it." She hurried away from them. His brother chuckled. "You think she's ever done any muff diving?"

"You're a jackass," he said and strode away.

Conner grabbed his shoulder. "I was kidding. Don't leave. We haven't talked in a couple weeks." He frowned. "Wait. Where'd you put the rubber?"

"In my pocket. Or would you rather I whip it out and make a balloon animal?"

Conner smiled. "See, you're funny when you want to be." He hesitated then raised an eyebrow. "Hold up, you still know what to do with it... don't you? Twisting it into a giraffe isn't exactly what the manufacturer had in mind."

Alex's annoyance faded. He couldn't help smiling at his brother's audacity. "Screw you, dipshit."

"Get *yourself* screwed, man. I just had my pipes cleaned by the coat check girl about ten minutes ago. I'm good for about another half hour."

Alex smirked. "You're my hero."

"You never answered my question," Conner reminded him.

"What's that?"

"Are you and the nanny a couple?"

Alex regarded his brother suspiciously. "Did mom ask you to talk to me about this?"

"Since when do Medusa and I conspire? Just curious is all."

A gang of tuxes had joined the circle of women Ella stood with. Alex frowned. She laughed at something one of the men said, though he couldn't see the guy's face.

"Cause if you're not, I'd like to take a shot."

Now he frowned at his brother. "What did you just say?"

Conner nodded in Ella's direction. "Your nanny. I'd like to take a shot."

"You're telling me you want to hit on my date? To my face?"

"Hit on her? No. Fuck her brains out? Yeah," he said, with a grin.

"Don't go near her," Alex warned then noticed Ella leaving the group with a man he recognized. Keeping his eyes on the two he reiterated, "Understand me, Conner? Don't even look at her."

"So she *is* yours?" The younger man asked.

Alex ignored his brother. Ella and the blonde man made their way to the veranda. Her companion set his hand on the small of her back, directly against the smooth white skin revealed by the low draping fabric of her gown. He led her through the double doors and they disappeared from view.

A loud pop broke his concentration. Sharp pain bit into his skin. He held up his hand realizing he'd snapped the stem off the champagne flute. Cuts on his palm and two fingers welled with blood.

"Dude, what the hell's wrong with you?" Conner pulled a handkerchief from his pocket and handed it to him. His brother knelt to retrieve the glass shards from the floor. Alex pressed the fabric to his injury and started toward the veranda.

"Wait a second." Conner stood and grabbed his shoulder. "Where're you going?"

"To get what's mine."

A chilly breeze ruffled Ella's hair and raised a wash of goose bumps on her arms as her companion led her out onto the garden grounds. The lightning and thunder had ceased, leaving in their wake the melodic trickle of water.

The air had grown chillier than when they had arrived and she shivered, wondering if she should go back inside.

"It's nice out here, huh," Brian said, wrapping his arm around her waist. She wasn't sure she liked his touchy feely nature, but she didn't mind the warmth radiating from his solid frame.

She breathed in the invigorating scent of damp air mixed with late blooming flowers and smiled as he led her to the edge of the building's wide patio. "It is," she replied, changing her mind about returning to the party. There was no one inside she wanted to see anyway.

The evening had been a mess so far. A lovely bone thin blonde had informed her the dress she wore was a three season's old Carolina Herrera, apparently an epic sin. Bulimia Barbie headed a group of saline-chested inquisitors and among their unending blitz of personal questions came, '*How did you land Alex?*' When she assured them she hadn't '*landed*' anyone and worked as Eric's nanny, the saline squad had sniggered. Their '*that explains everything*' looks made her stomach churn. They assumed she slept with the mayor of Magnolia Falls. What hurt most was that as of a day earlier, they weren't far off.

She'd done her best to avoid Alex all evening, partly because she didn't want anyone else to make assumptions about their relationship, but mostly because her feelings were still hurt. He'd meant to attend this fiasco with another woman. She couldn't stop thinking about that. Jealousy didn't sit well with her. She had no experience with the emotion and didn't like the way it twisted her heart.

But in avoiding her boss she'd had no choice but to interact with strangers. Many of the attendees were celebrities. Some of them had engaged her in conversation, others had no clue she existed. She didn't follow politics or the latest fashion trends. She had nothing in common with these people. For the most part she felt like a fish out of water among Alex's peers.

And the males in Alex's family had been even worse. His younger brother had openly undressed her with his eyes. His father barely said two words when he met her. And the red-headed man that Alex had introduced as Wilson Boggs, otherwise known as uncle Wilson, had eyed her like she strangled kittens for a living and then he'd stalked off.

Diane York, his elegant mother, was the only one she had enjoyed speaking with, but their conversation had been short lived. The woman was master of ceremonies, function organizer and namesake of the charity ball, not to mention last year's recipient of a fifth Academy Award. She'd had the media, as well as hundreds of guests to attend and had been tugged in every direction.

She'd been about to call a cab when she'd met Brian Sutherland. Diane had introduced him as a close family friend.

Tall, blonde, blue-eyed, the handsome gym franchise owner oozed sex appeal, even if he didn't give her the tingles like Alex did. Sure he was nice to look at and filled out his tux like a champ, but the urge to tear Brian's clothes off, slather him in whip cream, and lick him like an ice cream cone simply wasn't there. The mere thought of her employer, however, gave her a craving for Maraschino cherries and chocolate syrup that rivaled any she'd ever known.

Jeez Louise, my employer.

She was sick and tired of allowing all of her thoughts to center on her boss. On Alex.

Cut it out Ella. Look at Sutherland. She glanced at him. *He's hot. Why can't you forget Alex and have a little fun with this guy?* She resumed listening to the man's conversation.

"You'd love my Porsche. It's red and…"

That's why.

She smiled and nodded, feigning interest while groaning inwardly. Scanning the sky, she suddenly wished for a resurgence of the storm. A nice bolt of lightning might help end his insufferable chatter.

Alex stepped onto the veranda and squinted into the darkness beyond the building's lights. Three or four couples mingled on the patio. Others strolled the garden paths in distant silhouettes.

He scanned the lamp lit gardens hoping to find her. He should have stuck to her like glue. Letting Ella evade him during the benefit had been the last thing he wanted to do. Now he paid for the mistake.

Were the hell did they go?

Striding past the rose beds, their blooms weighted down with the preceding rain, he noticed a gazebo further along the path.

Two people stood within the freestanding structure.

He'd found her.

And she stood close to her companion.

Too close.

Their proximity infuriated him.

He remained in the shadows, closing the gap between him and the gazebo. Ella nodded like she absorbed every word the guy said. Her red lips curved in a smile. Her hair glistened gold in the lantern light. The sparkling black dress clung to her body, emphasizing her small firm breasts and the gentle curve of her hip.

Heat tightened his groin. Memories flooded his head. Looking into her eyes, kissing her lips, tasting her breasts. *They're mine. She's mine.*

The heat roared into fire, igniting a powder keg of anger when the man caressed her shoulder and leaned down to kiss her. A violent inferno boiled his blood. Without thought, Alex rushed the gazebo.

Ella was nearly through hanging out with Brian when something behind him caught her attention. A man silhouetted in darkness stalked toward them, keeping to the shadows.

Alarm jump started her pulse. She raised her hand to point out the weirdo creeping up on them. Brian mistook her intent and drew her closer as he blabbed on and on, sounding a lot like the teacher from the Charlie Brown cartoons.

When a sliver of moonlight glinted off black hair and a scowling face she suddenly knew exactly who the creep that stalked them was.

Alex!

Is he spying on me?

He inched closer. Steam exited her ears.

He is *spying on me.*

"—and I really want to kiss you."

Ella switched focus. Brian grinned a la Pepé Le Pew. "Huh?" She blurted.

"I said I really want to kiss those hot sexy lips of yours."

"Oh," she said, while she watched Alex in her periphery.

Then a wicked impulse tickled her brain.

Brian caressed her shoulder.

"What the heck. Lay one on me, Butch," she said, puckering up, hoping Alex would get an eyeful. *He's not the only one who can seduce someone he doesn't care for.*

His lips touched hers, but before she could truly enjoy her moment of triumph, Brian was tackled from her side.

Chapter Twenty-Two

Brian smashed through the railing and tripped into a fountain beyond the gazebo. Alex grabbed the dazed man by the lapels, hauling him out of the shallow pool. He dragged him to his feet then shoved Brian into a nearby tree. The bare branches shuddered, dumping rainwater on their heads.

Ella hurried off the gazebo, hand to her mouth, while the two men grappled. Brian threw a punch. Alex ducked it. His fist connected with Brian's jaw. The blonde stumbled but kept his feet and tried another left jab. The blow found its target. Alex's head snapped back, but his right hook caught Brian in the nose a split second later. A sickening crack and the man hit the ground.

"Are you insane?" Ella shrieked, gaping at Alex. He stood over Brian, scowling. The man sat in the grass, cupping his nose, blood oozing between his fingers.

Alex didn't react to her question. He didn't seem to notice the crowd of people hurrying toward them. Nor did he seem to care about the pointing and whispering.

"You stay away from her." Alex's sexy southern drawl had morphed into the low growl of a lion, steely and unwavering, a quiet menace that held vicious threat.

Brian stood. He wiped his hands on his trousers, lips and chin still covered in blood. He spat onto the grass then smiled at Alex with red teeth. "It's like déjà vu, huh, Lex?"

Alex jerked forward. Before he reached his opponent, a group of men grabbed him, holding him back. He struggled for a second, dragging his captors with him. Finally subdued he stood still. He shrugged out of their grasp, glared at Brian, and turned around to walk away.

Brian shrugged spitting blood onto the grass again and blotted his nose with a handkerchief. Ella scanned the onlookers. A few of them had out their camera phones.

This isn't good.

Lifting her gown, she ran across the lawn to catch up with Alex. He'd bypassed the veranda striding around the building toward the main entrance.

"Wait a second."

He ignored her.

"Wait. What the heck's wrong with you? Why'd you attack him like that?" She yelled.

He strode beneath an arbor slapping a low hanging vine out of his path.

"I'm asking you a question, you Neanderthal." She had to hurry to keep up with his long-legged pace. He reached the valet parking desk and dug through his pocket.

"My car," he ordered and slapped his ticket into the valet's hand.

"Are you gonna explain yourself?" She asked, finally catching up. "Who do you think you are?"

He glared at her. The muscles in his jaw flexed as he gritted his teeth but didn't answer.

"Fine. Don't say a word. I'll answer for you. You're one of those egotistical jerks who think he rules the world. You think you can do whatever you want, whenever you want, to whoever you want, and you don't care who you hurt in the process." She poked him in the chest, vaguely aware of the onlookers waiting for their cars.

"You have no business spying on me. Or throwing people through railings. Why don't you just pound your chest and sling me over your shoulder while you're at it. Then you'd really be acting like a caveman."

Finally through, her heart slammed against her chest. Her blood boiled.

The Mercedes pulled up to the curb and a young man hopped out, held the door open, and smiled brightly. "Hope you had a great evening, Sir," his happy voice chimed.

Alex glared at the valet. The kid's chipper grin disintegrated, and he stepped aside. Alex moved past him and descended on Ella. She backed up, unnerved by his ominous expression.

Before she could run, he grabbed her by the waist, slung her over his right shoulder and strode to the passenger side door. A collective gasp rang out among the onlookers. Ella slapped at his back and kicked her feet, trying to break his vice grip on her hips. "What are you doing?" She yelled as he pulled open the car door and shoved her into the seat. "Stop it. Who the hell do you think you are?"

He leaned close, "I'm a caveman, remember?" He punched his chest with his left fist. "Ugh," he grunted, then slammed the door closed with his right.

Chapter Twenty-Three

"Where are we?" Ella glanced at Alex as he pulled the car into the gravel driveway of a partially constructed home.

He shifted into park. Eyes straight ahead he gazed at the darkened structure.

"This is my house." He stated plainly without shifting focus. It was the first thing he'd said since they left the gala and his deep voice made her jump.

Moonlight bathed a weed choked lawn in silver. Large sections of stonework were missing from the facade. There was no mailbox, no shrubs or flowers. The house seemed to have been abandoned mid-construction.

"Not mine exactly," he continued. "It was supposed to be for Eric. A gift. I bought the property a little over a year ago." He gazed at the house. "I thought a change of scenery might help him... forget."

She hadn't spoken to him at all for the last twenty minutes since they left the benefit either. She'd still been angry after being spied on, man-handled and tossed into his car. And even though his admission tugged her heart she didn't believe she'd ever speak to Captain Brow-Ridge again after this evening.

He took off his seat belt and got out of the car. He crossed the dismal lawn and ascended the steps. Standing on the front porch, hands on his hips, he stared at his feet. Or maybe the floor boards. He appeared to be waiting for something.

Her.

She opened the door and slid out of the car. The damn magnetic attraction between them still had strength.

"Why are we here?" She finally asked when she reached the first step, hugging herself against the chill. "I want you to take me home, please."

His handsome face shone resolute in the moonlight. "I'll take you home. I promise. Just come inside for a minute, out of the cold."

His deep mesmerizing voice disarmed her will. The strengthening attraction pulled her toward him, making it difficult to breathe.

He turned a key in the lock and entered the dark house.

A moment later she followed.

The house was warm regardless of the temperature outside. Unlike the exterior, the interior appeared nearly complete in the bright moonlight that poured through floor to ceiling windows. Through a two-story entry she followed him into an octagonal room. Covered in a huge expanse of shiny black granite, an island dominated the space dividing the kitchen from the stop sign shaped room beyond. Her eyes traveled upward. More moonlight flooded the area, let in by a large round skylight set in the high domed ceiling. The unconventional architecture mesmerized. But scanning the space she realized there wasn't a stick of furniture.

"You've disrupted my whole life."

His voice startled her. He stood by the windows gazing into the backyard. Slowly, he turned and faced her.

"You speak your mind, bring home a dog against my wishes, dye my son's hair green," he hesitated. "There's never any pie left in the kitchen. I get barely any work done because of you. You're bossy and stubborn, and you infuriate me more than anyone I've ever known."

Ella put her hands on her hips. "So tell me how you really feel... Mr. Perfect."

"I intend to." He stepped forward, casually, until he stood in front of her. "I hired you thinking you'd make my life easier. I thought by having you around I wouldn't have to worry about Eric. He wouldn't have to be near a father he blamed for his mother's death."

She frowned not understanding.

"That's right," he said with mild sarcasm. "You don't know the whole story." He shoved his hands in his pockets and took a deep breath. "Let me fill you in.

"I met Deidre in law school and then married her soon after I graduated. Our goals for my future were political and Deidre hoped I'd take my father's seat as soon as possible." He scanned the room and then rubbed the back of his neck. "I wanted that, too. Following in my father's footsteps and doing good for the country has always been very important to me, but at the time I needed to stay closer to home. She had just given birth to Eric and I wanted to be a part of his life. For me, mayor instead of senator, fit both aspirations."

Ella waited patiently for him to say more. When he remained quiet she very softly said, "Alex?"

He gazed at the floor, but started talking. "She told me about the affair one night in bed. Said it like she was talking about shopping or the goddamned weather." He focused on her. "Supposedly she'd been dropping hints for weeks, wanting me to find out, but she said I never paid her any attention." He shrugged. "I didn't... not anymore. To be honest, she'd changed after I was elected mayor. She'd had visions of the White House. And though I'll never stop wanting that as well, I really enjoy presiding over the town I grew up in. I love the area, the challenges, the people. I know most of the families in Magnolia Falls by first and last name. I've been invited to their daughter's weddings and their son's little league games. I've eaten at their tables and listened to worries about their homes and schools and jobs. I realized putting off my dreams of a higher office for a little while longer would enable me to help my community as well as raise Eric. I wanted to be there when he said his first words and stood up and walked. I wanted to see his excitement when he started his first day of school and played pee-wee football."

He drew in a deep breath, letting it out slowly. "After her affair I couldn't stand the sight of her. Couldn't forgive her. I wanted to kick her out of the house. But I let her stay for Eric's sake."

He stared out the back windows into the black night. "Despite her faults she was a good mother. Eric loved her, and I didn't want him to suffer through a divorce... so I let her stay." He paced a few steps and rubbed the back of his neck.

"Six months later I came home from a meeting, about two in the morning. I always checked on Eric first, but he wasn't in his room. I found him downstairs asleep on the floor in the den. I didn't want to wake him so I covered him and went upstairs. I walked into our room and there she was, in *my* bed, with her boyfriend."

Ella drew in a breath.

"In *my* bed. I threw the son-of-a-bitch out of the house. She screamed at me, blamed me for everything, told me she screwed him there on purpose, that I deserved what I got. She told me she never loved me and planned on leaving me for him."

His eye's changed. Their color darkened with raw emotion. "I was furious. I couldn't think straight." He drew in a ragged breath. "I forgot about Eric. Whether Deidre knew he'd fallen asleep in the den or not, I don't know. We yelled back and forth for a while, until I finally told her to get the hell out and never come back. She said fine, she'd be better off without me. The last thing I said to her was... and I'd be better off if you were hit by a truck." His frown deepened. "I said that exact thing, word for word." He shook his head. "When she stormed out of the house I realized Eric was hiding under the dining room table. He must have woken up and followed the yelling. He'd heard every word I'd said to her."

"Oh my God," Ella whispered.

"On her way to wherever she'd been going after our fight she was hit by a drunk driver, killed instantly. It was raining. The semi hit her head on. She didn't have a chance." His gaze speared the floor. He closed his eyes, squeezed them shut and then looked at her, pain wrinkling his brow. "How does something like that happen? What are the odds that what I shouted in anger would come true?"

Ella sat heavily on the window seat, stunned by his story.

"Eric said four words to me that next morning before he stopped talking for good." A muscle flexed in his cheek. His eyes closed and he took a deep breath. Exhaling softly, he looked at her. "You made mommy die."

Ella's heart beat skid to a halt. She stood and stepped toward him but hesitated when he held up his hand. He faced the bank of windows, both hands clasped behind his neck.

Clearing his throat, he said, "Three years old and the kid had to witness his father wishing his mother dead. Jesus." He set his palms against the window. "For a while I blamed myself for her death, too. No one should say what I said to her. Not for any reason. And, shit, look what happened after I said it."

Ella stepped beside him, wishing she could see his face. The anguish in his voice at that moment gave her an image of what his expression might be.

"He wouldn't talk, or smile, or laugh. He barely ate and lost so much weight." Alex pulled away from the window.

"He wouldn't play with his toys anymore. Any time Maggie found him in the play room upstairs he'd be crying, curled in the blanket his mother had knitted for him." His lips pressed in a grim line. "I ended up locking the door so he wouldn't be reminded of her. That's why I initially built this house," he said, gazing at the structure. "I thought we'd move away so he'd have a chance to heal. But he was so fragile his doctors feared the stress of relocation might be too much."

He glanced at her. His green eyes were clouded with shame. "He hid whenever I was home, wouldn't come near me. Maggie said when I wasn't around he'd eat better and didn't cry as much. He didn't wake up with so many nightmares. So I... stayed away, buried myself in work... thinking that was best for him. And then I was asked to run for governor. I'd always wanted more, still dreamed of bigger and better things, so I accepted. I figured the rigor of campaigning and the greater responsibility would keep me away from home and my mind off the guilt that was slowly tearing me apart. It broke my heart to know I was the cause of his suffering. I didn't want to keep torturing him with my presence."

He tucked a stray wisp of hair behind her ear. The contact of his fingertips against her skin sent electricity through her veins, but she didn't pull away.

"I didn't think I'd ever see him smile again or hear his voice. I didn't think I'd ever get my son back... until I found you."

Her heartbeat quickened as his fingers lingered at her jaw. They slid to her neck, lightly tracing the skin below her pulse point. His eyes, darkened by pain a moment earlier, changed.

They devoured her.

"The last thing I wanted to do tonight, Ella, was take that woman out. I feel nothing for her at all, and when she called to cancel I couldn't believe my luck. I wanted to go with you... but..." A grim smile crested his full lips. "You were pretty pissed."

"I was," she said with a nod, but flashed a small smile of her own.

"I was surprised when you agreed to go. I figured someone upstairs must be looking out for me. Until I saw you with Brian." He scrubbed the back of his neck and then let his hand fall to his side. "I attacked that guy for two reasons. First," he said with the merest trace of a smile, "I refuse to share you with another man. And second," his voice growing cold, "Brian Sutherland is the bastard who slept with my wife."

Ella raised her fingers to her lips. "Oh my God," she whispered. "Alex... I'm so sorry. I had no idea."

"Don't apologize. It's not your fault." With the lightest touch his fingers skimmed her shoulder. "And actually, before tonight I thought I'd come to terms with the whole thing. Believe it or not, after my wife was killed, Brian's role in the affair didn't even matter to me anymore," he said, shaking his head, a smirk on his handsome face. "Death puts things in perspective. So I decided, if I ever *did* see him again, I had no reason to confront him. But... when I saw him with you..."

He strode toward the kitchen island. His back turned he set his hands on the granite surface gripping the beveled edge. "I wanted to kill him, Ella... and not because he had sex with my wife."

She moved toward him. In profile his lips were a tight line. "I wanted to kill him because he had his hands on *you*."

After a moment he shook his head and then smiled at her. Breaking the tension he shrugged broad shoulders. "I said you've disrupted my life. You infuriate me. Drive me absolutely nuts. What I failed to mention, though..." He caressed her cheek. "...all of that only makes me want you more... Cinderella."

She blinked. "What'd you just say?"

"That you drive me nuts."

She raised an eyebrow, cocking her head. "No... the other thing."

He chuckled. "When I had that investigator make sure you never held up a gas station or cooked meth, the first thing I learned was your birth name."

Her jaw dropped. She slapped his shoulder. He ducked before she could smack him again. "You knew that ridiculous name the whole time?" She groaned.

"What's the big deal?"

"Don't even think about saying my middle name out loud."

He chuckled and grabbed her, swung her into his arms and sat her on the granite countertop. "I think both names are kinda nice." He grinned, "Oh, and by the way, why is Cinderella wearing combat boots to the ball? Aren't these things supposed to be made of glass?" He teased, lifting the edge of her gown to reveal the scuffed, black boots and then tugging on the laces.

"Glass gives me blisters." She smacked his hand away.

"Is that right?" He smiled back. A breath later his expression altered. Lifting the hem of her gown over her knees, he exposed smooth, pale thighs. He stood between her parted legs and took her right hand. Drawing her palm to his lips he kissed the warm skin. He pressed her fingers against his cheek. "It's like I'd been holding my breath until I met you," he whispered against her flesh.

She smoothed her left hand over his shoulder, tracing his collar. Her fingertips brushed the fine hairs on his neck and grazed the hollow beneath his ear.

The feather touch nearly buckled his knees.

The look she gave him said one thing—desire. He cupped her face. "It's those eyes of yours."

"My eyes?" A small laugh escaped her throat.

Moving closer still, he nuzzled her neck, drew in her intoxicating scent, shared her sweet breath. Turning his face just slightly he set his lips against the corner of her mouth and murmured, "Your eyes take hold of me and don't let go."

His kiss electrified her, setting her skin abuzz with sensation and filling her head with Ginger Ale. She melted against him reveling in the feel of his full lips. The warm velvet of his tongue stroked hers, igniting a fire in her belly that spread to her extremities. The inferno grew, fueling an ache, tightening her core with seductive pain.

She drew back and held his face in her hands. Their eyes met. "I owe you an apology."

He took her hands and held them in front of him, running his thumb gently over her wrist. "For what?"

"For misjudging you." She lowered her gaze, shaking her head. When she raised her chin again she added, "I thought you cared more about work than you did your son. I was so wrong." She stroked his cheek. "You're a good man, Alex. A loving father. I know that now, and I'm sorry I doubted you."

"Stop," he said, taking her hand and holding it in front of them again. A slow smile curved his lips. "I didn't give you a reason to think otherwise." He moved closer and kissed her softly.

She shivered in his embrace. Could her heart explode from sheer pleasure? Her blood raced in time with her mounting pulse as if in answer to her question. *I can't think of a better way to die.*

"Ella," he whispered, his forehead lightly touching hers. "I stayed away for two reasons. For years I thought I was doing what's best for Eric." He looked at her. "Today showed me how wrong I've been. He needs me and I need him. I won't make that mistake again. But more recently I stayed away for your sake."

She frowned.

"I've wanted this..." he held her face in his hands and kissed her slowly, softly. After a blissful few seconds he pulled back. "I've wanted this from the moment I met you," he said, staring into her eyes. "You're all I think about, from the minute I wake up to the second I fall asleep every single night." He smiled. "I couldn't keep you out of my dreams either. And I tried, I... honestly tried. But I'm done fighting my feelings for you." He kissed her deeply, tasting her warmth and sweetness. He couldn't get enough of her and when he finally broke away he whispered against her mouth, "I've wanted all of you, Ella, every inch of you, and I plan on taking what I want, right here and now."

He shrugged out of his tux jacket. Tossing the black fabric onto the floor he took hold of his shirt collar. She stopped him.

"Let me," she said, the rush of blood from his admission stirring a cauldron of unexpected daring. He moved closer, lifted his chin slightly to let her unbutton the neck of his shirt. One, two, three. The buttons slid from their holes with ease.

Her fingers should have fumbled. Nerves should have tied them in knots. But Alex's eyes, the way they feasted on her, gave her courage she'd never felt before.

Four, five, six. With an intake of breath, she pushed the crisp halves of his shirt open.

Granite.

Smooth, but hard, the tanned curves of his chest muscles, divided by a striated groove down the center of his breastbone held her attention. She swallowed and ran her hands over his hot flesh, trailing a finger over a small, flat nipple and feeling it stiffen beneath her touch. She took hold of his shirt and tugged it from his pants. In her haste she tore the remaining buttons from the fabric.

"Sorry," she cringed.

He peeled off the shirt, let it land in a heap on his discarded jacket and smiled. "I'm not." He moved in like a predator, shirtless and beautiful. Thick shoulder muscles and powerful sinew rippled beneath her fingers, but before she could explore further he whispered, "My turn."

Chapter Twenty-Four

Alex reached around Ella's neck. He felt for the pins in her hair and with a couple of flicks, the long golden waves fell past her shoulders.

A whiff of summer. That was the only way he could describe her scent—sunshine and flowers. Her white-gold hair reminded him of June or July—glowing, warm, fragrant.

It drove him wild, and he pressed his lips against her neck so he could breathe her in.

He buried his hands in the silken curtain of her hair and unclasped the hooks that held her halter in place at the top of her spine. Letting go, the narrow strips of fabric slid down her shoulders, past her delicate collarbones, and lower still.

The plunging neckline collapsed and fell open to reveal luminous skin the color of porcelain.

His breath hitched. He'd seen Ella's breasts before. He'd kissed them. Licked them. Grew hard just thinking about them.

But not like this.

Moonbeams flooded the skylight and lit the bank of windows to her left. Her nipples and the soft flesh above them were bathed in silver. The full, rounded curves beneath each rosy peak glowed a creamy shade of white.

"You're so beautiful," he said in a hoarse whisper, eyes locked with hers. She shook her head, but he kissed her when she seemed like she might disagree. He moved lower nipping her jawline, nuzzling the pulse point in her throat, licking the heated skin of her chest until his lips captured her nipple. He drew the pebbled flesh into his mouth and suckled until she leaned into him and gripped his hair in her fist.

A mewling sound escaped her throat and he moved to her other breast, sucking and licking until she arched her back, moaning. He moved lower, running his tongue over the scalding skin of her stomach. He kissed every inch of her torso then pulling away he knelt to unlace her shoes.

The heavy leather boot loosened. Falling, it clunked against the floor. The other dropped near its mate and he gently kicked them aside. He tugged her thin socks off her feet and took her right instep into his left hand. He kissed her ankle. Ran his palm over her calf and followed its path with his lips. Moving higher he squeezed the toned length of her outer thigh. Still higher, he nudged beneath the lacy edge of her panties. He gripped her ass with one hand and traced the baby smooth skin of her inner thigh with his other.

"Your skin is like silk," he whispered against her leg and shifted to a standing position so she straddled his hips. He pressed his other palm against her thigh to grip the rounded curves of her ass with both hands.

"Lie back," he commanded gently. She bit her lip, but obeyed, eyes gleaming. Lying flat on the counter she gasped when he jerked her hips to the edge and pressed the stone length of his cock against the sensitive nub of her sex.

Fabric against fabric couldn't shield the heat of her body, but he needed more. He brushed his thumb over her panties, running the digit up, down, and in between the damp, silky groove. Her breath came out in soft huffs. Her knees rose on either side of him. Her legs spread wider. He fought hard for control when she threw her head back and whispered, "Alex, please... I want... you."

His hand slid up her thigh, her belly, her rib cage until he reached her breast. Rolling her nipple between his fingers, he lowered his face and kissed her through moist fabric. Her hands fisted at her sides. Her back arched and he nipped her clitoris until she cried out.

"Oh God." She writhed beneath his mouth. "Yes..."

He took hold of the lacy waistband and slid her panties down over her hip bones past the narrow strip of neatly trimmed blonde curls. Sliding the fabric over her knees, past her calves and ankles he tossed it on the floor. He gripped her gown and much like the underwear, drew it down the length of her body until it lay in a heap with the other clothing.

On the counter dressed in nothing but moonbeams, Ella was a goddess. But looking at her wasn't enough. He wanted to possess her. Needed to possess her. Wanted to bury himself inside her and absorb her heat.

He slid his arms beneath her neck and knees, lifting her easily. He kissed her and continued to kiss her as he carried her to the bay window. A wide cushioned window seat had already been installed and he set her on top of it.

He unfastened his belt. Unbuttoned and unzipped his fly and was about to shed his pants when he felt the outline of something in his pocket. Suddenly thankful for his brother's inappropriate gift, Alex pulled the foil package from his pocket and stepped out of his pants.

Ella watched him undress. Nothing compared to the sight of his perfectly honed body. He'd stripped down to a pair of snug black boxer briefs and she nearly sighed just looking at his thick shoulders, rounded biceps, and defined abs.

Letting her gaze fall lower she bit her lip.

She was ready for him. The slick, liquid heat between her legs and the mad rush of endorphins spiking her pulse told her so.

But as he removed his underwear, sliding the elastic over his narrow hips she realized with sudden fear *he* was ready for *her,* too. His erection jutted between his thighs, thick and rigid. The moonlight illuminated a smooth head crowning a long shaft. Her heart slammed against her chest.

He stepped forward. She cringed, suddenly realizing she'd been staring. The primal need reflected in his eyes mirrored his obvious physical desire.

What next?

Oh, she knew the mechanics of intercourse. She'd taken Sex Ed in high school, listened to people talk and watched movies for goodness sake. But personally?

She'd never gotten this far with a man. Never. A few kisses followed by a hasty retreat were the extent of her sexual experiences.

All these years it seemed she'd been saving herself for... him. For Alex.

And though she'd been teased for being a 'prude' she was never more thrilled... or more terrified to be a virgin than she was at this moment.

He took hold of her, lifting her from the seat to stand in front of him and then crushed her against his naked body. He captured her lips in a searing kiss. Her body turned molten and her excitement tripled, realizing she liked the ferocity, the intensity of his mouth ravaging hers.

He broke away. His head bowed and his hands moved in the mere inches between them. He tore open a small square package. Watching him roll the thin latex slowly over the length of his erection was so erotic her clitoris actually twitched.

He kissed her again and pressed his finger into the slick, wet folds between her legs, rubbing the most feminine part of her body with gentle strokes until her knees buckled.

He held her close, keeping her from collapsing, used his big body to nudge her back against the window seat until she sat down.

Pressing her against the cushion, he knelt between her thighs continuing his assault on the incredibly sensitive nub. His finger rubbed and slid over her flesh, igniting sparks of pleasure that caught fire and roared out of control until the inferno burst inside her like an explosion.

The orgasm surprised her with its intensity. It ripped through her core, spreading up into her belly and out her fingertips and toes. Her entire body convulsed in sweet spasms of ecstasy so extreme she thought her spine would snap.

Her nipples, already hard, turned to diamonds in his mouth and as her release peaked she screamed out his name.

"Alex... oh... my... yes." She shuddered breathlessly between each word until the last was drawn out like a song ending on a lyrical gasp. Her lungs filled and deflated as the delicious waves of pleasure gently subsided.

She purred like a cat and finally opened her eyes.

"I'm not done with you yet," he murmured with a smirk.

She ached for him. The clenching muscles in her core craved what she knew only he could give, but a sudden, consuming fear of the unknown got the better of her and she jerked away.

Positioned above her, his powerful arms rigid as columns on either side of her he frowned.

"I'm sorry," she said hastily.

His green eyes narrowed, and he gently smoothed the hair from her forehead. "Why are you sorry?" He asked softly, his expression patient and concerned.

The look on his face calmed her racing heart. Instead of trying to hide her nudity she rose on her elbows. She bit her lip trying to think of the right words to say. "I... I'm not sure."

"Are you okay? I didn't hurt you, did I?"

That made her smile. Hurt her? Far from it. "I... I've never." She bit her lip again. "I've never done this before."

He'd shifted back a bit when she rose on her elbows and the moonlight caught his hair. The short, glossy waves shown blue-black under the silver beams. His eyes glowed green against his tan face.

Alex was the biggest man Ella had ever known. Roughly six-five, broad shouldered and ripped from head to toe she figured most people might find him extremely intimidating. He resembled a pro-quarterback more than a mayor.

But the way he looked at her now with understanding in his gaze, her doubts and fears melted away.

"You're a virgin?" He asked without the slightest hint of accusation or mirth.

She nodded slowly.

He hesitated for a moment and then kissed her forehead. "Why didn't you tell me sooner?" He asked softly. "We could have taken things slower."

"I'm twenty-five," she said with a half smile and feeling much more confident in light of his understanding. "I think I've taken things slow enough." She touched the fine stubble of his cheek. "I just got nervous I guess."

He turned his face and kissed her palm. "I don't want to make you nervous."

His expression jump-started her pulse. "I'm not anymore."

He smiled and dipped his head. She gasped when the heat of his tongue drew her nipple into his mouth. He sucked firmly igniting a renewed shower of sparks and then glanced up at her suddenly. "You sure?" He asked with another cocky grin.

She laid back, took hold of his neck and pulled him closer. Kissing his full lower lip, she bit gently. "Positive."

He settled between her legs, shifting so the length of his body hovered over hers. "I'll go slow."

She nodded.

The heat of his penis pushed against her folds. He directed the smooth head beyond the slick nest of curls and stopped at her tight entrance. All the while he watched her. Looking into her eyes. Holding her gaze.

Her breath hitched. Her blood pounded. But desire won out.

Without saying a word, she communicated her need, wrapping her legs around his waist and drawing him in. She got her reward when in one powerful lunge he buried himself inside her.

Pain ripped through her, biting and sharp, but the discomfort was short lived as pleasure replaced the sting.

In and out he slid.

Deep and then shallow.

She rolled her head back on the cushion. Eyes closed. Taking him in. She absorbed the controlled power of his hips and moaned softly with each exquisite thrust.

The divine friction sentenced her to death. Killing the part of her that held nothing but mistrust and pain.

She'd fallen for Alex.

Everything about him swelled her heart.

Tears gathered and she squeezed her eyes shut against them, but they fell nonetheless.

He stopped suddenly. "Ella?" Still deep inside her, concern creased his brow.

She gripped him harder. Pulled him closer. "Don't stop," she breathed. "Don't ever stop."

He moved inside her again. Stretched her. Filled her. Kissed the tears from her cheeks, then increased the motion.

She cried out in ecstasy, meeting him thrust for thrust, digging her nails into his back as sensation built higher and higher.

Faster.

Harder.

Until he stiffened. Muscles flexed, skin damp, he shuddered his own release. He continued to move inside her a few more strokes until finally he collapsed on top of her.

Her legs remained wrapped around his waist. His body still sheathed inside her. She ran her fingers through his thick, soft hair and reveled in the feel of his heavy body pressed against hers.

She smiled.

Death wasn't as bad as she thought it might be.

Chapter Twenty-Five

Ella woke to bird song. She blinked at the sunshine, shielding her eyes with her hand to gaze out the window. Ruffling its feathers and then puffing out its chest, the little beige and brown bird belted out a second chorus. Its perch, a leafless Japanese Maple, turned her view into art.

The drape of her sleeve caught her eye. She lifted her hand from her brow and gazed at the cuff as it slid down her forearm. Alex's tuxedo shirt. He'd buttoned her into the soft fabric last night... after they had made love.

She turned from the symphony outside and peered over the edge of a window seat that hadn't been wide enough for two.

Alex lay on the floor, a few inches away.

Last night he'd found a drop cloth in one of the unfurnished bedrooms and had used that as his mattress. Shirtless, wearing black boxer briefs, he slept on his back, his elbow bent beside his head, his forearm serving as his pillow.

She shifted onto her side to get a better look at the sleeping man she'd given herself to.

Given herself to...

The thought should have scared the crap out of her. It should have made her sick inside. But it didn't.

Instead, she felt warmth and peace, and trust... and happiness.

A smile gouged dimples into his cheeks.

Ella rose onto her elbows, frowning. "Are you awake?" She asked in a whisper, hating to rouse him if he was merely in the middle of a pleasant dream.

"Yes," he answered, eyes closed, still smiling.

She reached down from her perch and poked him in the chest. "How long have you been lying there pretending to be asleep?"

His head turned her way. One eye closed against the brightness of the sun, he chuckled. "Not long."

"Did you know I was awake?"

Lifting a hand to shield the glare, he squinted. "I could feel you looking at me."

"I wasn't looking at you."

He grinned and dropped his hand, closing his eyes and then nestling into his flat, paint spattered mattress. "Yes, you were," he said with a smile.

She raised an eyebrow.

"But I was watching *you* earlier, so we're even," he added.

She reached down and shoved him playfully. He grabbed her hand and her hip and then pulled her down on top of him. She yelped and tried to squirm away giggling, but he shifted over her.

They wrestled in each other's arms until the smile in his eyes shifted into desire.

Giggles and squirming ceased.

She gazed at him. His heartbeat thumped against hers.

"Ella…"

Her name whispered with such passion stole her breath.

He drew closer. His kiss, soft and warm against her lips, turned hungry. Need sent her pulse into a frenzy.

She threaded her fingers in his hair, drew her knee up against his side. He gripped her other thigh, drawing it higher, guiding her leg around his waist. He kissed his way to her throat, seeking her collar-bone and then the rise of her breast. He tore her shirt open, ripping thread and sending the remaining onyx buttons clattering across the floor to let the sun bathe her naked flesh. She gasped when his tongue drew her nipple into his mouth.

She hadn't bothered to put her panties back on last night. They had been hard to spot in the dark. And now she was thankful for her neglect. Nothing slowed his progress.

Suckling one breast and then the other, he reached between her thighs, seeking the moist heat that throbbed there. A few strokes, slick and wet, and she arched into him.

"Alex," she said, nearly breathless. Emboldened after a single evening she slid her palm down his torso until her fingers grazed the bulge in his boxers. In the next instant she gripped his penis through the fabric, squeezing firmly and running her thumb over the head.

His response, a seductive rumble in his throat, ended in a kiss that curled her toes. As his lips ravaged hers he pulled down his boxers, shoving them past his hips and over his knees. With a hand on his cock he slid the head up and down against her clitoris, once, twice, three times, drawing whimpers of pleasure from her until finally he entered her in one deep stroke.

Still tight, but no longer a virgin, she gripped his shoulders in ecstasy. No pain, no worry, no mistrust, just Alex. Just desire. Just… love.

She hadn't simply fallen for him, she loved him.

She'd never been so sure about anything in her life.

He moved inside her, building the slick friction between them, looking into her eyes, kissing her lips, forging their bond.

Unbreakable. That's how it felt. Her connection to him was and forever would be unbreakable.

She closed her eyes, intensely happy. When he kissed her again, her lids fluttered open. Their gazes met as she wrapped her legs tighter, pulling him in deeper.

He rose to his knees, lifting her hips and tugging her closer. Cupping her backside, he thrust into her again as she gripped the cloth beneath her.

Supporting her with one hand, he used the other to reach between them. As he continued to thrust he rubbed her swollen nub with smooth, wet strokes.

She gasped at the sensations radiating into her belly, nipples, fingers and toes. Every inch of her hummed like she'd been electrically charged. He filled her, stroked her, plucked her like a harp until the build of tension exploded, spiraling out of control.

She cried out, clutching his thighs, shuddering and praying that the heart-stopping pleasure would cease and go on forever.

Her orgasm lasted longer this time. It was stronger and reached its peak as Alex continued to move inside her. Her release barely finished as his began.

His thrusts increased, in and out, in and out. Her internal muscles convulsing around him. "Ella," he breathed, pulled out of her and spilled himself onto her belly.

He leaned forward using an arm to keep himself from crushing her beneath him. Breathing heavily his strong body stiffened with each wave that coursed through him.

Finally spent, he slid his arm alongside her. He pressed his forehead against hers. She could hear the smile in his voice. "I only had one condom..."

He drew back slightly and peered down between them. He scanned the floor and located his boxers a few feet away. Shifting to his side, he gently wiped her stomach.

She didn't rise, letting him clean her skin, but watched him while she lazily stroked the muscles of his back. She didn't admit it then, but had been intensely aroused when his liquid heat had pooled on her stomach. Now she felt liquid herself, like a mass of quavering flesh devoid of bone.

Satisfied, Alex folded his boxers and set them aside. His back to the window, he shielded her from the sun. "You're probably sore," he said softly.

She smiled just as softly. "It's a good sore."

He smoothed aside her bangs and trailed a finger along her cheek. "How'd you sleep?"

"Like a baby."

A raven eyebrow rose high. "On that thin cushion?"

"It's surprisingly comfortable," she said, glimpsing the window seat behind him. Nodding, she added, "The owner has impeccable taste."

Dimples. She loved when he flashed those dimples.

"How'd *you* sleep?" Grimacing, she made a fist and thumped his bed, the rigid floor beneath her.

"I would have slept like a baby, too... if someone didn't snore."

Her jaw dropped. "I do not!"

He laughed. "Yeah, you do. But it's cute. Like a baby bulldog with a sinus infection"

"What?!"

"Or Darth Vader with hay fever." He chuckled, ducking when she tried to shove him.

"Vader, huh?" She asked, laughing and then lying back down. "See, now that one's a compliment. I'm a proud *Star Wars* nerd."

"I know," he said, plucking a dust bunny from her hair.

She lifted onto her elbows. "How?"

He rose to his feet, naked and beautiful.

"What are you doing?" She asked.

"One question at a time, and I'm getting my pants," he said as he walked across the room and retrieved them from the pile of cast-offs on the floor. He stepped into a leg, but hesitated in pulling them up. "Unless you're interested in round three?" He raised a sexy eyebrow, still clutching his waistband, but only wearing half of his pants. "Say the word..."

Her belly warmed with the idea, but she needed a little rest. She *was* sore, deliciously so, but sore none-the-less. Twice in one night. She felt like she'd been plopped into one of Maggie's novels. "I'm good... for now."

Dimples flashed again and he stepped into the other leg and then zipped them up. After securing the buttons he continued with, "And getting back to your first question, it's obvious you're a fan. You wear Star Wars t-shirts nearly every day, and at your apartment there were two framed *Empire Strikes Back* posters hanging on the wall." He raised an eyebrow as he came closer. "I'm going out on a limb here, but I'm assuming they're yours and not your mothers."

She'd shifted to a sitting position and while she gathered the drop cloth to hide her nudity she said, "So you've been paying attention."

"When it concerns you, always." He sat down next to her with a wink.

She couldn't help the thrill that shot through her veins. "Trudy prefers *Return of the Jedi*." She bristled. "A planet populated by teddy bears? I think old George dropped the ball on that one. Besides, everyone knows *Empire* is, hands down, the best."

"Obviously," he mocked with a grin, leaning back against the window seat and crossing his long legs out in front of him.

She smirked at him and then smiled with a memory. "Last week Eric and I watched a *Star Wars* marathon on TBS. He also likes *Empire* the best. Such a smart cookie." She sucked in a breath. Her hand flew to her mouth. "Oh God, Eric!" She shot from her seat.

"Don't worry. He's fine."

She spun toward him. "But... what time is it?" She scanned the large room and nearby kitchen. The green display on the stove blinked, one-forty-five. Obviously the clock needed to be set.

He stood up and drew his phone from his pocket. "It's seven thirty-two." He smiled at her. "Relax. I called Maggie about an hour ago. She's got it covered."

She sighed. "Whew... I..." She shoved her bangs back and rubbed her scalp. "I can't believe I forgot about him." She gazed up at him, frowning. "I feel like a jerk. I'm a terrible nanny."

He drew her close and kissed the tension in her forehead. "You didn't forget. You were just… distracted."

She drew back as something occurred to her. "My job."

He smiled. "I told you not to worry. Maggie's taking care of him."

"No, I mean… continuing to work for you, after last night… it wouldn't be right."

She couldn't remain on as his employee, getting paid while she slept with him. *Jeeze, talk about inappropriate.*

Or was she jumping the gun? Maybe he'd had his fill. Maybe to him last night was just a onetime thing.

No. Don't think that way. Don't fall backwards. Move forward.

He nodded, appearing to digest her point. "Then there's only one thing you can do."

"What?"

He caressed her cheek. His expression, his eyes, the way he seemed to see deep inside her made her believe she wasn't just a fling. She meant more to him than that… she was sure of it.

"You need to move in with me."

"But I'm already staying in your house," she said, confused.

A soft smile tugged his lips. "No, I mean move *in* with me. Not as an employee, but someone I care for."

Someone he cares for. She drew in a deep breath, her heart swelling like helium in a balloon. Were her feet still firmly planted on the ground?

"I'm home now. Maggie can help out when I'm at the office or in town at a meeting, but other than that I'll be home from now on. I'll take care of Eric. You can start class again. I know you've been saving to finish school. So let me pay for it."

She frowned up at him. Her heart deflated. "How is that any different from before?"

"What do you mean?" He shrugged. "It's completely different."

She stepped back. "I appreciate your willingness to fund my education, but I wouldn't have earned it. It's not right."

"Wait a second." He held up a hand. "You need money. I have it. It's as simple as that."

"No it's not. My father never earned anything in his life. He took what he wanted, or swindled it from people. I promised myself I'd never sink that low. Never."

"But you're not sinking anywhere. I'd be doing it because I care about you."

"And I'd have to refuse because I care about *you*."

Hands on his hips, he studied her. A muscle in his cheek twitched. He glanced away, brows knitted. Turning, he strode to the kitchen island. After a moment he set his hands on the granite, fingers splayed on its surface.

She hiked the drop cloth higher under her arms. "Do you understand why I can't accept?"

He said nothing at first and then glanced to his left, out a nearby window. The little bird, or one of its many feathered friends, had resumed its symphony. Its happy song penetrated the glass and filtered into the room.

Alex finally turned to gaze at her. The bird's performance hadn't lightened his expression. "I understand," he answered. He held out a hand to her. She lifted the stiff fabric off her feet and padded across the floor to reach him. Their fingers touched and he drew her into his arms. She pressed her cheek against his chest and listened to his heartbeat.

"I understand, but that doesn't mean I like it," he whispered into her hair.

She stepped out of his arms and shifted next to him to lean against the counter. "Eric's doing so well now."

"I know. He's pretty damn amazing."

"He is. And now that you're in his life, he'll be amazing without me."

"Ella, he loves you," he said, stepping in front of her. "He needs you... as much as I need you. I want you in our lives."

Magical. She could think of no other word to describe the way her pulse fluttered when he said things like that. "I will be." She grasped his hand. "I'm not going anywhere." She realized she meant those four words, felt no fear. She ran her fingers across his knuckles and then met his gaze. "Not really. I mean, it's best that I move out, but I'd still like to see you and Eric."

He squeezed her hand gently.

"Besides, I miss having my mom as a roommate."

It was a win-win situation. She could run interference with Trudy in case Clyde showed up, and no longer employed by Alex, she could concentrate on building a healthy relationship with him.

A healthy relationship.

Was it possible? Could this be the beginning of exactly that?

"And I'll find another job," she added with confidence she hadn't felt in years.

"What about your degree?"

"I have every intention of finishing school. I have nearly enough to pay for the semester in full, thanks to your overzealous efforts to hire me." She smiled. "When you agreed to fifteen hundred a week I nearly fell off my chair."

"I was ready to pay you five thousand. You got taken."

She laughed. "Well, regardless..." Her smile softened. "Thank you."

He nodded and then drew her into his arms. His kiss seared her lips.

When he drew back he asked, "You hungry?"

"Famished."

He reached the pile of clothes and retrieved her evening gown. He handed her the glittering fabric. "Good. I'll take you home and make you and Eric breakfast." He glanced at his phone's screen. "He's got to be up by now."

She pursed her lips. "I'm curious to see what Mr. Wheat Germ's idea of breakfast will be."

He'd shrugged into his dress shirt. As he tugged on his socks he smirked at her. "What's wrong with waffles?"

She had discarded her drop cloth robe and stepped into last night's dress, hiking it up to her hips. "Dusted with wheat germ?"

He chuckled. "Powdered sugar."

"Now that's what I'm talking about." Wiggling her butt into the snug column and then covering her breasts with the halter top, she grinned from ear to ear.

"Do that again."

"What?" She asked, fastening the clip at her neck.

"Wiggle," he said, eyeing her seductively.

"No no." She stepped closer, grabbed his shoulder, spun him around and pushed him toward the door. "You had me at powdered sugar. Go start the car. I'm salivating already."

He turned, pulled her against him, and buried his face in her hair. Lips brushing her throat, he murmured, "So am I."

His stubble tickled the flesh beneath her ear.

A jarring ring jerked her back down to Earth. He growled and straightened to dig his cell phone from his pocket. "It could be Maggie," he said, but frowned when he scrutinized the screen.

He swiped the lock icon. "Hello?"

The response was loud enough for Ella to hear. She immediately recognized Diane York's cultured voice on the other end of the line. She stepped away to give him some privacy, but he took her hand to keep her from leaving his side.

"Are you busy today?" Diane said as Alex mouthed, *sorry* to Ella.

"I've got plans, yes," he said into the receiver.

"Business or personal?"

"Either way I'm still busy."

"I see."

"What did you need?"

"Well, we were hoping to visit this evening. Your father wants to discuss a strategy concerning last night's slugfest."

Alex smirked. "Slugfest?"

"Mr. Boggs has already spoken to Mr. Sutherland. I feel he can stave off any bad press with the man's cooperation. Sutherland's not pressing charges and has refused interviews, so that's good."

"I can take care of Brian Sutherland."

"Why would you get in a fight in the first place? And in public."

"I've got my reasons."

"Have you seen the paper?"

"Not yet."

"Well, it's not good. They're saying your volatile and that you lack self control."

"I'll take care of it."

"You don't sound concerned."

"I've got other things on my mind."

Diane paused long enough for Alex to ask, "You still there?"

"I am. I'm just worried. We're not exactly a low profile family. Unfortunately my job brings yours and your father's careers under an even brighter spotlight. The story is local right now. We'd like it to stay that way.

Would it be okay if we stopped by? We'd like to visit Eric. We've been so busy it seems like an eternity since we've seen him."

"I think he'd like that."

"Wonderful. See you at eight?"

"Sounds good," he agreed.

"See you then," she said and then finally hung up.

Alex buried the phone in his pocket and smirked. "I think her hearing is going. She talks loud lately. You heard her?"

Ella nodded.

"I know you're planning on moving out, but I'd like you to stay for dinner tonight. Hang around a little longer?"

"Sure."

He kissed her on the cheek and then on the lips. After he'd sufficiently curled her toes he straightened and said, "I'll warm up the car," and left her side for the front door.

He had nearly walked outside when she called out, "You told her you were busy all day today." She hoped he didn't intend on spending the day at the office.

"Yeah, with you," he said with a wink and then closed the door behind him.

Ella blushed. She tugged on her combat boots and nearly floated down the hallway. Before she reached the entry hall she turned for one last look. The room they had made love in was flooded with sunlight. She felt as warm as the glowing rays.

Warm and confident that heartache was behind her and a bright future lay ahead.

Chapter Twenty-Six

"You sure you don't want to come to the aquarium with us?" Alex asked Maggie through the driver's side window. Ella sat beside him and echoed his invitation, hoping her friend would give in and join them.

The woman chuckled. "I'll be harpooned and then air-lifted into a tank with the other whales if I set foot in that place."

Eric giggled in the back seat.

"Oh, you think that's funny, do you?" Maggie asked the little boy with a smirk on her round face.

Eric nodded, flashing adorable dimples.

"So you want to press your face up against the glass and watch old Mags swim by?" She sucked in her cheeks and made a fish face.

"Yes," he said giggling again. "Just like a mermaid."

"That's right, my apron, my support hose and my size sixteen hips will be *just* like a mermaid." Maggie reached in through the back window and tickled Eric's ribs. He squirmed in his seat, laughing until tears sprung up in his eyes.

Letting him breathe, Maggie ruffled his hair and then stepped back. She peered in through Alex's window again. Her eyes crinkled at the edges as she smiled first at Ella and then at Alex sitting beside her.

"Thank you for the invitation, but I'll stay here, let the harpooners have the day off. You three go have fun."

"Thanks, Mags," Alex said.

"No... thank *you*."

"For what?"

"Oh, just for making an old mermaid happier than a clam."

Eric giggled again. "Maggie's a mermaid, Maggie's a mermaid," he sang.

Alex chuckled at his son in the rearview mirror and then nodded at Maggie. "Ok. We'll see you later."

"Take your time. Faust and I'll be here when you get back... though he might be gagged and hog-tied in the basement by then," she said with a raised eyebrow. "Old goat gets on my nerves." With a wink she waved goodbye and ascended the front steps.

Alex glanced over his shoulder at Eric. "You ready, Buddy?"

The little boy nodded, spun the propeller of his toy plane and then smiled at his father. "Yes, Daddy."

Ella noticed Alex's Adam's apple bob in his throat. His son had called him daddy again. His smile deepened and he said, "Me, too." Shifting his gaze from Eric, Alex smiled her way and they left the house.

They spent the morning and part of the afternoon at the Georgia Aquarium. Ella had never found time to visit the attraction and gawked at the amazing array of marine life. After the aquarium they ate a deliciously greasy lunch at The Varsity and then, giving Eric the choice of what to do next, they had ended up close to home at the park she had been taking him to every day since she'd started as his nanny.

They arrived at about five and circled the lot for a space. Every Saturday in October and on through to Thanksgiving Magnolia Falls hosted an antebellum festival with crafts and food carts set up on the perimeter of the sprawling lawn. This particular Saturday, the lawn itself was the stage of an elaborate Civil War reenactment. Soldiers dressed in blue and gray aimed replica rifles at each other. The periodic boom of cannon fire vibrated in the air. Ladies cinched into hoop skirts and corsets, wearing bonnets and ringlet curls mingled with dandies donning beaver hats and starched collars.

The festival she'd fainted at had marked the beginning of the *Magnolia Falls Margaret Mitchell Celebration*, since the *Gone With The Wind* author had supposedly spent the night in one of the towns oldest bed and breakfasts before her untimely death.

To Ella, on a gorgeous day like today, it appeared that most of the residents, as well as hundreds of tourists shared their desire to join in the celebration. The huge park overflowed with noisy activity.

She'd been visiting *Scarlett and Rhett Park* since she was a little girl. Her favorite spot, a bulbous mass of stone lying off the beaten path, resembled an Elephant sleeping on its side in the grass. Its front leg, eroded smooth over time, had been her thinking spot, sometimes her crying spot, and often her dreaming spot.

After watching some of the battle and a quick stop for funnel cakes they strolled toward the rear of the park where her elephant slumbered. Eric high-tailed it for the monkey bars, his favorite, and the only play structure nearby. She figured he liked the dome shaped lattice so much because of its height off the ground. He'd lock his legs through the bright blue metal bars, sit on a rounded joint and lift his toy plane into the sky above him.

She watched him there now, swooping the little red twin engine up and down, side to side. "Vroom, vroom, vroom." His happy voice carried over on a breeze. He had the monkey bars to himself. Most of the kids running around seemed to prefer the mock battle raging just beyond the hill, the brand new jungle gym erected a year earlier, or the elaborate wooden pirate ship that had been beached on the farthest end of the park back when she'd turned seven.

Alex took a seat next to her. He laced his fingers into hers and kissed her knuckles. "Eric told me you've been taking him here every day." He smiled, squinting in the sunshine.

"Yep. I love this place and it's such a short walk from the apartment."

His smile faded and he switched focus to watch Eric. "I've been wanting to talk about that some more."

"What?"

"Your apartment."

She studied his profile, couldn't tell what he was thinking.

"I want you to stay with us... for longer than just this evening." He leaned forward, resting his forearms on his knees.

"Alex..."

He glanced at her.

"I can't do that. I told you already."

"What's wrong with us living together?"

"Because I'm not going to be some chick sponging off the mayor of Magnolia Falls."

"You wouldn't be sponging off me. And you're not just some chick."

"Yes I am. And I happen to have a checkered past to boot."

"You don't have a checkered past."

"There are things I bet even your investigator doesn't know about me."

"Hey," he said softly, taking her shoulder and swiveling her back toward him. "Look at me." He waited until she met his eyes again. "That's one of the reasons I want you to stay. I want to get to know you better." He flashed those attractive dimples, "Checkered past and all."

"And what if getting to know me better puts your campaign at risk?"

"It won't... I'm bowing out of the race anyway."

She frowned. "For governor? What do you mean? Since when?"

He shrugged. "Since recently."

"But I thought you said you've always wanted this. That you still dream of bigger and better things. You've made amazing changes in Magnolia Falls, Alex. Just think what you'd be able to accomplish as governor."

"My priorities are different now."

"Don't ignore the things that are important to you."

"I know what's important... you and that little boy over there." He nodded toward Eric and smiled. After waving at him he resumed speaking. "If taking a break for a while brings me closer to both of you, then it's worth it."

I'm telling you right now, that blonde has and will screw up everything!

Had Wilson Boggs been right? *Was* she screwing up everything? The media buzz surrounding Alex's campaign had been incredibly positive so far. According to some of the political journalists on TV, he was a shoe in for governor and possibly even president one day. He'd been a force for good in Magnolia Falls. She and a lot of other people believed he'd make a difference on Capitol Hill as well.

She'd been trying her best to do the right thing all her life, the opposite of what her father might have done. Clyde hurt people, his own family, stole their dreams and kept them from reaching their goals. She couldn't do that to

Alex. She refused to be the one holding him back. But she suddenly felt stuck.

She'd wanted to continue seeing him, even if she didn't continue living with him, but suddenly, more of what Wilson Boggs had said made her rethink that desire. The man had had a point and she couldn't help echoing his concerns. "Alex, living with the daughter of a criminal isn't good for your image, whether you're mayor *or* governor. My father's crimes *will* become fodder for speculation on your values, just like your friend said."

He studied her for a moment. "So this has to do with what you overheard yesterday in the backyard. I knew it. What else did you hear?"

"Very little."

"I bet," he muttered. "Wilson's got a big mouth."

"But he's right. Whether you run for governor or remain mayor, your involvement with the daughter of a criminal isn't going to help your career. "

"Your father's done his time, paid for his mistakes."

"I'm sure he'll find himself behind bars again very soon, paying for new mistakes. It's the only thing he's ever been good at. That and hurting people."

He sighed and shook his head.

"You shouldn't forget what he is. I won't."

"And what about forgiveness?"

"He doesn't deserve forgiveness."

Alex frowned.

Eric called out, "Daddy, look." He sat atop the monkey bars, pointing to a vender on a nearby hill. Children and parents flocked around a man holding a massive floating bouquet of helium balloons.

"You want one?" Alex asked Eric, whose perch was no more than fifteen yards from their sleeping elephant.

The little boy scratched his head and then shrugged dramatically.

Alex chuckled. "Well if you make up your mind, let me know."

"Okay," he said and resumed flying his plane.

Alex watched Eric for a moment more and then glanced at Ella. "So, what about Eric? Do you think he shouldn't forgive *me*?"

"Alex—"

"No, wait a second. I've done some pretty shitty things over the last few years. I've robbed him of time with me. I've robbed myself of time with him. I've cheated that little boy out of two years of his childhood. Two years he didn't talk or laugh or know whether his father loved him or not. Jesus Christ," he said, arms thrown wide, "*I* should be jailed for what I've done."

Her stomach twisted in knots.

"But after all that... after everything I've done," he glanced at Eric. A brilliant smile lit the boy's cherub face and he waved his little hand. Alex smiled and waved back. After a moment his smile faded and he gazed at her. "After all the shit I've put him through, Eric's forgiven me."

"I sympathize with you, I do... but your sins don't compare with my father's."

"Your father wronged strangers. I wronged my own flesh and blood."

My father wronged *me,* his flesh and blood, she wanted to say, but stayed quiet. She didn't want to continue souring a wonderful day.

"I'm just as guilty," he added.

She shook her head. "No, you're not."

His chuckle lacked humor. "Man, you're stubborn." Shoving a hand through his hair, he stood up. Without looking down at her he said, "I'm gonna go get Eric a balloon." He took a few steps and then glanced back at her. "Think about what I said, Ella... whether you believe it or not, everyone needs forgiveness." He buried his hands in his jacket pockets and walked away, putting distance between them.

He doesn't get it.

He had always loved Eric. He'd gone through a tragedy and had been devastated by Eric's withdrawal. She didn't blame Alex for his failings as a parent. She sympathized with him. He was doing all he could to make up for lost time. But her father had been deficient from the start. He'd never shown interest in her. He'd always been a dead-beat. And he'd always done the wrong thing.

She didn't want to be like him. She didn't want to do the wrong thing. And to her, the wrong thing would be keeping Alex from following his dream. If she moved in with him and became a part of his life, she'd be doing just that.

She rose from her seat and took a few steps toward the monkey bars as Eric swung down into the bark chips beneath the latticed dome. He spun round and round, arm extended, twin engine "*vrooming*" in descent. With a plop he sat on the ground and guided the plane to a safe landing. He rolled it along the runway, having an important conversation with the tiny pilot.

She smiled. To her, Eric was completely healed. He acted just like a healthy five year old should act. He'd grow up loved by his father, acknowledged by him, nurtured and guided by him.

Forgiveness couldn't have happened to a better man. Alex deserved forgiveness... Clyde did not.

"Hey there, String-Bean."

The soft, gravelly voice came from behind her. Her gut dropped, a sickening stone weighing it down.

She turned around and came face to face with Clyde Slipper.

Chapter Twenty-Seven

At first glance, her father looked the same as she remembered him, tall, lanky, blue eyed and fair skinned. But closer inspection revealed subtle differences. Though he stood a good five inches taller than her, the width of his once broad shoulders sagged beneath the sleeves of his plaid shirt. His posture made him appear less sturdy, older, a little shorter even. His blue eyes mirrored the brilliant fall sky, but the light within, the twinkle that her mother had often said revealed his devious mind, seemed to have dimmed. And though his light blonde hair had always been closer to white than wheat, the wisps of gray that peeked from his temples and the cowlick on his forehead were further reminders of his advancing age.

A breeze whipped the edge of his plaid shirt aside, revealing the wrinkled t-shirt beneath it. Ella glanced from the bright orange and green *Hicks Landscaping* logo on his chest to his face. "What are you doing here?"

He shivered, hunched against a chill she didn't feel. Rough hands disappeared into his jean's pockets. "You always liked this spot." He nodded toward her granite elephant. A small smile tugged his lips. "Even as a kid."

"You didn't answer the question."

Unfazed by her tone he shrugged. "I don't know. Years back we always knew we could find you here, after school, weekends, for hours on end. I guess I hoped I'd find you here now."

"The last time we spoke I made it clear I don't want to see you."

He said nothing at first, toeing the dirt with his scuffed boot. After nudging a pine cone aside he finally squinted at her. "That was years ago. I was hoping time might have softened you towards me." His brow wrinkled. He seemed to be waiting for a response.

She gave him none.

He changed the subject. "I saw your mom. She looks good."

"Stay the hell away from her."

"String-Bean—"

"Don't call me that."

"Ella—"

"You don't get to call me that, either."

He blinked, looking dumbfounded.

What'd he expect? A tearful reunion? A kiss and a hug? An, Oh daddy, you're back?

"What should I call you, then?"

"Nothing. The only thing you should do is turn around and walk away."

"I haven't seen you in years."

"Yeah, because you were in prison where you belong."

He flinched. "I did my time."

"You took a plea deal. You should have done longer."

"It wasn't much of a deal. The judge had it in for me. I served six years... most guys like me do no more than two, three tops."

"Guys like you?"

He glanced left and right like he feared someone might be listening.

"Oh, I'm sorry, Clyde, am I talking too loud? Afraid someone might find out what you really are? Not just some *guy*, but a career criminal?"

He stared at the ground.

"If he'd really had it in for you that judge would have had *thief* tattooed on your forehead. Right here." She ran her index finger across her brow. "Then everyone would know what you are."

He didn't say anything, but his Adam's apple bobbed like he tried to swallow a tennis ball.

"Turn around and walk away. And don't seek my mother, or me out again."

Clyde's troubled gaze shifted to something behind her. She nearly turned to investigate when she felt a tug on her pants leg. Eric stood beside her, eyeing the man curiously.

The little boy craned his neck, looking up at her. "Who's he?" He whispered, clutching her hamstring in one hand, his plane with the other.

Ella squatted. She smiled brightly and plucked a wrinkled leaf off his sweatshirt. "You're done playing?"

He nodded, but didn't take his eyes off Clyde.

Clyde squatted, smiling at Eric.

Ella stood up and stepped in front of the little boy.

Clyde cocked his head. "Hi there. How're ya doing?" He asked when Eric peeked around her leg at him.

Unaware of the man's character, Eric answered, "Good," loud and clear, friendly grin and all.

"I saw you flying that plane earlier," Clyde said to him, pointing to the toy he held.

"You've been watching us?" Ella held Eric closer.

Clyde dropped his hand, stood up and cleared his throat. "Not in a creepy way... just..."

"Just what?"

"Hold on now." He flashed his palms. "I've been sitting over there," he nodded at a bench nearly concealed under the stringy branches of a naked willow tree, "And saw you three come up the hill. I laid low for a while, that's all."

"The definition of creepy," Ella said.

"No... I didn't know how you'd react seeing me. I guess I was nervous." He scratched his head, ruffling the cowlick and muttered, "Rightly so."

"Who are you?" Eric's inquisitive voice cut in.

Clyde smiled at him. "I'm Ella's—"

"Don't you dare," she warned.

He cleared his throat. "Friend. Just a friend."

"And it's time for him to leave," Ella said.

"Do you live here?" Eric asked, like he hadn't heard her. She drew in a deep breath. *Why'd he have to choose now to test his voice out on strangers?*

"At the park?" Clyde chuckled.

"Noooo," Eric giggled. "People don't live at the park. Just squirrels and chikmumps."

"*Chikmumps,* huh?" Clyde asked, still smiling.

"And pigeons," Eric added with a nod. "But they fly."

"That they do... just like that plane you're holding, huh?"

Eric nodded, absently spinning one of the twin engine's propellers with his index finger.

Clyde squatted down to Eric's level again. Ella tried to step between them, but Eric let go of her hand and moved closer to the man.

"You know, Ella used to love those swings over there," Clyde pointed to the closest play area bustling with kids, "When she was no bigger than you are."

Eric studied the swing set and then raised an eyebrow at Clyde. "When she was little?"

"Yep. She liked that blue one in the middle the best."

"Did you push her on it?" Eric asked him.

Clyde's smile dimmed. He gazed at Ella when he finally answered, "Not as much as I should have."

"That's enough," Ella said, unimpressed. She took Eric's hand and ruffled his spiky black hair. "Why don't we go see what your daddy's up to?"

"What about the man?" Eric asked, glancing at Clyde, worried.

"He's leaving now," Ella assured him.

Clyde stood up and brushed off the knee of his jeans. His lips drew into a grim smile. "Yep, better be on my way."

"Daddy's back," Eric said.

She turned and realized Alex strode their way. A red balloon bobbed above his head.

Eric broke free and ran to his father. Alex squatted, tied the balloon around his wrist and then patted his bottom, sending him scurrying off toward the monkey bars.

He stood and held out his hand. "Hi, I'm Alex."

"I recognize you, our young mayor. Been reading about your

accomplishments over the years. I've been away for a while. Things've really changed round here. For the better it seems. Looks like we have you to thank for the improvements." Clyde shook his hand.

"Thank you. I appreciate it."

Ella glared at the man. *He's been keeping up with current events in jail?*

Clyde added, "In fact, I saw an article in the paper this morning." He glanced at Ella and then back at Alex. "You had your fists balled up. Some guy with a bloody nose was on the ground in front of you. You and Ella were in a few pictures, too, all gussied up."

Alex frowned. "I haven't seen today's paper yet."

The stone in her stomach grew. So the press *had* gotten wind of the fight. One of the guests with a camera phone must have tipped them off. A brawl at a charity event couldn't be good for his ratings. Hopefully Mr. Boggs had had an effect on Brian and the story would go no further.

"Your mom's that actress, right?"

"She is."

Ella couldn't believe Alex sounded so calm, like he made the news for knocking conceited gym owners on their butts every day.

"And your father's Senator York?"

Alex nodded.

Clyde whistled. "Must be money coming out of the wood work in your house, huh?"

Ella stepped closer to the older man. "That's enough. You need to leave. Right now."

"Ella, it's fine," Alex said, frowning.

"No, no..." Clyde flashed his palms. "She's right. I'd better be on my way. Got work to do. Gotta pay the bills." He shrugged and backpedaled slowly. "Was good to meet you, Mister Mayor." He glanced at Ella, nodded and then turned around and walked away.

Clyde, hands buried in his pockets, shoulders hunched against a stiff breeze skirted the play area. In seconds he disappeared over a hill.

"Ella?"

She rubbed her left temple.

"You okay?" Alex asked, a frown tugging his raven eyebrows.

She stood taller. "What makes you think I'm not?"

"That was your father."

"No, that was an ex-con."

"He's still your father. Even if I hadn't seen his mug-shot, it's obvious you're related to the guy."

"I look like my mother."

Alex glanced in the direction Clyde had gone. Nervous, Ella checked over her shoulder. No sign of the man. *Good.*

"What did he want?" Alex asked her.

"Money."

"He asked you for money?"

"No, but that's what he was leading up to. It's all he's ever cared about."

"You're sure?"

"Of course I'm sure. Didn't you hear him mention your wood work?"

"I heard him. It sounded like an observation, nothing sinister."

"Whose side are you on?"

"Your side."

"Then stop sticking up for him."

He shook his head, smiling. "I'm not sticking up for him. I'm telling you what I heard."

"Well, you heard wrong. You don't know the man like I do. He's plotting something. He's always scheming and plotting. It's in his blood."

"You're right," he said, moving closer to her. "I don't know him like you do. And, to be honest, I don't blame you for worrying, but..." He reached out and clasped her shoulders. "Give the guy a chance to redeem himself before you tie a noose around his neck."

"He's not after redemption," she said, frowning up at him.

"Maybe, maybe not. But you never know."

Her frown deepened. "I don't get why you're defending him."

"It's what I used to do for a living, remember? Innocent until proven guilty."

She tried to respond but he kissed her. Warm lips turned her knees to mush as she let him draw her closer into his arms. He caressed her cheek, and though she couldn't see it, she felt his smile against her mouth. Stepping back he held her hand. "You gave *me* a chance, steered me in the right direction. Hell, I'm curious to see whether that constant nagging of yours will work on someone other than me."

"Nagging, huh?" She gave him shove, but said, "Uh oh," when Eric hurried toward them.

"Daddy?"

"Yeah, Buddy?"

Clutching his plane and balloon in one hand and his crotch in the other, Eric bounced on his toes, grimacing. "I gotta pee-pee."

"Waited until the last minute, huh?" Alex scooped up his son with a chuckle.

Ella pointed toward the small building in the distance near the crowded line of vendors selling their crafts. Father and son left her side and as they hurried toward the bathrooms people waved to their mayor, shook his hand, clapped him on the shoulder. Alex's constituents had been praising him all afternoon. He was incredibly popular. He'd been a force for good since his election and Magnolia Falls was a better place because of him. She imagined he'd be just as popular as governor. The state of Georgia needed him. The country as a whole needed a man like him.

She slumped on her elephant in dismay.

I'm bowing out of the race. His admission looped in her mind. Guilt jerked her in two directions. She wanted to be a part of his life, but in doing so she'd be steering him from the political career he'd said he'd always wanted.

And to make matters worse, hurricane Clyde had just thundered into the picture.

Why'd he have to show up?

Why couldn't he leave her alone?

Alex wanted her to give him a chance, but the man had had dozens of them. And no amount of nagging or begging or pleading had ever changed his ways.

And his appearance now, so soon after he'd been paroled could only mean one thing. He needed money. It had happened before. He'd been released from jail and the first thing he'd done was slither into their lives begging for a hand out.

Got work to do. Gotta pay the bills, he'd said a minute ago.

Yeah, right. *Got cons to pull. Gotta pay my bookie*, is more like it.

Even if Alex followed through with his plan to give up the governor's seat her father's crimes would surely poison his success as mayor if she were to continue seeing him. Proof of that was in the paper her father had mentioned. She'd been the cause of the violence at the benefit... *her*, a woman raised by a criminal. The realization tied her gut in knots. Alex's critics would use last night's altercation against him. He'd lost control in a public arena.

The whole thing had smear campaign written all over it.

Chapter Twenty-Eight

Ella sat rigid on the leather sofa in Alex's library. Eric knelt on the floor in front of her pushing his twin engine along the herringbone wood floor. She thought the little boy would have been exhausted after a full day at the aquarium and then the park, but his animated play and unending pilot chatter gave no indication he'd be retreating to his bed any time soon.

She, on-the-other-hand, wanted to do a face plant on her own pillow.

She'd never been more tired in her life. But her exhaustion had nothing to do with physical activity. It was all mental. She wanted to curl up in the covers and sleep for a hundred years. Maybe then, after waking in a different century, time would have diluted her feelings for Alex and the emotional roller coaster she'd been riding would have lost its momentum.

He strode into the room, a smile on his irresistibly handsome face.

The roller-coaster hurtled into a nose dive and she realized that no amount of distance, whether in years or geography, could ever lessen her feelings for him.

"I heard voices downstairs. I'm pretty sure my parents are here," Alex said to her. He knelt next to Eric and watched his son play for a moment. His smile grew and he tapped the little boy on the shoulder. "Hey, Buddy?"

"Uh huh," Eric said, concentrating on guiding his plane to a smooth landing.

"Someone's here to see you."

The twin engine came to a halt. Eric, brow wrinkled, squinted up at his father. "Who, Daddy?"

Before Alex could answer the Senator and Mrs. York entered the room.

Ella stood up. Her hands turned clammy.

At the ball, Alex's father had seemed unimpressed by her and his mother, though friendly and gracious, had still intimidated the crap out of her. How the heck could she stand next to the genius who'd won a fifth Oscar just ten months earlier without feeling star-struck?

But the unease gurgling through her gut right now had nothing to do with celebrity or a little senatorial snubbing.

It had to do with the man who strode into the room behind Alex's parents. Wilson Boggs.

The tall, pudgy, red-head made a bee-line for Alex and clapped him on the shoulder with a hearty hello. Alex returned the greeting. It appeared their previous argument might have been swept under the rug.

A light touch on her thigh drew her attention. Eric had scrambled to her side when his grandparents arrived. She drew him close in reassurance. His little body went rigid at her side. She wondered how he'd respond to them since he'd recovered his voice. Alex had mentioned it'd been a long while since they'd gotten together as a family. She hoped he wouldn't revert to silence.

"Ella, so nice to see you again," Diane said, moving closer. She smiled and then shifted focus to her grandson. Eric's head tilted back as he studied the elegant woman.

"Hello, Eric," his grandmother said. "It's wonderful to see you, too." Her bright smile lost some of its glimmer, fading slowly into an expression tinged with sympathy. She squeezed his little shoulder and then addressed her son. "Thank you for having us—"

"Grandma, I got a dog."

Diane sucked in a breath and gaped at her grandson.

"He's a Golden Recieber," Eric chirped proudly, unconcerned by his grandma's surprise.

Alex left Wilson's side and hoisted his son into his arms. "Receiver," he gently corrected the little boy, a twinkle in his eyes.

Eric nodded. "Oh... re-seeee-ver," he sounded out carefully.

"My heavens." Diane's eyes were wide. "He's speaking," she said with a stunned laugh. "Alexander, he's speaking. It's wonderful."

Alex winked at Ella. "It *is* pretty wonderful."

"Grandma?" Eric's dimples set off a charming grin.

"Yes, dear?" A hesitant smile peeked through her fingers.

"Daddy said I can keep him even though Chewbacca's fur makes his nose all red and he sneezes a lot."

His grandmother's hand lowered to her collar bone. Her smile broadened. She took a step closer. "Is that your dog's name? Chewbacca?"

Eric's head bobbled up and down. "Yup."

"Such a nice name. Did you pick it out yourself?"

"Uh huh," he said with another head bobble.

She held his little hand and then focused on her husband. The senator had joined them, his jaw agape. "Did you hear your grandson, Richard?"

"I heard him." The senator's smile warmed his entire face. Ella suddenly realized where Eric and Alex had inherited their dimples. "Is he a puppy, Eric?"

"Nope" Eric grinned. "He's this big." He leaned forward in Alex's arms and held his hand out above the floor. "You can play with him if you want. He's good at fetch."

Diane set a hand on Eric's knee. Tears glittered in her eyes. "That's wonderful. We'd love to play with both of you."

Eric giggled. "Just don't step in his poops, though. They're really big, too." He wrinkled his little nose and added, "And smelly."

Diane laughed along with him. She touched her grandson's hand and then gazed at Alex. "It's like heaven, hearing that little voice again."

"You have no idea." He set Eric on his feet and patted his head before he scampered off. "It's changed my life."

Eric plopped onto a nearby chair and rolled his plane along the carved arm. The Senator stood beside his wife. After a moment he shifted focus from his grandson to his son. "How long?" The older man asked quietly.

"Has he been talking?" Alex clarified.

The Senator nodded.

"Weeks."

His salt and pepper brows drew together. "Why didn't you tell us?"

"I tried. We played phone tag off and on. I showed up at the house once or twice, hoping to catch you in between meetings. I called the office last week and finally gave up after your secretary put me on hold for ten minutes." He focused on his mother. "And I tried to tell *you* last night."

"Is that what you wanted to talk to me about?" She glanced at Eric and then back again. "I'm so sorry. The event took up all of my time, Alexander. I was in twelve places at once."

"We're both so busy, son," his father said.

Alex nodded, grim faced. He glanced at Ella. They exchanged a look of understanding. "I've been busy, too. But I'm working hard to change that."

Eric ran up to Alex and tugged on his pants leg. "Daddy? Can I have one?" The little boy pointed at Mr. Boggs. The man held a Hershey Kiss in his open palm.

"Sure, Buddy. But just one. We're going to eat soon."

"Okay." Eric sped off and let the man peel the silver foil for him.

A light sniffle caught Ella's attention and she realized the tears in Diane's eyes had finally fallen.

"Mom?" Alex set his hand on her shoulder.

Diane patted his knuckles. "I'm fine. Just happy. It's so good to hear his voice again. We... we feared he'd never recover."

"It's like he's been speaking all along. Like he never stopped." The Senator watched his grandson resume playing, looking misty eyed himself. "I can't tell you how happy I am for you."

Alex gazed at his son. The little boy smiled, his teeth coated in chocolate. "He amazes me every day." He reached for Ella's hand. "And I owe it all to this woman."

"Pardon me."

They turned toward the voice. Maggie stood at the doorway, unconsciously smoothing her crisp apron. "Dinner's about to be served."

"Thanks Mags," Alex said. "We're coming."

She nodded and left the room.

Alex glanced at Eric. His son laughed at something Mr. Boggs said and then laughed harder when the burly man tickled his ribs. "Why's Wilson here?" Alex asked his father.

"Well, I was supposed to meet with him tomorrow morning. He had something urgent he wanted to discuss. Maybe it couldn't wait. He showed up at our house as we were getting in the car to come here. You don't mind that he tagged along, do you?"

Grim faced, Alex sighed. "No."

"What's wrong?" His father asked. "You know what he's all hot and bothered about?"

"Yeah, I think I do."

"He must still be worried about that Sutherland fellow."

"We can talk about it later."

Ella stared at the area rug while father and son spoke. She had a good idea what Mr. Boggs was all hot and bothered about, but it wasn't the fight. Alex's admission to him in the back yard was probably more like it. He planned on quitting governor. She felt bad knowing more than Senator York did. His son was about to do something that would affect the trajectory of his life… and she was a big reason Alex would ignore his internal GPS and take an alternate route. She wished she could slip away, blow off dinner, run home and leave all of her worries behind. But Diane had stepped aside to answer her phone and she had been left pinned between the two men and the couch without an escape.

"I don't feel like listening to another of Maggie's lectures on the evils of letting the food she slaved over get cold," Alex assured the senator. "I say we go eat before she breaks out the rolling pin."

"Sounds good to me." The senator rubbed his hands together. "I'm starved."

The six of them moved toward the hall. Diane, Alex, Eric and the senator exited the library first. Mr. Boggs stood aside to let Ella pass through the doorway. "Thank you," she said and smiled at him.

He smiled back, but the curve of his lips didn't appear genuine.

A little over an hour later, Ella, stuffed with fried okra, wood fired shrimp, creamy cheese grits, heirloom baby tomatoes tossed with sautéed spinach, buttery corn muffins and the best apple pie she'd ever tasted, volunteered to carry a sleeping Eric up to his room and tuck him into bed. The little boy had finally nodded off at the dinner table, cheek flattened against the linen, little mouth open with soft snores, clutching his twin engine in one hand and a forkful of pie in the other. Alex had kissed him on the forehead before handing him into her arms. The senator gently smoothed his grandson's unruly hair and whispered 'see you tomorrow little fella.' She left the men to continue debating the merits of the Falcons rookie quarterback and scanned the hall and nearby rooms for Diane. She wanted to give Eric's grandma a chance to say goodnight, but the woman had been called away on another phone call concerning her next film and was nowhere to be found. Neither was Mr. Boggs, who had excused himself from the table a few minutes earlier, though she wasn't concerned with his absence in the slightest. The man had been perfectly polite at dinner, but she still recalled his outburst in the yard, his rudeness at the ball and the way he'd given her the stink eye during dinner. Subtlety didn't appear to be one of his attributes.

Ella ascended the stairs, careful not to wake her sleeping bundle. She held him close, pressing her cheek against his temple, cradling his bottom on her forearm. She stroked his back and breathed in his baby shampoo scent.

A few days ago, holding him, this little boy she adored, would have warmed her heart. But in the blink of an eye everything had changed. Now all she felt was dismay.

She couldn't continue on as Eric's nanny, not anymore. Not after the passionate night she'd shared with his father. And though the decision left an icy void in her chest, she couldn't, in good conscience, continue on in a relationship with Alex either.

There was no longer any doubt in her mind. She had to break things off with him to keep him from making the biggest mistake of his life.

Swallowing the lump in her throat she set Eric in his helicopter bed, drew the covers over his shoulders and kissed him softly on the cheek. "Goodnight," she whispered.

The little boy stirred and snuggled against his pillow. Eyes closed, a small smile on his lips he mumbled, "Night, mommy."

Ella straightened. Eric's sleepy confusion stabbed at her soul. She backed away from his bed.

She wasn't his mother... though she suddenly wished she could be. Her heart ached with love for him.

Tears stung her throat and she turned from the sleeping boy and hurried from his room. She closed the door with a soft click and stood in the hallway trying to compose herself.

A cleansing breath in and out didn't help. In fact, a messy, snotty, blubbering cry felt seconds away.

She squeezed her eyes shut, fighting the urge to sob.

What's wrong with you? How are you gonna explain a red puffy face to Alex and his parents? Get a grip!

She opened her eyes and straightened her spine. *You can do this. You've hardened your heart in the past... you can certainly do it again.*

She turned from Eric's door determined to continue on downstairs as if her world wasn't coming to an end, but something lying on the carpet a few feet away shattered her resolve.

Eric's little red twin engine.

As she'd carried him to his room she'd heard something thump onto the floor. She'd known Eric must have dropped his toy, but she'd ignored it, determined not to wake him.

She bent to retrieve his prized possession. The die cast metal still warm where his dimpled hand had clutched it.

Her vision blurred. She couldn't fight the tears any longer. She swiped at her cheeks and hurried down the hall. She had to leave. Right now.

Turning the corner she plowed into the worst possible person.

Alex.

He steadied her shoulders. "Ella?"

She turned away from him, not wanting him to see her cry. Why hadn't she turned left instead of right? If she'd taken the rear stairway she would have never run into him. *Why am I always running into him?*

"Ella," he shifted to see her face. "What's wrong?"

"Nothing." She fought hard to reign in her emotions.

His warm hands melted her flesh. He shifted again, but she dodged his scrutiny. "It doesn't look like nothing. What happened? Why are you crying?"

"It *is* nothing," she blurted, tugging from his gentle grip. She stepped back. "I... I stubbed my toe. That's all."

He glanced at her shoes. She wore steel toed combat boots. She could have dropped an anvil on her freaking foot and it wouldn't have hurt enough to merit an *ouch* let alone tears. He raised an eyebrow. "You sure?"

"I'm sure." She softened her voice even though she felt trapped. She had to break free before she collapsed into his arms a whaling mess.

A muscle flexed in his cheek. He obviously didn't believe her.

"I need to go."

"Go?"

"Home. I need to go home."

"Now?"

"Yes, I'm sorry." He deserved a goodbye, some kind of explanation for why she needed to leave him and his son, but she wasn't ready. Not here, in the hall, holding his little boy's plane and the shattered pieces of her heart in her hand.

He shoved his fingers through his hair. "Did Boggs say something to you?"

"No." *I can't do this right now...*

"Don't listen to anything he has to say, Ella."

"He didn't say a word to me. This has nothing to do with him. I just need to go home."

He drew in a breath and let it out on a sigh. Very softly he said, "Stay here, with us. This is as much your home as any."

That sexy, sweet voice of his tugged at her heart. Everything about him drew her nearer. She felt the magnetic pull radiating from his big, strong body and feared being lured into his arms with no way... or no desire to escape.

Lie! Say something, anything! "My mom needs me."

"Trudy? Is she okay?"

"She's worried my dad's gonna weasel his way into her life again. I promised I'd sleep there tonight so we can talk."

"Why didn't you say that in the first place?"

Because I just pulled the lie out of my butt. She shrugged and forced a smile. "I'm tired. I'm not thinking straight."

"Well, family comes first. I don't blame you for wanting to be with her."

"I knew you'd understand."

"You want me to give you a ride over there?"

"No," she answered a little too quickly.

"Okay." He nodded toward the staircase. "My parents are leaving in a little while. They wanted to say goodbye to you."

"No," she blurted a second time. "Can... can you tell them I wasn't feeling well and went home? I... just... I want to hurry."

His frown deepened. He stepped closer and held her hand. She should have pulled away before the electrical spark of his touch zipped up her arm, awakening every nerve in her body.

"Are you sure you're okay?" He took Eric's toy from her and set it on a console table so he could hold both of her hands. He gave them a squeeze.

"I'm sure." She squeezed back, meaning to end the conversation and tug from his grasp, but he drew her closer, buried his hand in the hair at her nape and pressed his lips against hers.

His cinnamon apple scented breath, soft full lips and fiery heat sent the roller coaster speeding through her soul on another perilous nose-dive. Her gut flip-flopped and a familiar, hungry ache tightened between her legs.

She would have been lost if not for a single chunk of bone lodged in the quivering mass of vertebrae that made up her spine. Its support gave her the strength to summon will power she didn't think she possessed.

She broke his seductive kiss, slid her palm over his muscular shoulders, flashed a content smile to keep from revealing her pain and then stepped out of his embrace.

He nodded toward the stairs. "I'll walk you to your car."

"I'm fine." She broadened her false cheer. "I know the way. Besides, you have guests. You shouldn't leave your parents and Mr. Boggs all alone. They're probably wondering what happened to you."

"They'll wonder what happened to you, too."

She swallowed hard. "Tell them goodbye for me?"

He smoothed a fringe of bangs from her eyes and smiled. "Sure."

"Thank you." She turned away from him.

"Drive safely."

She glanced over her shoulder, nodded and then hurried down the rear stairs.

She remembered setting her purse on the round table in the entryway when they'd returned from the park and grabbed it off the polished wood, hoping she wouldn't run into anyone else on her escape. In a few steps she was out the door and taking the front steps two at a time. Opening her purse she rummaged through the contents as she jogged the walkway to her car.

Stepping onto the driveway she found her keys and finally looked up.

She jerked to a stop.

The second worse person she could have run into on her flight from Alex's house, stood blocking Pepto, smoking a cigarette.

Wilson Boggs.

"Where're you off to in such a hurry, Blondie?" Illuminated by the glow of porch and lawn lights his bright smile looked as about as natural as Tori Spelling's boobs.

"I'm going home," she answered, unwilling to fabricate a smile of her own.

He took a deep drag on his cigarette and then exhaled out the corner of his mouth. At least he had the decency not to blow smoke in her face... "Hope everything's okay, sweetheart," he said, blowing a different kind of smoke instead.

"Like you care." She was done pretending with this guy.

He raised a ginger eyebrow. "Touché."

"Can you move out of the way, please?"

The man stood his ground, inches from Pepto's driver side door. He took another unhurried puff and then flicked the cigarette on the ground. Crushing the smoldering butt with the toe of his shoe he finally gazed at her. "This is good thing."

She scowled at him. "What is?"

"You're quick exit."

"If you'd step aside it'd be even quicker."

He chuckled. "I think under different circumstances I'd really enjoy your company."

"I can't say the same."

Another chuckle. He drew in a deep breath and let it out as he tilted his head back to gaze at the stars. "You know, you never answered my question."

She glanced over her shoulder at the front door, worried Alex's parents or Alex or Eric or even Maggie might appear. "What question?" She asked, frowning at him.

He shrugged. "What's the hurry? What's got you running out the door?" He raised an eyebrow. "Don't tell me there's trouble in paradise?"

She shifted her purse and shuffled her keys in her grasp. "Mr. Boggs, I get that you don't like me. I'm not sure why, since we barely know each other, but you've made it abundantly clear you're not a fan. How 'bout you forgo the pleasantly contrived chit-chat and tell it like it is?"

"Well, if you say so." He stepped forward. "You don't belong in his world. You're beneath him. You're blood's not even the same temperature as his much less the same color. You have nothing to offer him other than a pretty face and if you stick around you'll be sorry."

"Are you threatening me?"

"Threat— No... no, nothing like that," he blurted. He held up a hand, stepped closer and for the first time since they met his expression seemed sincere. She recognized worry in his knitted brows. The corners of his mouth drooped along with his shoulders. He shook his head and then smoothed his comb-over. "I wouldn't do that." His frown crested in a grim smile. "I might not be the most likeable guy. Hell, I've been called a dick on more than one occasion, but... I'm no monster. I'd never hurt a fly. And I didn't mean to imply that any harm would come to you. I'm just..."

The dread coursing through her veins diluted. Her gut told her he was telling the truth, but she remained wary. "You're just what, Mr. Boggs?"

"Look, I love Alex like he's my own. I watched him grow up. I've listened to his hopes and dreams. I've even helped him achieve a few." He ran a meaty palm across the back of his neck. "To tell you the truth, I wouldn't mind helping him achieve a few more. You gotta understand something here. That kid is one in a million. His future is as big and bright as the sun."

I know... and he's about to give it all up.

Mr. Boggs stepped closer. Gently he said, "Do you really want to be the one responsible for extinguishing that ball of fire? By allowing him to do something you'll both regret?"

No. It's the last thing I want...

"I know *I'd* certainly regret it if he gave up on his future."

"So are you worried for his career or for your own?" She asked before she could stifle the urge.

"Yeah, I get how it might sound that way. And you're not far off. I'm not gonna lie. Being a *king maker* of sorts is a hell of a great job to have, but whether a couple of big wins help me look like a hero or not, Alex has always come first. I truly only want what's best for him. And right now, as painful as it might be to hear... Ella, Honey, I'm sorry, but you're just not it." His gruff voice had softened. He'd tried to lessen the blow.

His sudden kindness might have been soothing had she not already come to that same conclusion herself. "I know that."

He frowned. "You do?"

"Yes... I do. This state needs a man like Alex. He's an amazing mayor. He'll be an incredible governor. I can't let him give that all up. I won't let him. He's better off without me." She raised her chin. "I may not belong in Alex's world, Mr. Boggs, but I know what I need to do to keep that sun shining down on it."

His frown faded. He narrowed his gaze, but not in accusation. She couldn't help thinking his expression bordered on respect. He stepped aside to allow her access to her car. "I'm sorry I've kept you."

She shrugged. Pepto behaved and let her open the door on the second yank. She slid into the seat and turned on the engine.

Mr. Boggs leaned down to her level. "You're doing the right thing, Miss Slipper," he said with a nod.

She nodded back and closed the door.

Driving off she wondered why doing the right thing suddenly felt so wrong.

Chapter Twenty-Nine

"What's he doing here?!" Ella blindly tried to hang her purse on a hook, once, twice, three times. Finally giving up, she threw it on the apartment floor.

Anger boiled her blood as she stormed into the center of the studio.

Her mother sat on her favorite chair, a shaggy upholstered number that resembled a boxy sheep dog.

And sitting next to her, making the lie she'd just fed Alex a reality, was Clyde-effing-Slipper.

He had the decency to straighten his posture as she barreled closer, but he didn't tuck tail and sidle out the door as she'd hoped.

"String-Bean—"

"Don't you String-Bean me." She glared at him and then shifted focus to her mother. The woman seemed okay. No handcuffs, no ropes. Nothing tethered her to the chair right next to her ex-con ex-husband other than her own skinny butt and an abundance of furry white fabric.

"Did he break in?" Ella asked her.

"Don't be ridiculous."

"Then he tricked you, forced his way in."

"Ella, please, honey, sit down."

"No, Mom." She flung her arm out, pointing at the man without looking at him. "Not with him here."

"String-Bean..."

She shot Clyde a warning glare.

He cleared his throat. "Ella, please. Hear me out. That's all I ask."

"Hear what out, Clyde? That you need money? That you've gotta pay your bookie or he's gonna break your legs?" She stepped closer. "Or you've got a get rich quick scheme you want to share with us... you just need to empty our bank account to get it started?"

"Ella, please," her mother whispered.

"What's wrong with you? Why would you let him in the house? You said this was over. You said you'd never fall under his spell again." Ella studied her mother's expression, but the look of compassion on her face made no sense.

"Ella, sit down," Trudy said, softly.

When she didn't obey her mother raised her voice, repeating the order.

Her chest continued to rise and fall erratically, and she shot venom Clyde's way, but finally relented and took a seat... as far from the man as possible. "What?" She barked.

"You know you're acting like a child right now," her mother accused. "You're a grown woman, Ella. We should be able to sit here, all three of us, and have an adult conversation. This is a tense moment for you, I know, but you need to take a breath and trust that no one's here to hurt you... or me for that matter."

She hated being lectured, but her mom had a point. When it came to her father, she had always turned into an angry, screaming, yelling, inconsolable child, no matter her age.

She drew in a deep breath and let it out slowly. After a second inhale, exhale, she raised her chin and said, "I'm listening," through her teeth.

After a long pause he finally said, "I'm here to apologize."

She raised an eyebrow.

He hesitated another moment and then continued. "I've never had the strength or the decency to say that before. But more than anything, I want to say it now. I'm really, truly sorry... for everything."

Her eyes narrowed. Something in his voice... Despite her feelings for him, she couldn't help thinking he sounded... sincere.

"Why now, Clyde?" Her mother asked without malice. "Tell her what's changed."

Change. Right... like a skunk loses its stink. The notion stole the ounce of compassion that had sneaked into her heart. He'd never changed before. Why now, exactly.

He cleared his throat and shoved a hand through his cowlick. Leaning forward he braced his elbows on his knees and stared at the floor. "I'm afraid it's too little too late, Trudy. My daughter hates me... and I don't blame her."

Oh boo hoo.

"It can't hurt to talk it out. Just try. Tell her what you told me, Clyde."

He ruffled his cowlick again and sighed. Still concentrating on the braided area rug he said, "I should have changed my ways for you from the start." He picked at a tiny hole forming in the knee of his jeans.

"You tried to set me straight, but... I... just didn't have the courage, or the confidence to be a better man. It was easier to be a criminal than a provider. Easier to steal money to pay bills than work to pay them."

After a long hesitation he added, "I let my little girl down from the start."

Ella rolled her eyes. "So if it wasn't your own family that supposedly straightened you out, then who? Who's the miracle worker that turned a piece of dirt into a *shining example* of society?" She cocked her head and laid the sarcasm on thicker. "Was it God, Clyde? Did you find God in jail? Are you born again?"

Clyde said nothing. His head remained bowed. He sat hunched over his knees and completely still until a vibration shook his shoulders. His body quaked softly and he covered his face with both hands.

Ella's jaw dropped. *He's crying?!*

Tears streamed down his cheeks, dripping off his chin. He tried to wipe them away but they kept falling. She'd never seen the man cry before. The raw emotion etched on his face thawed a bit of the ice encasing her heart. For the first time in her life she felt sorry for him.

Clyde dug in his pocket and withdrew a handkerchief. He mopped his cheeks and wiped his nose.

Alex's voice echoed in her head, *He's done his time. Give the guy a chance before you tie a noose around his neck.*

"I'm... sorry. That was... I shouldn't have said those things to you," she managed to say past the lump in her throat. He'd never merited an apology before, but his tears... they affected her in a way she'd never thought possible.

A grim smile tugged his lips. "I don't blame you." He wiped his face again and then clutched the damp square of fabric in his fist. "I've never given you any reason to think otherwise of me." He sniffled a few times, blew his nose and then gazed at her. "It wasn't divine intervention that saved me, Ella... it was you."

Me? The daughter you abandoned? Was he playing her? Was he doing what he'd always done, telling her what she wanted to hear? Had she been wrong to feel sympathy for him?

His watery eyes never wavered. "I've been in contact with your mother since the beginning of this last incarceration."

Ella glared at Trudy. "You promised me you wou—"

"No, believe me, Ella," Her father interrupted. "It was a one sided correspondence. I never even knew if your mother opened my letters."

"Is that true, Mom?"

Trudy raised her chin. "You know as well as I do that I didn't respond to him for years. Now give someone the benefit of the doubt for once in your life."

Ella sighed. *Benefit of the doubt. Benefit of the doubt. He's cried, he's apologized. Just give him the benefit of the doubt.* She glanced at her father.

"I was put in a cell with a guy doing fifteen years. He'd been in and out of prison all his life, like me. He was an okay dude, but he never shut up. He always talked about his kids, always brought them up, day in and day out."

"How terrible. A man devoted to his children," Ella spat as her heart re-froze.

Clyde focused on the floor. "For me, it was the worst thing he could have talked about."

"I don't have to listen to this." She shot from her seat and stormed toward the apartment door.

A rough hand caught her wrist. She tried to yank free, but her father held tight.

"Let me go you selfish son-of-a-bitch." She couldn't help the tears that blinded her or the lump that distorted her voice. She'd felt sorry for this man? What had she been thinking?

"Ella, please, listen."

She jerked harder. "No. If family is the worst thing you can talk about with someone then I want nothing to do with you."

"I couldn't talk about it, Ella. Not with my cell-mate, not with anyone. I wouldn't allow myself to think of you or your mother. Being reminded of what I had done to you both, how I'd acted, tore me apart inside." He clutched his chest in anguish. "I left you because I didn't... I couldn't face you. You were good and decent, such a sweet, smart little girl. You trusted me and I think you even loved me once." He shifted to grab her attention. In a broken voice he said, "You tried to be like me. Remember? When you were twelve."

Ella recalled the incident. She'd wanted to get her mom something special for her birthday, but didn't have any money. A lack of funds had never stopped her father, so she'd emulated Clyde Slipper, the thief, and had shoplifted a boxed set of scented lotions from a local Kroger. She'd been caught and should have been prosecuted but the store manager had pitied her and let her go. The incident would be forever etched in her mind as the lowest point in her life... the moment she'd done the wrong thing.

"I didn't want to drag you down with me," he continued, choking on his words. "I didn't want you to grow up like me. And I was too weak to change, so I left. I'm so sorry." Tears streamed down his cheeks. "I'm so very sorry."

She stopped struggling. The emotion in his voice tore her in two. Part of her wanted to flee. He was a liar, a thief, a criminal making up a story.

Another part of her wanted... him... her daddy, to gather her into his arms and hug away any doubt.

"I've chosen the wrong path every single minute of my life. When I should have turned left I turned right and the mistakes I've made have caused me and you and your mother nothing but pain. Instead of leaving you..." He reached for her, hesitantly. When she didn't pull away the tips of his fingers grazed her forehead, feathering her bangs aside. She wasn't repulsed by his touch. In fact, ever so slightly, she leaned into it. "...Instead of running away," he repeated, "I should have had the courage to stay and be more like you."

He flashed a sad smile and then squeezed her shoulder before leaving her side to take a seat next to her mother.

"Ella, sit with us." Her mother's voice broke as she patted the seat next to her.

Seconds later she lowered onto the sofa, sitting between her mother and her father.

"Clyde, tell her." Trudy's fair brow creased.

"I'm not sure she'll believe me," he said.

"Let your daughter be the judge of that."

He mopped his cheeks and drew in a deep breath. After stowing the handkerchief back in his pocket he set his elbows on his knees. "Like I said, I wrote dozens of letters to your mom while I was inside. Most of it was nonsense. I'd ask her for money to buy cigarettes. I'd beg her to take me back when I got out. I'd even blame her for my troubles now and again." He glanced at Trudy, sorrow etching deeper lines in his face. Another fortifying breath and he switched to Ella. "At first she didn't write me back. Years went by with nothing, not a word. But I guess she got fed up with me and one day about a year ago she finally sent a letter."

Ella glanced at her mother. She should be furious with her for lying, for saying she'd never speak to the man again and then going behind her back, but things had changed. In the space of minutes her feelings had altered.

"The letter was all about you."

Ella blinked. "Me?"

"Your mother wrote six pages, front and back, on everything you'd accomplished. Graduating from high school while you worked afternoons and weekends. Going to college while you worked full time to pay for tuition and help with bills. Helping to keep your mom's store afloat. Volunteering with her. Getting accepted into grad-school. And now you're on your way towards earning your masters and a teaching certificate." He set his hand on her knee. "Even with a role model like me you found the courage to take care of your mother and make something of yourself. You were choosing the right path... and I was so proud of you."

His grizzled hand caught her attention. Veiny and riddled with age spots it resembled the appendage of an elderly man. Her father had aged in jail. Not only in appearance, but in attitude. The years had smoothed his rough edges. He'd lost his overly confident swagger. He'd left his ego in a cage.

"I had been so sure you were gonna follow in my footsteps. I imagined you in juvie, doing time for drugs or theft. But you rose above that. You broke the cycle and after I'd read your mother's letter I realized I wanted to prove to you that I could be a better man for your sake." A grim smile creased his lips. "My counselor called that an epiphany."

"You went to counseling?"

"Still do. My PO set it up for me. He's a good man. Helped me get a job, too."

"A job?" Ella asked, wide-eyed. She couldn't remember the last time her father had been employed."

He nodded. "It's not much. I mow lawns for Hicks Landscaping, but..." he shrugged, "It's honest work and with my history, I'm lucky to have it."

Ella marveled at her emotions. She'd harbored so much anger and mistrust for her father for so long, that it seemed crazy to believe anything he said. But, remarkably, she did. She suddenly realized that even through the worst times, when her hatred for him had been most potent, she still loved him and wanted desperately for him to love her in return. And he had, he'd just feared the consequences.

A lot like Alex before he'd reunited with Eric. He'd feared the consequences.

"I don't expect you to welcome me back." His Adam's apple bobbed in his narrow throat. "And I don't expect your sympathy either. I'm not asking for a place to stay or a helping hand... or for money. What I need from you is worth much more." He bowed his head. After a long pause he looked up again. "I'm hoping for your forgiveness."

She'd listened to every word and honestly believed that he wanted to make a new start. He had apologized, cried, attended counseling and even landed a job, all of which were unprecedented. And most important, she recognized now that she had loved him all along and that he loved her, too.

But she stopped short of saying three words.

I forgive you.

The phrase stuck in her throat.

She no longer hated him. Oddly, the weight of that emotion had left her with as much effort as removing a coat. But could she forgive him for all the pain he had caused? For her mother's sadness? For the tears she had shed as a little girl missing her father? For the court dates and handcuffs and lawyer's fees that had made up her childhood? For her negative feelings toward men and relationships and love?

And what if he relapsed?

What if things got tough and he resorted to crime again?

It could happen. It *had* happened, many times before.

No... it was too soon, too scary, too raw. She couldn't forgive him. Not now. Not yet.

The consequences were too frightening.

"I can't."

"Ella," her mother said.

Instead of responding to Trudy, she rose from the sofa. "I'm sorry, Clyde," she said softly.

Her father's sullen smile said it all. *It's okay. I understand.*

"Ella?"

She didn't answer her mother, just kept walking toward the door. She picked up her purse and turned the knob. The stale scent of the stairwell wafted in.

She turned to gaze at her mother and father. Worry etched lines into both of their faces.

"Ella where are you going?" Her mother asked.

Her father stood up. "I'm not staying here. I have a place to bunk. Hicks, my boss, he's putting me up. I don't want to chase you from your home." He stepped forward. "Stay here, I'll go."

Ella considered his offer. She couldn't go back to Alex. And she needed a place to sleep, but spending the evening in the apartment didn't sit well with her either. The night's events, the heartbreaking decision she'd made earlier, were mentally draining. She feared her mother's influence would only make things worse. "I have to go back to work," she lied. "They're expecting me, so... I'm gonna go."

"Ella..." Her mother stood.

"Trudy." Clyde reached for her mother's hand, grazing her fingers. "Let her be. Give her some time." He glanced at Ella. "It's not easy to digest... my being here, asking for so much." He paused a moment and then his mournful smile returned. "You looked good together, like a family. The three of you... today at the park."

Her heart lurched.

"You deserve some happiness in your life, String-Bean."

"Thank you," she said. And as she turned to leave she realized that happiness had already slipped away.

Chapter Thirty

For the second morning in a row, Ella woke to bird song. Only this time, instead of a symphony the grating vocalization of a crow penetrated the window. She grabbed a pillow and smashed it over her ears.

"Shut up," she yelled, when the rasping melody penetrated the lumpy barrier.

Caw, caw, caw.

She jumped out of bed, stormed across the room and threw open the motel door. "Shut up!"

The big black bird flapped off the railing like she'd fired a gun. But in frightening the animal, she'd also scared a woman and child walking past.

Wide eyed, the woman gathered the little girl closer as they hurried down the walkway.

"Sorry," she called out, shielding her eyes from the morning sun. "I was yelling at a bird." Realizing how ridiculous that sounded, she frowned and returned to her room.

The unit she'd been given smelled like moth balls. The matted shag carpet had seen better days and the seventies era decor reminded her of Greg Brady's basement bedroom, but to her surprise, everything appeared pretty clean. The price fit her budget, too. Thirty-five dollars a night. She'd driven past the little motor-lodge countless times in the past and often wondered about the people staying within its dreary walls. Were they desperate, alone, running from something?

She flopped into bed.

She didn't have to wonder any longer.

As of last night, she'd become one of *those people*.

And her reasons for being here were probably as depressing as theirs.

After leaving her mother and father she'd driven straight to *Arthur's Camelot Motor Lodge*. She figured the cement block exterior had been modeled after a castle, though the single story expanse looked more like barracks. It fell short on aesthetics but it was cheap and she hoped it would be quiet.

Except for the distant rumble of interstate traffic and this morning's avian annoyance, it had been.

The peace had given her time to think.

And cry... and then think some more.

She lay in bed last night with two names in her head, Clyde and Alex. After hours of deliberation one of them took a back seat to the other. She still wasn't ready to forgive her father, though his apology and his tears had softened her heart. That alone amazed her. For over a decade she'd felt nothing but hatred for him, had shaped her entire outlook on paternal animosity, but in less than a half hour he'd melted her icy exterior to reveal feelings she'd buried long ago. *Love...* she loved her father and finally accepted that she had all along. True, she couldn't imagine skipping through the grass hand in hand with him or planning daily father daughter picnics, but she could see herself thinking of him as dad instead of dead-beat and believing his *epiphany* might finally set him straight.

Her feathered alarm clock and Clyde's reemergence in her life, however, had not been what kept her from enjoying a restful night's sleep.

Her insomnia had been due to the other name in her head.

Alex.

She loved him, too.

But instead of revealing her feelings for him, she'd have to bury them.

And just as heartbreaking, she'd have to bury her feelings for his son.

The popcorn ceiling blurred. She blinked hard and then scrubbed away gathering tears. She'd shed enough last night.

With a sniffle she got out of bed and made her way to the bathroom. She used the toothbrush and toothpaste she'd bought along with a few other minor toiletries at the CVS across the street. After she washed her face and combed her hair she wandered back into the bedroom. Picking up her purse she opened the door. The first truly frigid day of the year welcomed her.

It was time to leave.

It was time to see Alex.

And then she'd never see him again.

Ella parked her car in Alex's driveway and turned it off. Pepto continued to cough and sputter, wheezing like an indignant old woman. Normally she'd ignore her refusal to shut down, but today she wondered if *Miss Ah-Bismol* wasn't trying to tell her something.

Don't do this... put, put, put. Drive away... put, put, put.

Her father had left to keep her safe and ensure she reached her goals. He hadn't offered a reason or explained his actions at the time. He'd just left.

Maybe that's what she should do. Just leave. No explanation, no anguish. Like tearing off a Band-Aid, quick and painless.

Yeah, right.

She'd been in pain all her life because of Clyde's decision. Leaving her without saying goodbye had never felt like protection. To her, an impressionable young girl, his absence had been a rejection.

She glared at herself in the rear view mirror. "Is that what you want Eric to think? That you don't care? That he means nothing to you? That you've rejected him?"

No.

The last thing she wanted was to wound the little boy so deeply that he'd carry the pain for the rest of his life. He'd already survived one traumatic event. She didn't want him struggling through another. He'd be upset, but unlike her father, she'd lessen the blow with a goodbye.

Alex, on-the-other-hand, was an adult. He'd forget about her. She didn't suppose it would take very long, either. *He's handsome, rich, available. He's the mayor for goodness sake! He'll find someone else and I'll simply fade from memory.*

Though she clung to that reasoning, her heart rejected it completely. Imagining him holding another woman, kissing her, sharing his love for Eric with her, ripped into her gut like a rusty knife.

She rested her forehead against the furry steering wheel, willing tears not to fall. Why did love have to hurt so badly?

Pepto finally gave up the fight and shuttered her last. The interior went quiet as misery wailed inside Ella's soul.

A thump on the door jerked her upright.

Alex stood next to the car, smiling. "What are you doing out here?" His voice muffled by glass and metal.

She swallowed the lump in her throat. "I... nothing."

He tugged on the handle. The damn thing opened right away. A chill breeze whipped her bangs from her forehead.

"Trudy doing okay?"

She frowned at him. "Huh?"

"Your mom? Did you guys talk last night?"

"Talk?" *The lie you told him that came true, you moron!* Realization finally dawned on her. "Yes... we talked."

"Good." He held out his hand. "Come on. Let's go inside, get out of the cold."

When she hesitated his dimples grew deeper and he leaned closer. "Maggie made another apple pie... It's still warm."

She channeled Boggs and fabricated a smile.

He helped her from the car and then turned to lead her up the front steps. "Are you all right?" He asked when they entered the house and he'd helped her out of her coat.

"Yeah, I'm fine." She rubbed moisture from her eyes and then blinked hard like she tried to clear something from her lids. "Dust from my car I think."

His brow furrowed. Concern etched his face. "Last night and now... something seems off with you. You're sure everything's okay?"

"Yes." She drew in a deep breath. "Mmm, I can smell pie from here," she said, desperate to change the subject.

He kissed her forehead. The warmth of his lips shocked her resident butterflies into a fluttering frenzy.

"The woman's been baking all night apparently." He shrugged. "When she's really worried about something she turns to pastry. I think she made a dozen pies. We're gonna be eating them breakfast lunch and dinner."

The butterflies fell into the pit of her stomach. "What's she worried about?"

"Who knows? All she said was that her psychic warning bell is ringing off the hook. You know how she is."

She'd gotten to know Alex's housekeeper very well. The woman had once said she could divine the future. Had she divined what was about to happen?

"Hey, I have a surprise for you." He took her hand and led her deeper into the house. "UPS delivered it this morning."

"No... Alex... I..." She shuffled behind him, trying to slow things down. This wasn't going as she'd planned. She shouldn't have set foot inside. She should have asked him to bring Eric to her. She should have said her goodbyes at the car and then left.

"Come on," he said, grinning over his shoulder. "It's in the kitchen. Eric helped me pick it out."

Her heart sank. "Alex, I don't want you buying me presents." She tugged her hand from his.

He set his palm against the swinging door, but didn't push through. "Come on, you're gonna like it."

"No."

A good natured chuckle escaped his lips. "No?"

"No. I can't accept it."

He stepped closer.

She stepped back.

"Ella..."

The lump in her throat turned into a boulder. "I..."

He stepped even closer.

She backed into a table. Something teetered and she spun to catch the lamp before it fell. Setting it straight she meant to back further away, but he gathered her into his arms and drew her close.

"Come on," he whispered, looking into her eyes. "Tell me what's wrong."

"I..." the words stuck in her throat.

"What happened?"

"Alex, we... need to talk... about us... I can't do this."

He opened his mouth to reply, but the kitchen door banged open. Eric sprinted toward them. "Ella, Ella! I got you a present," he cried and grabbed her hand. He wore a napkin tucked into the neck of his t-shirt and a thick milk mustache on his upper lip.

"Get back in the kitchen you squirmy little tadpole." Maggie joined them, wiping her hands on a dish towel. "You've still got a full plate of breakfast in there," she scolded. She used the corner of her apron to clean his mouth and smiled at Ella. "He jumped out of his chair like he had ants in his pants."

Eric giggled. "I got ants in my pants."

"Said he heard your voice out here," Maggie added. She shrugged. "The boy's got superhuman hearing. The only sound I heard was my own chewing."

Alex had stepped away from her during the exchange. Ella glanced at him now. He watched her carefully.

"Come on, Ella," Eric grunted as he tugged on her fingers. "I wanna show you."

The pull of Alex's gaze threatened to draw her back into his arms. She broke eye contact and focused on Eric instead. But that didn't help. His dimpled excitement was her undoing. Instead of fleeing the house, she followed the little boy into the kitchen.

"See," Eric said, pointing.

The gift sat on the kitchen counter amongst at least ten fragrant pies. The package, a large, slightly mashed rectangle, wrapped in Darth Vader wrapping paper had been topped with a shiny black bow.

Eric scampered to the counter. He stood on tip-toes to pat the edge of the package. When he turned to gaze at her, big green eyes twinkled. "I helped Maggie wrap it." He grinned from ear to ear.

"You did such a good job." Ella cleared her throat, having choked on her words. "Vader's my favorite."

"Daddy?" Eric flew past her. He shoved the swinging door open and held it still. "Are you gonna watch?"

Maggie and Alex stood in the next room. They glanced her way... as if they'd been discussing her.

"Daddy?"

Alex smiled at him. "Yeah, Buddy?"

"Can we watch her open it now?"

Alex's green eyes settled back on her. His visual caress warmed the remaining pieces of her breaking heart. She swallowed hard and severed contact, turning away.

"Sure we can."

Alex entered the room, set his hand on her shoulder, squeezed lightly and then left her side. The heat of his touch seeped into her flesh. She made a mental note of her body's reaction. A wash of Goosebumps prickled her arms. Her knees turned to jelly. The butterflies had resumed flight and swirled in her core.

Alex lifted her gift and set it on the kitchen table. "Here, sit down, Eric, so you can see better." He patted one of the chairs. His son, bobbing on his toes, hopped up and knelt on the seat.

"Come on, Ella. Open it. Open it." His child's voice, that sweet little sound that had once been silent, became another mental note. She never wanted to forget it. She prayed she'd carry the memory with her for the rest of her life.

"Okay," she said softly. A few steps and she reached the table. Alex stood a few feet away. Maggie watched from the doorway.

"I helped Maggie wrap it," Eric repeated, very proud of himself.

"I know. And you did a beautiful job, too." Ella patted his head and then honked his nose. His grin lit the room.

She glanced at Maggie. The woman smiled at her, but her expression failed to brighten her eyes. *Sweet, intuitive Maggie. Could she really be psychic?* She pushed the thought aside. "Thank you... for helping him."

"My pleasure, Honey." Her smile deepened, but her gaze remained troubled.

The package sat before her. It wasn't right to accept it... but she plucked the bow off the top and stuck her finger into a taped seam. She wouldn't rob Eric of his excitement.

The paper ripped. Rich black leather peeked out. A split down the center and another small swipe and the entire gift was revealed.

No, not this. She covered her face and crumpled into a seat. Misery sliced through her chest.

"What's wrong? Don't you like it?" Eric touched her shoulder.

She fought her emotions. Anguish and tears would only make what she had to do harder. Not only for her, but for everyone.

She took Eric's hand and forced another smile. "I love it." She squeezed him close and then drew him off his seat and onto her lap. She hugged him tight. "I love it very much."

"You're breaking my bones," Eric grunted.

She chuckled despite her sadness at the comical way he'd said it. Releasing her strangle hold on him she held his face between both hands and rubbed the tip of her nose against his. "I'm sorry. I didn't mean to break your bones."

He smiled and wiggled off her lap, returning to his seat. Grabbing her gift, Eric opened the flap and showed her the interior. "It's for school. You can put lots of papers in it and erasers and crayons and a ruler and that pointy thing we used that day to draw circles..."

She smiled in spite of her pain. "A compass."

He nodded. "Yeah, a compass and maybe some chalk and scissors... and even your Star Wars lunch box."

Made of soft buttery leather with a short sturdy handle, a long strap and loads of internal compartments, the messenger bag was less stuffy and structured than a brief case. Black with a silver buckle, the color and shape were exactly what she would have chosen for herself.

Only, she hadn't chosen it. A generous father and son had picked it out for her. *For her.* They had taken the time and the consideration to find a present that reflected her personality and goals. They had given her a wonderful gift... she didn't deserve.

Tears threatened, but somehow she kept them at bay. "I think it's beautiful," she whispered. "Just what I always wanted." She stood up and began gathering the wrapping paper, trying her best to avoid meeting eyes with Alex.

"I'll get that," Maggie said.

Ella handed the wad of paper over, avoiding her gaze as well. She stepped back from the table. She focused on the floor. *How will I make it through this?*

"Ella... let's go out back. We can talk... if that's what you want." The earlier playfulness in Alex's southern drawl had vanished. Now his voice only held concern.

She closed her eyes.

He stepped closer. "Or we can take a ride somewhere instead if you'd rather."

She needed to say goodbye to each one of them... but she couldn't go through that pain three separate times. It was best to tell them now, while they were all together. Otherwise she'd lose her nerve. "I'd like... I want to..." She cleared her throat. "Can we... just talk in here?"

"We'll give you two some privacy," Maggie said, reaching for Eric.

"No... please, Maggie. Both of you stay." She took the woman's hand. Her fingers closed around her plump palm. "You're part of their family."

"So are you," Maggie whispered and squeezed gently.

Her words shattered another piece of her heart, but she steeled her spine and drew her hand from her grasp. Maggie backed away and took a seat at the kitchen table.

Like a band-aid... quick and painless.

"I... I'm sorry, but I have to leave."

"On a trip?" Eric straightened. "Like to Disney world?"

"No, sweetheart. Not Disney World."

"Daddy, can we go to Disney World?"

Alex smiled at his son. "Soon, Buddy. I promise." Like Maggie, his expression didn't reach his eyes.

"Then why do you have to leave, Ella?" Eric's smile drooped, thoughts of Goofy and Mickey quickly forgotten. "When'll you be back?"

"I... honey..." The jagged boulder in her throat grew. "I have to leave for a very long time."

Eric frowned. He glanced at his father and then back at her. He'd been kneeling on his chair, but sunk onto his heels. "A long time?"

"Yes..." She'd rehearsed this last night, alone in her motel room, with an olive green lamp, a chipped pitcher and an ice bucket standing in as the family she'd grown to love, but the pain stabbing her chest was so much worse in person.

"Where're you going for a long time?"

"I'll be at school."

He brightened. "My school?"

"No, honey. That would be lots of fun, but my school is far away. I'm going to have to move. So I can't be here with you... or your daddy anymore."

The urge to glance over her shoulder at Alex assaulted her, but she focused on Maggie instead. The older woman dug a tissue from her pocket and pinched her nose. Her eyes shined and when she blinked a single tear slid down her cheek.

Eric's shoulders sagged. He slid off the chair and stood in front of her. He stared at the floor. "But I don't want you to leave."

Ella knelt in front of him. She clasped his thin arms. "I know. I know you don't. But it's going to be okay. You'll be okay. You have Maggie and your dad and Chewbacca. You're about to enroll in a real school and you'll make lots of friends there." She squeezed gently when his lower lip quivered. Her voice broke and she pulled him close to hide her agony. Hugging him she managed a hoarse whisper, "I'll never forget you. You're my favorite little boy."

His arms encircled her shoulders. He hugged her back.

He smelled of chocolate milk and Play-Dough. She breathed him in and stroked his hair. "Be good for Maggie and your daddy, okay?" She choked on her words and pressed her forehead against his.

He rubbed his nose against hers.

Tears spilled against her will.

A muffled sound came from Maggie. The woman held the tissue over her mouth. Her eyes were squeezed shut.

Ella swiped at her cheeks and then stood up.

"Come sit with me." Maggie held out a hand to Eric. He left Ella's side and let the woman lift him onto her lap. She hugged him close, holding on to him like a life line.

"I don't want her to leave," Eric mumbled into her plump bosom.

"I know. None of us do," Maggie crooned, rubbing his back as he began to cry.

"Ella." Alex's voice startled her. He'd been silent for so long, she'd hoped he'd left the room. Things would be easier that way. If he simply didn't care.

But she knew in her heart that he did… and that awareness crushed her soul.

Alex said her name again, but she couldn't answer. His son's quiet whimpers affected her more than if he'd wailed at the top of his lungs.

She focused on Maggie. "I… I'm sorry. I know this is abrupt, but it's best for everyone if I simply make a clean break."

"Ella, look at me."

She kept her back turned toward Alex, still addressing Maggie. "Thank you for everything." She prayed for the strength to continue speaking. "For welcoming me into your home and treating me like a part of the family—"

He clutched her arm and turned her toward him. "Look at me."

Eyes glued on the floor she pulled from his grasp. "Mayor York, I appreciate everything you've done for me." Barely choking out, "Goodbye," she ran from the kitchen.

Tears blurred her vision. She sprinted through the house and flew out the front door. Stumbling on the steps, she caught her balance and then rushed toward the car.

"Ella," Alex called behind her.

She grabbed the car handle and yanked hard.

"Damn it, Ella. Will you look at me?"

Tears blinded her as she jerked on the stuck door.

His hand covered hers. She tried to shake it off, but he took hold of her shoulders.

"No, Alex, please don't..." She turned away and used her sleeve to quickly dry her eyes.

"Don't, what?"

"Don't stop me."

"I'm not letting you go."

"You have to."

"Why?"

"Because it's best for everyone."

"Will you please look at me?"

She couldn't.

He shook her gently. "Look at me."

She closed her eyes. *Don't do it. Don't do it.* But the magnetic pull of his gaze forced her to obey.

Pain and confusion clouded his handsome face. "Why are you doing this?"

"Because it's what's bes—"

"Stop saying that." His frown deepened. "How is your leaving best for everyone?"

In her rehearsals last night she'd planned on telling him the truth, that his career would suffer because of her. That he'd resent her in the end if he gave up his dreams for her. She'd wanted to tell him that she loved him more than words and for that reason needed to do the right thing.

Honesty had worked well in theory, but now...

Telling him she loved him and always would wasn't going to get the job done. He'd look at her with those sensual eyes and touch her with those skillful fingers and she'd melt like a chocolate bar in summer. He wasn't some jerk out to get into her pants. He was kind and sweet and obviously hurt by her decision to end things. He'd convince her to stay and she would, and in the end he'd resent her just like he'd resented his wife.

Telling him she loved him would only make things worse.

Her fingernails gouged her palms. She had to hurt him instead. "I can't do this."

His hands dropped to his sides. "Do what?"

"Pretend anymore."

His eyes narrowed.

She stiffened her shoulders and pressed her nails deeper. "That I care."

"About what?"

"About you!"

A muscle in his cheek flexed.

"It's exhausting. I'm tired of it. I got what I wanted out of this arrangement. So I'm done pretending."

"Why are you saying this?"

"Because it's the truth."

He shook his head. "No it's not."

"It is!"

"You don't care about me?"

"No."

His mouth set in a hard line.

"I saw an opportunity to make some easy cash and took it. That's it." She shrugged. "Like father like daughter. Clyde taught me well." The wind dried the remaining moisture on her cheeks. She hardened her gaze.

"The other night. That meant nothing?"

"Nothing."

A frown was his only response.

"Can you move out of the way so I can open my door and get the hell out of here?"

He didn't budge. "Everything was good until last night. What happened between then and now?"

"Get out of the way." She tried to grab the door handle.

He shifted, blocking her access.

"Move!"

"What happened, Ella? And don't give me a bunch of made up shit you think might hurt me. I want the truth."

"I told you the truth. You're a meal ticket. I've played this little game long enough. I'm bored. It's time we parted ways. You're just too pig-headed to see it."

"Well I might be pig-headed, but I'm also in love with you."

The blood racing in her veins screeched to a halt.

"I've loved you from the start." He stepped closer. "And that little boy inside loves you, too."

The mention of Eric crushed her soul to dust.

"I don't know what happened last night, but I do know one thing. You care for him. You can't fake that, Ella. You love him... maybe as much as I do."

The boulder in her throat dropped into her gut. Its weight sent shock waves of despair through her body. He wasn't taking her bait, but she couldn't let him see her anguish.

"I never said I don't care about your son. He's... he's a sweet kid." She lifted her chin. "I simply don't care about you."

"Is that so?"

"I used you. Plain and simple. And you were an easy mark."

"That's what I am to you? A mark?"

"That's it."

He pointed at the house. "You were in tears inside. You could barely speak."

"I'm a good actress."

"Yeah, okay." He shook his head and gazed at the sky. A humorless chuckle escaped his lips as he looked at her again. The frown returned. "You care for me. I know you do."

"I care about your money."

He grabbed her arm and pulled her close. His heart beat against her breast.

She wanted to struggle, but couldn't. His heat held her prisoner.

"You care about me," he whispered against her hair. He'd pinned her against the car, his hard body molding her curves. He nuzzled her ear, threading his fingers into her hair. "I can feel it."

"No…" she said, breathless. His lips trailed her jaw. She couldn't think straight.

He cupped her face. Green eyes searched hers. "You're scared, Ella. Something spooked you. That's why you're trying so hard to hurt me." He set his forehead against hers.

She closed her eyes. She wanted to be with him, wanted to be loved by him.

"But I'm not falling for it." He stroked her back. "Tell me what happened. Talk to me."

She couldn't help melting against him.

His warm breath fanned her cheek. "Please, don't do something we'll both regret."

Regret.

Alex is one in a million. His future is as big and bright as the sun. Do you really want to be the one responsible for extinguishing that ball of fire? By allowing him to do something you'll both regret?

The echo of Boggs's warning strengthened her resolve. She pushed out of his embrace. Regret and resentment went hand in hand. He'd end up regretting this day, the day he talked the woman who would end his political dreams into staying with him. And then he'd resent ever meeting her and end up leaving.

Shattered beyond repair, her heart no longer called the shots. She went numb, running on auto-pilot. "There's nothing here for me." Her own voice sounded foreign to her.

"Don't," he whispered. "Don't do this."

She took hold of the car handle. It opened without a struggle. She got inside and tried to close the door. He stood in the way.

She stared at his feet, her vision unfocused. "I need to leave."

He didn't move.

She held the door, arm extended, waiting.

Finally, after what felt like an eternity, he stepped aside.

She slammed it shut, turned the key and pumped the gas. The engine sputtered to life.

She heard her name called out as she pulled away. *Eric?*

"Ella!"

Her attention snapped to the rearview mirror. It *was* Eric. Framed in the back window he leaped off the front porch and sprinted toward her.

"Stop, wait. Ella!" The little boy cried out, running to catch up with her moving car. "Don't go! Please…."

His anguished cries penetrated metal and glass. Not even the sputtering engine could drown him out.

She swerved onto the main driveway and nearly skidded into a tree. She jerked the wheel, tears blinding her, until she righted the car, shifted gears and increased speed. *I'm so sorry. Please forgive me.*

"Ella, I want you to be my mommy. I love yooooou," were the last words the little boy cried before he gave up the chase.

And the last thing she glimpsed through the rearview mirror and a haze of burning tears was a father comforting his broken hearted son.

Chapter Thirty-One

Two weeks after she'd left his home, Alex stood in the narrow hallway outside Ella's apartment. It had taken him that long to seek her out again.

His first reaction when she'd left was denial. He figured she'd been scared, something had spooked her and after she thought things over she'd come back to them. He'd refrained from calling or showing up at her door, wanting to give her space. But when days had turned into a week and he realized she might not be coming back, hope had turned to anger. She'd devastated Eric when she ran off. The little boy had cried and pleaded with him to make her come home but when he'd explained how much she wanted to teach and that she needed to leave, not because she didn't love him, but because she wanted to work in a school as badly as he wanted to pilot a real plane one day, his son seemed to understand.

Eric's sniffling acceptance should have calmed him down, but his anger had only escalated. He realized how lucky it was the boy hadn't reverted to silence in the first place. Her actions could have easily caused a relapse and he blamed Ella for making him worry over his son's mental health.

But, thankfully, Eric hadn't fallen silent. In fact, he'd been full of questions. *Why did she leave? Where did she go? Will she ever come back and see me?* They were questions he couldn't answer because he wondered the same damn things himself.

So his temper had finally cooled.

He'd been absent for a good chunk of his son's life, had been the initial cause of his silence.

Hating her for leaving Eric would be hypocritical.

Another week passed and though he was miserable without her he'd stayed away.

She didn't want him.

Whatever her reasons, she'd made that abundantly clear. And though he'd find himself picking up the phone to call her or even in his car on the way to her apartment, he'd quickly come to his senses and hang up or make a U-turn

185

before the promise of her scent and body and hypnotizing eyes could draw him any nearer.

He'd pleaded with her to stay with him once before... his manhood wouldn't allow him to do it again.

That is, until Eric found the messenger bag they'd bought for her hidden in a box in his office closet. His son had made him promise to try and find her and give her the present she'd left behind.

He'd been so against seeking her out he'd nearly broken the vow he'd made his son, but the thought of deceiving the hopeful little boy had wracked him with guilt.

So here I am.

He knocked on the door again. Paint chips flaked off, sprinkling the welcome mat beneath his shoes.

"Trudy, I know she's here. Her car's parked at the curb. I promised Eric I'd give her something." The groaning and shifting of a passing truck was his only answer.

He raised his fist to knock one last time when the door cracked open.

Eyes remarkably like Ella's peered out at him. "Her car's here, but she's not." She tried to close the door, but he shoved his shoe in the way. She blinked at him through the narrow space. "Do you mind?"

"I promised my son."

Trudy glanced away.

"I wouldn't be here otherwise."

She focused on his face again. Her brow creased.

"He wanted her to have this." He held up the messenger bag Eric had been so proud of.

Trudy glanced at the bag and then closed her eyes. A few seconds passed and she opened them. "Can you move your shoe?"

Shit.

He withdrew his foot, feeling like a dick for shoving it there in the first place.

Sorry, little guy. I gave it my best.

She shut the door in his face.

He turned to leave, but the security chain slid from its slot and the door creaked behind him. He faced her again.

"Come in," she said, softly.

He flashed a grim smile. "Thank you."

The delicate scent of Ella's favorite lotion lingered in the interior. His heart rate increased. He scanned left and then right, realizing how desperate he suddenly was to see her, but other than her mother, the apartment seemed empty. Even her posters were gone. He reigned in his emotions and breathed through his mouth.

Trudy took a seat on the edge of a fuzzy white chair. "Ella's in Virginia."

"Virginia?"

"She's in a comparative education program there. She's interested in working with inner city and low income kids, children from broken homes.

She's earning credits toward her masters. She's been wanting to do this for a while, so she was thrilled to make it in."

Virginia?

She just up and left the state?

He'd come to terms with the idea that she didn't want him, but the realization that she was really gone, so far away, hit him hard. His heart was being ripped from his chest. "When will she be back?"

Trudy shook her head. "I don't know. She's sharing an apartment with three other students. She bought a one way bus ticket. I think her stay might be permanent."

And the shit load of cash she earned working for me obviously paid for the opportunity. Irony's a real bitch.

Trudy eyed the messenger bag. "Gift or not, Mayor York, you shouldn't have come. Ella made things very clear before she left. She doesn't want to see you anymore."

"That's the thing. She *wasn't* clear. She didn't give us a reason, just ran out." He itched to say more, but kept his mouth shut. He'd already blurted too much. He wanted closure for Eric, but not at the expense of his pride.

She picked at a tuft of white fuzz without responding.

He sighed and set the bag on the coffee table. "This is hers. We want her to have it, Eric and me." He turned to leave.

"Please... wait...."

He stopped without facing her.

"Your son?" She stepped in front of him. Her troubled gaze met his. "Is he... is he doing okay?" She bit her lip. "He's still talking?"

"Constantly."

Her shoulders relaxed.

"He's in school, Magnolia Falls Elementary. His teacher says he's doing great. He comes home excited to tell me what they did in class." His smile faded. "And after he's done telling me about his day, he asks about Ella."

Her smile faded, too.

"He wonders what she's doing. If she likes school as much as he does." He rubbed the back of his neck. "He wonders if she misses him."

Her frown deepened.

"He loves her."

Trudy nodded. Sadness darkened her sky blue eyes.

His hand fell away from his neck. He drew in a deep breath and let it out on a sigh. "I'm gonna go now. School's almost out. I like to meet him at the bus stop and walk him home."

"Of course," she said and led him to the door. She opened it and let him pass.

He stepped into the hallway.

"I'm truly glad to hear he's doing so well," she said softly.

"It's thanks to your daughter that he is."

Trudy lowered her gaze, a sad smile crossing her lips.

"I wish her nothing but the best."

She looked up at him. "Thank you."

"I won't seek her out again," he said and walked off, though like most politicians, he had no intention of keeping his word.

Ella stepped out of the bathroom. She stared at the closed apartment door. Her gut clenched as she glanced at her mother.

Listening to Alex mention Eric, knowing the man she loved was only feet away, had been torture. She'd sat on the edge of the tub, weeping into a bath towel while her mother did what she couldn't... face him.

Now, she forced herself to stay put instead of running to the window to catch a glimpse of him getting into his car. She wanted desperately to see him again. Watch the fluid movement of his strong body. See the wind tousle his dark hair. But she fought the urge.

She had to stick to her guns. *This is best for everyone.* "Thank you," she managed.

Her mother glared at her. "I'd wrestle a rabid bear for you Ella, but I refuse to ever lie to that man again. Did you hear him talking about his son?"

Ella closed her eyes. She covered her face with her hands, trying to compose herself.

"Did you?"

Her hands fell away. "Yes."

Her mother sighed. "When your father left you were heartbroken. And now you're doing exactly the same thing to someone else."

"I'm not Eric's parent."

"No, you're not, but it's obvious you mean the world to him. And I'm not just talking about a little boy."

"Why are you making this more difficult?"

"You're the one making things difficult by sabotaging your happiness."

"I have good reason."

"That's right, I forgot. You're trying to save his career." She folded her arms over her chest.

"You say it like that's not important."

"It's incredibly important, Ella, but don't you see what's going on here? You're following in your dad's footsteps."

"No, I'm doing what's right."

"What's right about ending a relationship that made you happy?"

Her stomach ached.

Her mother paced and then speared her with a glare. "This all started with that fight. A silly, meaningless fight that everybody's already forgotten about."

"I haven't forgotten. That fight was over *me*. The mayor of our town and gubernatorial hopeful lost control because of *me*. People took pictures. Those things are never erased from the internet. The story will be there forever."

"Yeah, well I saw those grainy pictures and read the articles, too. And you're right, Ella. It *was* big news… for about twenty-four hours… until that Kardashian chick announced she's pregnant again and the handful of people who gave two flips about the fight realized her drama is much more interesting."

Ella opened her mouth to object, but her mom cut her off. "And the fight you were so worried about didn't hurt his appeal in town at all. In fact, the Civil War museum he's funding has made him as big a celebrity here as his mother."

A flash of crimson caught her eye. A fat Cardinal had landed on a tree limb near the window, puffing up its feathers against the cold. Ella drew nearer, amazed the animal didn't fly away. Its perch had to be less than a foot from the fogged pane. She pressed her palms and nose against the chilled glass, heart weighing heavily in her chest. The Cardinal reminded her of Eric. The boy used to love watching the scarlet birds squabble over seeds and then take flight just like his little red twin engine.

"Ella? Are you listening to me? The man's image hasn't suffered a bit. He's just as popular as he's always been. He'll win the governor's seat by a landslide."

She stepped away from the window. "I know he will." Clearing her throat, she tried to speak past the lump lodged there. "And without me at his side he'll get there for sure."

"What makes you such a detriment?"

She frowned at her mother. "Um, where do I start? Let's see…" She held up her hand, counting each answer on a finger. "I have a record, my father's a multi-convicted criminal and it's because of me that Alex was slammed in the news after the benefit. I'm a triple threat."

Her mother frowned. "You *don't* have a record, that store manager let you go. Your father's no longer a criminal, he did his time and even bad publicity is publicity. Like I said, he's as popular as ever. And that guy, what's his name, Bands, Bones, Bags…?"

"Boggs," Ella muttered, rubbing the bridge of her nose.

"That's the one. You said he's his campaign manager, right? Well, he ended up spinning the fight to look like a little rough housing between friends. You sacrificed yourself for nothing."

"It wasn't nothing. Even if he quit the race for governor today, he's still mayor. The man in charge of Magnolia Falls doesn't need someone like me on his arm."

"I can't believe you just said that."

She shook her head. "See, this is why I moved out. You don't understand and you never will."

"I understand perfectly. It's obvious you're scared, Ella."

"Of what?"

"Of commitment."

"That's not true, and that doesn't have anything to do with this."

"It has everything to do with it. You should go see your father's shrink. Then you'd realize I'm right."

"You're not right."

"I am." Her mother stepped closer, sparks in her eyes. "I'll break things down for you. When you were a little girl you were happy. Then your father left and broke your heart. You met Alex and you were happy again, but then worry weaseled its way into that blonde skull of yours."

"What worry?"

"That Alex would have left you, too. So instead of waiting for that to happen, you decided to nip it in the bud, leave him first. That stupid fist fight was just an excuse. And the excuses are still piling up as we speak."

"That's ridiculous."

"No, it's the truth. And my proof is hearing you say that you're not good enough for him. You know damn well that's a lie. You've never been self-deprecating or apologetic of who you are in your entire life. Stop lying to yourself and me and be honest. Why did you really leave him?"

"I left so he'd have the future he's always wanted."

Trudy threw up her hands. "Did you ever stop to consider that maybe he wants you in that future?"

"If he did he would have come after me when I left."

"He did, just now."

"No, he came for Eric. I heard him. He wouldn't have shown up otherwise."

"Yeah, you *heard* him. You didn't see him. I did. I saw the sadness in his eyes. He misses you, too." Her mother stepped closer. "Sweetheart, you were happy with him. He was happy with you. Your dad said you looked like a family together."

"He saw us in the park and formed a snap opinion of our relationship. Do you know what Alex and I were arguing about when he came along thinking we looked so sweet together?"

Her mother sighed.

"Whether it was right for me to continue living with and working for him. And it wasn't. I'm surprised the media hasn't thrown that in his face yet. I can see the headline, *gubernatorial hopeful caught boinking the help.* That'd be just what he needs."

"Oh, Ella."

"Don't oh, Ella me. He helped me earn enough money to finish my masters with a chunk left over to rent an apartment. I'll be damned if I'm going to repay him with scandal."

"I see... so you're going to keep lying to yourself... and me?"

They stood silent, both of them glaring at one another. The standoff seemed to last forever until the hard glint in her mother's eyes finally softened. "He told you he loves you." She took Ella's hand. "And you told me you love him, too. Why would you deny your feelings?" She squeezed lightly. "Or his?"

She pulled away, turning toward the window again. She scanned the limbs for the Cardinal, but the little bird had flown off.

"Ella?"

I'm in love with you. I've loved you from the start. Her vision blurred on the branches as his words looped in her head.

"Has he expressed any concern that being with you might hurt his chances at winning governor or his career as mayor?"

The tree shifted into focus. He hadn't, but that didn't mean it wasn't on his mind.

"I'll assume by your silence it's a no." Her mother touched her shoulder. "Ella, if it wasn't worrying him, then it shouldn't have worried you." She gently turned her so they faced each other. "Unless, of course, I'm right about your real reasons for ending things."

The pesky lump returned. She tried to swallow the sadness, but it wouldn't budge.

"Don't do what your father did for so many years. He convinced himself that leaving was for the best. It obviously wasn't. And if all you've told me is true, Alex made the same mistake, too, with his own son."

"That's exactly it, though. Don't you see? When things got tough he left the little boy he adored. What if..." She dropped into her mother's chair. "What if things get tough somewhere down the road and he decides that things are easier without me?"

"Why would he ever think that? You're smart and funny and beautiful. And he loves you, wardrobe, junk food addiction and all."

"Yeah, well, love is fickle. One day it's kisses in an unfinished house and the next it's pain and disappointment."

"Jeez Louise, you're a pessimism machine. Is this what you've become? Someone who only thinks doom and gloom all the time?" She shook her head. "I don't know, Ella... I looks like I really failed you somewhere along the way."

Ella stood and hugged her mother. She held her at arm's length and smiled. "You didn't fail me. I'm strong and smart and driven. I don't need a knight in shining armor to sweep me off my feet. I can ride my own horse, thank you very much."

"You've never ridden a horse in your life."

She lifted her chin. "Then I'll learn."

Her mother brushed her bangs from her eyes and then drew her closer to kiss her forehead. "I want you to be happy. That's all I've ever hoped for."

"I know." She squeezed her thin shoulders. "And I will be. I'm going to finish the rest of my credits and student teach and then I'll get hired and have my own class of students. I'm inches from my goal, mom. And that makes me incredibly happy."

"Really?"

"Really," Ella assured her... even as the pain of Alex's final words, *I won't seek her out again,* echoed in the void that had once housed her heart.

Chapter Thirty-Two

Two weeks after he'd shown up at Ella's apartment only to learn she'd fled town, Alex waited for Eric to come home from school. His bus stop happened to be situated on the sidewalk about five feet from where Ella had fallen and skinned her knees. The tree branch that had tripped her had been cleared, but the memory of that morning, the weight of her body cradled in his arms, the scent of her hair brushing his neck, the warmth of her soft skin, remained.

He couldn't get her out of his head. Everything reminded him of her.

Including an empty stretch of asphalt.

As Eric's bus rolled up to the curb he shook his head. *It's over York. Get that through your skull.*

"Hi Mayor York," the first little girl that exited the bus said. She hurried toward the group of moms waiting for their kids. He waved at his neighbors, said a couple of hellos and then focused on the bus. Three more children came out before Eric ran down the steps and hopped onto the street.

"Daddy, I saw her!"

Alex waved at the bus driver as she closed the door and drove off.

"Daddy."

"Yeah, buddy," he said, taking his son's hand and leading him toward the sidewalk.

Eric hopped onto the curb and flung his back pack off his shoulders. It thumped on the grass.

Alex stooped to pick it up. "What are you doing?"

"I saw her." He bounced on his toes.

"Who?"

"Ella."

Alex frowned. "Eric, she's in Virginia."

His chin zipped back and forth. "No she's not. I saw her at my school."

"At your school?"

"Yep."

"Where?"

"At my schooooool."

"I mean where at your school? When?"

"We were on my bus and Jason found gum on the floor and Matt dared him to eat it, but he didn't want to and then Laura said, *Look at the pink car over there.* I looked and it was Ella. It was *her* pink car."

"Was she driving?"

"No, she was stopped. She got out of her car and was walking to the bus rider lane. She had my present I gave her. I tried to open the window to say hi, but it was stuck and Laura said I'd get in trouble, but I still tried. I waved to her but she didn't see me. I yelled her name and then the bus driver told me to sit down cause we were leaving."

Ella? Here? Since when? Had she just come back? Was she home for good?

A dozen emotions filled his head, everything from elation to anger.

"Can we see her, Daddy?"

Alex reigned in his feelings and glanced at his son. "Eric..."

What could he say? He wanted to see her as much as Eric did. A part of him wanted to hug her and kiss her and tell her everything would be okay. Another part of him wanted to shake her, yell at her, force her to explain why she'd broken his son's heart as well as his own.

He drew in a deep breath and set his hand on his son's shoulder. "Not yet."

Eric's excitement dimmed. "Why not?"

As much as he still loved Ella, he hated her for putting him in this position. She'd helped him reconnect with Eric. Their relationship was stronger than ever. He'd vowed never to hurt him again... but now... because of her, causing him pain seemed inevitable. "Because she has to do some things first."

Eric scratched his head and then dropped his hand to his side. "Cause she gots to go to school like me?"

"Yeah," Alex said softly.

"Can't we just go over her house?" His expression brightened. "We could bring her Oreos."

Alex forced a smile. The hope in his son's voice tore his heart from his chest. "Maybe one day."

"Tomorrow?"

"No, Buddy. Not tomorrow. Let's give her more time than that, okay?"

Eric's frown darkened his entire face.

"Okay?"

Eric walked away.

"Eric?" Alex followed him.

"What?" He asked, striding purposefully toward their house.

"Wanna play some ball later?"

"I guess."

And those were the last words they spoke before they reached their driveway and Eric sulked off to his room.

Forty-five minutes later, with his last business phone call behind him as well as the bulk of his paperwork Alex strolled upstairs to get Eric for dinner.

He frowned when he entered his room. Underwear, socks, shirts and sweaters, shorts and pants littered his floor. Four or five pair of shoes lay in a heap near his closet. Most of his dresser drawers were open, clothes hanging out, as if he'd been searching for something. Either that or there'd been a tornado in the house he didn't know about.

"Eric?" He strode to his walk in closet. "You in there?"

Nothing.

He left the mess figuring his son might have gravitated to the room next door. Months earlier he'd unlocked the playroom after Eric had begged him to. He'd been worried about reminding his child of his mother, but Eric hadn't appeared saddened at all when he'd entered the room for the first time since her death. In fact, he'd seemed happy to rediscover toys he hadn't played with in years. Eric's resiliency amazed him.

A quick perusal of the playroom came up empty as well.

He found Maggie vacuuming in the library. "Where's Eric?"

Shutting off the machine she wrinkled her brow. "In his room, isn't he?"

"I just checked. He's not there." He frowned. "And didn't I tell you to stop with the vacuuming? Let Faust do that."

"That old rattlesnake would rather scowl me to death than do *women's work* as he calls it. I'm perfectly capable of pushin' this machine around."

"Well, how about you let me give you a hand now and then?"

"Why don't you concentrate on being a daddy and a mayor and leave me be you big pain in the keester?"

"Just trying to help."

"If you wanna help then go fetch your son. He's probably in the back yard. Make sure when he comes in he's washed up for dinner. I'm serving the chicken and dumplings at five sharp, with or without you."

"Okay, oaky." He chuckled and left for the yard. Eric had probably gone out back to play with Chewi, though he knew better than to head outside without telling someone.

Fifteen minutes later, panic turned his blood to ice water. No Eric, anywhere. Cold dread pooled in his gut. He'd searched the house frantically. Maggie had taken the second floor. Faust inspected the third floor and attic while he checked the first floor, basement and outside.

At first, he'd thought Eric might be playing a game. Then he worried he was still upset with him about Ella. He could be hiding on purpose. But they checked closets and cabinets, under beds, behind desks and doors, curtains and sofas. They'd searched every inch of the house, inside and out.

Eric was nowhere to be found.

Alex hurried into the kitchen, about to pick up the phone. Faust had beaten him to it. The old man's bushy gray eyebrows were ruffled. "I'm on with the police. They're sending a car over immediately, Sir."

"Did you tell Chief Mills it's Eric?" Alex asked.

"Yes, Sir. He's sending officers to check the area."

"I'm going out, too."

"Sir, would you like me to accompany you?"

"Thanks but stay—"

Maggie pushed through the kitchen door. "I found this!" She clutched a sheet of notebook paper. "In Ella's old room."

She handed it to Alex.

Im going to her hows
I miss her.
Im soree I stold sumthing

"He ran away." *Jesus.* "I'm gonna look for him. When Mills gets here tell him not to stop until he's found." He didn't wait for a response and sprinted to the garage and got in his car.

The woods flanking the drive up to his house were dense enough to hide a little boy and his dog. Chewbacca had disappeared, too, and though he was scared to death that his son had gone missing he held out hope the two were together. He rolled slowly along the bricked drive, scanning the trees and the bushes, calling out Eric's name. He'd already looked here, but he couldn't help trying again. When he pulled past the front gate he stopped at the street.

Left, or right?

God, where is he? Which way do I go?

A gust of wind blew through the open car windows. Leaves skittered noisily across the pavement to his right. He made up his mind and turned in that direction.

Two blocks away, he finally let out a grateful breath. *Thank God.*

In the waning light, under a lattice of bare tree limbs and flanked by houses on either side, Eric made his way down the wide street pulling a rolling suitcase behind him, carrying what looked like his school lunch box in the other hand and wearing a knit ski cap. Chewbacca followed obediently without needing a leash.

Alex parked the car at the curb and got out. He jogged down the street, closing the distance between them.

When he came within ten feet of his son he stopped. "Eric?"

The little boy turned. He seemed surprised at first, but determination quickly replaced confusion. "I don't need your help."

"Eric, wait. Stop. Talk to me." Alex kept his voice neutral and calm even though his heart raced. *Thank God I found him. Thank God. Thank God. Thank God. Thank God.*

Eric frowned. His suitcase, a small zippered rectangle, bulged. "I'm gonna get Ella."

Alex swallowed hard. He took a deep breath. *This is my fault.*

"I wanna see her. I miss her. She's not in Birginia anymore so I'm getting her."

"Eric..."

"You won't get her back, so *we* will." His furry companion had taken a seat, tongue lolling out, tail swishing from side to side. Eric glanced at his friend. "Right, boy?" Chewbacca barked and licked his face in answer. He glanced back at his dad. "We're gonna find her."

"You were going to walk all the way to her house?"

"Yes."

"Do you know how to get there?"

His lips pinched, eyebrows bunched together. "...No."

Alex took a few steps closer. "Eric you scared me. I had no idea where you went.

His little boy stared at the street, shoulders drooping.

"I thought something happened to you. I was really worried."

"I left you a note."

"I know, I know, but you still scared me."

After a long hesitation he looked up. "I'm sorry, Daddy."

"It's okay. I'm just glad you're safe." He shoved a hand through his hair and then ran his palm across his neck in agitation "Why didn't you come tell me what you wanted to do?" He moved closer and sat on the curb.

Eric stood next to him, still clutching his lunchbox and suitcase handle in gloved hands. "I did."

Alex realized he *had*, at the bus stop, not an hour earlier.

"You didn't listen to me," Eric added and carefully set down the suitcase. He dumped his lunchbox, which smelled faintly of tuna fish, on top and joined him on the curb. His cheeks were rosy from the cold.

Alex nodded. "You're right. I didn't, did I?"

"Nope." Eric stared at the street. Chewbacca barked once, sniffed the lunch box and turned soulful brown eyes on his mini-master.

"Is that your dinner in there?" Alex pointed at the lunchbox the dog seemed to covet.

"Uh huh. We were gonna eat it later. I fixed tuna sandwiches when Maggie wasn't looking. I made one for Ella, too, but I didn't put Beggin' Strips on hers."

"You don't think Ella'd like a few Beggin' Strips on her tuna fish?"

Eric didn't look at him, but giggled lightly. "No. I didn't put any on mine either. Just on Chewbacca's. He likes them even though they smell like barf."

"Barf, huh?"

"Yeah... Barry Weisberg barfed on the floor right next to Mrs. Lewis's desk after he ate three kid's hot dogs, two tostadas and a green popsicle at lunch yesterday... so I know what it smells like. It's gross."

Alex chuckled. "I'll remember to stay away from the Beggin' Strips then."

They remained quiet for a minute, both of them staring at the street. Chewbacca gave up on chicken of the sea, mayo and barf scented dog treats to lie on the asphalt, snout resting on Eric's sneaker.

As the seconds ticked by Alex's humor faded. He felt worse and worse. His reluctance to reconnect with Ella had upset his son enough that the kid had packed up and ran off.

"Daddy?"

"Yeah, Buddy?"

"Are you mad at me?"

"Mad?" He set a hand on the boy's knee. "I was scared to death when I couldn't find you, but mad? No, son. I'm not mad at you."

"But I stole something."

He'd forgotten about the alleged theft. He cocked his head. "What did you steal?"

Eric stared at the pavement.

"It's okay. You can tell me." Alex couldn't imagine his son stealing a cookie, much less something valuable.

Eric patted Chewbacca's head and then slid his foot out from under the dog's snout. He shifted and knelt to unzip his suitcase. Before he opened the flap he glanced at his father. His somber expression whispered, *promise you won't be mad.*

"Eric... it's okay. You can show me."

He slowly opened the flap, resting it on the street. The contents of the suitcase were finally revealed. His twin engine sat on top. No self-respecting pilot-in-training would ever embark on an adventure without it. Eric set his prized possession on the dormant grass. Next he lifted out a rumpled t-shirt, the one he and Ella had decorated one rainy afternoon when they couldn't play outside. They'd painted a scene on the front—Ella and Eric as Jedi knights, wielding light sabers, side by side.

Alex smiled. Ella's influence on his son warmed his heart.

Eric pulled out a few other articles of clothing—a mismatched pair of socks, a baseball hat and five more t-shirts. No underwear, no pants. Apparently going commando wasn't an issue for his runaway son.

Surprisingly, though, oral high-gene made the cut. His electric toothbrush sat on top of a lumpy pillow jammed into the bottom of the suitcase. Eric frowned. "I forgot toothpaste."

Alex shrugged. "We can get some later."

Nodding, Eric set the toothbrush on the street. Chewbacca sniffed the cast-off and quickly licked the bristles.

Alex chuckled. "I guess we'll get another one of those later, too."

Eric laughed and swiped it from his dog's fat tongue. "Chewbacca," he scolded and stuffed the toothbrush in his back pocket.

Alex studied the pillow shoved into the base of the suitcase. It belonged in Eric's room. He figured the boy worried he'd get in trouble for taking it. "It's okay that you brought your pillow, Buddy."

Eric frowned. "Huh?"

Alex pointed at it. "The pillow from your room. Taking it isn't stealing."

"Oh..." He shook his head. "I didn't mean that."

"Then what were you talking about?"

He drew the pillow out slowly.

A lump formed in Alex's throat.

The only thing left in the suitcase, the item his son believed he'd stolen, looked back at Alex, a soft smile on her still lips.

"I stold *her*," his son said, eyes downcast. He gently picked up the angel statue that his mother bought for him years before she died.

Eric hugged the figure to his chest, gazing down at her pale, painted face. "She looks like Ella." It seemed Maggie had been on to something when she'd concluded the statue might be the reason Eric had spoken to Ella in the first place.

Eric held the angel out for him to see.

The statue's delicate arms were drawn in close to her body. Her hands, one on top of the other, pressed against her breast, over her heart.

"Doesn't she, Daddy?"

Alex glanced at his son. The little boy smiled at him, hopeful for his answer.

The lump in his throat grew. "She sure does," he said, softly.

"I'm glad you unlocked the playroom."

"You have a lot more toys now, huh?"

He shrugged. "I guess." He studied the winged statue. "But that's not why. Now I can see her whenever I want."

"The angel?"

"No... Ella." He smiled sheepishly, flashing twin dimples. "Since she looks like her, I pretend she can hear me." A frown replaced his grin. "But Faust told me I shouldn't talk to in... in-mid... in-add-mint... objects."

"*Inanimate* objects."

"Yeah, that." His brow wrinkled.

Alex raised an eyebrow. It was time he had a word with his surely valet. "There's nothing wrong with pretending."

Eric set the angel in the suitcase. "I know. That's why I taked her. So me and Chewbacca would have a mom on the trip."

Alex's heart broke for his son. "A mom?"

He nodded. "Ella. We want her to be our mommy."

It wasn't the first time his son had said that. He loved Ella as if she'd given birth to him. "You miss her, huh, Buddy?"

"This much." He held his arms stretched wide as they could reach.

"I miss her, too."

"You do?" Eric cocked his head, peering up at him.

"Very much."

"So can we go tell her?"

He'd planned on letting her finish school, maybe even land a teaching job before he sought her out again, but Eric's decision to run off had changed everything. His son needed hope. And so did he.

Chapter Thirty-Three

Late Saturday morning Ella dropped onto the sofa in her basement apartment and drew a pillow onto her lap. She set a bowl filled with three scoops of salted caramel ice-cream, a Sasquatch fistful of M&Ms, chocolate syrup, two heaping tablespoons of crunchy peanut-butter, a mountain of Ready-Whip and crushed Double Stuff Oreos on top.

Her mother would have a cow if she saw her ready to wolf down this particular breakfast. But worry over yesterday's events had her craving a real artery clogger, so she didn't really care.

Ordinarily she would've been thrilled to meet the principal of the school she'd been assigned to student teach. But yesterday, to her dismay, that school turned out to be Magnolia Falls Elementary, the one Alex had mentioned Eric attended.

When she'd realized the risk she'd immediately asked for a transfer, but the assignment might as well have been set in stone. Guilt tore her up inside, but she'd had no other choice. If she wanted to teach she had to show up at MFE. So she'd planned on introducing herself to the principal around three, when she hoped most students would be in their classrooms. She didn't want to chance running into Eric before she even got hired. She didn't want to upset him. *What if I end up working with his class? What if he hates me for leaving him? What if... What if...What if...*

Of course, a traffic jam on 316 had skewed her *brilliant* plan and she'd ended up parking Pepto just as students were piling into their buses. She'd done her best to fade into the background in case Eric sat among the hundreds of kids on their way home...but just as the second to last bus lurched into traffic, she'd caught a glimpse of wild black hair bobbing up and down in one of the rear windows.

Eric.

She hadn't seen his face, but she'd know that adorable little head anywhere. She'd turned away quickly and had hurried into the building without looking back.

She'd been such a fool, telling lies about leaving the state, hoping the fictional distance would keep Alex from pursuing her. What a dumb-ass plan. They lived in the same small town. Chances were she'd run into father or son, or both... and then they'd hate her even more for adding dishonesty to abandonment.

She took a bite of breakfast.

It didn't taste as good as it should have.

In fact, nothing tasted or smelled or looked or felt like it should anymore.

Everything had gone gray.

She set her concoction aside and sat back on the sofa, closing her eyes.

Alex...

His images sprang up in her subconscious like a Jack-In-The-Box.

She couldn't get him or his adorable son out of her head... and she feared memories of their time together would plague her with insomnia for the rest of her life.

She rolled onto her side and pulled a pillow under her cheek, squeezing her lids tight.

She kept telling herself she'd left for his own good, so that he'd win the governor's seat, but a day after her mother had accused her of following in her father's footsteps, she'd read that Alex had officially pulled out of the race. The article had shocked her. *Why did he give it all up? Why throw in the towel when there was no longer anything standing in his way?*

And why were her mother's words, *I'm right about your real reasons for leaving him,* so loud in her head?

A rap at the door startled her. She sat up, frowning. No one but her parents knew her address. In fact she'd learned about the apartment by accident, eaves dropping on a gossiping professor. He'd had some legal work done by the owner, a widowed mother of three little girls. Cecily had been looking for a female to take up residence in her finished basement and they'd hit it off immediately. Ella had only moved in about a week and a half ago, but she already felt comfortable in the cozy space. Priced right and close to campus her new home came complete with a mini kitchen, a sitting room, a bedroom and a full bath. She couldn't have asked for a better set up.

She might have been supremely happy... if she wasn't always so incredibly sad.

She swiped a hand across her cheek and ambled across the room to open the street side door.

Clyde stood on the stoop.

A month earlier she would have told him to leave her the hell alone. She would have sneered at him, spouted criticism and then slammed the door in his face.

But ever since his tearful apology, things had changed.

He had changed.

For the better.

"Hey String-bean."

"Hey." She smiled and stepped aside to let him in. "No work today?"

He wiped his boots on the welcome mat, nodded with a smile of his own and then stepped inside. "Nope, got the day off. I'm not interrupting ya am I? Probably should have called first."

She led him into the sitting room and sat at the sofa. "No, I was just..." She glanced at the melting ice cream and chuckled lightly. *Feeling sorry for myself.* "About to have breakfast."

"Is that what you call it?"

She shrugged. "Breakfast of champions.

"Your mom would have a cow if she saw that mess."

She grimaced. "I was just thinking that." She patted the cushion next to her. "You wanna sit?"

Her father took off his coat, set it neatly over a chair, drew off his gloves and then took a seat. After running his calloused hand over his chin stubble he flashed a concerned smile. "How's it going?"

She forced a grin. "I'm doing really great." The lie soured her tongue.

"You haven't been by the apartment in a few days. Your mom and I've missed you. I know you want to be on your own, but we enjoy having you around."

Once upon a time she would have been furious knowing her father now lived in the studio she once shared with her mom.

But that was all in the past. So much had changed. She no longer hated the man. In fact, she was happy her mother had asked him to move back in.

"I've been so busy with school and work. Any free time I have I sleep."

"You sure it's just your schedule sapping your energy?"

She smirked. He'd gotten as good at bullshit detection as her mother. "Yeah. I'm sure."

"Classes during the day, library job at night? Everything's working out for you?"

"Yeah. It's a good set up." She'd landed a job shelving books at the college library and though it paid minimum wage, the hours didn't clash with her classes and she even had down time to study.

He nodded. "Good." He cocked his head and then scanned the room. "I'm glad you found this place. It's real cozy. Ms. Harlow seems like a nice lady, too."

"She is. I like her a lot. Her girls are so cute."

"Got three, right?"

"Yep."

His blue eyes dimmed. "It's been how long since she lost her husband?"

"Two years."

"She spoke very fondly of him when we helped move you in. Bet she misses him, huh?"

Ella nodded. "They were high school sweet hearts before they married."

"Really?"

"Met in ninth grade I think she said."

"Since his death, she's never dated anyone else?"

Ella frowned. "No. She told me she'd never marry again. She lost the only man she'll ever love."

He absently rubbed a patch of calluses on his palm. After a moment or two he glanced at her. "You believe that? That there's only one person in the world for you?"

She did. She believed it with all her heart. She'd found the only person she would ever love... and then she'd pushed him away. "I don't know," she answered, not wanting to open that wound.

"I believe it," he said, softly. "I think you have one chance at real love. True love. The kind that makes your heart sing."

"That's pretty poetic coming from a rough guy like you."

A faint smile crossed his lips. "I've gotten soft over the years."

"And mom? You think she's the only one for you?"

His smile grew. "I *know* she is. I'm lucky to have her and so damn grateful she took me back, forgave me." He lowered his gaze and resumed tracing the calluses.

Her throat went dry. His tone hadn't been angry and, clearly, he hadn't accused her of anything, but guilt ravaged her none-the-less. Since that first night he'd asked for it, he'd never mentioned the word forgiveness again. Instead, he'd slowly inched his way back into her life, gaining her trust, proving he'd changed. He'd been working a steady job, earned a model employee plaque, leased a small pickup truck from his boss, continued weekly therapy, moved back in with her mother, helped pay rent and bills and even attended church every Sunday. He'd not only become a model citizen, he'd evolved into the father she'd always wished for.

Though, she had yet to grant *him* his wish... just three little words.

I forgive you.

A fourth word crossed her mind, *unfair.*

He'd been incredibly patient.

And she'd been... incredibly *unfair.*

Very little time had passed since he'd come back into her life, but her feelings for him had altered dramatically. He deserved to know that.

"Dad?"

He grimaced. "Sorry. It's getting weird in here, huh? Kinda embarrassing talking about love while you're sitting alone with your old pop."

"No," she smiled. "No, that's okay. I'm not weirded out, I'm just..." She swallowed hard. Her hands turned clammy. Tearing down walls had never come easy. "I want you to know something." She reached for his wrist and set her palm against his rough skin, squeezing lightly. "I'm sorry it's taken me a while to come around." Her brow wrinkled. "I guess I've been scared. We've got this new life, me, you and mom, and I don't want anything to change it."

"What's worrying you, String-bean?"

She shrugged. "The past."

He frowned. "I hate that my past darkens yours."

"No..." She patted his hand. "No, that's not what I'm talking about. I... That night you told me why you left us. I haven't wanted to revisit it." She flashed a grim smile.

"You don't have to. There's no need to bring that up again, especially if it upsets you."

"Actually, there is. I thought that if I said what I'm about to say to you pain would come flooding back... but," she shrugged again. "Now that I'm saying it, I realize my worries were pretty silly."

"Sorry, String-Bean. I'm not following you."

She smiled. "I know, sorry." She drew in a deep breath and let it out. "What I'm trying to say is that like mom... I... forgive you, too."

He went very still.

"I forgive you for everything."

A pained sound escaped his throat. His blue eyes filled with tears and he reached out to pull her into his arms. His hug suffocated her, but she welcomed the squeeze.

Hugging him back she closed her eyes. "I love you, daddy."

He cried harder, struggling to speak. Next to her ear he managed a choked whisper, "I love you, too, String-Bean. I love you, too."

She hugged him tighter. "And I'm so proud of you."

He drew back slightly to smile at her. Tears coursed down his cheeks. "Ditto, baby girl." He kissed her forehead and used the pad of his thumb to wipe moisture from under her eye. He let her go, ran his sleeve across his own cheeks and chuckled. "Did you ever think an old jail bird like me would be such a cry baby?" He grabbed some tissues off the coffee table and blew his nose. "I'm like a five year old girl here."

She laughed and used a tissue to dab her eyes. "We both are."

They took a moment to dry their tears. When he finally composed himself her father said, "Thank you, Ella, for forgiving me. It means more than you could ever know."

"You're welcome."

A tear slid down his cheek. "So much time lost. So many regrets. Promise me, honey," he said in a choked whisper, "You'll do everything you can to live a happy life without regret... without fear."

She swallowed hard. After a moment she nodded, but couldn't find her voice.

He pulled out another tissue and rubbed his nose. Standing he ran his hand through his cowlick. "Whew... all right. I think I'm okay now. No more water-works." He drew in a deep breath and then let it out. "You know, you've made me the happiest old man on Earth. You've given me so much... but..." He chuckled lightly. Um... I gotta ask one more thing of you. A favor. It's for your mom."

Ella smiled. "She need me to pick up a case of Final Net?" She asked, but frowned when she noticed something. "Dad, you arm's bleeding."

He swiped at the abrasion on his freckled forearm. "I cut myself on a fence while I was trimming a hedge yesterday. I keep breaking open the scab. You have a Band-Aid?"

"Yep. Come with me. I'll patch you up."

He followed her into her bedroom. She sat on the edge of her bed, opened the nightstand drawer and lifted out a small first-aid kit. She handed him a Band-Aid and then stowed the case back where she'd found it. She nearly closed the drawer when something caught her eye. Smooth macaroni beads and red yarn peeked out at her from under a stack of magazines.

She used to wear Eric's gift all the time, even after her break up with his father. But the longer she'd spent away, the more it hurt to be reminded of her time with them. One day she'd finally taken off the necklace and had hidden it away.

She drew it out carefully, memories flooding her head—*Eric smiling, chasing Chewbacca, flying his little cast-iron plane, hugging her and laughing... Alex... gazing at her, kissing her... telling her he loves her.*

"What's that?"

She held the necklace in her lap, running her fingertips along the mini pasta beads. "Something I was given."

He remained quiet.

She glanced up at him. "Eric and I made it when I was still with..." She swallowed the lump in her throat. "He wanted me to have it."

"Can I see?"

She handed it over. He smiled, examining the workmanship of a little boy. "Why's it in the drawer?"

"I don't know... memories."

"Good or bad?"

"Good, but..." She frowned. This was exactly why she'd hidden the necklace away. Her stomach suddenly ached and a vice squeezed her heart. "A lot of times, good memories have a weird way of making me feel bad."

He nodded as if he understood.

"I've gotten pretty good at distancing myself from that sort of thing."

"You learned from the master," he said softly. He eyed the necklace, working it through his knobby fingers like a rosary. "But... you need to unlearn it." Stepping forward he stretched the yarn over her head. The beads settled against her skin. She peered down at them. Warmth pumped life back into her heart. She'd forgotten how much Eric's gift meant to her. Or, more likely, she'd forced the feeling into a lock box in her mind.

He brushed a fringe of bangs from her eyes. "Running from the people I love never worked out for me." He leaned against her dresser. "How's it working out for you?"

It's not.

"Do you still have feelings him?"

"Dad, let's not start this."

"It's a simple question. A yes or no works."

"Simple? Try amazingly complicated"

He smirked. "It's only complicated in that blonde melon of yours."

She shook her head and focused on a pile of clothes she had yet to fold. *Let it go, Dad. Just let it go.* "What was it mom needed?"

"We'll get to that later. Right now I'm kinda likin' this turn in our conversation. I suddenly feel like Dr. Friedman."

"Too bad you don't have a degree like your therapist." She raised an eyebrow.

"I don't need a degree to see what's obvious."

"So I'm right? You've graduated from jail-bird to bullshit detective?" *Trudy obviously snagged a very willing recruit.*

"Huh?"

She waved a hand and stood up. "Never mind." Drawing the necklace off her head, she bent to stow it back in the drawer.

"Wait. What're you doing?" He took it from her.

"I'm putting it away."

"This was a gift, Ella. It was meant for *you*, not a drawer."

"Dad, please."

"When I put this on you a second ago, your expression changed. Your face softened and that wrinkle between your eyes smoothed out—"

"I have a wrinkle between my eyes?" She touched her forehead.

He smiled. "Yes, and you're gonna look older and grayer just like me if you don't let yourself be happy and stop worrying *what if* all the damn time."

He stretched the yarn around her neck again. "I got old in jail. I wasted my life in that hole." His hands dropped to his sides. "And you know what? You've built your own cell. You sit in there all alone, pushing people away and avoiding happy memories because they make you sad. You've locked yourself up, Ella. Just like I did."

"I'm living my life." Her response sounded shallow even to her ears.

"No. You're living a lie. You didn't break the law or commit a felony, but you're serving a life sentence none-the-less."

She tried to take the necklace off, but he stilled her hands.

"Wear it. Let the memories come."

The lump filled her throat.

"Let them come and instead of focusing on loss, focus on what it felt like to be loved."

Tears stung her eyes, but she held them back. "I can't. All those memories do is depress me."

"Why?"

"Because... I can't be with them."

"Who's keeping you from being with them?"

The vice squeezing her heart cranked tighter.

"Who, String-bean?"

She studied the floor. She couldn't look at him. His tone of voice and expression assured her he knew she knew the answer, but wouldn't admit it.

"You. Ella." He tipped her chin higher and gazed at her. "The only person keeping you from being with them is *you*."

She bowed her head and closed her eyes. Pain ripped through her heart.

"I was the only person in the way once, too. I lost years I'll never get back." He touched her shoulder. "I spent a lifetime away from you. And I regret every day I lost... every minute... every second."

Tears fell. She couldn't help it.

"God knows I've made some huge mistakes, but the last thing I want is for my only daughter to follow in my footsteps." His features were etched with sorrow. "You have to take a leap of faith every now and then. I didn't know if you'd accept me back into your life. I was scared to death you'd reject me..." He drew in a deep breath and let it out slowly. "But I didn't want to let that fear define me. I'd been doing that all my life... letting fear define me."

She used her sleeve to blot the steady stream of tears dripping from her chin. He was right. Right about everything. But she couldn't visualize herself running back to Alex. Too much time had passed. She'd left him and his beautiful son. Hurt them.

She'd missed her chance with them.

It's too late.

"I'm not a college graduate, Ella. And I'm not the smartest guy around, but I've got enough sense in this old cob-webby brain of mine to realize that some of my faults have been passed down to you. Difference is... you're strong. Stronger than any person I know. You can survive anything the world throws at you. You've proven that time and again." Pausing, he absently rubbed the calluses on his palm. A few seconds passed and he gazed at her, blue eyes watery but bright. "But your strength is also one of your biggest weaknesses. It hardens your heart. And you don't think you deserve happiness."

She swiped a tissue off the nightstand and wiped her cheeks and then her nose. She wished she could stop crying. She wished she'd never opened that drawer. She wished things could be simpler.

"But you do... deserve happiness. You know that don't you?"

"I do," she said with a sniffle.

"Then why don't you grab it? Take that leap?"

"Because happiness always ends up hurting too much."

He gathered her into his arms, hugged her close and stroked her hair. "I did this to you. I'm so sorry," he whispered. "But it's not supposed to feel that way. If you give it a chance you'll see how powerful love really is."

He stepped back, holding her at arm's length. "It's a lot stronger than sorrow, I can tell you that much. Take it from someone who knows."

He squeezed her shoulders and then reached behind her to lift her hair from under the necklace. The macaroni beads settled more comfortably around her neck. "It suits you," he said with a wink.

She touched the pasta and ran her fingertips against the fuzzy yarn. Visions of Eric and Alex floated in her head.

"Now, about that favor, String-Bean..."

"For mom?"

"Yeah."

She sniffled.

"Actually, it's for me, as much as her." He said, leading her into the living room. He pointed to her kitchen table. "You sit." He picked up her ice cream soup and dumped it in the sink. "I'll explain while I cook you a real breakfast. And then after you eat you can start."

"Start what?"

"Learning to smile again."

She frowned.

"Come on, String-Bean. It's easier than you think."

She stared at the floor.

"Come on."

She gazed back at him. "I'll try."

"Good. That's all I ask." He clapped her on the back and then strolled into the kitchen. "Now what are ya craving?"

"The ice cream you dumped in the sink for starters."

He smirked and then opened the fridge. "How 'bout some eggs and bacon?"

She smirked back at him. "It's not salted caramel, but I guess it'll do." While he busied himself preparing her meal, Ella sat quietly at the table. She fondled the macaroni necklace, gently running her thumb against the beads.

What if I seek him out and he's already moved on?

What if he hates me for breaking Eric's heart?

What if he regrets ever loving me?

Her father wanted her to learn to smile again, to love... but she worried she'd never breach the wall of *what ifs* standing in her way.

Chapter Thirty-Four

Ella stood on stage, dressed in fur trimmed crimson with bells on her toes and a smile on her face. If not for Clyde she'd be bundled in flannel, prone on the couch in her apartment doing her best sloth impersonation while binging on caramel corn and watching *A Christmas Story* on Netflix.

Instead, dear old dad had talked her into granting the favor he'd asked of her that morning.

Clyde's boss, Mr. Hicks, recalled when his favorite employee had been a stage performer and had asked Clyde if he'd headline the Magnolia Falls Retirement Village's Annual Christmas Extravaganza. But her dad needed a partner and since Trudy had come down with a stomach bug, Ella had taken her place.

She'd spent the bulk of the day rehearsing with *Count Clyde The Magnificent*, though she didn't feel capable of filling her mother's shoes... literally... the woman had freakishly narrow feet and the curly-Q Mrs. Claus slippers she'd lent her were pinching the crap out of her toes.

She grinned and bared it, glancing to her left, watching her father work his magic.

He waved his hands, chanted a goofy rhyme and then with a puff of smoke a white dove flapped from under the scarf he held. Their ancient but spry audience erupted in applause. She clapped along with them, genuinely entertained.

"*And* now, with Mrs. Claus's assistance I will achieve the amazing." Her father strode to the free standing closet in the center of the stage. "Mrs. Claus, please open the portal."

Ella curtsied and obeyed. Opening the door while trying to gesture as theatrically as her partner, she showed their audience its contents.

"Nothing," her father shouted, since a good portion of the onlookers wore hearing aids. "As you can see, there is absolutely nothing inside this closet." He nodded at Ella. "Now you may close the portal, Mrs. Claus."

She played her part and with a sweep of her arm shut the door. She couldn't wait to see their audience's reaction when Mr. Hick's seven grandkids, all dressed as Christmas Elves, materialized from the cramped space like clowns from a car at the circus.

They turned the closet round and round, careful not to disturb the black curtains that hid the illusion's secrets. She smiled in anticipation as the door finally faced the assemblage.

"Ladies and gentleman, this is a passage straight to the North Pole. For all our sakes I hope a hungry Polar Bear hasn't wandered too near." Clyde's dramatic announcement echoed in the theatre. His audience chuckled.

"Tinsel, bows and falling snow." He gestured wildly and then smacked the door with his wand three times. "Come forth!"

The door burst open... but instead of seven little elves, a rotund man in an elaborate Santa suit stepped out of the closet. He strode past Ella, reached the edge of the stage and took a bow.

As their audience erupted in applause she glanced at her father perplexed. He shrugged, mouthing *'just go with it.'*

'Who's he?' she mouthed back.

Instead of continuing their silent conversation, he shouted, "Ladies and gentleman, look who it is."

Her father clapped the man in red on the shoulder. "I'm so glad you came to join us Saint Nick." Clyde glanced back and waved her forward. "Mrs. Claus, why don't you greet our guest with a kiss under the mistletoe."

Mistletoe?

Luckily she didn't see any mistletoe... until, with a slight of hand, her father pulled a bundle out of thin air.

She hesitated, unwilling to lock lips with some stranger stuffed into yards of velvet, but their audience had other ideas. *Kiss, kiss, kiss,* they chanted as if they were seniors in high school instead of senior citizens.

"Give the old boy a good smooch, Doll," a gray haired man in a wheelchair called out.

She raised an eyebrow at her father, but he simply flashed a grin and then faced his rowdy audience again.

"Don't be shy, Mrs. Claus," A woman with horn rimmed glasses shouted out.

Ella ambled across the stage and stood next to her father. "Seriously?" She muttered to him out of the corner of her mouth.

Clyde ignored her sarcasm while lifting his hand high to dangle the sprig of mistletoe in the air. Then he took an evasive step back and she suddenly found herself standing beneath a bunch of white berries and a little too close to Kris Kringle.

Kiss, kiss, kiss. Their chant filled the small theatre.

With a sigh she smiled. Their audience's enthusiasm got the better of her and with a chuckle she waved her hands in surrender. "Okay, okay."

The chubby guy in red turned and gazed at her.

Her heart screeched to a halt.

About fifty pounds of padding, a snowy beard, mustache and a set of glued on brows camouflaged his face, but Santa's piercing emerald eyes were a dead giveaway.

Alex!

She jerked back, but her slipper hit a slick spot on stage and she lost her balance.

Alex steadied her. "Whoa, there, be careful."

She instantly recalled their first encounter. Out of her head with dehydration, she'd barely been able to make out his features, much less his expression that afternoon, but at this moment... she registered every detail with exhilarating clarity—his light grip on either side of her waist, silver whiskers framing the soft smile playing on his lips... the glimmer of awareness in his gaze.

Once upon a time she'd struggled to define that sultry look.

But that felt like a lifetime ago.

She was no longer untried or untested.

No longer a virgin.

A zillion butterflies swarmed in her belly. The fluttering made her bold... she took a leap... and kissed him.

His whiskers were bristly and tickly against her cheeks and chin. She pressed her lips against his with firm persistence.

Her eyes were open.

So were his.

Applause? Is that applause?

Wait! What am I doing?

She tugged from the intensity of his gaze, but Alex squeezed her closer, softened his lips... and ignited a scorching fire.

Her core blazed, burning butterfly wings to ash. Every nerve in her body sizzled with electricity.

She closed her eyes... and melted.

The laughter, the cheers, the whistles and clapping faded.

It was just her and him.

God how she'd missed this.

On tip toes, with the taste of him still on her tongue, she broke the kiss and whispered his name against his lips.

He paused, his breath warm against her cheek. "Ella..." He squeezed her shoulders and then stepped back. With a tug he drew off his hat. His beard, mustache and brows came next. He stowed them in his pocket, eyes locked with hers, as their audience broke out in another wave of applause.

"It's the mayor," someone shouted, breaking through her haze. "Mayor York's here," another called out.

Alex turned toward the gathering with a small smile and a wave.

Just past his shoulder, partially hidden in the shadows off stage, a flash of white-blonde hair caught Ella's attention.

Trudy?

Shocked to see her dressed in red sequins and fresh as a sprig of Holly instead of sick as a dog, she frowned at her mom as the woman quickly ducked behind the curtains.

Ella shot her father a questioning glare, but caught him in what appeared to be an attempt to shoo Trudy out of sight. He grimaced when he realized he'd been discovered.

What the...?

Then she noticed Alex, who was being beckoned off the low stage by his fans. He stepped into their smiling embraces, let them clap him on the back and sing his praise. He glanced over his shoulder at her and shrugged.

It suddenly occurred to her that this goofy reunion might not have been his idea at all.

More than likely it had been orchestrated by the meddling goof-balls she shared DNA with.

Embarrassment, humiliation, even anger heated her cheeks.

She'd practically thrown herself at him just now, *in front of everyone*. Had he even wanted to kiss her? *Oh God...*

She spun to retreat backstage, but ran into her father.

"String-Bean, wait. Where're ya going?"

Clyde's magic closet and its curtains blocked her second escape route. She shifted direction and hurried off the stage, down a side isle and toward the double doors.

She ran through the main dining room, vestibule and then out the front entry. A blast of icy wind hit her in the face, nearly knocking her back. She gripped her collar tighter, shrugged deeper into her velvet shawl and then sprinted toward her car.

Squealing out of the parking lot it occurred to her that taking a leap felt a lot like a fall.

Chapter Thirty-Five

In her basement apartment, Ella sat on the edge of her bed and rubbed her feet. She glared at her discarded Mrs. Claus slippers.

What a fiasco.

Pinched toes were the least of her worries.

I can't believe I kissed him.

What was I thinking?

What must he think?

What were my parents thinking?

She squeezed her eyes shut, gritting her teeth.

The Albino twins had obviously conspired to get her and Alex together tonight, executing an elaborate ruse and a convincing illness. Her mother had actually moaned in bed earlier, clutching her gut as if her colon might pull an Old Faithful.

Ha. What a miraculous recovery.

The woman had some nerve hiding in the shadows to spy on their handy work! Clyde had given an Academy award performance today as well.

But the worst... the very worst part of the evening had been of her own doing. She'd taken what her father had said to heart, took a huge leap of faith and had fallen right smack into Alex's face.

His face.

Even hidden by whiskers he'd snared her attention. Those eyes, that smile. The heavenly scent of his skin.

It seemed like forever since the last time she saw him... breathed him in... kissed him...

She frowned, realizing her finger-tips had gravitated to her mouth. Gently, she touched her lips, but instead of embarrassment a bolt of desire zipped through her body.

She'd wanted that kiss.

She'd wanted it with all her heart.

It had felt wonderful and right... and... if she had the chance, she'd do it again.

She stood up.

I'd do it again.

In a freaking heartbeat!

Her pulse rate tripled.

Suddenly everything clicked.

Yes she'd fallen when she'd taken that leap, but not to her death.

She'd fallen in *love*, all over again.

Falling wasn't so hard after all… it was a revelation! And like a coward she'd run from it.

Her father had feared rejection and damn if it didn't terrify her, too, but it was time to pull up her big girl g-string. It was time to kick fear in the patute, as Maggie would say.

"Oh, Mags, how I miss you and your pies. And, Eric. God I miss you so much!"

Kicking the curly-Q slippers aside she grabbed her combat boots and yanked them on. With a tug she righted her velvet cape, strode out of her bedroom, grabbed her purse off the counter and rummaged for her keys.

No more walls, no more barriers, no more prison of my own making.

Screw fear.

Not only did she miss his family, but she missed Alex, too, more than anything in the world. She should've never left him, never wasted so much time worrying over the endless *what ifs*.

Winning him back suddenly consumed her.

Finding her keys she sprinted to the front door, flung it open and yelped.

Alex grabbed her, yanked her into his embrace and pressed his lips against hers.

He tasted like peppermint and smelled like heaven.

Wind howled in her ears, but the gale was a whisper compared to the pounding of her heart.

His hands were everywhere at once, buried in her hair, cupping her face, stroking her shoulders and spine, gripping her backside. He stepped toward her, maneuvering her into the apartment. With a kick he slammed the door shut.

"Alex." She barely found breath to utter his name.

"No," he said and kissed her again, curling her toes right inside her boots. He held her face in his hands, narrowing his gaze "Don't say anything. I'm not letting you talk your way out of this. Not again."

She opened her mouth to speak.

He barked out a, "No." His gaze narrowed. "You're not leaving."

"Well of course I'm not leaving."

He straightened. "You're not?"

"Nope… this is my apartment. If anyone's leaving, it'd be the giraffe in my entry-hall."

His frustrated frown made her smile.

"You're screwing with me." A pleasant quirk lifted his lips.

"Um, yeah."

"So you're not kicking me out?"

She shook her head no.

"And you're not planning on sprinting out of here the minute I let go of you?"

Her smile softened. A small blob of dried glue remained above his left eyebrow. She couldn't help plucking it off.

"Ouch."

She chuckled and handed him the remnants of his costume. Gazing into his eyes she said, "I'm done sprinting away from you."

He cocked his head. "Since when?"

"Since I realized I need you."

A slow, sultry smile crested his lips. "You're just now coming to that conclusion?"

She left the warmth of his embrace. "I've known all along." Turning toward him again she took a seat on the arm of the sofa and shrugged lightly. "It's just taken me a while to accept it." She glanced at her feet and then up at him. "You might have noticed... I'm a tad stubborn."

He flashed those gorgeous dimples. "You? Stubborn? Never."

Rising she stepped forward. With a gentle touch she traced his jaw-line and then caressed the flesh along the column of his throat.

His expression turned serious.

Her fingertips trailed his collarbone. She set her hand over his heart. The vibrant thump, thump, thump beneath her palm buoyed her courage. Eyes locked with his she said, "I'm in love with you."

His smile returned. It lit his face and dented his cheeks. With a tug he pulled her close and wrapped his arms around her.

She hugged him tight, pressing her cheek against his chest and murmured, "I can't believe you gave it up."

He leaned back to frown at her. "Gave what up?

"Governor. It was everything."

His grin faded. With a gentle stroke he smoothed the bangs from her brow. "No, Ella. Everything is you. Everything is Eric." He kissed her left cheek and then her right. His hand closed around hers and he pressed her palm against his chest again. "My heart is yours. It beats for you and a little boy." He kissed her slowly, sweetly. "I already have everything."

After a moment, he reached into his jeans pocket. He withdrew something then held it out for her to see.

She inhaled sharply and immediately patted her throat. "My necklace. I didn't even know I'd lost it. Where'd you find it?"

He stretched the long, macaroni strand over her head and arranged it around her neck. She beamed at it and then at him.

"It must have come off when you left the show. I found it on one of the steps." His brow wrinkled. "Why'd you leave? You were there one minute, kissing me, and the next you'd vanished."

She grimaced. "Momentary lapse. You know, that slight stubborn streak I have?"

He chuckled.

"How'd you know I'd be there tonight?" She cocked her head. "Let me guess, Freckles and Final Net clued you in?"

"Your parents?"

She smirked.

"Sort of. I went to them yesterday wanting to know where you lived. But *they* came up with the ambush idea."

She noticed his jeans and then tugged the sleeve of his gray t-shirt. "Where's your Santa suit?"

"I left it with the reindeer."

"Aren't you allergic?"

"Only to endless questions."

She raised an eyebrow. "Well what would you rather be doing?"

He took a few steps back and sat in the Lazy Boy. "Why don't you come sit on Santa's lap and I'll tell you?"

With a smile she obeyed. With a wiggle she sat side saddle and snuggled in close. She wrapped her arms around his neck and asked, "So what do you want for Christmas, Santa?"

His expression changed. His loving gaze reached into the depths of her soul. "All I want is your heart," he said softly.

"It's yours." She kissed him gently and then added, "It beats for you and a little boy."

Epilogue

Ella followed the slow moving procession. They wound their way in between seats and then up through the center aisle. Each step brought her closer to triumph. Her heart raced. Her cheeks flushed.

It's happening.

It's finally happening.

She could barely contain the energy racing through her veins.

A few more steps and she reached the stairs. The announcer steadily called one name after another, his voice loud and clear. *Pomp and Circumstance* played in the background teasing the butterflies to dance in her belly.

Five ahead of her.

Four.

Three.

Two.

Don't trip on your gown, don't trip on your gown...

She crested the final step onto the stage just as the announcer called her name, "Mrs. Cinderella Ariel York."

Her stomach flip flopped and her face ached from grinning, but she didn't care. It was all worth it. Striding to the center of the stage she looked the presenter in the eye and took her diploma in her left hand. She made sure to reach over her treasure with her right hand and shook his vigorously.

"Thank you," she beamed. "Thank you, thank you so much!"

"You're welcome Mrs. York.

Ella turned toward the audience, shifted her tassel to the opposite side of her cap and smiled from ear to ear. She waved at her mother and father. She waved at Maggie.

With tears of joy in her eyes she waved at her husband, Alex, the man holding her heart, and the little boy who had brought them all together.

THE END

216

ABOUT THE AUTHOR

My name is Tamara LeBlanc. I'm a fiction writer and author of contemporary, paranormal and historical romances layered with eroticism that builds into a satisfyingly happy ending… in more ways than one.

I've been writing all my life, creating characters, fashioning plots, researching ideas. Writing jump starts my heart. It fills my lungs and fuels my soul. I hope my stories of love and passion do the same for you.

I love hearing from you.

To connect with me on Twitter go to:

https://twitter.com/Tamaraleblancrw

or on Facebook at:

https://www.facebook.com/tamara.leblanc.16

Happy reading and best wishes,
Tamara

www.ingramcontent.com/pod-product-compliance
Lightning Source LLC
Chambersburg PA
CBHW061146170626
46809CB00003B/1005